Vambran of House Matrell

Vambran reached the wall of the Matrell estate and heaved himself atop it, then he stopped and listened for the sounds of someone nearby, even as he carefully peered into every shadow, stared at everything that might be a figure hiding in the darkness. He heard and saw nothing. Clenching his teeth in determination, he walked along the wall for a while, tuning all of his senses to his surroundings.

Inside, the man burned for vengeance. They had dared to threaten his family. They had come after his whole House, and he would not stop until he hunted them down and made them accountable.

He would not stop.

The fate of his family,

and his city,

falls into his hands.

Is he ready?

THE SCIONS of ARRABAR TRILOGY

...

BOOK I

THE SAPPHIRE CRESCENT

BOOK II

THE RUBY GUARDIAN
November 2004

BOOK III

THE EMERALD SCEPTER
August 2005

Also by Thomas M. Reid

R.A. SALVATORE'S WAR OF THE SPIDER QUEEN, BOOK II

INSURRECTION
Available in paperback December 2003

GREYHAWK

THE TEMPLE OF ELEMENTAL EVIL

STAR*DRIVE*

GRIDRUNNER

THE SAPPHIRE CRESCENT

THE SCIONS of ARRABAR TRILOGY · BOOK I

THOMAS M. REID

Author of *Insurrection*

THE SAPPHIRE CRESCENT
The Scions of Arrabar Trilogy, Book I

Distributed in the United States by Holtzbrinck Publishing. Distributed in
Canada by Fenn Ltd.

Distributed to the hobby, toy, and comic trade in the United States and
Canada by regional distributors.

Distributed worldwide by Wizards of the Coast, Inc. and regional
distributors.

Cover art by Duane O. Myers
Family Tree by Dennis Kauth
First Printing: November 2003
Library of Congress Catalog Card Number: 2003100836

9 8 7 6 5 4 3 2 1

US ISBN: 0-7869-3027-6
UK ISBN: 0-7869-3028-4
620-17991-001-EN

U.S., CANADA,   EUROPEAN HEADQUARTERS
ASIA, PACIFIC, & LATIN AMERICA   Wizards of the Coast, Belgium
Wizards of the Coast, Inc.   T Hofveld 6d
P.O. Box 707   1702 Groot-Bijgaarden
Renton, WA 98057-0707   Belgium
+1-800-324-6496   +322 467 3360

Visit our web site at **www.wizards.com**

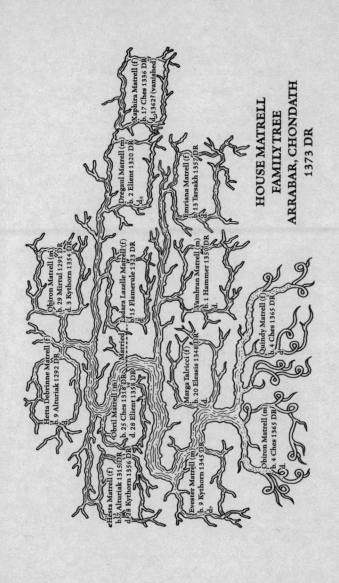

HOUSE MATRELL
FAMILY TREE
ARRABAR, CHONDATH
1373 DR

Xaphira Matrell (f)
b. 17 Ches 1336 DR
d. 1362? (vanished)

Dregaul Matrell (m)
b. 2 Eileint 1320 DR
d.

Emriana Matrell (f)
b. 13 Tarsakh 1357 DR
d.

Obiron Matrell (m)
b. 29 Mirtul 1291 DR
d. 3 Kythorn 1354 DR

Ladara Lazelle Matrell (f)
b. 15 Flamerule 1323 DR
d.

Vambran Matrell (m)
b. 1 Hammer 1350 DR
d.

Herta Debrinne Matrell (f)
b. 9 Alturiak 1292 DR
d.

Obril Matrell (m)
b. 25 Ches 1318 DR
d. 28 Eileint 1356 DR

married

Marga Talricci (f)
b. 20 Eleasis 1348 DR
d.

Quindy Matrell (f)
b. 4 Ches 1365 DR
d.

Hesta Matrell (f)
b. 7 Alturiak 1315 DR
d. 28 Kythorn 1356 DR

Evester Matrell (m)
b. 9 Kythorn 1345 DR
d.

Obiron Matrell (m)
b. 4 Ches 1365 DR
d.

PROLOGUE

Flamerule, 1362 DR

Xaphira Matrell stumbled into a narrow alley and against the back wall of a net mender's rough wooden shanty, where she slumped down behind a small stack of barrels, her left leg throbbing in pain. In the near-darkness of the moonlit night, she held still, hoping the clammy mists and the shadows of her hiding place were deep and dark enough to keep her concealed from pursuit. The salty scent of the bay was heavy, tantalizing her with the nearness of the quay, where she could gain refuge aboard a ship in the harbor.

Beyond her hiding place, along the fog-shrouded street that went past the alley and down to the docks of Arrabar, a trio of armed watchmen jogged into view, their booted feet slapping loudly on the damp cobblestones. They paused there, peering into the alley uncertainly. Xaphira held her breath and tightened her grip on the crossbow in her hands, ready to fire if it became obvious that she had been spotted.

One of the soldiers muttered something low and unintelligible to his companions, who both shook their heads. Just when it seemed that the trio was about to move closer and begin searching, a shout, muffled by distance and the muggy air, turned their attention away from Xaphira's location. They turned and sprinted out of sight. When the woman could no longer hear the sounds of their footsteps on the street, she sighed heavily in relief and closed her eyes.

The immediate danger past, the woman's attention was forcibly turned once more to the excruciating pain in her thigh, where she could see the silhouette of a crossbow bolt protruding from it. She knew she was going to have to yank the missile free, yet she hesitated. It was not so much out of fear of the pain. That she could handle. It was the fear that she would cry out and give away her hiding place that stayed her hand for the moment.

She leaned back, brushing aside the rivulets of sweat that drenched her face, keeping them clear of her eyes. Then she closed those eyes in weariness and sorrow and slumped against the rough wooden wall of the shanty, half listening for the inevitable sounds of soldiers coming into the alley and thinking back to the beginning of the evening, when her nephew had first approached her with his terrible news.

...

"Aunt Xaphira," Vambran Matrell said softly, his voice tight with fear as he approached his father's younger sister. "I think I killed someone."

Xaphira Matrell gasped softly as she jerked her head to stare at her nephew. He was standing beside her on a secluded patio overlooking the Lord of Arrabar's gardens, a finely crafted crossbow in his hands, the stock inlaid with silver and lapis. The matching quiver with its blue-fletched bolts hung by its strap from one shoulder. She recognized the weapon instantly, a recent gift from an uncle. Two of his friends—Adyan Mercatio and Horial Rohden, both proud scions of merchant families themselves—flanked him, staring with wide, round eyes. Behind her, inside the Generon, the palace of the Lord of Arrabar, the din of other guests attending Eles Wianar's annual Night of Ghosts festival began to fade as the twelve-year-old boy's words made the blood pound in the young woman's ears.

Xaphira grasped Vambran by the shoulders and held his gaze firmly.

"How?" the mercenary officer said, clenching her jaw and fighting to keep her voice low so that no one could hear. "Where?"

The younger man's face was faintly illuminated by both a series of rounded, pierced silver lanterns sitting in a row along the top of the balustrade and the waxing moon shining down upon the port city arrayed below them. Even in the dim light, the woman could see that his visage was grave and pale.

"It was an accident," Vambran whispered fiercely as the implication of his own deed hit him squarely. "We were just shooting plantains out of the trees, I swear!" he insisted, pointing down into the palace gardens below. "We didn't mean to . . ."

The boy's words faded away as he understood the futility of explanations.

"Are you certain?" Xaphira asked her nephew, locking eyes with him still. "Or is it just a trick of the festival? Someone playing at ghosts?"

Vambran shook his head and replied, "No. I fired a shot, and we heard it hit someone; they yelled in pain. We ran to see what happened and found a man."

"He's over there, in the trees," Horial offered softly, pointing down into the orchard that was part of the garden.

Xaphira groaned to herself, lamenting her nephew's ill fortune. And foolishness.

Shooting blindly into trees. . . .

"Has any one else seen you?" she asked, straightening and peering around the balcony to see if other guests were near. "Was anyone else down there in the gardens with you?"

Vambran shook his head no.

"Have you told anyone else?" Xaphira demanded.

"No," Vambran replied.

"Are you certain he's dead?"

"He was bloody," the boy replied, shrugging helplessly. "When we saw, we just ran."

"Then take me to him," Xaphira insisted. "Show me where he is."

Despite her calm, firm demeanor, Xaphira's heart was pounding in her chest. She felt pity welling for Vambran, pity mixed with the devastated disbelief that something so tragic could have befallen her family again. She feared they would not recover from another setback.

Waukeen, please let him still breathe, the mercenary silently pleaded. Don't let my nephew have to live with a death on his hands.

The tiles beneath Xaphira's boots were slick with humidity as she followed the three boys toward broad, shallow stairs that would lead down into the gardens, leaving the sounds of the party behind them.

Just as the four of them reached the top of the steps, a voice called to them from behind, "Xaphira, there you are." It was Dregaul, the mercenary officer's older brother. The functioning head of House Matrell strolled closer as Xaphira and the three boys halted. "I've been looking for you. I wanted you to meet someone back inside. He's a—"

"There's been an accident," Xaphira cut in, keeping her voice low and motioning for her brother to do the same.

Dregaul cocked his head to one side quizzically, then his eyes widened slightly in surprise.

"What?" he asked.

"Just come on," Xaphira said, turning back and gesturing for the boys to lead on. "Someone's hurt."

"Oh, by Waukeen, what's happened now?" Dregaul murmured softly as he fell into step beside his sister. "What's going on?"

"Vambran might have accidentally injured someone," Xaphira replied as she and Dregaul followed the trio, staying close as the boys led the way onto the vast expanse of grass that demarcated the beginning of the gardens. "They're taking me there now."

"What?" Dregaul said with a strangled cry, stopping and turning to face his younger sibling. "How did this happen? Vambran, what in the Nine Hells were you doing?"

"Shh!" Xaphira whispered insistently. "Keep your voice down or others will find out." She stared at her brother until he got the point and snapped his mouth shut. "He didn't know," the mercenary added.

"Didn't think, is more like it," Dregaul hissed. Out of the corner of her eye, Xaphira could see Vambran flinch. "Are you trying to ruin us, boy?" Dregaul added, shaking his head in disbelief. "Pray your victim still lives."

The five of them continued on, and none of them said a word. Indeed, Xaphira peered around as they progressed, watching and listening for any signs that others were nearby, others who could discover the victim and raise the cry before she and Dregaul could get the situation in hand. The Lord of Arrabar had invited many guests, and the Generon and its grounds were overflowing that night, but thankfully, no one seemed nearby at the moment.

The three boys pushed through a gap in the low, thick fronds of lush undergrowth near a row of plantain trees, and Xaphira could see several hunks of the fruit lying upon the ground there, slashed and pierced where they had been violently removed from the trees themselves. The boys' targets, she surmised.

"We were back there, shooting," Adyan began to explain, delivering the words in his usual lazy drawl, jerking a thumb over his shoulder. "When Vambran took a shot, we heard a grunt and came to see what happened. We found him right . . . here," the young man finished, pointing toward the bank of a pond a few paces farther ahead.

Xaphira pushed past the boys and brushed aside damp, clinging foliage. She peered into the moonlit evening, followed closely behind by Dregaul. It was, if possible, even more humid among the lush greenery. She could see a form lying still upon the ground, right near the water's edge. It was a man, very obviously a party guest, judging by the lavish cut and style of his clothing. Then she spotted the fletched end of a crossbow bolt protruding from the man's chest, a dark stain spreading from it into the white linen shirt the man wore.

Damn.

Xaphira had hoped against hope that something else had hurt the man her nephew had found, but it was apparently not meant to be. She stepped closer and knelt down, feeling for any signs of life.

"Is he still alive?" Dregaul asked, looming over Xaphira's left shoulder.

"No," the woman replied miserably, rolling the body over onto its back.

"Who is it?" Adyan asked quietly from behind, cautiously peering between the two adults at the corpse.

Xaphira started to shake her head, for she did not recognize the man's features, but at that moment, a call arose from nearby, in another section of the gardens.

"Rodolpho, where are you?" It was a woman's call, a cheerful, laughing sound. "Rodolpho, you hide too well. Come out now and take me inside where it's cooler for some iced punch."

Dregaul gasped as he heard the mysterious woman's words.

"By Waukeen," he breathed softly. "You've killed Lord Wianar's cousin, you fools," he said, his voice cracking in near-panic as he spun around to stare at the three boys.

Xaphira's heart fell. She was fond of Vambran. She had been almost fourteen when he was born, and she thought of him as a younger brother. In fact, she had practically raised her nephew herself and felt somewhat like his protector.

And now this, she lamented.

The Lord of Arrabar's cousin was dead, by the hand of Xaphira's nephew. However innocently slain, it would be called murder, and Eles Wianar would have his retribution upon the guilty. Upon Vambran.

"Rodolpho! What kind of a rake leaves a lady wandering through his gardens?" The woman called, very clearly closer than she had been previously. "Rodolpho, answer me! This is no longer amusing."

Xaphira could hear the woman's footsteps by then, strolling through the orchard toward them. Farther in the distance, others were also calling for the man, moving across the grounds of the palace.

"What were you thinking?" Dregaul demanded quietly, almost pleading, as though an answer might change the situation. Vambran could only shrug helplessly, miserably.

The other two young men stood aghast, utter despair plain in their widening eyes. Adyan's mouth hung open as he stared back and forth between Dregaul and Vambran, while Horial clutched at his midsection and staggered away a couple of steps, shaking his head in futile denial, looking like he was about to be sick.

"This can't be happening," Dregaul muttered help-lessly, his gaze locked on nothing, his stare distant. "The House," he said, his tone forlorn. "The estate. We'll lose it all."

His hands went to his temples, his fingertips first grinding into his skull and running up and through his swept-back, graying hair. The man opened and shut his mouth several times more, unable to find the words he needed.

Xaphira shook her head.

"No," she whispered firmly, trying to reason out some way to extract Vambran from the situation. "It was an accident. We can explain it to Lord Wianar, have him bring priests, fund a resurrection. Surely he will under—"

"Don't be a fool," Dregaul snapped. "You know the game. The family is responsible for killing Lord Wi-anar's cousin, and now House Matrell is at his mercy. He will crush us. Or worse, manipulate the situation to his advantage, and House Matrell will be his to use as he wishes. All because my foolish nephew," Dregaul said, turning back to Vambran, who stood with tears running down his face, "the son of my dead brother, could not be bothered to consider the consequences of his actions. Your uncle Kovrim should never have given you that wretched weapon, and I should never have allowed you to bring it to the Generon tonight. You cannot fathom the doom you have brought upon us all, most especially upon yourself. And I cannot help you."

He turned away from the rest of them, his shoul-ders slumped, and he took several paces to distance himself.

Xaphira watched, heartbroken, as Vambran stood silently sobbing, tears running down his face as his hands clenched and unclenched by his sides. She wanted to take hold of him, crush him to her like she had when he was a small child, but she dared not. She could not take his guilt from him, no matter how hard she tried.

Or can I?

The idea came so suddenly, it nearly knocked Xaphira flat. If her heart seemed to have been pounding before, at that point it felt as though it would burst from her chest. It was a way to redeem Vambran, a way to allow him to reclaim his life—for he was still merely a child in so many ways, and had so much still to look forward to—but at the same time, it terrified the mercenary officer. The implications . . .

Xaphira acted before she could think, before she could change her mind.

"Wait," she called to Dregaul.

Xaphira peered through the hedge and could see the woman who had been calling out. She was moving slowly toward them, her head scanning back and forth uncertainly, one hand rapidly airing herself with a fan spread wide. As she peered about, she moved her other hand up and testily brushed aside damp, limp ringlets of hair that had plastered themselves to the sides of her face from the dampness. She had not spotted them. Carefully, silently, Xaphira motioned for her four companions to crouch down, out of sight. She moved close to them.

"There is a way out of this," she said, her voice barely even a whisper. "For you."

Dregaul looked at his sister sharply, his incomprehension clear.

"What are you planning, Xaphira?" he asked, just as softly. "What foolishness now?"

Instead of answering her brother, Xaphira slipped off her ornate officer's breastplate and turned to Vambran.

"Give me the crossbow," she said, her hand outstretched.

The boy looked at her, puzzled.

"Now," she hissed, peering up momentarily to see

what progress the woman had made.

Rodolpho's huntress was definitely closer, though she had stopped and was turning back as others out playing the hiding game had called to her and were moving to join her. Xaphira nodded in relief and turned her attention back to Vambran.

The boy handed the crossbow to his aunt.

"Now the quiver," Xaphira demanded, reaching for the strap.

Quickly, Vambran shrugged out of the container and passed it across.

"What are you going to do?" Dregaul asked again, reaching out and laying his hand across Xaphira's arm. "Tell me, Xaphira."

"I'm going to give you back some hope," the mercenary officer replied, "and Vambran his life."

"What?" Dregaul blurted in a strangled voice, finally understanding. "You can't! Don't be a—"

"Shh!" Xaphira hissed. "You will ruin it if you don't be still." Then, taking a deep breath, she said, "You know this is right, Dregaul. You know this is the only way to spare the family.

"And you," she said, turning back to Vambran and handing him her breastplate, "keep this. And do good in the world. For me."

Her nephew stared hard at the armor for a moment, its polished silver and gold surface glinting faintly in the dim light, then his eyes went wide in understanding, and he lunged toward Xaphira, clenching her tightly in a hug.

"No," he said. "Please, don't do this."

Gently, Xaphira disentangled herself from her nephew's embrace, though she wanted in the worst way to grip him just as tightly.

"I do it for you, Vambran—" He began to shake his head and protest, but Xaphira placed her finger on his lips to quiet him. "Don't worry for me. I can make my way in the wider world just fine. You're still young,

and you have endless futures ahead of you, to do with
whatever you want. Don't waste my gift to you; make
it count."

Vambran was crying again, perhaps realizing for
the first time that he would never see his aunt again.
He clung to the breastplate she had given him.

Xaphira began to unwrap her uniform sash from
around her waist as she turned back to Dregaul.

"Get them out of here," she said. "You cannot be
seen near the body."

Dregaul nodded and replied, "And you cannot be
caught, or the plan is ruined."

"I know," Xaphira replied, wrapping the sash
around her head, disguising her face. "I won't be."
She managed to conceal her face entirely, hiding all
except her eyes beneath the red cloth. "Tell Grandmother Hetta that—" and she had to stop, for she was
choking back her own sobs.

Dregaul took her hand in his and nodded.

"I will," he said, his voice tight, too. "I'll tell them
all."

Xaphira nodded back, then motioned for them to go.

Vambran lingered, staring hard at her, but she
turned away, to watch the oncoming guests and to
avoid his gaze. Finally, she heard him slip away, pass
back through the gap in the hedge. She closed her
eyes once in sorrow, thankful the cloth would hide
her tears.

It was time to vanquish her emotions then, time for
the real test at hand. Taking one long, deep breath,
Xaphira cocked the crossbow and set a bolt into the
channel, then watched and waited. The woman had
been joined by two others, a man and a second woman,
more guests of the Night of Ghosts festival.

Momentarily, Xaphira wondered if they would
even believe her as genuine. They might instead
perceive her as just another of the many hired enter-
tainers instructed to pretend to be ghosts, abruptly

but playfully scaring the guests throughout the evening. She would have to make certain they recognized her as a legitimate threat right away.

When the trio of guests drew close enough, Xaphira darted out of the protection of the undergrowth, as though she was fleeing from something behind her. She paused for a moment, staring back, waiting for the guests to take note of her.

"Hey there!" the man in the group called as both of the women gasped. "You're quite a frightful little spook," he added, laughing, the women joining in.

Xaphira whirled to face them, letting a low snarl escape her. She raised the crossbow and fired, aiming low, right at the wide skirts of the first woman, the one who had originally been calling for Rodolpho. She squeezed the release on the weapon and felt it jerk as the bolt jumped free. The missile whistled through the air, slicing through the expensive dress, and struck the trunk of a large pear tree behind her with a loud and solid thunk. The woman gasped again.

"Beware!" the other woman cried out, realizing Xaphira was truly threatening them. "He means to strike us down!"

With those words, the woman stumbled backward, trying to flee from the would-be assassin. Beside her, the man and the woman with the ruined dress stared in confusion for a heartbeat, then they, too, began to retreat, shouting for help in frantic voices. Xaphira made a defiant gesture at the three of them, then turned and sprinted away, working to reload the crossbow as she did so.

That ought to draw everyone's attention, the mercenary officer thought. Now to see if I can get over the walls before the cry is raised in full.

For a moment, Xaphira allowed herself to think of Vambran, of her family. She prayed to Waukeen that her actions would be enough to draw the attention from them. She hoped that Dregaul would be clever enough to conceal their involvement, to tidy up the loose ends. And she began to doubt the wisdom of her decision, wondering if she had been rash.

Too late to change my mind now, she realized grimly. Farewell, Vambran, she thought, sending her thoughts out to her nephew. Do good in the world.

Xaphira dashed around the edge of the pond toward the opposite side, leaving behind the frantic calls for aid, hoping that the moonlight was bright enough for the trio she had threatened to see which way she had fled without making it impossible to hide later. She tore through blooming plants and shoved her way past tendrils of hanging vines, all of which soaked her billowy white shirt and gray trousers with moisture. She was thankful she was not wearing the breastplate then, for it would not only have been cumbersome for such light-footed work, it also would have made her even more miserably hot than she was at the moment. Even without it, she was soon gasping for breath, almost choking on the warm, cloying air. Finally, she broke clear of the dense undergrowth and was running through the orchard itself. The woman turned directly toward the perimeter of the palace grounds, then, sprinting between two rows of tall peach trees, ducking low to avoid the occasional dipping branch.

As she neared a wall, Xaphira spied a way to get to the top. As she approached, she did not slow down much, but instead slung the crossbow across her back. Reaching the wall, she redirected her momentum upward, planting her feet against the stone and jumping at the same time. As she rose high off the ground, she spun in the air, turning back toward the nearest tree. A single thick limb jutted out from its trunk, parallel to the ground, and it was that branch that Xaphira hoped to grasp. The leap seemed to go on forever, her fingers outstretched desperately as she drifted toward the limb.

She had given herself just enough of a push to reach
the branch, and once she had a hold of it, it was a simple
matter to swing her legs back and forth a couple of times
until she could fully flip over and get her weight on top
of it. Xaphira was just struggling to her feet when the
first of the palace guards began to arrive. The mercenary officer knew that, even in the thick, concealing
leaves of the tree, her white shirt was too easily seen
in the moonlight. She dared not slow her ascent and
look back down. She frantically climbed higher in the
tree as a crossbow bolt sliced through leaves near her
shoulder, working her way toward another limb that
might be close enough to the top of the wall.

A second and a third palace guard arrived, and
each of them began to fire missiles at her, even though
she was difficult to see. She wasn't bothering much
with stealth, so perhaps they were tracking her by
the sounds of rustling leaves.

The mercenary officer swallowed hard and flinched
as a bolt struck the trunk of the tree near her head,
showering her with splinters of bark. Thankful that
the sash wrapped around her head protected her from
the stinging chunks of wood, she eyed her jump. It
didn't seem terribly far, but then again, if she missed,
it was a long way down, and the fall would drop her
into a hornet's nest of guards, too. Mentally urging
herself on, Xaphira took three quick but careful steps
along the branch, propelling herself forward toward
the wall and thrusting her arms out slightly to each
side to try to keep her balance. As the branch began
to sag under her weight, she took one additional step,
practically running, and leaped again, lunging up
and forward.

She ignored the scratching of leaves and branches
along her face as she dived out into space, reaching
forward toward the edge of the wall, where a walkway
traversed its length. She heard the sound of another
crossbow firing, felt the bolt zip past her ribs, rustling

the cloth of her shirt, but she steadfastly kept her attention on the edge of the walkway. Her hands hooked over the edge of the stone and held tight as she slammed against the wall with a grunt.

"He's getting away!" one of the soldiers called from below. "Shoot him! Shoot him, damn you!"

"To the wall, to the wall!" another guard shouted.

Gasping for breath, Xaphira smiled slightly to herself, glad that her pursuers still mistook her for a man. Her deception was intact, at least for the moment. Deftly, she began to swing her legs side to side. After three or four times, she had enough momentum that she was able to get a leg up and over the side of the walkway. From there, she quickly pulled herself up the rest of the way and rolled out of sight, just as two more crossbow bolts clacked against the stone wall where she had been.

Xaphira lay on her back, taking two or three deep breaths to regain some of her endurance, but she could not tarry. Already, she could see more soldiers coming at her along the walkway, having gained the top from farther along its length. Never hesitating, she arose to her feet once more and peered over the far side of the wall.

It was a long drop, longer than the side Xaphira had ascended, but that did not stop her. Swiftly, the mercenary officer swung herself out over the edge, just as another shot was fired at her, whistling past her head and into the night. Holding firmly to the parapet top, she dropped out of sight and hung there, stopping her momentum for a heartbeat. Then she let go and dropped the rest of the way down to the soft ground below, using her hands and feet against the wall to slow her fall a bit.

The woman was on her feet and running almost instantly after touching down, looking back only once to spot soldiers converge on the point where she had eluded them.

Xaphira had thought that, once she had escaped the confines of the Generon, she would have been able to disappear into the city. But it was not the case. Somehow, the patrols all throughout Arrabar knew to look for her, and the easy stroll she had expected turned into a desperate flight. She had at first thought to return to the Matrell estate, to perhaps gather a few things before vanishing, but it quickly became apparent to the woman that she would be lucky to reach the docks unscathed.

About two streets from the quay, that luck ran out. Xaphira was half walking, half jogging along one of the streets toward the docks, ducking from shadow to shadow, when a patrol appeared suddenly from around a corner just ahead of her. The four soldiers were surprised for a heartbeat longer than she, which gave her the chance to react.

Spinning on one foot, she lashed out with her other boot at the closest soldier, raking her heel across the side of his jaw and snapping his face sharply to the side. At the same time, Xaphira reached out and grabbed the soldier's weapon arm, which was just bringing a slender short sword up and into play. Using her own torque from the kick and levering her hip underneath the soldier's, the mercenary officer drew the young watchman forward, between herself and the other soldiers. The move prevented two other guards from attacking, as they had leaped forward to cut at her with their own blades, pulling up short at the last possible moment to avoid striking at their mate. Xaphira continued the throw, flipping her off-balance soldier completely around and away, but before she released him, she yanked his blade free of his grasp and sent it flying across the street with a clatter. The watchman tumbled to the street several feet away, grunting in pain. She ignored him and pivoted back around to face the other three adversaries.

The fourth member of the group, who had not yet engaged Xaphira, fired a crossbow at her from perhaps ten paces away. She shifted her weight reflexively and slashed out with her hand, slapping the bolt aside just enough to redirect it past her hip. The remaining two watchmen who had been forced to pull their attacks short before fanned out and dropped into defensive crouches, waiting to see what she would do. Xaphira did not hesitate, for she wanted to flee, not fight. Before the soldiers could maneuver around to surround her, the mercenary officer feinted a punch at one then spun and kicked low toward a second foe.

The first target flinched back, but the second one, thinking his quarry was turning her back on him, stepped in too confidently. He barely managed to hop over her kick when she suddenly shifted her weight over and brought her other foot up and back around toward him. The heel of her boot raked inches from his nose and he stumbled back, scowling. With him out of range, the woman darted in close to the last of the four, making several quick jabs and kicks designed to drive him back a step or two, while at the same time she rotated her position around him, placing him between herself and the last remaining threat. Then she darted in quickly, striking at the flat of his weapon with her palm open and snapping his blade free of his hand. At the same moment, Xaphira went low with a sweeping kick and hooked his heel, tripping him.

With a second soldier down, Xaphira ran forward, leaping high over his prone form and at the crossbowman standing a bit farther back, who had just reloaded and was about to fire again. Before he could get the weapon up and aimed properly, Xaphira planted her right foot squarely into his chest and kicked off of him, sending him skidding backward several feet and reversing her own direction in the process. The woman used her momentum to spin and kick at the only soldier still standing, snapping the instep of her left foot into his ribs. He flinched sideways and crumpled to the ground, moaning.

Xaphira landed on her feet and turned quickly in place, noting that all four of the soldiers were prone but not seriously hurt. She turned to jog off, leaving them to recover on their own, when a crossbow bolt whistled out of nowhere and plunged into her thigh. The mercenary officer gasped in pain and went down to her good knee, swearing. Her hidden opponent had fired from a rooftop across the street, and she could see the silhouette of a figure crouched there, reloading. At the same time, a shrill whistle erupted from nearby.

Xaphira turned to see the first of the four soldiers she had downed up on his knees, holding a whistle in his mouth. She shook her head in frustration. Reacting quickly, the woman mouthed a quick prayer to Waukeen while making a slight undulating gesture with both hands to either side of her body. A thick, damp mist rose up from the cobblestones, thicker than the light fog that had risen up naturally from the cool night air. In a couple of breaths, the mist had completely enveloped Xaphira.

Not waiting to see what the crossbowman on the roof would do, she turned and limped away, fleeing down the closest alley, then along another street and into a second alley. From there, Xaphira sought a place to hide, ducking down behind the barrels near the net mender's shack.

Thinking quickly, Xaphira grabbed one of the bolts from the quiver hanging from her shoulder and considered it carefully. It would do, she decided, and wedged the thick wooden shaft of that bolt between her teeth.

Biting down hard on the wood, Xaphira prepared to jerk the bolt from her leg. She closed her eyes and placed both hands on it, gripping the end of the missile firmly. She took one, two, three deep breaths and, before she could think about what she was doing, withdrew the shaft from her flesh.

The motion was like burning steel sliding through her, and she gave a deep-throated howl of agony, biting down hard into the wood of the bolt in her mouth. She had to bury her face in her shoulder to stifle the cry. A single shudder passed through her body as she trembled from the pain, breathing hoarsely. Finally, the initial nauseating waves of torment subsided enough that she was able to refocus.

Grabbing at the medallion that hung from a small chain down inside her shirt and between her breasts, Xaphira kissed the image of the Merchant's Friend and softly muttered a second prayer to the goddess of trade. Then she pressed both of her hands palms down against the freely bleeding wound and held them there for several moments. As she felt the slight tingle of healing course through her leg, Xaphira breathed a sigh of relief. When she removed her palms, all that remained was the torn and bloodied breeches and a pink, puckered scar on her flesh.

Xaphira examined the bloody bolt that had wounded her. As she gazed at it, her eyes narrowed and she gritted her teeth in anger. She tucked the missile away for safekeeping and prepared to flee the city. Peeking up over the top of the barrels, she saw that the alley was clear. Rising slowly, she tested her leg, putting weight on it gradually. It felt a bit weak, but she could stand on it.

Cautiously, the mercenary moved out from behind the wall of barrels and prowled toward the end of the alley. She peered around the corner into the street itself and saw no one. Carefully, fearful that she was being watched from some unseen place, she took the first cautious step out into the open. Then another. She slowly worked her way to the end of the street, down to the docks. When she got there, she slipped into the water and swam toward a ship that sat at anchor a few yards off the pier. Carefully and quietly, she climbed up the side of the ship and slipped over the side onto the deck.

By dawn the next morning, the ship and Xaphira were well gone from the port of Arrabar.

CHAPTER ONE

10 Tarsakh, 1373 DR

Only the glow of the waxing moon shining through vine-covered trellises shielding the balcony where Emriana crouched let her see her surroundings. Even with such muted light, she could clearly make out the grounds of the estate far below her. She spotted three house guards wandering along one of the paths that meandered through the hedges and trees of the gardens. There to keep unwanted guests from gaining the grounds, they were usually easy to elude when coming from the other direction, from inside the house. The panthers were another matter. She knew that they would catch wind of her if she got too close.

The breeze carried the smell of bougainvillea and passion vine blossoms, of wandering hearts and orchids. There were so many of the blooming vines and plants—climbing the trellises, dangling from hanging planters, and overflowing from large pots and basins—all around the balcony that their fragrances were almost overwhelming, blending together with the fainter scent of the citrus trees in the gardens below. She hoped they would help to mask her smell from the great cats.

Beyond the walls, in the streets of Arrabar, the girl could hear throngs of people celebrating Spheres. The sounds of the festival were muted from where she crouched, but they wafted in just the same. She imagined the crowds, all dressed in bright clothing and dancing in the streets, waiting for the parades. She craned her neck to hear the voices and the music drifting across the warm, damp air like the cloying scent of the large blossoms all around her. Hints of laughter and singing rose up from time to time, clearer than the general din. Perhaps that would help muffle any unintentional noises she herself made.

With a faint smile, Emriana checked to make certain the three guards had passed, then she turned and crept over to the last trellis in the row, reaching out and giving it a gentle shake to make sure it was still firmly anchored to the wall. When she was satisfied at its stability, she deftly hopped up onto the balustrade, swung out and around to the outside of the trellis, slipped her foot into one of the small openings, and began to climb.

Careful to disturb only minimally the leafy vines coiled about the trellis, Emriana rose at a steady pace, ascending all the way to the top of the frame, where it was attached to the overhang that protected the balcony below. Easing herself up, she swung one leg over the top of the portico and went flat on the gently sloped roof, catching her breath for a moment and peering back down to see if anyone in the gardens had been close by and managed to spot her. Satisfied that she had not been discovered, she spun on her stomach and shimmied to the top of the roofline.

At the high end of the inclined porch roof, the wall of the estate rose up another two stories. To either side of the space where she hunched against the wall, windows pierced the surface, broad openings that let light into a long hallway inside the building. The window frames themselves were formed of blocks of stone that protruded outward from the wall itself perhaps the width of Emriana's hand when she spread her fingers wide.

Standing with her back to the wall and keeping herself as flush against it as possible, the girl let out one deep, calming breath and lifted her left foot up, jamming it against the side of the window frame at an angle. Then she shoved upward and planted her right heel against the opposite frame, so that her legs were in an inverted V shape and her own weight kept her wedged and prevented her from slipping back down. She shoved her hands into a similar position, bracing herself firmly. Carefully, a little at a time, Emriana began to climb up, shifting her weight back and forth and inching her hands and feet higher on alternating sides.

The going was slow and nerve-wracking, for Emriana had to keep herself pressed flat against the wall to avoid tipping forward and losing her balance. She thus could not lean out to peer down and monitor her progress. It all had to be done by feel. Fortunately, she had climbed that wall a number of times and no longer felt her insides doing flip-flops at the thought of slipping and falling.

Finally, Emriana reached the limit of the lower level of windows and could stand on the top of the frame and rest her shaking legs. Catching her breath, she surveyed the grounds again, even farther below her. If she slipped then, she would fall to the inclined roof of the porch and quite possibly tumble over the side and fall the remaining story to the grassy lawn below. The girl forced that thought out of her head and took another deep, calming breath before continuing.

The higher set of windows were more difficult to wedge into, simply because they started a few feet above the top of the lower openings. She could bend her knee and bring one foot up, but she would have to actually jump up in order to bring the second foot high enough, all the while still pressing firmly into the wall, and there was no room for half-hearted efforts. She considered it the hardest part of the climb.

Emriana began to will herself to succeed, taking several strong breaths, and, before she could think about failure, she shoved her left leg up against the frame, bent her other knee as much as she dared without overbalancing, and shoved up as hard as possible. Again, she could not look down to spot where her feet must be planted—the girl simply had to work by feel.

The sudden lift was agonizingly slow, her heart pounding in fear that she would not get high enough. As she reached the apex of her hop, she shoved her right foot out to the side, thankfully feeling the solid form of the jutting stone against her other heel. She rammed her legs apart hard to keep from slipping and just froze there, trembling.

One of these days, I'm going to have to hang a rope out here, she thought, closing her eyes in relief.

Carefully but quickly, Emriana began to work her way up again, until at last, she was near the very top of the second row of windows, fully twenty feet above the roof of the porch. She was actually glad she couldn't look down to see how far the drop was. Her hands rested on the top of the window frames, and she could go no higher and still use them for support. Slowly, still in danger of losing her balance, the girl brought her arms up to either side and over her head, keeping them pressed flush against the wall the whole time.

Overhead, Emriana could feel the top of the wall, where a parapet surrounded a platform. The platform was the highest point of the house and had been made into an observation deck, perhaps for looking out over the walls of the estate to the city beyond or just to study the stars above. The top of the wall was smooth stone, with no protrusions or crenellations to make it easier to grasp. She rested both hands there, palms to the wall and thumbs pointing out away from her body, hooking her fingers over the top and taking some of the weight off of her rapidly weakening legs.

Drawing yet another deep, slow, calming breath, the girl gathered her strength and prepared for the last effort to get over the wall. She rebraced her legs and twisted her right hand around a full turn, swiveling it in a complete circle and once again grasping the top of the stone. Then she released her other hand and crossed it over her right, allowing herself to roll out into space and make a half turn with her whole body. She lunged around and caught hold of the top of the wall with her free hand and hung there, facing the wall, her nose pressed against it. Her toes found a hold on the top of the window frame, and from there it was easy to drag herself up and over the top of the parapet and to the platform.

Emriana collapsed in a heap there, breathless. She had done it. She had managed to scale the wall. She closed her eyes and sighed in relief. From that point, getting out of the estate was a simple process.

"Sneaking out again, O sister of mine?" came a voice from the darker shadows on the far side of the platform.

Emriana nearly shrieked in fright before she realized it was Evester, her oldest brother.

"Waukeen! You scared the hells out of me!" she fussed at him, flopping her head back onto the tiles and waiting for her heart to stop thumping. "What are you doing up here?"

Evester laughed softly and stepped out from where he had been standing, hidden in the murky darkness of a great chimney.

"I could ask you the same thing, Em," he said, coming to lean over the parapet next to Emriana and peer down over the edge, where she had just ascended. "At least I used the stairs to get here. You could have broken your neck."

"But I didn't," was all the girl replied, feeling a little smug. "You and Uncle Dregaul can't seem to figure out that I'm not a little girl anymore. I can take care of myself."

"That may be," Evester replied, still leaning on his elbows as he stared out over the city beyond the walls, "but only children take such foolish chances just to prove others wrong."

Emriana pursed her lips and refused to answer her brother. She sat up finally and looked at him. Everyone in the family said Evester resembled their father, with his strong jawline and piercing black eyes, but Emriana really couldn't have said one way or another; she was too young when Obril Matrell died, barely over a year old, and she didn't remember him. The only thing she had to go on was a great portrait of her father when he was much younger, which hung over a fireplace in her grandmother's sitting room.

Emriana thought Evester looked older than the person in that painting, much older than she would have expected for his twenty-eight years. He appeared old enough to have been her father, though he certainly didn't much act like one, nor did he seem much like a brother. In truth, she saw more of Evester's twin children than she did of him lately.

"How's Uncle Dregaul?" Emriana asked finally, just to change the subject.

"Fine, I would assume," Evester answered absently, still gazing out over the lights of Arrabar. "He's in the offices still, looking over some bills of lading."

Emriana grunted, not really sure what her brother was talking about and not really caring. To her, all of the musty old parchment sheets and columns of figures Dregaul and Evester poured over every day were the worst kind of boring.

Evester didn't seem to notice her sour reaction to his answer. He merely stared out over the city, his arms folded across the parapet.

"Do you realize how much of this city is controlled by only a handful of families?" he asked.

"No," Emriana replied, thinking it was time to go. "A lot?"

"Nine-tenths of this city's wealth is tied up in half a dozen family holdings. Ninety-nine one-hundredths is controlled by perhaps fifteen Houses. It really is remarkable. And it makes it exceedingly difficult for any true business breakthroughs to occur. No one is willing to explore the possibility of joint ventures, mergers, anything bold, because that would involve risk. And when you take a risk, there are other Houses perched around the periphery, waiting to gobble up your failures."

"Are you going to tell Uncle Dregaul that I snuck out, or not?" Emriana asked at last, tired of playing the waiting game with Evester to see what his intentions were. "You know that tonight is Spheres. I really don't want to miss it."

"Er, what?" Her brother replied, apparently drawn out of much deeper thoughts. "No, Em. That's between you and him. But if you ask me my opinion—"

"I didn't."

"—I would suggest," Evester continued, ignoring the interruption, "that you think seriously about what's to be gained versus what there is to lose. It's really all about acceptable risk. A night on the town against possible danger to life and limb and a scolding from Uncle Dregaul. Every time you climb up onto the roof, every time you prowl the streets of the city unescorted, you are risking much more than what you gain. In the business world, you'd be considered a poor investment. Too much risk."

Emriana rolled her eyes.

"Look," she said, "my birthday is in three days, Vambran is returning tonight with presents, and there's a festival in the streets. I'm not sitting here while all of the fun is out there."

"Ah, yes," Evester replied. "My prodigal brother returns from high adventure on the open seas once again. No wonder you're so eager to be on your way." He shrugged and added, "Suit yourself, but be careful. You know what kind of trouble roams the streets on a night like this."

"I won't be wandering alone," Emriana explained. "Uncle Dregaul is sending the carriage to fetch Vambran, and I just want to ride along." The girl gave an exasperated sigh and muttered, half to herself, "I don't know why he wouldn't just let me go. I'm not a child."

She rolled her eyes again, though she realized Evester probably couldn't see the expression.

"Besides," she added, "Vambran said he had a surprise for me, made it seem like he was standing right next to me, whispering in my ear. Can you imagine how he pulled that off?"

Emriana gushed, smiling as she got to her feet. She twirled once, imagining what it must be like out there, watching the Waukeenar clergy parading through the streets as they flung the glass spheres filled with coins, cheap trinkets, and tiny gems up into the air.

"And if you're still worried, don't be," the girl said, "because I've got this...."

She withdrew a slender bejeweled dagger where it had been nestled in a finely tooled scabbard, which itself was tucked into the sash at her waist. The dagger had been a present from Vambran, brought all the way from Aglarond.

"Do you even know how to use that?" Evester asked.

"Yes," Emriana retorted, rolling the dagger deftly through her hands then flipping it through the air before smoothly resheathing it. "I got Argen and some of the other guards to teach me a few things."

Evester snorted. "A little sleight of hand is far different from a street fight, you know. And you'd better not let Uncle Dregaul catch you hanging around the barracks. You know he won't consider *that* very proper."

"Duly noted," Emriana replied sarcastically, using a phrase both Evester and Uncle Dregaul seemed fond of and employed frequently. "If there's nothing else, then, dear brother, I'm on my way."

"Em," Evester said, looking pointedly at the girl then.

"Yes?" she said, pausing before hopping up onto another section of wall to begin her descent toward the perimeter of the estate and the streets of Arrabar beyond.

"Be careful."

Emriana smiled.

"I will," she said, and waved once before she crossed over the wall and began to tiptoe along the peaked roof of the estate.

She could feel Evester's eyes still on her as she reached the edge and dropped down over the side. From there, it was a simple matter to cross over to the kitchen, and the barracks, by way of the roofs. The back side of the barracks was close to a zalantar tree that grew near one wall of the property. Emriana dropped down into it from the roof of the barracks, using its many fanned-out trunks to stabilize herself. Making her way across carefully, she reached the wall and scrambled onto the walkway atop it.

She swung her legs out over the smooth parapet. Settling onto her stomach, she carefully lowered herself down the other side. She sought a small, jutting stone that she knew would be there with her toe and, when she found it, she eased her weight onto it. She then slithered down the rest of the way and dropped behind some shrubs that ran between the wall and the cobblestone street.

Emriana smiled in the darkness, pleased with herself at her successful escape and somewhat breathless with the excitement of her misbehavior. The sounds of Spheres were definitely louder, and she could tell that the crowds were just a street or two over. She quickly slipped out of her dark, snug clothing and boots and exchanged them for a colorful, tight-fitting dress and matching slippers that she had hidden in the bushes earlier in the day. Then she stood in the shadows, waiting for the carriage that her uncle had sent to fetch her brother to roll past. It wasn't long before the black, open-topped vehicle swung into view, drawn by a pair of white horses. Emriana saw Prandles, seated smartly on the driver's bench.

Perfect timing.

Emriana stepped out of her hiding place in the darkness and into view, almost skipping in delight.

. . .

"Remember, now, I don't want to see your ugly faces for a whole day," Vambran Matrell said to the pair of soldiers standing before him on the deck of *Lady's Favor*.

He stared down at the satchel resting at his feet, and toward the gangplank, then turned back once more and caught them both smiling.

"Aye, sir," Horial Rohden said, snapping to attention and giving Vambran a sharp, if mocking, salute. "Twenty-four hours, on the nose."

The man's three-day beard and disheveled black hair contrasted noticeably with his pretensions of formality.

"A whole day, lieutenant? Are you sure you can bear to wait that long?" Adyan Mercatio drawled, a twinkle in his eye, his own grin exaggerating the white scar that ran diagonally down from the middle of his chin to the jawline on his left side.

Vambran dismissed their jibes with a quick wave of his hand.

"One day isn't going to be nearly long enough," he replied in jest. "Now get out of here. I'll see you at the Crying Claw tomorrow night."

The lieutenant motioned for the two men to depart, and the pair eagerly grabbed up their own satchel bags.

As the two men turned toward the gangplank, Horial turned back to Vambran and gave him a quick, meaningful look.

"Are you sure you're all right?" he asked quietly, and Adyan turned around, too, sharing the concerned look.

Vambran nodded and motioned again.

"I'm all right," he said, trying to sound reassuring. "It's only for a few days. Now go."

Horial and Adyan frowned together, but they finally nodded in return and turned to go, scampering down the gangplank and disappearing into the hustle and bustle of the quay. Vambran watched his longtime friends vanish and sighed, not feeling nearly as confident as he tried to appear to the concerned pair.

Can I stomach my family for that long? he asked himself.

He wasn't sure he knew the answer. The carriage Uncle Dregaul would have sent for him hadn't arrived, but that wasn't surprising, given the fact that it was the evening of Spheres. The streets would be packed with revelers, and Prandles, the carriage driver, would be having a hard time of it. Still, the lieutenant knew it was more than a lack of a ride that had kept him standing on the deck of the ship for so long. He was simply stalling. After casting one more meaningful look around the deck of *Lady's Favor,* he finally, reluctantly, scooped up his own bag of personal effects and started down the gangplank.

Once he was standing on the pier, the lieutenant had to pause for a moment and get his balance. It still amazed him how much adjustment was necessary to go from the gentle roll of the ship to the unwavering feel of dry land, and he had been aboard *Lady's Favor* for merely four days. He could only imagine how hard it must be for a true sailor, living almost his entire life at sea, to get rid of his sea legs.

Then again, the man thought, I guess it wouldn't be any harder than when I first boarded a ship.

As he stood there, remembering how to walk without listing to one side or the other, Vambran sighed, already dreading his visit. Every homecoming to Arrabar was a bittersweet affair, the palpable strain that existed between his uncle and him intertwined with the delight of returning to familiar surroundings. As if to reinforce that point, the familiar scents of Arrabar's docks wafted past him, the smells triggering boyhood memories. Besides the sharp, tangy smell of pitch mixing with the stale odor of filthy saltwater in the harbor, the lieutenant caught a whiff of hot, spicy thaek buns from a shop nearby.

Hurrying up the pier, he turned onto the quay and moved briskly past the other ships in the harbor, deftly sidestepping the endless morass of longshoremen and sailors, merchants and harbor officials, and the endless stream of goods they loaded and unloaded, even at that time of the evening. They all worked ceaselessly under the light of huge lanterns hung from posts along the entire length of the harbor, and the light was more than ample for the lieutenant to move quickly and confidently.

Thaek buns and dockside memories aside, Vambran wasn't terribly happy to be back in Arrabar. Just thinking about coming face to face with Uncle Dregaul put his stomach in knots. The older man rarely had much to say to his nephew when Vambran returned home, and when they did speak, it was hardly warm. The lieutenant knew that Dregaul still greatly resented the trouble he had caused for the family, and he couldn't say that he blamed the man. They seemed to have come to a mutual if unspoken agreement to keep their distance from one another. Trips home to Arrabar were short-lived for a reason.

But beyond that discomfort, the lieutenant simply found life as a mercenary commander much preferable to the staid environment of a wealthy merchant House. Evester would eventually inherit the reins of the business and seemed to have a knack for it, which was all well and good, Vambran often told himself. He had no desire to be a part of bookkeeping and letters of credit.

Perhaps knowing I will never inherit it makes it easier to scoff, Vambran thought.

Just as quickly, though, the lieutenant dismissed the notion as wishful thinking. The truth was, the free and carousing lifestyle of a mercenary commander in Waukeen's own private military was satisfying. He was a prince among loyal men, he enjoyed visiting the many exotic locales throughout the Sea of Fallen Stars where his duties often sent him, and he could always find himself in the company of a lady if he so desired.

With all that life in the Sapphire Crescent had to offer, though, Vambran wasn't foolish enough to discount the benefits of being a member of a prominent mercantile family. His rank in the mercenary company, though not purchased, had been enhanced by his family connections, he knew. And even if he was one of the Crescent's best and brightest—or so his

captain had claimed—the monthly stipend he received
from Uncle Dregaul was nothing to sneer at, for it was
in actuality far more than his lieutenant's pay. And
truthfully, he got along well with most of his relatives.
He was looking forward to seeing his grandmother,
and Emriana of course. Thinking of his younger sister
put a smile on Vambran's face, albeit a brief one.

Uncle Dregaul—and Evester too, more and more—
apparently felt the need to make Vambran miserable
whenever he returned home from a tour of duty. What
was so galling to the lieutenant was the way the older
man so prominently displayed his antipathy, despite
the fact that only a small circle of older family
members knew the truth. There always seemed to be
questions surrounding his choices, out-loud musings
concerning what he was really doing with his life.
That, even though it was common knowledge he would
never hold the reins of the family business himself.

Hell, Dregaul was the one who encouraged me to
join the temple, Vambran thought, though he knew
good and well that, at the time, the man was simply
trying to get his nephew out of his sight. Anything
to avoid reminding him of what happened, Vambran
mused, sighing.

Even so, Vambran knew that soldiering was not
what Dregaul had had in mind, and he made a point
of expressing that any chance he could. And that was
really what the lieutenant's reluctance was all about.
Every time Vambran returned home, his uncle and
his older brother would poke and prod, hoping to hear
that he was finally going to give up the soldiering, join
the ranks of the true temple clergy, and rise to a position of prominence, which would in turn strengthen
House Matrell's position with the Waukeenar. He
hated it, and he wanted more than anything just to
avoid the whole issue.

When are you going to grow up? the lieutenant
could hear his uncle asking. When are you going to

stop wasting your time and opportunities doing a
common man's work?

What you really mean is, when am I going to make
amends by being more useful to you, right, Uncle?

Just thinking of the impending confrontation set
the lieutenant on edge. Common or not, Vambran
liked commanding soldiers, and he wasn't planning
to give it up any time soon. But though the young man
might have the firmest of convictions, Dregaul had a
habit of manipulating his nephew with guilt. Sooner
or later, his uncle would win. He always did. Standing
up to Dregaul just made Vambran's stomach roil.

Though that could be hunger, too, Vambran
thought, smelling the thaek buns again. He supposed
he was hoping a little wry amusement would ease his
tensions, at least for a time.

Turning onto a cobblestone-paved street winding
up the hill from the harbor, Vambran left the wharf
behind and moved deeper into the city of Arrabar,
keeping half an eye out for the Matrell carriage.
The street was alive with people gathered together
or moving in large clumps, many of them dressed
gaily and laughing together or singing. Lengths of
rope or chain had been strung between buildings or
along balconies, from which dangled hundreds of lanterns and multicolored pennants and streamers that
wafted in the lazy, salt-laden breeze. The celebration
of Spheres was in full swing, he realized.

Vambran spotted a thaek bun cart offering the
delicious meals and his mouth began to water. He
shifted his satchel to his other shoulder and pulled
his coin pouch free of the hidden pocket where he
kept it inside his *naraebul*. He fumbled a pair of
coppers out, slipped the pouch back underneath the
short cloak, and strolled up to the cart. The proprietor passed him a large bun and took his coin with a
smile, and Vambran was on his way, biting into the
snack gingerly. His first mouthful rewarded him

with spicy meat, mushrooms, and onions soaked in a tomato-and-peppers sauce. He closed his eyes in contentment, savoring the taste.

It's always the food I miss the most, the lieutenant mused, taking another bite.

At the next corner, Vambran was forced to stop, for the crowds there had gotten a lot thicker, and he could see why. One of the many parades common to Spheres was passing by, led by a mitered Halanthi bedecked in his overly gaudy vestments. Even from that distance, Vambran could see the numerous gems and thread-of-gold sparkling all over the Waukeenar priest's scarlet cloak, as well as the robes themselves. The lieutenant thought he recognized the Halanthi, though he wasn't certain. Not that seeing an unfamiliar face bedecked in Waukeenar vestments would have surprised him. The temple swelled with new priests almost every day, drawn to its resurgence since Waukeen had returned to Brightwater. In the two years since the Merchant's Friend had reappeared, the temple's ranks had nearly doubled.

The priest waved and smiled at everyone as he strolled past, followed by a horde of musicians playing a lively dancing tune. They in turn were followed by a large oxen-drawn wagon, also brightly decorated, upon which sat a handful of Telchar and Coins, the most novice of priests in the temple. As they rumbled by, those young men and women alternated between smiling and waving at the crowds and tossing fist-sized spheres of glass up into the air that were filled with cheap pretties—small imperfect gems, a few coppers or silver coins, and perhaps a necklace of beads or two. The spheres shattered whenever they struck anything, though they had been magically altered so that the fragments of glass became as soft as parchment afterward. The crowds who'd gathered along the parade route laughed and ran, trying to scoop up the treasures where they landed, or even attempting to catch the delicate orbs as they fell from the night sky.

A drunk man, amber foam flecking his thick beard, staggered past Vambran, his eyes twinkling in merriment, one cupped hand holding a combination of sphere fragments and coppers, the other a beaten tin belt cup half full of frothy beer. He wore three or four colored necklaces around his neck, and as he neared a woman standing next to the lieutenant, the man paused, smiled broadly, and attempted to pull one of the strands free, presumably to give to her. Unfortunately, he went for the necklace with the belt cup still in his hand and wound up tipping beer out onto the cobblestones. He stopped and stared forlornly down at the widening puddle as the lady laughed, then leaned in a gave him a quick kiss on the cheek before trotting off, disappearing into the crowds. The drunk man watched her vanish, then turned and gave Vambran a wink and a smile before staggering on his way.

Vambran laughed, deciding that, for the moment at least, he was happy to be home. He hadn't remembered it was Spheres until they were only a day out of Arrabar, but it was a good if unintentional welcome-back celebration, he decided, and he was glad for it. He turned to see if he could find a way through the crowds since the parade had passed and thought he heard someone calling his name. He stopped and peered around, uncertain if he'd imagined it.

"Vambran!" the call came again, and that time, the lieutenant heard it clearly.

He turned in the direction of the sound and was nearly knocked to the ground as a woman in a brightly colored dress launched herself at him and wrapped him in a bear hug. He nearly dropped the remaining chunk of thaek bun to the street in surprise. It took him another heartbeat to recognize the shoulder-length tresses of windblown black hair, slightly damp from the sultry air.

"Em!" Vambran cried, returning the hug and laughing. "I didn't recognize you!" he said, pulling back at last to get a better look at his sister. "By Waukeen, but you must have grown a foot since I last saw you."

Emriana rolled her dark eyes at him.

"It's only been two months," she chided, but her beaming face told Vambran that his comment delighted her.

In truth, the girl only came up to Vambran's chin, but she still seemed to have matured considerably. He raised an eyebrow at her rather snug dress.

"Been teasing Denrick again?" he asked, gesturing at her figure, which he realized was no longer that of a little girl's.

His sister was rapidly becoming a woman, and a startlingly pretty one, at that.

Emriana smirked, rolling her eyes again.

"Please," she said with more than a hint of disdain. "Don't ruin the evening by mentioning *him*." The girl cocked her head to one side, staring Vambran squarely in the face. "Three?" she asked, obviously puzzled.

The lieutenant started to shake his head quizzically, then he realized she was referring to the three painted dots upon his forehead.

"Ah, yes," he said, nodding and smiling. "That's my new surprise. I've been working with one of the other Crescents, and I've managed to learn a few simple tricks."

Emriana's eyes widened, first in surprise, then in delight.

"Really? You have to show me! That's wonderfu—" The girl froze as something occurred to her. "Wait," she said, turning her head sideways, looking at her brother askance. "Is that how you sent me your message?" she asked, growing excited again. "That was wonderful! You must teach me."

Vambran shook his head and held his hands up, trying to calm his sister down a bit.

"No, no," he said, laughing at her exuberance. "That was something else entirely. I'm not *that* good with the magic, yet."

Emriana glared at her brother.

"You know what Uncle Dregaul will say, once he sees that on you," she scolded. "Sometimes I think he's convinced that every wizard in town is secretly preparing to bring back the magic plague."

Vambran started to tell his sister that he had no intention of letting his uncle see the third mark and risk his wrath unnecessarily, but he never got the chance. Emriana lunged at Vambran again, hugging him tightly once more.

"Oh, it's good to see you home," she said, her voice muffled in his shoulder. "When I got your strange message that you'd be home tonight, I knew I had to come down and meet you. Sorry I'm late. I'm glad I didn't miss you."

Vambran pulled free of her embrace and stepped back.

"Only you?" he asked, his mouth beginning to curve in a barely concealed smirk. "Sneaking out again?" he added, his tone teasing.

"No, not just me. Prandles has the carriage on the other side of the road," she said, pointing toward the black vehicle with its attendant horses. "But Uncle Dregaul wasn't going to let me come. I'm going to turn sixteen in three days, and he still treats me like I'm five."

"So how did you change his mind?"

Emriana smiled and said, "I didn't." At her brother's bemused smile and mildly shaking head, the girl pretended to grow indignant. "Stop it! I missed you!" She gestured toward the remains of the thaek bun in her brother's hand, and at the celebration going on around them. "And I knew it would take you forever to get home with all this going on, and I couldn't stand waiting."

"So you snuck out." Vambran said, still smirking. "Again."

"Yes," Emriana replied, stamping her foot in frustration. "Why does everyone keep bringing that up?"

Vambran laughed.

"Well, it's no skin off my nose, but don't be hiding behind me if you get caught," he said, pretending to sound stern. "I may command an entire company of professional soldiers, but Uncle Dregaul is still the man to answer to in House Matrell." He chuckled and added, "At least this way, if you sneak back in, you have to pretend you haven't seen me yet and I get a whole new set of hugs."

In response to his teasing, Emriana stuck her tongue out at him playfully. Then she took his free hand and they turned toward the carriage together. As the pair of them approached, Prandles hopped down, bowing repeatedly at Vambran.

"Evening, Master Vambran," the driver said, his voice somewhat rough and gravelly and his accent common. "Good to have you home again. Do you have other things for me to fetch?"

Vambran shook his head and replied, "We can send a wagon to get them off the ship tomorrow, Prandles. Let's just go home."

"Very good, sir," the driver said.

He climbed up onto the bench once Vambran and Emriana were seated and the door was properly shut.

Soon, the carriage was on its way, making reasonable progress through the crowds, which were thinning somewhat because the parade was long past.

"So," the girl said as they rolled out of the port district, climbing the gentle hills upon which Arrabar had grown. "What did you bring me from Sembia?"

They were moving into the trade district by then, where the buildings were spaced more widely apart and loomed behind formidable walls. Imposing estates of white stone with highlights of burgundy, deep green, azure, or any of a dozen other rich colors sprouted numerous golden-spired domes and towers. Those were the palatial homes of the city's wealthiest merchant-nobles, and among them rested the Matrell estate.

Vambran snorted and said, "What makes you think I brought you anything?"

Emriana laughed and playfully punched her brother in the arm.

"Because it's almost my birthday, Meazel-face!"

Vambran feigned shock and dismay.

"It is?" he teased. "Oh, that's right . . . Em's birthday."

He tapped his chin, pretending to contemplate that news.

Emriana glared at her brother again and said, "And I know you're smarter than to show yourself around here without bringing me a birthday present."

Vambran mimed horror at the suggestion, then grinned again.

"You're not sixteen yet. You'll just have to wait until your party to see what it is."

Emriana growled in exasperation, but her delight wouldn't allow her to hold the scowl.

"Grandmother Hetta is planning something amazing, so I hear from Jaleene," she gushed. "But no one will tell me anything," she continued, pouting again. "It's supposed to be a complete surprise."

"As well it should. It's not every day you turn sixteen, you know."

The carriage continued on, passing the houses of the truly great merchant families. On the left was the ever-private House Darowdryn, whose occupants all sported hair so fair as to be almost white. Several blocks down and on the right was the sprawling

Cauldyl estate, home of the most sneering and pretentious family Vambran had ever had the displeasure
to meet. Up the next rise, the spires of House Mestel
rose up, peeking over a whole grove of suth trees stra-
tegically planted around the entire perimeter of the
grounds, just behind the outer wall, for privacy.

Vambran grimaced slightly, thinking of the Mestels, and how his grandfather had been born a bastard
to one lordling of that family. Even after Obiron Matrell had changed his name and made a fortune with
his own merchant company, the Mestels still looked
down their noses at what they considered cousins born
on the wrong side of the district. Vambran doubted
it would ever be any different. House Matrell was a
fine merchant empire, but it was small compared to
the half-dozen or so truly ancient ones, in existence
almost since the founding of the city.

The lieutenant shook his head, ridding his mind
of such unpleasant thoughts.

Instead, he turned to his sister and said, "So, Em,
tell me what's been going on in the great halls of our
beloved homestead. How's Mother?"

Emriana shrugged and replied, "She's fine. Spends
all day with Grandma, or staring out the window day-
dreaming, as usual."

"Hmm," Vambran grunted. "How about Evester?
How are the twins?"

"Evester is turning into Uncle Dregaul more and
more every day," Emriana replied with a sour tone.
"The two of them go off to the offices and hunch over
their books all day. He hardly has time for his own
children, much less me. But the twins are fine, though
I can't keep Quindy out of my rooms, lately. She wants
to try on my clothes all the time. And Obiron is just
a wild thing. He actually went running through the
garden the other day with a loaded crossbow, screaming at the top of his lungs. I thought he was hunting
one of the panthers or something."

Vambran swallowed hard at that image and shuddered. Emriana seemed not to notice. Recovering, the lieutenant forced a chuckle.

"Now you see why I joined the Crescents. Too much niece and nephew is never a good thing."

"Yeah, well, I've been lobbying Grandma to build me a private wing. After the crossbow incident the other day, I think she was almost convinced."

Vambran laughed out loud at that. He could only imagine how Grandmother Hetta, the matriarch of the family, would have reacted. He found himself honestly smiling again, thinking fondly of seeing her. He doubted she would have retired for the evening—the woman kept long hours, even at eighty-one years of age. Uncle Dregaul might have managed the day-to-day operations of the family business, but Hetta Debrinne Matrell was still the head of the household.

It's good to be home, Vambran decided.

He turned to his sister to tell her so, but the words never came out. A loud, desperate scream issued from an alleyway between two blocks of shops, cutting him off.

CHAPTER TWO

S tay here," Vambran instructed his sister.
He stood up in the carriage and leaped
over the side to the street before it had even
come to a stop. The lieutenant broke into a run
even as he hit the ground, sprinting full-out
in the direction of the screams still reverber-
ating from the alley, which was flanked by
a bakery on one side and a chandler's shop
on the other. Both businesses were dark and
shuttered, as were the windows on the stories
above, where the shop owners and their families dwelt. Only the light of the moon showed
the soldier the route into the alley.

As he dashed down into the deeper darkness between the two businesses, Vambran
slipped a narrow-bladed steel sword free of
the scabbard that hung on his left hip. With
the weapon in one hand, the lieutenant

deftly reached inside a pocket of his shirt, pulling free a scrap of parchment with the other. Another scream echoed through the air, definitely the voice of a woman. That was followed closely by a second cry, delivered by a man. It was a cry of pain.

Surging forward, Vambran rounded a bend in the alley and into a small courtyard with no other apparent exits. The backs of several more shops and homes formed the barrier to the open area, which was perhaps twenty paces across at its widest point. In one corner, a handful of figures gathered in a clump.

Slowing for a moment, Vambran closed his eyes and muttered a quick prayer to Waukeen. He pulled out a gold medallion that hung from a chain around his neck and that displayed the Merchant Friend's profile. He brought the coin to his mouth for a quick kiss, the scrap of parchment held between his lips and the coin face. Crumpling the parchment and moving it in a circular motion around his body, he finished the prayer. The lieutenant felt the parchment fragment dissolve into dust in his hand and he opened his eyes to confirm that a shimmering, glowing aura surrounded him. He stepped out into the dead-end courtyard and advanced openly toward the gathering of thugs.

Half a dozen of the attackers were huddled with their backs to Vambran, weapons drawn. Most of the figures were standing, gathered around a trio of others who were down on the ground. One of the standing shapes held aloft a lantern, and by its light Vambran could see that two of the figures lay motionless on the cobblestones of the alley, while the third held a thin dagger in his hand. The kneeling figure thrust the blade into the body closest to it, which convulsed once at the attack, then lay still again.

"Hold!" Vambran said, slowing his pace only slightly as he closed the distance toward the assailants. "Stand down!"

Even as he spoke those orders, Vambran advanced
warily, in a crouch, ready for the fight he was certain
was coming. A part of him wondered what he was
getting himself into.

As the group of assailants turned to face Vambran,
the mercenary realized they were more than simple
thugs. All armed and armored alike, with half-spears
and crossbows, they wore matching clothing: dark-
colored breeches with a white shirt. The lieutenant
also noticed for the first time a crest or logo upon each
man's breast, and as the group in front of him realized
they were under attack themselves, they fanned out,
bringing their weapons to bear.

Vambran skidded to a stop, his boots sliding on
the damp cobblestones of the alley. The symbol of
Arrabar—three golden balls on a field of white—shone
visibly in the lanternlight on the group's breastplates,
marking them as city watch.

Vambran frowned even as he held his free hand up
in a placating manner. Something there didn't feel
quite right, but that thought, along with the notion
that he needed to diffuse the situation, passed through
his head in the blink of an eye. Unfortunately, he was
not quick enough to demonstrate that he recognized
the soldiers as official watchmen, for one of them fired
his crossbow at the lieutenant.

In his unbalanced position, having just skittered
to a stop so close to the men, Vambran had no way
to twist clear of the missile. The bolt flew straight
at his shoulder and would have pierced his flesh,
had it not been for the magical protection he had
thrown around himself just moments before. The
glimmering aura of magic saved him, turning aside
the bolt at a funny angle but wrenching his shoulder back painfully in the process. Vambran grunted
and stumbled back, throwing his other arm up to
protect his face well after the missile had already
flown past.

"Easy!" Vambran managed to call out as he spun away from the group and went down to one knee, making his body a smaller target as a second bolt flew past. "I yield, watchmen!"

He heard a snort from behind him, and several footsteps closing, but no more shots were fired.

"Drop your blade now, pretty boy!" Vambran heard one gruff voice call out, even as two more soldiers fanned into view on either side of him, leveling their half-spears at his head.

Calmly, gently, Vambran laid his steelblade down in front of him and lifted both of his hands well out to either side of himself.

"All right, easy," he said, peering at the two men who were in view. "It's down, no need to get worked up."

He tried to offer a disarming smile, but he got nothing but scowls in return.

"Stand up! Get away from the weapon," the same gruff voice demanded.

Vambran did as he was instructed, backing away from where he had laid his sword down.

"Now turn around," the guard commanded.

Vambran spun slowly in place, keeping his hands up and out, trying to look as unthreatening as possible.

"I didn't recognize your uniforms in the dark," he started to explain as he turned in place, "I thought you were muggers or—"

"Shut up!" the soldier commanded, stepping closer as Vambran completed his turn. The lieutenant was facing the fellow and noticed that he was marked as a sergeant. "You have a death wish?" the sergeant asked.

He was a short, stocky, dark-skinned fellow, with darker hair that sat in greasy waves on his head. A full, unkempt beard matched the hair, and even in the weak lanternlight, Vambran could see streaks of gray in both. The man's eyes were dark and sunken, with big circles under them, like he hadn't gotten a good deal of sleep. As he stood in front of the lieutenant, he brought his free hand up to bite at the fingernail on his thumb, studying his counterpart.

"Of course not," Vambran answered, shaking his head. "As I said, I didn't—"

"Yeah, yeah, I get it. Shut your trap."

The sergeant motioned for one of his men to move closer, then stood back and watched as the soldier handed his half-spear to a companion and stepped forward to search Vambran, patting him down.

Vambran suffered the examination quietly, but his sense that something was out of place was growing steadily. Though their clothing marked them as guards, none of the men had the bearing of city watchmen. He couldn't quite put his finger on it, but they seemed somehow less professional than he remembered. That alone wouldn't be enough to convince him, he knew, but then there was the matter of the two other individuals, who still lay motionless on the cobblestones behind the row of guards.

Vambran peered in that direction, trying to see who was lying there as the guard completed his search of the lieutenant's body. From that distance, with the light so bad and with the soldiers screening his view, he could make out very little, but it was clear that a man and a woman were both back there, dressed in fairly simple clothing.

Once the guard was finished searching Vambran, he stepped back into the line. Vambran lowered his hands to his sides.

The sergeant noticed Vambran trying to get a better look at the two corpses and moved closer, blocking his view.

"Keep your eyes on me, and stop getting your nose into business that doesn't concern you!" the fellow barked.

Vambran's eyes narrowed. He was not fond of that one. In most cases, when the watch encountered a man dressed in the markings of a mercenary of the temple of Waukeen's private army, he could expect a certain amount of deference. Even when that was not the case, however, city guardsmen rarely displayed such a brazen lack of manners.

"It seems awfully odd that the Arrabar city watch is in the business of slaying people in dark alleyways," Vambran said, his voice cold, "especially as I don't see any weapons on those two."

The man in front of him cocked his head to one side, his jaw beginning to jut out in what Vambran could only believe was belligerent insult.

"Oh, a thinker, eh? Well, not that it's any concern of yours, pretty boy, but them two back there were running from us after we tried to question them about three dots on their foreheads." He stepped closer still, putting his face right up next to Vambran's, though the guard came up only to the lieutenant's nose. "The same three dots that mark your head!"

Vambran blinked, taken aback a little bit.

"What?" the mercenary asked. "They were wizards?"

"No," the sergeant replied smugly, smiling for the first time and showing a mouth full of yellowed and blackened teeth. "That's the whole point. They weren't wizards, but they were pretending to be. And you know what the penalty for pretending at sorcery is, right?"

Vambran nodded, not liking where the discussion was going at all.

"I can assure you, my own markings are completely legitimate, and I'll be happy to—"

"Hey!" one of the other soldiers cried out, turning and scampering across the alley toward the exit. "Someone's spying on us!"

The guard sprinted across the cobblestones to a pile of wooden-slatted crates stacked haphazardly near the back door of one of the buildings.

Vambran groaned as almost all the other soldiers either turned to peer at what their companion was chasing or wisely tightened their grips on their weapons as they surrounded him. He turned to look at what the guard was pursuing, too, already knowing what was about to happen.

As the guard got closer to the stack of crates, there was a shrill squeak, and a figure flashed up and away, running awkwardly back in the direction of the end of the alley. But the mysterious spy was not fast enough and the guard quickly grabbed her, yanking her to a stop.

"Ow! Let me go, you big orc!" the figure cried out.

It was Emriana, just as Vambran feared. The guard twisted her around and held her at arm's length for a moment, eyeing her critically. Then he reached out and pulled something free of her sash and proceeded to haul her back by her wrist toward the gathering in the courtyard.

"Stop yanking on my arm!" Emriana continued to complain as she was dragged against her will, digging in her heels.

Her slippers skidded fruitlessly across the damp cobblestones, unable to keep the man from making progress. Vambran saw that the guard had confiscated a dagger from his sister, and indeed, he then recognized it as the very same one he had given to her for her birthday a year previous.

The leader of the surly band of watchmen hissed in vexation as his underling towed Emriana into the lanternlight, still thrashing and yanking her arm, trying to pull free of her captor.

"Who the blazes is this?" the sergeant demanded, jerking his gaze back and forth between the girl and Vambran.

"My name is Emriana Matrell, of House Matrell, and you will let go of me immediately! My uncle—"

"Em! Enough," Vambran growled, staring hard at her. "Didn't I tell you to wait in the carriage?" he asked, his voice hard-edged with anger.

"You know her?" the leader asked, forcing Vambran to turn his attention back to the guard.

The lieutenant nodded and said, "Yes, she's my sister. We were on our way home when we heard the screams and I came running. She's out past her bedtime," he added, raising his voice and directing this last bit at Emriana, hoping to drive his point home, "and should not be here."

The girl glared at him but said nothing.

"And why shouldn't I assume that you two are actually friends of my two deaders—" the sergeant jerked his thumb over his shoulder, indicating the pair of bodies lying in the courtyard behind him—"sneaking in here to help them?"

At that, Vambran nearly laughed. The word of a lieutenant of the Sapphire Crescent should have been good enough for the soldier, but everything about the man just seemed wrong.

Shaking his head and with disdain clear in his voice, Vambran said, "Well, of course you should suspect us. You wouldn't be doing your duty if you didn't insist that I demonstrate my ability right here and now." The lieutenant was just baiting the man, then, seeing how well the sergeant knew procedures. "So, what do you say? Shall I prove to you that I have the right to mark myself thrice with the chalk?"

He turned his palms up, waiting to see whether he should proceed or not.

After a moment of eyeing him warily, the sergeant gave a nod to the soldier who was holding Emriana, and said, "Keep her close, and slip her own blade into her ribs if this one tries anything."

Emriana squeaked again, and Vambran opened his mouth in anger, ready to argue with the sergeant, but the man held up his hand to indicate he would hear nothing from his prisoners.

"If you are who you say you are," the sergeant said, "then you've got nothing to hide, and if you aren't, then I'm not giving you a chance to charm us all with your stinking magic. Now make a show, and no tricks."

Vambran sighed, equally angry at both the sergeant and Emriana, and considered what he might show them that wouldn't be construed as an attack or threat of any kind. Then, he got an idea. He only hoped Prandles would understand. Outwardly, he nodded.

"I use this little trick to rally troops on the battlefield, to signal for reinforcements to move out, or to indicate any of another few special instructions. It's just a simple magical flare, so don't get excited when it goes off, all right?"

The sergeant squinted at the lieutenant suspiciously but then nodded, indicating for Vambran to proceed.

Taking a deep, steadying breath, Vambran uttered a single magical syllable, and about twenty feet directly over his head a dazzling burst of bright white light went off, hanging there for several moments, illuminating the entirety of the courtyard. All of the city watchmen murmured in mild surprise, and the sergeant cocked his head, then finally nodded in reluctant approval. But Vambran wasn't watching. He had taken the opportunity to get a good, long look at the two victims lying on the ground behind the row of soldiers.

The male of the two was turned face down and away from Vambran, and the mercenary couldn't get a clear view of the man's face. But the woman was on her back, her simple white dress stained with her own blood, her eyes staring sightlessly up into the night, as though she, too, were watching the flare overhead. On her forehead Vambran could see three fuzzy marks, apparently dots made with a bit of blue chalk, though they were not the neat, orderly marks he would have expected to see on someone vain enough to paint herself as reader, writer, and wizard. They seemed to have been applied hastily.

The flare fizzled out after a moment, returning the courtyard to relative darkness, and Vambran turned his attention back to the sergeant, cocking one eyebrow expectantly. He realized quickly that the soldier could not see his expression, though, because he had gazed into the light of the magical flare and was suffering an inability to see clearly in the darkness.

"Well?" Vambran demanded at last, tired of waiting for the foolish man to admit that the lieutenant was who he said he was and no threat to the city watch.

"All right," the sergeant said at last, waving Vambran away. "You've proved your point. You and your sister can go." He motioned for his underlings to let the pair pass unhindered, then turned back to Vambran. "But let this be a lesson to you, and don't go barging in where you aren't wanted or needed."

Vambran sniffed in bemused disgust. The suggestion that he was doing anything other than what was noble and right appalled him. That just wasn't like the city watch at all, to go around insulting members of the merchant families, or of the mercenary companies, for that matter. There might be some resentment or even jealousy on the guards' parts, but rarely was there such a level of animosity and lack of respect.

At that moment, there was a commotion from the opposite end of the courtyard, where the alley emptied into it. A new group of city guards had arrived, a full squad of twelve, moving out into the open with the obvious self-confidence that Vambran was used to in Arrabar. From the first sergeant's expression, it was plain to Vambran that the man had neither expected nor welcomed the intrusion, but he was at a loss as to what to do about it for the moment. More damning evidence against him, as far as Vambran was concerned.

Briefly, the lieutenant considered just outright accusing the original soldiers as imposters to the newcomers, exposing them through their own ignorance of proper procedure and letting the new squad arrest them for impersonation of city officials and, more important, murder, but he doubted it would end as simply as that. More likely, the original group would put up a fight, and Vambran didn't want Emriana in the middle of a skirmish.

On impulse, Vambran decided to try something. Taking another drawn-out breath, he focused his attention on the sergeant in a new way, drawing on his spiritual connection with his faith and his deity to sense the man's emotions, his surface thoughts. He let the sensation wash over him, building in strength. At first, all the lieutenant could sense was the presence of thoughts tumbling around, but then he was able to focus specifically on what the man was thinking.

The sergeant was standing there looking back and forth between Vambran and the new arrivals, frowning more deeply by the moment. The new squad of watchmen drew close, and Vambran could see that they were led by a captain, a crisply dressed woman with very short dark hair and a perpetual smirk. She was eyeing the first group askance.

She finally barked, "So? What's going on here?"

Vambran smiled calmly and replied, "We were just waiting for you to arrive. The sergeant here was just about to tell me where I should report tomorrow. For the debriefing, of course," he added, still grinning disarmingly.

All the while, he was still focusing on the male sergeant's mental emanations.

"The debriefing?" the man opposite Vambran asked, obviously confused.

The watch captain nodded and said to Vambran, "Right. You need to be at the district headquarters first thing tomorrow, at seven bells. Do you know where that is?"

Vambran began to read nervousness in the fellow's mind. He pushed a little further.

"Yes, absolutely," he answered agreeably. "Seven bells. And you'll perform the divine ceremony then, too, right? To contact the spirit of the slain victims? Standard procedure whenever there's a death, right?"

The female captain nodded in agreement.

"Ask for me," she said, "Captain Leguay."

Vambran nodded, but his attention was on watching the male and still focusing on the man's thoughts and emotions.

"Oh, uh, right," the sergeant said, befuddled. Vambran was reading clear uncertainty and panic in his thoughts by then. "You said you were with House Matrell?" the sergeant asked, and Vambran sensed desperation.

"Right," he answered, smiling even more. "It's just around the next bend, in fact."

"Well, uh, then be sure to report at seven bells, just like she said."

The captain looked quizzically at her male counterpart and said, "I don't recognize you. Are you stationed in this district?"

The male's eyes widened, and his fingers flexed, as though he wanted to go for his half-spear. Vambran sensed almost overwhelming panic, and he was afraid the man would lose his nerve and simply try to fight his way out of the situation, but instead, the greasy-haired fellow shook his head and said, "No, we're from the other side of the city. We were, um, working on a special assignment."

The female cocked one eyebrow, then shrugged it off.

"Ah, well. Saves me from having to fill out the report," she said. "Let's get the bodies to the station house."

The sergeant winced, then nodded and slunk off, just to get away from the woman's scrutiny. Vambran's smile grew even broader.

"That sounds fine," he said, and he was smiling on the inside, too.

The sergeant was clearly scrambling to maintain his facade, struggling to appear legitimate, when all he wanted to do was get away from there. The lieutenant was picking up another line of thought, too. The sergeant was very worried about Vambran finding out about the others, and what sort of threat that would be to him. Who the others were, the lieutenant could not get enough of a read on to figure out, but the sergeant was obviously afraid of them and would do whatever it took to keep them placated. It was, of course, what the lieutenant had hoped to glean from the man, figuring that thugs wouldn't go to all the trouble to kill someone and make it look like a crime on their own. Someone else had to be behind the deaths, and he figured the best way to find out was to the let the men get away with it, then track them down later.

"Tomorrow, then," the captain said, and Vambran sensed that it was time for him and his sister to leave.

"Of course," Vambran said, "We're on our way." He turned on his heel and moved over to where Emriana was still scowling at the soldier who had accosted her in the first place. "Come on, Em, let's get you home and into bed. I'm sure this is enough excitement for you for one night."

"But my—!" the girl started to protest, but Vambran clamped a hand over her mouth as he spun her around to lead her down the alley.

Emriana squirmed and tugged at her brother's hand, but when it was clear he wasn't going to let go, she relaxed and let him lead her away.

When they were far enough from the soldiers not to be overheard, Vambran released her mouth after whispering, "Don't make a scene. I have my reasons."

"They have my dagger," Emriana complained. "They never gave it back."

"That's right," Vambran replied. "I want them to keep it."

"Why?" the girl demanded, turning with a furious mien to face her brother. "That was your birthday present to me!"

"Shh!" Vambran admonished her, gesturing for her to quiet down. "Because I want to be able to find that first group of soldiers later," he explained as they passed out of the alley and back into the street. "Now I have a way to track them."

"What? How?"

"With magic," Vambran said.

Across the street from the alley, Prandles saw the two of them emerge, and his shoulders slumped in obvious relief. As the siblings approached the carriage, the driver jumped down to open the door for them.

"And why do you want to track them down?" Emriana asked quietly.

"Because I don't think they were city guards," Vambran replied. "I think something else was going on here."

He wondered if he was being as foolish as that comment just sounded. Even with all of the intrigue so common to Arrabar, thugs posing as the city watch seemed a bit farfetched.

"Then why didn't you report that to the others when they arrived?"

"Because, my incorrigible sister, you were in the middle of it, and if a fight broke out, you'd have been in a risky spot."

"I can take care of myself."

"Like you did hiding behind those crates?" Vambran asked sarcastically, scowling. "That was really foolish, you know."

"No more foolish than you running down an alley by yourself." Emriana replied smugly.

"That's different."

"Why?"

"Because," Vambran said, sighing in exasperation, "I'm a trained soldier, equipped to deal with the kinds of things found in dark alleys. I really can take care of myself. You aren't used to dealing with anything beyond the walls of House Matrell yet, though you may think you are. Em, didn't you see that woman lying there? She was dead, killed by those men. I don't want that to be you."

"Vambran," Emriana whispered, changing the subject, "I think I knew that woman."

"What?" Vambran said, spinning his sister to face him. "Who is she?"

"I don't know," the girl confessed, shaking her head doubtfully. "But I think I've seen her somewhere. Several times, in fact."

"Try to remember, Em," Vambran encouraged her.

"When I saw your signal, Master Vambran, I was about to drive home and fetch the house guards," Prandles said to the pair. "But thankfully, those city guards arrived. Is everyone all right?"

Vambran, realizing that they were standing in the middle of the quiet street, nodded as he turned Emriana and guided her to the steps of the vehicle.

"Yes," he answered as Prandles helped Emriana up into the seat. "The guards are taking care of it." He climbed in after his sister. "But we were lucky," he said, giving Emriana a stare as he sat down.

"You had me worried more than a man has a right to be, Mistress Emriana," the driver added, trying not to scold a superior, but making his point all the same.

"Prandles, the next time she tries to sneak off, even if she orders you to sit still and be quiet, you have my

permission to hold her down and sit on her to keep
her out of trouble," Vambran said, though he was still
looking directly at Emriana as he said it.

The girl bristled and started to open her mouth to
protest, but Vambran gave her a level look so scathing that she wilted under it and snapped her teeth
shut again.

"As you say, sir," Prandles replied, though Vambran
knew the man would never do any such thing.

All the way back to the front gates of the Matrell
estate, Emriana sat opposite her brother and scowled.
But Vambran was in no mood to soothe her feelings
right then. He was figuring out what he was going to
do about men pretending to be city guards.

...

Grozier Talricci, standing behind Bartimus and
watching the events taking place in the mirror,
made a strangled sound deep in his throat. Bartimus
couldn't blame the man; it was an amazing stroke of
bad luck that Vambran and Emriana Matrell had
managed to stumble onto the scene when they did, and
the arrival of a second squad of watchmen, legitimate
guards who had claimed the body and were taking
it back to the station house, just made everything
worse. The uniforms for the team had been meant as
a means of avoiding notice, but through terrible luck,
they were being forced to pose as guards for who knew
how long. Events had just gotten far more complicated
than they really should have been, and Bartimus was
very sympathetic toward Grozier's state of mind at
that moment.

The wizard waited expectantly for Grozier to give
him some kind of instructions, occasionally glancing
around at his study. There were only a few candles
burning, not really giving off enough light to make
everything out clearly, though that wasn't causing a

problem right then, since the scene the pair of them
were currently scrying was dark, too. But he had been
working by candlelight for quite a while, having run
out of lamp oil at some point and never bothering to
go fetch any more from the storerooms. So the place
was constantly dark.

Matters weren't helped by the dim décor of Bartimus's chambers. He had always liked rich, dark
furniture, things made of dark woods and leather.
He had plenty of it in there, with shelves lining just
about every wall, and more than a few chairs, tables,
and desks in what space was left over. Of course, most
of all that was stacked with piles of books, tablets,
and scroll cases, with even more spilling over onto the
floor in every imaginable corner. The few tapestries
that hung on the walls, mostly covered up by shelv
ing, had the same heavy colors, as did the rug on the
floor. There was more of the same in the other room,
where Bartimus slept. It was a consistent theme, he
realized. Somehow, it contrasted nicely with Bartimus's incessantly pasty skin.

The place needed a good cleaning, Bartimus noticed, looking around more earnestly then, though the
wizard told himself that at least once a tenday and
somehow never managed to do anything about it. Too
much else going on to take time for housework. And
there was no way he was going to bring anyone else
in there to do it for him. If he ever let anyone else into
his chambers to move things around, he'd never find
half his possessions again. Even having Grozier in
there was making him nervous; one wrong step, and
the man could send a whole pile of stuff scattering
across the floor.

Perhaps a special sort of servant spell could do
the trick, the diminutive wizard mused, pondering
briefly if he had ever acquired such an incantation,
and where it might be stashed in his collection of
scrolls, books, and other magical writings.

I'll have to dig through those Sembian letters sometime, he thought. I think there might be something in there. Later, though.

Bartimus turned his attention back to the moment, still waiting for his companion to say something. His scrying spell wasn't going to last much longer. Grozier just continued to stare into the large mirror, a finely wrought piece of furniture worth thousands of gold coins, resting on a large easel in the middle of the study. The image in the courtyard continued to show Captain Dressus and his men milling about, discussing what to do with the bodies lying there. The original plan had been for them to haul the pair to the nearest guard station in the city and deposit them thore, but it was obvious by then that the Waukeenar lieutenant's words had unnerved them, and they were uncertain what to do any longer.

"Oh, just run!" Grozier growled from behind Bartimus. He was beginning to pace. "Is there no way to talk to them through this damned mirror?"

Bartimus cringed as he said, "Unfortunately, no. It really only works one way. I could see if I have some other means of communicating with them, perhaps a scroll in my collection." He started to rise, completely enraptured at the thought of looking through some of his papers. "I think I might have just the thing," he muttered half-aloud, moving toward a distant shelf, "a little spell I acquired from a man I met in Cormyr several years ago. Let's see, I think I put those papers—"

"No, don't waste the effort," Grozier snapped, standing still and watching the scene again. "By the time you find something, it'll be too late. Besides, they've gone and mucked the whole plan up completely already."

Bartimus shrugged and sat back down as his counterpart sighed in exasperation.

"Dressus is an idiot," Grozier continued. "He should have just sent the Matrell boy away and cleared out of there. He got baited into that, you know."

Bartimus nodded, though he didn't, in fact, know that until just then, and he wondered how Grozier had come to that conclusion.

"Now," Grozier continued, "the city watch is concerned about our two dead victims, and Dressus is under suspicion. If not by the other guards, then at the very least, by the mercenary and his sister. We're going to have to take care of this ourselves."

He began to pace again.

Bartimus nodded, though he had no idea what his employer meant, and no desire to take the initiative to suggest some things until he knew more. He sat and waited while Grozier stewed.

Finally, the other man stopped his repetitive motion and said, "We're going to have to clean this up completely, you know."

Bartimus risked a glance over his shoulder at the other man, the head of House Talricci, to be sure he understood correctly.

"You want me to find someone?" the mage asked.

"No," Grozier replied, tapping the wizard on the shoulder. "You're going to have to do this yourself. I don't want to put it into anyone else's hands."

Bartimus swallowed hard.

"Me?" he asked, sounding more timid than he had intended, though he certainly felt a little intimidated at what his employer was asking him to do. "How would you like it handled?" he quickly added, hoping to cover his earlier hesitation.

"I don't know," Grozier growled. "You're the house wizard. You cook something up. But make sure you get rid of all the loose ends. And I mean all of them. I don't doubt for a minute that the mercenary is going to start sniffing around, trying to find out what happened tonight. I can just feel it."

He turned to go, then stopped and looked back at Bartimus through the gloom of his ill-lit room.

"And make it clever," Grozier added. "Something really good. Come find me and run it by me before you begin, though. I'll expect a first idea from you within an hour."

Bartimus nodded, inwardly sighing. Knowing Grozier, he was going to have to stay up half the night concocting something suitable to solve the problem.

CHAPTER THREE

You're teating me like I'm five!" Emriana shouted at her uncle.

She was slumped in one of the ornately carved high-backed suthwood chairs, with its claw-shaped feet and similarly formed arms, that surrounded the huge dining room table where the Matrell family was gathered. The seat was solidly padded, but that made it no more comfortable. The girl wanted more than anything to stand and pace, like her uncle was, but she had been told in no uncertain terms to sit down and remain there until she was permitted otherwise. Emriana looked to her mother for some measure of support, but Ladara Matrell was studiously gazing at her own robe, picking at the ornate fabric as the arguing continued. The mousy woman rarely stood in the way when her brother-in-law took the role of surrogate father over his dead brother's children. Emriana despised those times, and this moment was one of them.

The hour was late, and most members of the Matrell family were already dressed for bed. Only Quindy and Obiron, the eight-year-old twins, were absent. A handful of lanterns sat on the table itself, having been lit by sleepy servants who were roused by Uncle Dregaul when it became clear that a family meeting needed to occur. As such, the full complement of candelabra that hung from chains from the ceiling remained dark, so the spacious chamber was not as brightly cheerful as it might have been during a typical dinner. More than one yawn was carefully hidden behind the palm of a hand.

"Sometimes, you still act like you're five," Uncle Dregaul replied, moving back and forth on the far side of the table from Emriana.

His voice was like ice, and the thinly veiled anger in his countenance said all that needed to be said to the girl. Sneaking out had been bad enough, but as the rest of the story unfolded and it became clear that she had also disobeyed Vambran's instructions to stay in the safety of the carriage, Uncle Dregaul's mien had grown rock-hard. Emriana kept her defiant gaze mostly on her uncle, but she spared a moment or two of scathing glares for her brother, too. His return home for her birthday wasn't turning out to be quite the thrill she had hoped.

Vambran sat in another dark chair, the high arch of its back rising over even his tall frame. He stared at nothing, one leg thrown over the chair arm, pinching his lips together with his thumb and forefinger, oblivious to Emriana and obviously deep in thought. She was furious with him for so readily explaining the events of the evening, rather than holding his tongue about her involvement in the escapades. In fact, he had seemed bent on making a point of it, trying to get Uncle Dregaul to listen to his concerns about the veracity of the guards, even including the fact that Emriana herself believed she had recognized the dead woman. She doubted seriously if the entire household would even be having the conversation had Dregaul been told only that she had snuck out to ride down to the docks, safely in the carriage, with Prandles there to watch over her. But, of course, he was aware of it all and no doubt contemplating what sort of punishment to inflict on her for her insolence. She hoped that neither Prandles nor Jaleene, her personal maid, would get into trouble for their parts in it. Dregaul had never been adverse to firing house staff for similar shortcomings in the past.

"Sneaking out of your chambers after I specifically—specifically!—told you that you were not to ride to the docks with Prandles is bad enough," Dregaul said, interrupting Emriana's thoughts and ticking points off on his fingers. "But then to go and get in the middle of such an obviously dangerous situation in an alley in the middle of Arrabar is just plain brainless. Scuffles in alleys with mysterious figures is exactly the reason—exactly!—why I don't want you roaming around outside the walls. And yet, you don't have enough sense to see how dangerous it is. And you wonder why I treat you like a child. You act like one, Emriana, a very spoiled one.

"And you!" Emriana's uncle said, turning to face her brother. "How could you drag her into the middle of such a situation? You aren't home an hour, and already you're mixing it up with the common folk, playing at soldier. What's the matter with you?"

"I explained to you already," Vambran said, his own voice rising in resentment, "that I heard a scream and went to see who might be in trouble. There was no time to stop and wonder if it was wise to get involved, given that my younger sister was along."

"Naturally. You've never considered the consequences of your actions before, so why start now?" Dregaul sneered.

Emriana felt her eyes bulge as she stared at her uncle in amazement. He had never been a warm person, but that was downright vicious. She looked at Vambran, expecting him to retort angrily. Instead, the lieutenant bowed his head and stared at his hands, as though he had been slapped.

"When someone needs your help, you respond," Vambran said softly.

How can you take that? Emriana thought, hating to see her brother cower before their uncle. That's not like you.

"No, *you* respond," Dregaul replied. "The rest of us have enough sense to leave it for the city watch, which, as it turned out, was exactly who was already there, dealing with a problem. They certainly don't need your help to do their jobs."

"I'm far from convinced that the first group was actually men of the watch," Vambran said, looking up again. "I also told you that I specifically didn't call the imposters out, for fear of a fight erupting with Em standing in the middle of it. I—"

"Yes, yes, you've already explained to me your *theories*. Avoiding a confrontation was probably the smartest thing you did. But you shouldn't have been there in the first place. As usual, you're looking for trouble where there is none to find. Even if what you say is true, the other group arrived, and they'll clean it up. It's bad enough that you've taken to thrice marking yourself. Half the city probably knows by now that a member of the Matrell family—a member!—is dabbling in common arcane magic, rather than leaving it to the house wizards like sensible folk."

Emriana winced at her uncle's scathing comments, knowing how proud Vambran must be about his new talents. She watched as Vambran clenched

his jaw and shook his head in denial, obviously
fuming at Dregaul's derisive remarks. Off to one
side, Evester was nodding in agreement with their
uncle, acting as usual like the toady to his mentor.
Emriana had half a mind to admit that she had encountered her oldest brother on the roof earlier in
the evening, just to watch Dregaul's wrath turn on
Evester, but she held her tongue. She doubted the
ploy would come off as she expected. Nothing else so
far that evening had.

Beside Evester, his wife Marga was trying to hide
a gloating smile by turning her head away from the
scene. Emriana glared at her, but the red-haired
beauty never saw her.

"Uncle Dregaul," Vambran said, his tone deferential, "I already explained to you that bearing three
marks does not provoke the same fear and hostility in
other parts of the Reach that it does in Chondath, and
in fact it offers some benefits. The Rotting War was
nearly four hundred years ago. It's only in Arrabar
that uneducated fools still fear a return of the magic
plague that was unleashed. Everywhere else in the
Reach, the people are over it."

"Foolish or not, the fear is real," Dregaul responded.
"And it's powerful. Marking yourself is only inviting
scorn and suspicion, both upon you personally and
upon the House. It's a foolish risk that isn't necessary. But that never stopped you from taking foolish
risks before, so I don't know why I would expect any
different from you now."

"Don't worry," Vambran said through clenched
teeth, "I will certainly not 'disgrace' the family
further and raise your ire by continuing to wear the
third mark. I certainly wouldn't want the whole city
of Arrabar to cringe in fear, thinking I was bringing
the plague to one and all."

He threw his hands up helplessly, as if to say he
didn't know what else to offer to placate his uncle.

"Fine," Dregaul replied. "And as for this other matter with the guards, leave it alone. Don't drag the Matrell name any farther into it. Do you understand me?"

"Yes," Vambran said, rising up out of his chair abruptly. He stared hard at Dregaul, a dangerous gleam in his eye that Emriana had never seen before. "I understand exactly what's most important to you. I always have."

The girl realized she had gasped at her brother's reaction, and she wasn't the only one. Her mother was patting her chest in anxiety, obviously feeling the threat of a fainting spell coming on. Even Grandmother Hetta seemed taken aback, and very little got her excited. At the far end of the table, Evester frowned, but he didn't react much beyond that. Emriana was finding it harder and harder to read him.

For his part, Uncle Dregaul stopped pacing and stared right back at his nephew, his hands resting on the back of one of the tall, dark chairs. Emriana could see that his knuckles were white with strain, and she realized he was barely holding his own anger in check.

"You've made it perfectly clear what you think of me," Vambran went on, his voice dangerously soft. "I tried to give something back to the family, to you, as best I could. And when that didn't work, I tried to keep my distance, for both our sakes. But it's never enough to change anything, and I guess it never will be. So I'm through trying. I'm not going to ignore what I think is a murder ostensibly disguised as the city watch 'doing its job' "—Vambran's tone grew sarcastic—"just because it might temporarily put the Matrell family name in an unfavorable light. If you can't abide it, then I'll make sure none of my actions trouble you ever again."

Emriana's eyes widened in amazement. She couldn't believe what her brother was suggesting.

The girl realized her mouth was hanging open, and
she snapped it shut again, looking at Dregaul. The
man's face turned red as he sputtered, unable to speak.
Emriana turned to the rest of the family to see their
reactions. At the same time, she was beginning to
wish she could be somewhere else right then.

"Vambran!" Emriana's mother said, looking aghast
at her son. "You should not speak to your uncle that
way."

"I'm sorry, Mother," Vambran replied, "but he's left
me no choice. I can't continue to live under his baleful
stare any longer. I'll make my own way in the world,
on my own terms, if it means living in peace and
without his scorn and scathing remarks."

The lieutenant opened his mouth to say something
else, but Dregaul slammed his fist on the table.

"You insolent, selfish whelp! I will not be spoken
to in that manner. If it weren't for me, and for ...
you'd be ..."

He stopped, seemingly unwilling to finish his line
of thought.

Emriana's heart was pounding. She had never seen
either her uncle or her brother behave that way, and
she hated watching it. She wanted to sneak out of the
room and get far enough away that she wouldn't be
able to hear any more. She eyed the open, arched doorway that led away from the dining hall and into the
wing of the house where everyone's bedrooms were,
wondering if she could slip through it unnoticed.

"That's enough," came the quiet but commanding
voice of Grandmother Hetta, seated off to one side. Everyone in the room grew quiet and turned respectfully
toward her. The woman's face seemed tired and full of
sorrow as she looked from Vambran to Dregaul and back
again. "I'm too old to watch you two fight like this."

Dregaul nodded and said, "Of course, Mother. You
speak with the wisdom of many years. I only intended
to—"

"Dregaul, my son," Hetta interrupted, bringing up one wrinkled finger and wagging it at him in a gentle but stern way, "don't patronize me. You've never hidden your dislike of Vambran, and it disappoints me. I know you're feelings about—" Hetta paused, took a breath, and continued in a different direction. "I think it's time you let it go."

Emriana noticed her Uncle Dregaul's shoulders tense up, but the man said nothing.

What is she talking about? the girl wondered.

"And Vambran," the matriarch said, "I will hear no more talk of you leaving this family."

Vambran turned his gaze toward his grandmother and nodded, regret washing over his face.

The woman's voice softened, and she continued sorrowfully, "I've lost a husband and three children, and I will not sit by and watch what remains of my family tear itself apart like this."

"Now," Hetta said, her tone businesslike as she reached out her hand for Emriana's mother to help her to her feet. Ladara was there instantly, taking hold of her mother-in-law and providing support as the older woman rose up out of the chair. "It's late, and we're all tired and angry. I don't want to hear any more about this tonight. I want you two"—and she looked at Vambran and Dregaul, who still stood facing one another across the table—"to agree to put this aside for tonight and speak of it after a good night's sleep, perhaps tomorrow after breakfast. Your feud has gone on long enough. Resolve it."

She stood there, waiting.

Emriana turned, as did everyone else, to see how the two would react. Dregaul's jaw worked, clenching and unclenching, as though the man were struggling with complying with his mother's instructions.

Vambran, though, merely nodded.

"I'm sorry," Emriana's brother said, looking at his uncle. "I always have been."

Emriana blinked, confused by his words.

Sorry for what? she thought.

Dregaul eyed his nephew for a heartbeat, then shrugged and said, "I know. We'll talk about it in the morning."

He turned and left the room, heading for his own chambers, leaving everyone to stare at his back as he departed.

Emriana watched her uncle go, feeling a great sorrow emanating from him. It made her throat thicken in sympathy. As the rest of the family began to file out, Emriana turned to Vambran, wanting to ask him what he had meant about always having been sorry, but he was nowhere to be found. Frowning, the girl padded off to her room, dismayed that his homecoming had turned into such a disaster.

...

Breakfast turned out to be little better than the night before, though at least Vambran and his uncle had remained civil during the discussion. Still, the older man refused to recognize the evidence the lieutenant presented concerning the events of the previous evening. About the only thing they had agreed on was that Emriana should be kept out of it when it came time to discuss those events with the captain down at watch headquarters. Vambran had seen everything Emriana had, and from a better vantage point, and dragging her into it would only complicate things, especially given that she never could remember where she thought she had seen the woman prior to her death.

So it was that Vambran found himself headed toward the district headquarters alone, a little before seven bells. He had chosen to walk, seeing no need to take a carriage on such a fine morning. He preferred the stroll, anyway, enjoying the quiet avenues of the

merchant district and the salty air, which was still
cool enough at that time of the day not to soak him
through in sweat after only ten steps.

The streets were perhaps a little emptier that
morning, given the lateness that Spheres went the
previous night, though there were still plenty of folks
out and about, mostly the laborers rushing to their
jobs and servants of the wealthy doing the daily shopping. Scraps of shattered glass globes turned soft as
parchment were scattered along the streets or waft-
ing in the lazy breezes that blew in from the harbor.
Gulls screamed and dived for bits of breakfast as they
circled high overhead, shining in the morning sun and
set off against the crisp blue sky. It was turning into
an exquisite day, though with plenty of sunshine, it
would be a muggy afternoon for certain.

At last, Vambran arrived at the city watch headquarters in that part of the city. Like the rest of the
neighborhood, it was a nice building, a small compound surrounded by a low wall that served more
as a decoration than as a deterrent to trespassing.
Certainly, it was considered a choice assignment to
work the rich side of town, where the accommodations
were in keeping with the estates.

Vambran made his way through the front gates,
passing inside the low wall and almost immediately
into an open plaza, a tiled courtyard filled along
its edges with fruit trees, thick hedges, bamboo,
and climbing vines bursting to overflowing with
brightly colored blossoms. A fountain gurgled in the
center of the courtyard, a natural formation of rock
with a series of tiny cataracts that cascaded down to
a large pool filled with more lush vegetation. Swimming among the fronds and broad green leaves were
schools of large orange, yellow, and blue fish.

On the opposite side of the plaza was a desk shaded
by a gold and white awning. A civil servant wearing
a simple gold and white tunic with the Arrabar crest

stitched onto the left breast was seated there. The scribe was busy separating a stack of parchment forms into several piles and did not look up for quite a long time, even after Vambran approached and stood quietly.

Finally, the official glanced briefly at the lieutenant, and upon seeing Vambran's ornate breastplate, complete with the emblem of the Sapphire Crescent upon it, raised his eyebrows in mild surprise and scooted his chair back a bit.

"How can I help you?" the man asked, emphasizing the last word slightly as though wondering what a mercenary officer would need from the city watch.

Vambran smiled and removed his gauntlets, reaching out to offer a hand to shake.

"I am reporting here as ordered by Captain Leguay. I am to give a statement concerning a pair of killings from last night. My name is Vambran Matrell."

"Eh?" the scribe said, tilting his head to one side. "Matrell, eh? I don't think I have a record of your appointment," he added, looking down and thumbing through a series of pages in front of him. "Let's see," he muttered absently, licking his thumb as he lifted the pages up by a corner one after another. "Nay," the man said at last. "Nothing on my docket about you. Are you sure you're in the right place?"

Vambran shrugged helplessly and withdrew his proffered hand, wondering what the confusion was.

"Well, yes," the man continued, half to himself. "Obviously you came to the right station headquarters, since you mentioned Captain Leguay. I don't understand."

He flipped through the pages a second time, and when he reached the end, the official scratched his head.

"Let me check inside," he said, gesturing toward a bench to one side of the desk. "Have a seat, and I'll be back in a moment."

Vambran nodded his thanks and took a seat as the scribe hurried inside through an archway on the other side of his desk. As the lieutenant reclined on the rather uncomfortable wooden bench, studying the garden and listening to the gurgling of the fountain, he frowned, wondering if he had somehow been mistaken. It was possible that he misheard the captain, he reasoned, since he had focused so much of his attention on the sergeant's thoughts. But that seemed unlikely. Maybe the paperwork had just not made it through to the front desk, yet. With Spheres winding down, it was possible that there was a backlog, the mercenary officer told himself.

A pair of city watchmen entered the garden and headed straight toward the inside, giving Vambran a cursory if thorough look. He nodded and smiled at them, but they gave him only a slight nod in reply and were soon gone. Outside, beyond the low wall, he could see that the hustle and bustle of the city was beginning to pick up a bit more as the day got well underway.

A moment later, the scribe returned, shaking his head.

"I'm sorry," he said as he approached Vambran, "but there is no hearing for you this morning. You're free to go."

"What?" Vambran asked, standing. "But I'm sure I was supposed to—"

"Oh, you got your information correct enough, young man, but there won't be a debriefing. Captain Leguay said to tell you that you were free to go, and that the case was closed."

"Closed?" Vambran replied, growing exasperated. "But what about the two bodies? Aren't we going to commune with them this morning, find out their side of the story?"

"Isn't possible," the scribe said, adopting a more officious tone that implied he would brook little more of Vambran's arguing. "The bodies were destroyed last night. Burned. Carried the magic plague, apparently."

Vambran felt his face fall.

"I see," he said, trying to remain polite, but his mind was awhirl with the implications.

The bodies had been destroyed, so there would be no chance to commune with their spirits. But the plague? That seemed ridiculous. There had been no evidence of the magic plague inside the walls of Arrabar in several decades.

"Well, thank you," Vambran said at last, turning to go.

"If you want to find out more," the scribe said, his tone a little kinder again, "I suggest you go talk to your own people. It was a couple of Waukeenar priests who cleansed the bodies and everyone who came into contact with them. They actually showed up unannounced and informed Captain Leguay about the magical plague. We were all mighty thankful they did, too."

He gave Vambran a hopeful smile.

Vambran stared at the official for a moment, unsure what to make of that revelation. Priests of the temple of Waukeen, insisting the corpses bore the magic plague? How would they know before even examining the bodies? He meant to find out.

"Look," he said to the scribe, trying to sound both deferential and urgent at the same time. "Do you think Captain Leguay could see me for a few moments anyway? I really think she needs to hear what I have to say."

The official pursed his lips, staring at Vambran uncertainly.

Finally, he sighed and said, "I'll speak to her and see if she has a few moments to spare."

Vambran nodded in thanks and returned to the bench to wait once more. After a few more minutes, the official returned and motioned for Vambran to follow him.

"Make it quick," he warned as he turned and led the way inside.

The lieutenant nodded again and followed the scribe, thankful for the coolness of the interior and struggling to let his eyes adjust to the dimmer light. He followed the man into a hallway that passed several smaller offices near the back. The scribe stopped before one and gestured for Vambran to enter, then departed again almost immediately.

Captain Leguay was seated on a stiff-looking wooden chair with the traditional Chondathan high back, though it was very workmanlike in appearance, with none of the piercing, chasing, and bas relief Vambran was used to in more affluent décor. He stood and waited for a moment while the captain finished reading a scroll open in front of her. She clicked her tongue in exasperation once and took up a quill, scribbling some notes in the margin of the scroll, then she released it and let it furl up again. Slipping the quill back in its proper spot, she looked up at Vambran.

"Ah, yes. My mercenary from last night," she said. "I thought I made it clear you were no longer needed for questioning. Why are you still here?"

"I think you should hear what I have to say."

"I've got to go on patrol in another few minutes. Make it quick."

Vambran said, "I think there might have been more to last night's events than initially meets the eye. I think those other watchmen were imposters."

"That wouldn't surprise me in the least," Captain Leguay replied. "They somehow managed to slip off into the night while we were transporting the bodies back here, and I have put in a few inquiries this morning to try to find out who they were, with no luck."

Vambran was surprised that the soldier was agreeing so readily with him.

"Then are you tracking them down?" he asked, wondering if she would accept his help.

"I've got a couple of watchmen on it, but I doubt they'll find anything out."

Vambran tried to suppress his shock and asked, "Is that it?"

"Look, Master Matrell, I'm not sure what your concern is. Did you know the victims? Was there something stolen from you? What is it you want me to do?"

Vambran scowled. "I was hoping you might try to bring them to justice. They committed two murders, after all."

"We don't know that," Captain Leguay snapped. "Those two were thrice marked, and as best as I can tell, they had absolutely no arcane ability to speak of. You, I can easily accept. Them, no."

"But how can you be sure, when you let priests burn the bodies before performing a divination of any sort on them?" Vambran asked, his tone verging on sarcasm. "Did you happen to get the priests' names before you let them destroy evidence?"

"Master Matrell, they were a couple of common laborers. What difference does it make?"

"Beggar or king, we're talking about a possible murder. You should be out there, trying to find those imposters. I can help you track them, if you'll give me a chance."

"Are you presuming to tell me how to do my job?"

"No, I'm just asking you to do it properly!" Vambran could not believe how callous the captain was being toward the whole investigation.

"It's time for you to go, Master Matrell. I'm a busy woman, and I've got no time for pampered boys with delusions of grandeur."

"You're unbelievable!"

"Leave now, or I will have you arrested," she said, and her visage made it clear she wasn't kidding.

Vambran was so stunned he couldn't even retort. He simply glared for a full two heartbeats then, shaking his head, he stormed out of the station house.

Vambran was halfway back to the estate before he'd calmed down enough to take a deep breath. It was pretty common knowledge that the city watch functioned well inside the circle of intrigue of the city, just like every other major power player of Arrabar, especially given that they ultimately answered directly to the Shining Lord of Arrabar himself. Still, he would have thought it in Eles Wianar's best interests to see that some law enforcement remained consistent within the city, if for no other reason than to maintain stability for trade's sake. And of course, it was. So either the captain was simply a callous woman who cared little for the lower classes of people—which also wouldn't have been surprising, given her jurisdiction and the type of citizen she was charged with protecting—or there must be some other motivations influencing events. Most likely, Captain Leguay just didn't care enough to try to figure out what was going on.

But Vambran did. Seeing those two bodies the previous evening brought back uncomfortable memories for him, memories and guilt. He couldn't just let the crime go. If the watch wasn't going to do anything about it, then he would track the imposters down himself. But first, he wanted some advice. Nodding to himself as the seeds of conviction grew into certainty, he hurried down the cobblestoned road toward the Temple of Waukeen.

In his haste, Vambran completely failed to notice the pair of figures watching him from a corner, well back in the shade of an alley.

...

"Up, now!" Jaleene insisted, throwing back the screens to all of Emriana's windows and letting in the light. "You've lazed around in your bed long enough," the handmaiden said, and her tone made it clear she

was in no mood to listen to Emriana complain about
the early hour.

Emriana didn't care.

"Stop it, and go away!" she snarled, grabbing at the
sheet and pulling it tighter around her head, then
burrowing beneath the pillows to escape the intrusive
brightness. "It's too early," she groaned.

"Too bad," Jaleene replied, yanking the covers away
from Emriana and grabbing her by the arm.

The girl did not fail to notice the lack of honorifics
on the handmaiden's part that morning.

She must definitely be in a foul mood, Emriana
realized.

Opening one eye, she looked at her personal servant
and saw the tight expression on the other woman's
face. Emriana groaned again.

"Did Uncle Dregaul yell at you?" she asked somewhat timidly, sitting up when Jaleene pulled her by
her hand.

The woman's expression tightened further, wordlessly confirming the girl's question.

"You have a full day ahead, including a visit to
House Pharaboldi," Jaleene said briskly, ignoring the
issue of her own guilt in the previous night's escapades.
"Mistress Hetta instructed me explicitly to make sure
you were up and ready to go by eight bells."

Emriana groaned again. She had completely forgotten the tea that afternoon with Denrick. Sitting
around in the Pharaboldis' parlor in an uncomfortable dress, sipping tea and nibbling daintily on tiny
cakes while Denrick clumsily courted her was the last
thing Emriana wanted to do that day. She flopped
backward onto the bed again, sighing heavily.

Jaleene simply grabbed her by both arms and
hauled her completely to her feet, then guided her
toward her bathroom.

"I've already gotten a bath ready for you, Mistress Emriana. Get started while I prepare your

outfit for the tea. When we're finished, you are to go straight down to breakfast. Your grandmother wishes to speak with you before you depart for House Pharaboldi."

"Aren't you coming with us?" Emriana asked, already stumbling toward her private bath, stripping off her chemise as she did so and leaving it in a pile on the tiled floor.

Jaleene sighed as she followed the girl, picking up the garment.

"No," she replied, and the strain in her voice made Emriana pause and turn back. "I must have an extended conversation with Master Dregaul today," she explained. "My duties at the house, indeed my very future, are being called into question. I've already been warned that your presentation and timely appearance at breakfast this morning will be used to gauge my usefulness to the household."

Emriana's eyes bulged at the notion that her own personal attendant, who had been taking care of her since before she could remember, might be let go.

"Jaleene, no!" she said, putting her hands on her hips. "He can't blame you for last night. You didn't even know."

"It's my responsibility to know," the other woman replied softly, the look in her eyes pained.

Emriana felt the weight of guilt press down upon her, but she shook it off.

It's not right, she silently fumed. Uncle Dregaul cannot hold her responsible for my actions. I'm not a little girl anymore, and she can't be expected to keep up with me day and night.

"He's not going to do that to you. I won't let him. I'm going to go talk to Grandmother right now," she said, turning to find something to wear.

"Please," Jaleene replied, shaking her head, "just get to your bath and get ready. If you really want to help me, don't anger your uncle any further."

Her words were filled with desperation, and
Emriana felt pity and sorrow welling up in her. She
wordlessly nodded and headed back toward the bath.

For the rest of the morning, Emriana remained
somber and quiet, conversing little with Jaleene. She
dutifully got ready for her visit, bathing and dressing
without any fuss at all. Once she was finished in her
rooms, she gave her handmaiden one quick hug and a
meaningful look, then went downstairs to meet with
her grandmother.

Hetta Matrell was seated at the head of the same
large table where the heated debate had raged the
night before. When she saw her granddaughter enter,
she dabbed at her napkin and gave Emriana a warm
smile, then patted at the place setting next to her.
Emriana came to her grandmother and gave her a
quick kiss on the cheek, then sat down. Instantly, one
of the serving women came out of the kitchen carrying a platter of eggs, scrambled and mixed with cheese
and a sauce made of lemon and wine. The serving
woman scooped a spoonful of the eggs onto Emriana's
plate while another platter arrived with a baked fish
stuffed with sausages and potatoes. Then came a fresh
loaf of crusty bread already torn into chunks, and jars
of apple butter, fruit compote, and even fresh cream so
chilled and thick it literally mounded onto the hunk
of bread that Emriana grabbed. A goblet of freshly
chilled fruit juice mixed with just a hint of wine was
set beside her, and another pair of hands slipped her
napkin into her lap.

Once her plate was piled high with food and Emriana began to eat, her grandmother cleared her
throat.

"Sweetheart, I want to discuss last night."

The girl stifled a groan around a hearty swig of the
spiced juice and avoided rolling her eyes. She knew
it was coming, and in many ways, it was worse hearing about it from her grandmother, whom she loved

dearly, than from Uncle Dregaul, whom she didn't mind annoying in the least.

"All right," Emriana said at last, trying to put on a happy smile for her grandmother's sake.

"Oh, don't pretend you want to do this," Hetta said, chuckling. "I know you better than that, my dear."

It was true. Hetta had a way about her, an ability to read people and know exactly what they were thinking or planning, and precisely how they were likely to react in any given situation. It was how she and her husband, the first Obiron, had been so successful in business. Even though he had been the spokesperson during their business negotiations, it had been Hetta who had the shrewd business acumen and always advised the right course of action.

"I'm sorry, Grandma, but I'm not a little girl anymore. It's time to let me out of my cage, and Uncle Dregaul just doesn't seem to see that."

"You're absolutely right, Em. You're *not* a little girl anymore, and it *is* time you were able to make more of your own decisions. But child, getting caught sneaking out at night is not the way to prove that." It was funny to Emriana how her grandmother could tell her she was all grown up and still call her "child" in the same sentence. Somehow, it didn't sound wrong, either. "If you want Dregaul to respect your opinions and your adulthood, then you must first show him that you are capable of being smart, of making good decisions."

Emriana sighed.

"I know," she said quietly, "but I'm not so sure he has any better an idea of what's best for me than I do. He's always thinking about what's best for the family, and not the family members. I can't be someone I'm not, Grandma."

"Em, do you remember your Aunt Xaphira?"

The girl nodded and said, "A little bit."

"Your Aunt Xaphira was my youngest daughter. She was also the scamp in the family, and she drove everyone, your grandfather most of all, absolutely crazy."

"Why?"

"Because she was just like you. She wouldn't be tied down, wouldn't be sensible, like Obiron or even her older brothers wanted her to be. She had initiative, and ambition, and she went off and joined the Order of the Sapphire Crescent rather than allow the family to dictate what she did with her life."

"I understand," Emriana said. "I'll try to behave better."

"You're not listening to me, child," Hetta said, leaning in close. "Xaphira was, in some ways, the child I was closest to. I saw a lot of myself in her, just as I see a lot of her in you. You share that same spirit. Your future is not a game. I expect larger things from you, you know that."

Emriana actually blushed.

"Thank you, Grandma," she said. "What happened to Aunt Xaphira? No one ever talks about her."

"There was an accident," Hetta said softly, leaning in close to Emriana. "A man was killed, a very powerful man."

"Killed? What happened?"

Hetta sighed, obviously pained by recalling the memories of her revelation.

Her voice even lower, she said, "It's not really my tale to tell, child. Until the person involved is ready, I think it best that you keep this to yourself. But my point is, the blame on our family would have been a terrible tragedy that would have affected the whole household. Your aunt sacrificed herself to make sure that didn't come to pass. She did something selfless so that House Matrell would remain unscathed.

"Do not ever mention this again, though. It's a tale that must never come to light in front of the wrong people, for it could still cause problems, even today.

Keep it to yourself, and eventually, you'll hear the whole of it."

Emriana nodded, the sense of conspiracy genuinely frightening her. She was beginning to think that growing up wasn't just about getting to do what she wanted, when she wanted. Turning sixteen suddenly didn't seem quite as perfect and carefree as she'd once thought.

CHAPTER FOUR

Grozier Talricci did not look pleased when Bartimus arrived in his employer's study. Two others were there, each of them looking equally grim. Junce Roundface was sitting in one of the high-backed chairs, a goblet of something chilled in his hand, his feet sprawled out in front of him, the heel of one boot resting atop the toe of the other. Grozier's spy was staring down into the goblet in front of him, tracing his fingers through the beads of condensation forming on its outer surface.

The other man, Bartimus did not know so well. The wizard had only seen him once before, a priest of Waukeen. He stood in one corner of the study, staring out through the latticework of a vine-covered trellis that shaded the arched window from the midmorning sun beyond. He had his arms folded across his chest, resting on his ample stomach, and he was drumming his fingers, each of which was adorned with a gaudy ring replete with gems of every hue.

Bartimus waited by the door, unwilling to break the silence that hung so thickly in the air. Grozier had sent for him, though the wizard did not know why. He began to worry that the anger in the room was going to be directed at him, and the longer he could stave that unpleasantness off, the better. So he leaned against the side of the arched doorway and waited.

"I would have thought that eliminating the evidence would have dissuaded him from pursuing this any further," Grozier said, moving to sit on the corner of his desk. "I would think that a mercenary officer, or better yet, a young merchant scion, would have better things to do with his time. You're certain you picked up on his intentions correctly?"

"My divination functioned as it should have," the priest said, turning away from the window and looking directly at Grozier. "He was angry and determined to keep digging when he left the station house. But you underestimate his priorities. He has no duties, no responsibilities, in his house. He receives a monthly stipend to live on and spends his time wenching and fighting, like all men his age and in his circumstances do."

"Then why doesn't he go wench and fight," Grozier demanded, "instead of chasing ghosts that are better off left to drift away to nothingness?"

"In a way, this is his fight," the other merchant said. "He's made it his."

"Huh," Grozier grunted, seemingly unsatisfied with that answer.

"What he needs," Junce said, not moving nor looking up at either of the other two participants in the conversation, "Is a distraction. Something else to keep him busy."

"Or maybe a warning," Grozier muttered.

"No, your skulking man is right," the priest said. "A distraction would be best. It is more subtle than a direct warning, less likely to awaken his suspicion further." The Waukeenar was smiling, Bartimus saw, and had begun to rub his hands together as he spoke. "It has to be something suitably interesting to him, though. Something more interesting than playing at investigating this niggling crime before him."

"You have an idea already?" Grozier asked, looking expectantly at the merchant-priest.

"Yes. Remember what I said he likes?"

"Wenching and fighting?"

"Precisely. I'm sure we can arrange it so that he has ample opportunity for both."

"That's going to be interesting to try to pull off," Grozier said with a derisive snort. "He may already have some companionship of his own."

"A young man his age and temperament is always interested in a little more," the priest replied.

"What about his uncle?" Junce said, rising to his feet. "Didn't you say the mercenary was also planning to speak to him, drag him into this?"

"Kovrim Lazelle can be easily dealt with," replied the priest. "I will see to it personally. Do not involve yourself in the temple's side of things. Our connection to your financial endeavors must remain invisible."

"As you wish," Grozier said. "We'll keep on as before and leave these other matters up to you."

"Excellent," the priest said. He turned to go. "Are we still meeting in two days' time?" he asked at the doorway out of the study.

"Yes," Grozier replied. "The usual place and time."

The priest nodded and departed without even acknowledging Bartimus's presence.

Grozier, however, did.

"Bartimus, stop lurking over there and come sit down."

The wizard bobbed his head obsequiously and entered the rest of the way into the study.

"As you no doubt heard," Grozier continued, "our young mercenary is being quite persistent. I'm concerned about what he might yet find."

"I arranged it so that there would be nothing for him to find, as you and I decided," Bartimus said quickly, worried again that his employer was going to blame him for some shortcoming. "I can't imagine what else he could do."

Grozier snorted.

"Tell him what you and the priest discovered," the merchant said, looking at Junce.

The rogue chuckled.

"We followed Vambran Matrell today after he went to the watch headquarters to meet with Captain Leguay," Junce explained, flopping down onto the chair once more. "When she didn't give him any satisfaction, he left in a huff. The priest read his thoughts and discovered that Vambran seems to think he has a way of finding our phony watchmen. He seemed to have some notion of tracking down a dagger."

Bartimus frowned.

"Of course, I suppose that's possible, assuming that he knows of a particular dagger to track. Certainly, there are ways to do it, both arcane methods and divine incantations," he said. "But that wasn't something I would assume he had the capability to utilize, since first and foremost, he would need this dagger to be familiar, and secondly—"

"Enough," Grozier interrupted wearily. "I don't care how likely it is that he can do it. The fact is, he seems confident that he can. In those situations, I tend to trust that he knows what he's talking—er, rather, thinking—about. The question we should be asking ourselves is, what do we do about it? I don't intend to let the fate of all my planning rest in his hands," the merchant said, nodding toward the door where the

priest had departed. "Trusting in the possibility of
simply distracting him is a little too chancy for my
tastes."

"I can get over to Dressus's place and figure out
what dagger we might be talking about," Junce volun-
teered. "I can go ditch it somewhere harmless." Then
the spy began to smile. "Or, better yet, I can go slip
it somewhere rather dangerous, and let him wander
into a little trap."

"Ordinarily, I'd say absolutely," Grozier said, motioning for Junce to hold off. "But in this case, I don't
want to take any chances. I think it's time we got
Vambran Matrell out of the middle of this entirely."

"You want me to kill him?" Junce asked, his eyes
glittering. When Grozier nodded, the assassin said, "I
think I know just the group to help me do it."

"Then take care of it," Grozier replied, smiling
coldly.

After Junce departed, Grozier turned back to his
house wizard and said, "There's a possibility that our
friend Junce will fail. Vambran Matrell has proven
to be rather resourceful. If that's the case again, it
might not be such a bad thing for our pest to find
Dressus and the others."

"Pardon?" Bartimus asked, confused. "I thought we
didn't want him to learn anything from them."

Grozier sighed and said, "Right. I don't. However, I
think Dressus and his rowdies have begun to outlive
their usefulness. Even if we managed to get rid of the
dagger, nothing says Vambran Matrell doesn't have
other methods of finding them. I'd rather not take
that chance," the merchant said pointedly, looking
at his employee.

"Ah," Bartimus said, "so we'll let him find them,
but it will be too late."

"And I hope too late for him, too," Grozier added.
"I knew I could count on you to solve this problem
for me."

"Me?" Bartimus yelped, taking a step back. "I
can't—oh, wait. You want something else." He began
to think about his repertoire of magic. "There are a
number of different things I might try. Let's see," he
said, beginning to mentally tick off possibilities. "I
could—"

"I don't want the details," Grozier said impatiently.
"Just come up with something suitably nasty that's
certain to deal with everyone." The merchant was
nodding then, a pleased look on his face. "Yes. If
our nosy little mercenary lieutenant slips through
Junce's ambush and still wants to track down his
favorite dagger, we'll just let him. That should solve
our problems just fine."

...

As usual, the Temple of Waukeen in Arrabar was
bustling with activity when Vambran arrived. The
building itself soared from the middle of a vast open
lawn, a great rounded structure capped by a massive
dome and surrounded by various towers that were all
topped with sweeping, majestic spires, each one taller
than the next and reaching skyward. All of their
various surfaces were etched in gold inlay and precious gems, some of the stones large enough to glitter
brightly even when viewed from several blocks away.
No expense had ever been spared in the construction
of the temple, and its expansion continued even then,
as more and more space was needed to house the new
priests who pledged their lives to the Merchant's
Friend each day.

Vambran bypassed all of it with barely a glance,
for he had seen it many times before, and truly, such
a display of wealth did not impart the same impression upon him that it would most others. Still, he was
surprised by the amount of new construction going
up on the grounds. He gazed at the scaffolding where

another wing was being built, the walls already halfway up and the skeletal ribs of the interior floors
being put into place. Soon enough, the outer shell
would be complete, and workers would plaster and
paint those walls, embedding more gold and gems into
the surface as they finished.

The lieutenant stepped inside the main entrance.
In addition to the scores of worshippers who had come
to pray for a boon before their day's business dealings,
numerous priests moved through the spacious sanctuary, their robes, miters, and scarlet cloaks glittering
with precious gems, gold, and even divine light, the
result of magical orisons placed upon them. The effect
was designed to bedazzle all who looked upon the holy
men's and women's dress. More of the precious jewels
and metals covered nearly every surface of the interior of the temple, the only exceptions being the broad
arched openings that served as windows and doors, the
tapestries that hung on the walls—though those were
more often than not woven with thread-of-gold and
had tiny gems stitched into their images like elaborate stained-glass windows—and any surfaces where
adherents would need to walk. As a faith designed to
pay homage to wealth, the temple presented the right
message to its people.

Rather than moving into the main sanctuary, Vambran turned to move down a hall, heading deeper into
the interior of the temple, up into some of the spires of
the structure where many of the various offices were
housed. Even as he walked, though, Vambran nodded
in satisfaction that even on the day after a festival
that ran long into the night—or even into the small
hours of the morning, in some quarters—the devotion
to the goddess of trade, coin, and wealth was strong.

Vambran passed beyond all of that and wound his
way into the halls where the business of the church was
handled, where the priests responsible for all the various financial activities worked. He sought the offices

of his superior, Kovrim Lazelle, who was in charge of
many of the business-related activities of the Sapphire
Crescent. Vambran and Kovrim would spend the
morning together going over the business details and
financial documentation of the lieutenant's company's
most recent excursion, to Aglarond and Sembia. Vambran was certain Kovrim already knew that *Lady's
Favor* was in port. In fact, the older priest had most
likely already ordered its cargo unloaded. Once he and
Vambran went over the manifests together, the goods
would be put up for sale in temple-owned shops and
stalls throughout the city and in the bazaar. Vambran's
visit promised to be filled with tedious but necessary
paperwork, but he was looking forward to the day nonetheless. Uncle Kovrim was also family, the lieutenant's
mother's brother.

The lieutenant climbed a circling staircase that
spiraled just inside the main outer wall of one of the
towers, rising a couple of levels and passing narrow,
arched windows on occasion. When he reached a landing that let out into a large, open rotunda, he stepped
off the stairs. There, the temple was airy and bright,
exposed to the outside through numerous additional
arched openings set high in the dome overhead. The
indirect light of the morning sun shining through
those windows was further enhanced as it reflected
off the gold leaf of the ceiling. As was common in the
architecture of Arrabar, a fountain bubbled in the
middle of the rotunda, and all around the perimeter
of the chamber, doorways led into offices.

Vambran turned to one side and passed through
an arched opening, moving not into an office but out
onto a bridge that spanned the distance between the
tower he had ascended and a second one next to it. The
walkway was not long, and the protective walls along
either side of it not so high that Vambran couldn't see
some of the city from the vantage point if he wished
to, but it would require squeezing between the various

clay pots that were set at regular intervals along the span and filled to overflowing with blossoming greenery. Instead, the lieutenant simply enjoyed the warming sun that shone down and moved on into the next tower.

Inside that second tower, Vambran made his way up another rounded flight of stairs and into a similar rotunda. From there, he was before the doorway that led into his uncle's office chambers. Sticking his head inside, Vambran could see that Kovrim Lazelle was not in, though the mess of parchments scattered across the desktop told the lieutenant that his uncle was around somewhere. He went inside, stepping past the desk and the shelves filled with scroll cases and wood-bound books and through another arched opening to a balcony beyond. A brightly colored bird, mostly greens and blues, was sitting atop a wooden stand. It cocked its head sideways and squawked once as the lieutenant appeared.

Vambran smiled and lifted a bit of hard bread out of a bowl.

"Hello, Mackey," he said, holding the nibble out for the creature, which was perhaps a foot tall.

"Hello," the bird mimicked.

Mackey eyed the bit of food and darted its head forward and snatched the bite out of the man's hand, eating it in a single swallow.

Vambran smiled and ruffled the gorgeous bird's head feathers gently, then turned toward the balcony. Trellises formed a see-through wall, set where the railing kept occupants from falling to the ground four stories below. Tendrils of climbing vines covered the wooden frames, dappling and diffusing the majority of the light. Still, there was a narrow opening between the trellises, and Vambran moved there and leaned forward on his forearms to have a gaze outward.

Kovrim's office faced west, toward the harbor, so at the moment the sun was on the opposite side of the tower, keeping the near side in shade. In the afternoon, when the day was at its hottest, the sun would normally shine directly onto the balcony and into the priest's office, making it stifling. The trellises were a necessary relief from the afternoon heat. Still, on that morning, like every morning, the view from such a vantage was wonderful. Vambran could see the open expanse of the lawns below, green and lush, with a number of priests and visitors strolling in small groups or alone. Others had found a shady spot, either on stone benches or on the grass itself, beneath any of a number of large shadowtops that grew throughout the property.

Out beyond the temple grounds was the city, sloping gently down toward the harbor, where Vambran could clearly see the piers jutting out from the quay and the various ships currently in port. He spotted *Lady's Favor* in the same spot where he'd left her the previous night and noted that she rode high in the water. Her cargo had indeed been unloaded and she was waiting for a new one. In fact, as Vambran squinted, he could see swarms of men just beginning to shift crates around so that cranes could hoist them off the pier and down into her holds. The lieutenant estimated that she would be departing before nightfall. He felt a small pang of regret that he would not be going with her.

"Vambran!" Kovrim's voice boomed from behind, and the lieutenant spun to see his uncle walking into the office, a sheaf of parchment and a hunk of sealing wax in his hands. "Hello, nephew," the priest said, smiling broadly and dumping his work onto the desk so that he could properly greet his visitor.

"Hello, Uncle Kovrim," Vambran replied, smiling himself and crossing the distance between them to give his relative a hearty hug.

"It's great to see you home," Kovrim said, slapping Vambran on the shoulder before stepping back to look at his nephew. His face went from a smile to mild shock. "What's this on your forehead?" he asked, genuinely surprised.

"I've been studying with one of my men," Vambran explained, suddenly feeling a bit uncomfortable. "Not a whole lot, just enough to pick up a few tricks. I find them useful on the battlefield."

"I see," Kovrim said, tilting his head to one side, as though considering what he thought of the revelation. "The Lady's divine grace isn't suitable?" he asked.

Vambran frowned, trying to figure out a way to explain it.

"It's not that," he said. "I'm still very attentive to my holy studies. But there are some things I'm finding out work better this way."

Kovrim broke into another big grin.

"Well, then, good for you. I'd rather see you prepared for anything, you know. So, your trip went well, I gather," he said, gesturing toward a narrow, high-back chair in front of his desk.

"Absolutely," Vambran replied as he sat, relieved at his uncle's apparent approval. "Nothing at all like the last time," he said, grinning and remembering the skirmish he and his company had engaged in during the previous trip.

A local dispute had a horde of guildsmen up in arms in Procampur, and they had tried to blockade the ship to prevent it from offloading its goods. It hadn't been much of a fight, though relations with that particular guild were substantially cooler than they had been. The temple in Arrabar had already dispatched an envoy to Procampur in order to try to smooth things over.

"Well, that's good to hear, though I already knew it," Kovrim said with a laugh, gesturing at the pile of work on his desk. "There was a nice stack of new reports waiting for me when I arrived this morning. Another smoothly run business operation ready to be put to bed, thanks to you."

Vambran only smiled and said nothing.

"So, how's my sister?" Kovrim asked, leaning back in his chair. "How is everyone over at House Matrell?"

Vambran tried not to grimace.

"Mother's fine, as always," he answered, trying to keep his voice light. "She still spends most of her day helping Grandmother Hetta, who's still going strong. And Em's growing like a weed," he added with a laugh.

"I'll bet," Kovrim said, chuckling along with his nephew. "Well, I'm looking forward to visiting for Em's birthday in a few days. It'll give me a chance to catch up with the family. And I know Ladara will be happy to see me."

"Yes," Vambran said "Mother will certainly like that, and everyone would enjoy your company. Just don't show up without a big, expensive present for Em, or she'll never let you hear the end of it."

They both laughed.

"Well, are you ready to settle these accounts?" Kovrim asked, rising from his chair to grab a large, leather-bound ledger from a shelf behind his desk. "We can get these books in order and go have a bite to eat."

Vambran let the smile fade from his face.

"Uncle Kovrim, I have a problem," he said. "I need your advice."

Kovrim grew serious as well and sat back down.

"Certainly, Vambran, whatever I can do to help."

Vambran sighed, unsure how to explain things.

"Last night," he finally began, "On the way home from the docks, there was a killing."

Kovrim grunted, shaking his head in sorrow, but gestured for the lieutenant to continue.

"City guards accosted and 'dealt with' a pair of common folk in an alley near our estate. They claimed that the two victims were falsely marking themselves thrice."

"Oh? Haven't seen that in quite a long time."

"Exactly," Vambran said, leaning forward. "It struck me as odd, too. But besides that, these city watchmen just didn't seem quite right to me. They didn't really understand procedure, and they were downright surly toward Em and me."

"I see. Were you wearing your marks last night, too?" Kovrim asked, pointing toward Vambran's forehead.

Vambran nodded and said, "Yes, and of course they behaved rather poorly about it, too. Very accusatory, not surprisingly. But it was more than that. Even after I demonstrated my talents, they were downright rude, at least until a second squad of guards arrived."

"So what are you concerned about?" Kovrim asked, scratching at his balding pate. "Did something happen?"

"Not as such," Vambran replied. "But I decided to draw out the sergeant's surface thoughts, to see what he was really about, and what I read was unsettling. I just don't think they were actually watchmen. He seemed very worried about someone finding out what had happened last night."

"I see. So, what did you do about it?"

"Well, Em was there, and I didn't want a skirmish breaking out, so I just kept quiet. The second squad was led by a captain, and she certainly seemed to know what she was doing. They gathered the bodies and told me to report this morning for a debriefing. I was actually looking forward to it, because I wanted to see what came of the communing with the dead."

"And?"

"Last night, two Waukeenar priests showed up unannounced and ordered the bodies burned, due to magical plaque."

Uncle Kovrim's eyebrows shot up in surprise.

"Oh, really?" he said. "I haven't heard a thing about the plague breaking loose anytime recently."

"I figured you would be the one to know, if anyone did," Vambran said. "I think the magic plague is just a ruse. Someone is hiding something, and I'm worried about the implications that these two priests are involved in it."

"Yes," Kovrim said absently, scratching at his head again, deep in thought. "That doesn't sound good."

"I mean, it may be nothing, but a moment or two conversing with the spirits of the slain couple could have cleared it all right up."

"Yes, it could have. So, did you voice your doubts to this captain?"

"I did. She was not interested in listening to me. Claimed to have put a couple of her men on it, and that was that."

"And you're not satisfied with her efforts."

Vambran was silent for a long time. Finally, he looked his uncle squarely in the eye.

"You know what's troubling me," he said at last.

Kovrim nodded slowly and said, "You can't keep blaming yourself for that, Vambran. You were just a boy."

"You know that doesn't make it feel any better. It haunts you just as much as it still troubles me."

"That's different. I was an adult, I should have known better than to have given you that crossbow. If I hadn't—"

"So neither of us can forgive ourselves so easily. The fact remains that all I can think about is what Rodolpho's family must have thought when they heard the news and afterward. Bewildered, wondering why someone would assass—" Vambran clamped his mouth shut, unwilling to continue that thought. "Anyway, now, I see it happening all over again. I can't help but wonder how the families of these two are feeling, thinking their dead kin were criminals. It's not right."

"I understand your passion for this, Vambran, I really do. But I'm not sure you can do anything about it. I wish there were; maybe we'd both feel better afterward."

"There's something else," Vambran said, unwilling to let it go. "Em thinks she recognized the woman, though she can't remember from where. And," he added, wondering if his uncle would approve of what he was about to suggest, "the suspicious guards kept something of Em's, a dagger I'd given her and which they confiscated last night. I think I can track them down if I needed to."

"Hmm," Kovrim said, nodding. "You could tell the watch captain this, lead her to the men."

"I already offered. She still wasn't interested."

"A pity for her, but an opportunity for you." Kovrim leaned forward and gave a hard stare at his nephew. "I wish I could go with you, but these bones are getting a little too old for traipsing around the city in pursuit of criminals. I'll leave it to you. But if you do track on the dagger, you do not go alone, do you understand me?" Vambran nodded. "Take a couple more stout bodies with you. Someone you can trust."

Vambran nodded and said, "I think I know just the two."

"In the meantime," Kovrim replied, sitting back, "I'll help you any other way I can. I'll look into the two priests. If there's something going on that the temple's involved with, I'll find out what it is."

Vambran smiled.

"Thanks, Uncle Kovrim. I knew I could count on you."

...

The ride to the Pharaboldi estate was serene, if not terribly entertaining, inside the full coach. Emriana did her best not to fidget and complain, but she found the confines of her dress, the coach, and the company of her mother all to be very stifling. The vehicle

made its way through the merchant's district of the
city, the iron-rimmed wheels rolling loudly over the
cobblestones and jostling the occupants incessantly.
Emriana looked out the window, watching the hustle
and bustle of the city flow past them while Ladara
made small talk with Hetta and the attendants who
had traveled with them that day.

Emriana tried to tune her mother out, completely
disinterested in the latest gossip concerning the truly
wealthy of Arrabar, the plots and intrigues they were
involved with, and the speculation over what mar-
riages might be occurring between Houses in the
near future. She wished Jaleene were there to give
her some companionship that would be more to her
liking, but true to his word, Uncle Dregaul had ordered
the handmaiden to remain behind to be disciplined. At
least she wasn't going to be let go, for which Emriana
could thank her grandmother. Hetta had revealed to
the girl before they finished their breakfast that she
had informed Dregaul he was not to relieve the handmaiden from her duties, but that he could make the
threat to do so if it made him feel better. Apparently,
the man had taken his mother up on her suggestion.
Though she would not be losing her confidante and
friend, Emriana still felt no small amount of sympathy
toward poor Jaleene over the day she was bound to
have, being scolded by the master of the House.

"Em, I do hope you don't sulk like that when we
arrive. It is so unbecoming," Ladara commented,
drawing the girl out of her thoughts.

"What?" Emriana asked, blinking and looking up
to see the entire entourage of women watching her.
"Oh, I'm sorry, Mother," the girl replied, trying to
smile. She realized she must have been looking very
morose, contemplating her maid's fate. "I will try."

It wasn't easy, putting on airs, but she did it
because of what her grandmother had revealed to
her that morning.

The sooner I start pretending to be what they want, the sooner they'll quit scrutinizing me so much, Emriana told herself.

"And do try to be pleasant to Denrick today," Ladara continued, which almost elicited a groan from the girl before she caught herself and nodded, smiling. "The last time you visited with him, you were less than polite, you know."

Emriana stole a quick glance at her grandmother, who raised her eyebrows slightly as if to say, Remember what I told you.

Turning back to her mother, Emriana smiled even wider and said, "I will do my best, Mother."

Ladara smiled, apparently genuinely relieved.

"Thank goodness. Maybe you're growing up after all." The woman pulled a fan out of her handbag and opened it, waving it rapidly back in forth in front of her. "Mercy, but it's already unbearably warm this morning," she said.

That's because we insist on wearing all these ridiculous clothes, Emriana thought, wanting to scream.

It wasn't quite highsun, and the air was already growing damp and heavy, though inside the coach, where they had shade, it wasn't so bad yet. Once they arrived at the Pharaboldi estate, Emriana knew that it would be blessedly cooler inside, where she was sure the house wizards would have woven a spell or two to keep the temperature pleasant.

As if on cue, the coach arrived at the front gates of the estate of House Pharaboldi, which swung wide to admit them entrance. The coach rolled through the high walls and up the lane toward the house proper, which sat upon a large and gently sloped hill, and Emriana began to stare out the window once more, watching the large trunks of the shadowtops, planted at regular intervals, drift by. Emriana spotted several peahens and a few peacocks strutting about in the shade of those trees. Beyond them, on the open lawn, horses grazed, a large herd of them, for horses were one of the prized possessions of the Pharaboldis.

Eventually, the coach pulled up to the front of the mansion, coming to a stop in the rounded drive that encircled a great fountain and accompanying flower-filled beds. The home itself was several stories tall, and all four sides were surrounded by open-air porches pierced by arched windows that looked out on the grounds. The whole thing had been painted a warm shade of tan, with burgundy and pale blue highlights accenting the whole.

Attendants stepped forward from the shade of the porch to open the doors of the coach and assist the women in stepping out. Ladara climbed out first, then turned to help Hetta, with Emriana following to ensure the older woman didn't teeter and fall. Once they were all safely on the graveled walk, they flipped open their parasols and strolled together up the steps, which were flanked on either side by great planters teeming with a variety of tropical blooms. At the top of the staircase, standing regally on the tiled front porch, Anista Pharaboldi waited on her guests with a proud smile upon her face. It was not the first time the Matrells had come calling, but it seemed like each time Emriana remembered visiting, the woman practically glowed with satisfaction at the appearance of her stately home.

"It's so nice of you to come visit us today," Anista called out as the Matrell women made their way to the porch. "Please, come inside where it's bearable."

With that, the Pharaboldi matriarch turned and marched through the great front doors into the cooler, darker interior. Emriana followed her grandmother and mother inside, letting her eyes adjust.

Like the Matrell estate, the Pharaboldi home was a spacious, open-air place, allowing cooling breezes to blow through and keeping the warmth of the subtropical sun at bay. Cool tiles covered every floor, and countless planters contained ferns, vines, and even small trees, all of which were allowed to climb columns and walls, or to hang from above, draping over the sides of planter boxes clinging to balconies or hanging baskets that dangled from exposed beams running the length of the larger rooms. Trellises were used instead of solid walls to separate spaces in many rooms, thickly covered with bougainvillea and philodendrons and half a dozen other kinds of growth.

The group was led into one such room, a large central chamber two stories in height and encircled by a balcony on the second floor. The ceiling high overhead was vaulted, and near the very center, a small cupola rose even higher, with arched windows set on each side to let in light. A pair of channels were set into the floor of the room, running in a weaving path from one side to the opposite, and water flowed into them from a stone-walled pond, making them small, slow-moving streams. The pond itself was fed from a miniature waterfall, tumbling down one wall of the room with a pleasant splashing sound. The indoor streams flowed to either side of an island in the center of the room, joining together again on the far side and disappearing beneath a wall. A pair of foot bridges passed over the natural barriers, and the whole length of the streams had more planters lining each bank, so that palm fronds and miniature willow trees leaned out over the sides and grew up to further divide the whole place.

"Please," Anista was saying as the procession followed her to the middle of the room, onto the island, where a large table and a set of chairs had been placed, "Find yourselves a seat. First, we will have tea and visit for a bit, and later, we can move to the dining room for a proper midday meal. Oh, I can't wait to catch up with you and find out what sorts of interesting things you Matrells are involved with."

Emriana found a seat at one end of the table, off by herself, and sat. A serving woman dressed in a crisp outfit appeared beside her, placing a delicate Calishite porcelain cup and saucer before her and filling it with rich, aromatic Amnian tea. A second dish containing thin wafers made of sweetened bread topped with whipped honey was set beside the tea, and the servant was gone, leaving Emriana to her own devices.

The girl spent a few moments just taking in the room, which, though it was no more opulent than the Matrell residence, was nonetheless impressive in its luxuriousness. Sitting where she was, Emriana could see down into the waterway that encircled the sitting area, and she spotted a school of brightly colored fish, red and blue and all feathery fins, swimming lazily about. On impulse, she broke off a bit of the sweetened bread and tossed it into the water. In the blink of an eye, the fish swarmed toward the bits of food, darting toward the surface and slipping away with the crumbs. Several of the creatures began to fight over the unexpected meal, and Emriana watched as they darted and ran, making ripples in the surface of the water.

"Oh, Em, you are a vision today," Anista said, her high-pitched voice drawing the girl back to the conversation. "Denrick will be very impressed," the woman added, a knowing grin on her face. "I'll bet you'd much prefer to go visit with him than to sit around here with all of us stuffy old crones, now wouldn't you?"

Emriana opened her mouth to deny the notion that she would like to spend any time at all with the woman's boorish son, then snapped it shut again helplessly as she spied her mother boring a hole into her daughter with her gaze. It was clear to the girl that her mother wished her to be as endearing and cooperative as possible.

Emriana finally nodded and managed to croak, "Yes, ma'am."

"Well then, dear, I think he's out on the back porch, though you'd better hurry. I think I remember him saying he planned to go riding today. Patimi here can show the way, if you've forgotten."

Emriana silently groaned but got up and curtsied before hurrying along, following the attendant Anista had indicated. The woman led Emriana through the house and out onto a tiled and covered porch with awning-covered arched windows looking out over a broad field that sloped down the hill toward a rather massive barn.

"Master Denrick, the Lady Emriana Matrell," Patimi intoned, bowing toward a man perhaps four years older than Emriana.

He was tall and somewhat lanky, but with a carefully coifed head of hair and matching goatee that was thick and black. He looked up as the two women approached, and his smile was predatory when he spotted Emriana. Sure enough, he was dressed for riding, and a stable boy was standing at the bottom of a set of steps that ran down from the porch with a fine-looking horse in his care.

"Hello, Em," Denrick said affably, belying the hungry look in his eyes. "You're looking wonderful today."

Emriana forced herself to smile back at the young man. "And you look like you're getting ready to go riding," she replied, hoping he'd ask her so she could decline.

"Why, yes I am. In fact, I was hoping you'd find your way out here, so you could go with me. A picnic with you under the shade of a tree sounds like a perfect day to me. What do you say?"

Emriana had to work to keep the delight out of her voice as she apologized.

"Oh, I'm sorry, Denrick, but as you can see, I'm not dressed for riding today, and I'm afraid I didn't bring along any other clothes on this trip."

Denrick looked crestfallen, but for only a moment before he brightened again.

"You can wear some of my sister's!" he said. "She has scads of things still in her old rooms, and I'm sure some of them will fit you."

Emriana swallowed, feeling backed into a corner.

"Oh, well, I . . ." she stammered, trying to think of an out. "My personal maid, Jaleene, was indisposed today and could not come, so there's really no way I could change without help, and—"

"I'm sure Patimi can help you," Denrick said, his smile fading as he looked at Emriana expectantly. "Surely it's not that difficult to change your clothes."

Emriana sighed quietly and succumbed. "Well, then, I'd be delighted," she lied.

"Wonderful! I'll have Turcan prepare a horse for you while you change."

With that, the young man stood up and began instructing the stable boy to fetch Emriana a gentle horse and put a suitable saddle on it.

Patimi, meanwhile, led the girl back into the house and into the chambers of Denrick's older sister, Lobra Pharaboldi, who had gotten married and moved into her husband's estate a couple of years previous. Emriana remembered meeting the woman but once, a long time ago. Patimi showed the girl where the wardrobes were and helped her choose a suitable outfit for riding and assisted while Emriana changed clothes. The girl thought the servant seemed a bit subdued, for Patimi spoke very little, other than to offer a word of instruction, but Emriana was too preoccupied with her impending afternoon with Denrick to think to ask the woman what was wrong.

At last, the girl was dressed in a set of breeches and a shirt with a loose-fitting vest over it, accompanied by a wide-brimmed hat and durable gloves, perfect for riding. She had to admit that she was more comfortable than she had been in the stiff, sumptuous dress. She followed the servant back outside, where Denrick was waiting, already mounted on his own horse, a bay named Shert. Emriana's mount, held still by Turcan for her as she climbed into the saddle, was a slightly smaller palomino named Goldy. Once she was situated, she took the reigns from Turcan and nodded to Denrick. Emriana had ridden often enough to feel confident, if not completely at ease, atop the mount. Goldy proved to be a gentle creature, though, willing to follow Denrick as he turned Shert and headed around the side of the porch.

"First, we'll ride over to the back door of the kitchens and have the staff prepare a picnic basket for us," the boy called over his shoulder. "Then we can head over to a spot I like out toward the south wall."

"Lead the way," Emriana replied, determined to make the best of the trip and not give her mother any reason to frown at her.

The pair trotted slowly around to another wing of the estate, where Denrick hopped down and strolled inside a back door, which led into the kitchens. Emriana remained mounted, studying the door into which her riding partner had disappeared, suddenly ill at ease. Something was troubling her, something she needed to remember. She couldn't put her finger on it, but whatever it was, her stomach was roiling with nervous energy.

Denrick returned, followed by a kitchen maid carrying a large basket. One look at the woman in her simple dress and flour- and soot-covered apron made Emriana remember, and she nearly fell off Goldy in her alarm.

The woman who had been killed the night before had worked in the Pharaboldi kitchens.

CHAPTER FIVE

The rest of the morning went as smoothly as Vambran and Kovrim had hoped. He and his uncle spent it in the older priest's office, going through the manifests of the cargo that had been offloaded from *Lady's Favor*, cataloging it and reconciling it against the coffers of coin and goods that had been shipped out two months previous.

Standing watch over trade goods as they were shipped from one port to the next was certainly the least glamorous aspect of the life of a mercenary officer, but sometimes, no one needed the services of a professional fighting force, and when that happened the temple found other uses for its private army. Ensuring the safe transfer of cargo and funds in foreign lands—especially in places where the dealings didn't always go as smoothly as

the priests wished—occasionally fell on a division
or two of the Sapphire Crescent, as did sorting and
cataloging the goods afterward.

At last, Vambran and Kovrim finished their work.
Goods had been sold, other goods bought, and after the
ship's crew and the men of Vambran's company had
been paid, the temple would turn a good profit, which
would be plied into new goods to be shipped out again,
starting the process all over.

By the time the two men were done reconciling
the records, the sun was sitting high over the harbor,
and the day was hot and muggy. Kovrim set his quill
down, closed the leather-bound ledger, slid his chair
back, and rubbed at his eyes.

"Another good trip, indeed," he said. "So let's go
celebrate with a meal at Dark She Looks Upon Me,"
he added. "My treat."

Vambran grinned broadly at the mention of one of
his favorite *aszraun* in Arrabar. He quickly agreed,
thinking fondly of the roasted beef and lamb *talthaek*
he always ordered at that particular restaurant. Remembering how the rich, creamy brown sauce literally
dripped out of the meat pie made his mouth water.

Kovrim and Vambran made their way from the
temple and into the mercantile district on foot, chatting
about the events of the Sapphire Crescent's excursion,
the family, and politics in the city as they strolled.

Inside the *aszraun*, the crowds were already growing large, but a couple of Kovrim's coins in the right
hands quickly got the pair of men ushered into a private dining alcove where they could enjoy their meal
comfortably. The scents of the food at several tables
made Vambran's stomach rumble as he sat down opposite his uncle. After ordering their meals, Vambran
excused himself and made his way to the rear of the
restaurant to visit the jakes.

The privy was a long, narrow room with several
private alcoves in a row near the back entrance of

Dark She Looks Upon Me. Vambran strolled toward
the doorway of the jakes and was nearly knocked aside
by a young boy of perhaps nine years who rushed past
him and out the back door, into the yard.

Vambran at first turned back toward the dining
room of the establishment, thinking that someone
was perhaps chasing the lad, but even as he pivoted,
realization set in. The scoundrel had grabbed at Vambran's coin purse on his way past. Groaning in disgust,
Vambran quickly reached down and felt inside the
inner pocket where he kept the leather pouch and
discovered it was missing.

"Damnation!" he snarled, spinning back to pursue
the thief.

The lieutenant charged past the entrance to the
jakes and dashed out into the yard, where a number of
wagons were parked. The entire yard was enclosed by
the backs of other buildings, making it a completely
private area, with the only other means of egress
being a large wooden gate off to Vambran's right. At
the moment, the portal was shut. Of the boy, Vambran
could see no sign.

Stepping quickly out into the middle of the yard,
Vambran peered desperately in every direction,
trying first to spot some place where the thief could
have scrambled up and over a wall, or through a doorway or window, but no escape route was immediately
apparent. Rolling his eyes, the lieutenant began to
move among the wagons, checking to see if the lad
had simply slipped into a hiding place of some sort
or another.

"Don't you just hate it when they do that?" came a
voice from high up and slightly behind Vambran.

He spun around and peered warily up to the top
of a low roof, where a comely woman with close-
cropped hair the color of wheat lounged casually
on one elbow, smiling at him. She was dressed in a
loose, billowy shirt of fine white linen, over which she

wore a magenta vest. Both the vest and the shirt were
unlaced to midway down her belly, exposing ample
cleavage as she leaned forward to return Vambran's
gaze. Her shapely legs nicely filled a pair of snug-
fitting purple breeches and were tucked underneath
her rump.

"You saw the boy?" Vambran said, giving the
woman a hard stare. "Which way did he go?"

"Nowhere," the woman replied, shifting her weight
and rolling up onto her knees, all the while smiling
broadly down at him. "He just disappeared."

"You're quite the jokester," Vambran said icily,
turning so that he could watch the doorway back
into Dark She Looks Upon Me, in case the boy tried
to dart back inside from his hiding place.

Motion caught the lieutenant's eye, but instead of
the thief running inside, Vambran spied two figures
emerge from inside the *aszraun*. They didn't look
friendly, and they were staring right at him. The first
was a short, wiry fellow with long, greasy hair tied back
with a strip of leather. He twirled a pair of long-bladed
daggers in his hands. The second was a big, hairy man,
his face mostly hidden behind a thick, bushy beard and
mustache. He repeatedly smacked the steel head of a
wicked-looking cudgel into the open palm of his free
hand. They both stepped out into the yard and stopped
a few paces in, grinning malevolently.

Oh, terrific, Vambran lamented. I walked right
into it.

"What's this about?" he said, turning his gaze back
to the woman on the roof and cocking his head to one
side in accusation. "You already got my coin pouch."

He began to eye the yard, looking for the best place
to defend himself.

"Oh, it's not your gold we're after, mercenary," the
lovely blonde said, rising to her feet and slipping a
hand into her vest pocket. "But your day is definitely
taking a turn for the worse."

She pulled her fist free and tossed a handful of something small, like tiny reddish-brown seeds, into her mouth.

Vambran wasted no more time sizing up his opponents. He took several steps backward, away from the woman, drawing his sword free and turning so that his back was against a wall and he could see all three of his foes clearly.

The woman stepped to the edge of the roof and tilted her head back, then thrust it forward again, as though she was going to spit. Instead of the tiny seeds, though, a gushing spray of liquid spewed forth from her mouth, thousands of tiny droplets glinting in the noonday sun like a shower of rain. The burst of spray fanned out and cascaded over Vambran even as far away as he stood, fully five paces away from his attacker.

The lieutenant yelped and turned away from the fountain of liquid, raising his free arm up to protect his face.

The droplets showered over him, instantly sizzling on skin and clothing alike as they soaked him down. Vambran let out a scream of pain and staggered away from the spray, feeling acid burning him from head to toe. He nearly dropped his sword as his skin erupted in numerous blisters, red and swollen. He fell to one knee, swiping at his body futilely, trying to get the source of his agony off of him. He thought he was going to retch.

"Now," said one of the two men, who had both stayed well back until that point, obviously anticipating the magical attack.

Vambran struggled to open his eyes and catch a glimpse of the pair's intentions. It was difficult through the burning pain all over his skin. He could tell, though, that the thugs were separating and closing the distance between themselves and him. The one to the lieutenant's right, wielding the cudgel, began to trot toward Vambran, angling his body sideways and winding up to swing his weapon as he closed in, intent on putting a powerful hit on the mercenary. The other one, with the daggers, was circling around to come at Vambran's flank, still rapidly twirling both blades. He cocked his hand back as if to throw one.

Through clenched teeth, Vambran fought through the distraction of the acid burns and straightened slightly.

He stared at the man with the daggers directly in the eyes and said in his most commanding voice, "Flee!"

The word was a magical trigger, and Vambran felt the surge of energy leave his mouth and radiate straight toward the thug with the slender blades. The man took one last step and flung his weapon even as the cunning smile left his face and was replaced with a look of profound terror. The lieutenant's magic had disrupted his throw, and the dagger sailed harmlessly over Vambran's head, clattering against the wall behind him. Spinning, the thug ran toward the doorway back into the establishment, looking back once in abject horror.

At the same time, the mercenary tried to duck low to avoid the swing of the cudgel, but the combination of his pain-induced disorientation and the effort of casting the commanding spell made him a fraction of a second too slow. The swipe missed Vambran's head, but it caught him hard against his shoulder. The mercenary heard bone crunch and felt his shoulder pop in blazing pain. His arm went numb as he was knocked backward from the impact, sent sprawling several feet and landing with a thud, the wind knocked out of him.

Groaning, Vambran squinted up into the sun overhead and saw it suddenly blotted out by the silhouette of the thug. The man had his cudgel raised high, ready for another crushing blow. Desperately, Vambran tried to roll out of the way, kicking out at his foe's

knee, hoping to delay the strike long enough to get out
of range. The heel of his boot snapped into the man's
leg, twisting both it and the thug around, causing
the cudgel to slam into the hard-packed ground next
to Vambran's head. The blow was so solid, the thump
made the mercenary's head bounce. He struggled to
his knees and crawled as quickly as he could to the
side while the thug clutched at his knee and snarled
curses at the lieutenant.

Suddenly, Vambran felt the tingle of magic swarming over him. There was a hint of pain, a suggestion
of agonizing ache, licking at the corners of his mind.
The magic seemed to be trying to convince him he was
feeling the effects of the acid spray all over again, but
he steadfastly refused to give in to it, forcing the idea
out of his thoughts.

From overhead he heard a feminine snarl of exasperation and looked up enough to see the short-haired
mage scowling as she pointed a sharpened stick in his
direction. The lieutenant managed to give her a smile
as he rose unsteadily to his feet, his right arm hanging limp at his side, his sword lying on the ground.

Vambran staggered a few more steps to stay clear
of the enraged, cudgel-wielding thug, frantically
looking for a way out of the engagement. With his
sword arm useless and his magic limited, he would
be a fool to continue to stand toe to toe against the
pair attacking him, and it would only get worse when
the other one he'd sent running came back after the
magic wore off. He was in trouble.

The thug Vambran had kicked struggled to stand,
favoring his leg, and limped toward the mercenary,
his jaw jutting out in fury. Overhead, the mage was
digging into another pocket. Vambran frantically retreated, maneuvering so that he put a parked wagon
between himself and the cudgel-wielder. Then he gave
a measured look up at the mage and began another
prayer to the Merchant's Friend. At the conclusion

of the prayer, he opened his mouth wide and made
as if to scream, but instead of his own voice issuing
forth, a shrill and unnatural shrieking and whistling
blasted out.

The clamorous noise was aimed at and focused
on the mage, whose eyes flared wide. She dropped
whatever she had been pulling from her pocket and
clapped her hands over her ears, falling to her knees
as she did so. Vambran watched for only a moment as
the woman writhed in pain, trying in vain to escape
the horrific cacophony of noise. Already, he could see
trickles of blood running out from beneath her hands
where they covered her ears, and he knew that she'd
been deafened for the next few moments.

Maybe that'll stop all of her damned spell slinging,
he thought, turning once more to the cudgel-swinging
thug.

The large, hairy man was limping toward him
around the back end of the wagon, and the lieutenant caught a glimpse of the third of the trio step back
into the yard, his remaining dagger clutched tightly
in his fist. The moment the short, wiry fellow spotted
Vambran, his grimace deepened into determination
and he stalked closer.

Vambran backed himself into a corner and fumbled the pendant dedicated to Waukeen out of his
shirt with his good hand. He clenched it tightly as he
offered up a plea to his deity to protect and defend him,
then kissed the medallion once as he concentrated on
manifesting holy energy into a form in front of him.
Where the lieutenant envisioned, a glowing, pulsing
image of a cloud of coins filled the air, swarming
like a hive of angry bees. While Vambran continued
to clutch at the medallion, he could feel the mental
connection with the cloud of coins.

The larger of Vambran's two foes was closer, and
the mercenary quickly directed the spiritual weapon
in that one's direction. The bear of a man brought

his cudgel up defensively and backed off a step, but his retreat was ineffectual, and the coins teemed around him, causing him to cry out and flinch from the dozens of painful strikes inflicted. He stumbled away, swatting with his free hand all around his own head, trying get free of the zipping, stinging coins.

Vambran turned his attention to the shorter thug, who had cleared the front end of the wagon and was closing fast, long-bladed dagger thrust out for striking. The mercenary mentally whipped the cloud of coins in that direction, directing them to swarm over his wiry opponent before that dagger got too close. The attack had a similar effect, causing the diminutive thug to cry out and duck away, twisting around and covering his head to protect himself from the slapping, buzzing cloud.

Already, though, the bigger man had recovered and was running toward Vambran with hatred in his eyes. The lieutenant couldn't hope to keep both of his attackers back on their heels with his one magical weapon. The best he could hope for was to slow them down, but the magic would dissipate in only a couple more moments, regardless. He was running out of options.

Just as Vambran began to mentally direct the swarming coins back toward the larger foe, a flash of red caught the corner of his eye. He glanced over to see a figure swathed in crimson on the roof next to the mage, who had recovered somewhat from the lieutenant's sonic attack and was preparing for another bit of spellcasting. She never got the chance, though, for the figure in red began to pummel her with several well placed kicks and punches. The flurry of attacks drove the mage back and off the back side of the roof, out of sight.

Vambran gawked at the new arrival, wondering who he was and why he was lending a hand. At that moment, though, the mercenary heard a shout from the doorway leading back into the *aszraun*, and when Vambran glanced back over that way, Kovrim was standing there looking bewildered. At the sight of all the different reinforcements showing up, the two thugs lost their desire to fight and scrambled toward the large wooden gate. The big man was the first to reach it, and he shoved against it forcefully with his shoulder. As the gap of the portal widened, both men slipped through and disappeared from sight.

Vambran felt the magic of his cloud of coins wink out. Realizing the threat was over, he sagged down to the ground, overcome with exhaustion.

"What in the Nine Hells happened?" Kovrim exclaimed, running over to his nephew's side. "By the Merchant's Friend, you're a sight! Who were those brutes?"

Vambran could only shake his head. All of the pain, from the shower of acid and the crushing cudgel blow to his shoulder, was enveloping him then, and he was woozy from it. His clothes were ruined, burned to shreds by the acid. He simply slumped into the corner where he'd made his final stand and let the blackness slip over him.

...

Emriana could barely concentrate on listening to Denrick's conversation, which wouldn't have been surprising under normal circumstances if she had stopped to think about it, given that he spent most of the day talking about himself. They were almost all stories the girl had heard numerous times during previous meetings with him.

But her distraction went far beyond growing bored with an uninteresting peacock. Her mind kept wandering back to the face of the woman she had seen the previous night, pale in the light of Vambran's odd magical flare, and Emriana was more certain than ever that it was the same woman she remembered working in the kitchens. Of course, she had only seen the girl a time or two, and she couldn't even remember the scullery cook's name, but she did recall that the woman had a distinctive face, with honey-colored hair that often fell down in ringlets around her eyes, giving her both a timid and flirtatious mien at the same time.

The private revelation made her more than a little jumpy, for Emriana would think that the tragedy of a death among the staff would have put a noticeable pall over the house. In fact, when Emriana considered it in its entirety, the logical thing to do would have been to cancel the tea. That certainly would have been the case at House Matrell.

Unless they weren't aware of the death, Emriana decided. But was she the person who should inform them, if that was true? Surely someone from the city watch had come around to the estate by that point to let them know. None of it was making much sense. She wanted to solve the puzzle, but something unsettling was holding her back, as well as Denrick's droning. She needed a way to find out for sure if the Pharaboldis were even aware that one of their own had died in the night.

Emriana forced herself to return her attention to the young man's comments, to try to reestablish some semblance of a conversation with him, lest he grow suspicious of her distracted demeanor. She smiled at him and nodded, pretending to be enraptured by his story.

". . . and it was just at that moment that the boar came crashing out of the underbrush, heading straight for Jerephin."

He paused expectantly.

Emriana had heard it before. Jerephin was Denrick's older brother, and they had gone boar hunting a year or so before, at the Pharaboldis' country estate in the wooded hills to the southeast. She remembered something about Denrick supposedly saving the day from disaster, and she was pretty certain he was almost to that point in the story. He was waiting for her to give him the proper lead-in, she knew.

"So what did you do then?" she asked breathlessly, as though hanging on every word out of the pompous fellow's mouth.

"Well, of course I stepped between Jerephin and the boar and set my spear," Denrick replied proudly, standing with a flourish and acting out the motions for her benefit. "You have to keep your back foot turned sideways, like so," he explained, miming the position, "and put the butt of the spear up against the instep, like so,"—and he propped an imaginary spear in tightly—"then you just keep the tip of the weapon leveled at the boar and let it ram itself onto the sharp end!"

He burst out laughing at his own cleverness, and Emriana tittered along with him for a moment.

"Tell me something," the girl said, deciding the time was right to steer the subject to another path. "Have you ever seen someone killed?" she asked, trying to sound innocent.

Denrick blinked, studying the girl for a moment. Finally, he nodded, a little too vigorously.

"Sure, several times," he answered. "There are always executions, and I've seen a boar rip one of our porters practically apart when we—"

"No, I'm not talking about hangings or hunting accidents," Emriana interrupted, much to Denrick's disgruntlement. It was apparent to her that he took great delight in holding the stage and did not enjoy being trod over, even for a moment. "What I mean is, seeing someone killed, murdered, stabbed with a sword or a dagger right in front of you, where you were close enough to see the expression on the victim's face."

Denrick blanched the slightest bit.

"Certainly not," he said, "and with any fortune, I shall never have to. What brought on this morbid bit of conversation?"

The man was clearly uncomfortable discussing such grim matters, though whether he found the topic personally distasteful, or if he was just trying to act as the noble companion and spare Emriana the gruesome details, she wasn't certain.

"Vambran and I were witnesses to a killing last night," she said, hoping her comments still just seemed matter-of-fact. "The city watch slew two people who had falsely marked themselves as mages."

"Really?" Denrick replied, mildly surprised. "You don't hear about that sort of crime very often. Most people in Arrabar know better. What did you see?"

It was clear to Emriana that he had no idea of the identity of the victim. It was one of those instances her grandmother was talking about, Emriana decided. It was a time for subtlety, for keeping a low and congenial profile until she had a better grasp of what, exactly, was going on. She feigned disinterest.

"Oh, not a whole lot. We didn't get there until after it was all over, and the watchmen shooed us away before we could see much of what happened. But it was most unsettling, and I had difficulty getting to sleep last night."

Suddenly, Emriana knew who might know more about the scullery maid's death. She had to get back to the estate. Thinking quickly, she affected a yawn, waving her hand politely in front of her wide-open mouth.

"In fact, after last night's excitement and all of this sun and fresh air, I'm starting to feel . . ." and she faked another one, larger than the first.

"Oh, where are my manners?" Denrick said, rising to his feet. "I've kept you out here far too long. Your family is probably wondering where we are, and you must be exhausted. Come, we'll return home at once."

"But what of the picnic things?" Emriana asked, secretly pleased that he had taken her bait.

She was ready to be rid of the pretentious boy and could think of no quicker way to get him to do what she wanted than to swoon or do something else similarly ridiculous.

"Don't worry about them, Em. I'll send Turcan back here to collect them later."

Emriana nodded, feeling another "yawn" coming on, and even allowed Denrick to assist her in mounting Goldy. Quickly enough, they were back at the estate, and he was helping her inside to the coolness of the parlor. Almost immediately, she sped off, leaving him to deal with the animals while she departed under the pretense of changing back into her original clothes, Patimi in tow to aid her.

Once she was out of sight, though, the girl turned on the servant and looked her squarely in the eye.

"You know what happened last night," she said, her voice severe. "Tell me."

The woman, suddenly flustered, stumbled through apologies and denials, all the while unable to look Emriana in the eye. Shaking her head, Emriana grabbed her hand and dragged her deeper into the house, back into Lobra's old bedrooms.

"Enough pretending. You were moping about this morning when you were helping me to dress. I know you know what I'm talking about, because I can see it in your eyes. Now tell me. What was her name?"

Patimi started to shake her head again, but then the facade faded away and the woman simply pressed both of her hands against her face, her body wracked with silent sobs. Emriana felt slight remorse then, feeling compassion welling up for the poor woman who must have lost someone she cared for, and yet had to go through her day as if nothing were wrong.

The girl reached out, tentatively at first but when Patimi didn't shy away, more boldly, giving her a comforting hug.

"I'm sorry," Emriana said, patting Patimi's hair gently. "Tell me what happened."

Finally, the servant had collected herself enough to pull free of Emriana's hug and straighten her shoulders. She sniffed a couple of times and wiped her eyes, then nodded and began to speak.

"The soldiers came last night, late, after almost everyone was already abed. They told us that Jithelle had marked herself as wizard, had run from the soldiers. It was all so hard to believe, I just couldn't imagine..." Patimi's face screwed up with emotion again, and she cried softly for a few moments before continuing, "Jithelle would never have done that, ma'am. She didn't even know her runes, much less any magic tricks. She was a good girl and wouldn't get into any trouble."

Patimi sniffed again and looked at Emriana beseechingly, as if expecting the girl to somehow make it better.

Emriana sighed and consoled the woman again.

"Of course she wouldn't," she said. "But why were you pretending that nothing had happened? Why aren't the Pharaboldis mourning or even acknowledging her death?"

Patimi shook her head and replied, "Madam Anista said we don't want the scandal. Because of the plague mostly, but also just because."

"The plague? What plague?" Emriana asked, startled.

"Oh, the soldiers claimed that she and the other man—her lover, they say, though I don't believe it—the soldiers said that both of them were practicing dark rituals and were tainted with the magic plague. Said the bodies"—and Patimi began to sob as she finished—"had to be burned!"

Emriana sat back, stunned. If the bodies had been burned, that meant that Vambran couldn't have watched the communing spell to speak with the pair's spirits. And no one would hear their side of the story. A thought struck Emriana, then.

"Patimi, you said you didn't believe that the other one, the man who was with her, was Jithelle's lover. Why?"

"Because she had her heart set on someone else. She was never interested in Hoytir; no one ever even saw them together."

"Hoytir? That was the man? You knew him, too?"

Patimi stared at Emriana.

"He was one of the stable boys," she breathed, wiping her eyes again.

"What?" the girl exclaimed, sitting back, her eyebrows raised. "Here?"

The servant nodded and said, "A decent man, from what I heard, but he and Jithelle never looked twice at each other. He knew his place."

"What do you mean? Why wasn't it his place to see her?"

Patimi looked at Emriana for a long time before speaking, and the girl got the very uncomfortable impression that there was sympathy in her eyes.

"You don't know," the woman said at last, looking away.

"Know what?" Emriana demanded, forcing Patimi to look at her again. "Tell me," she insisted. "If someone murdered Jithelle and Hoytir, the only way the killers can be caught is if you tell me."

Patimi nodded and took a deep breath.

"Because," she said at last, "Jithelle was sharing a bed with Master Denrick."

...

When Vambran awoke, he was in his bed at the estate, and half the family was lurking over him,

worry creasing their faces. The first person to notice
the mercenary's eyes flutter open was Emriana, who
yelped softly from the chair she was occupying next
to her brother's bed.

"He's awake!" the girl cried out, hopping to her feet.
"Mother, Grandmother! Vambran's awake."

"Yes, child, we can see that," Hetta said calmly, sitting forward from her own chair on the opposite side
of Vambran's head from her granddaughter. "We're
not blind or deaf, Em."

Emriana pursed her lips but said nothing more.

Uncle Dregaul loomed into view as servants helped
Vambran to sit up.

"You're lucky to be alive," the man said, staring
pointedly at his nephew. "Kovrim said he got to you
just in time."

Vambran could see his other uncle lurking in the
background, behind Dregaul. He nodded in thanks
to the older priest.

"Yes," Vambran said, acknowledging Dregaul's
comment. "I was fortunate."

"Well, we're all very glad to see you back here, safe
and sound," Dregaul said, giving Vambran a single
pat on the shoulder.

Then he turned and was gone, heading out the door.
Vambran's mother pushed to fill in the void left by
Dregaul.

"How are you feeling, dear?" she asked, leaning
down to get a better look at her son. "Are you still in
any pain?"

Vambran shook his head and replied, "No, Mother.
I feel fine, actually. Just a little tired."

"Well, Kovrim said you'd be all right, but I wanted
to hear it from your own mouth. He said the scars
from the acid burns would fade in a couple of days."
Ladara Matrell's face scrunched up in emotion. "Oh,
Vambran, you must be more careful! You could
have—could have ..."

The lieutenant reached out with his hand—his right arm, which felt free of injury, he noted—and took hold of his mother's.

"It's all right," he said. "I'm fine. It was just a mugging, and I was a little careless. It won't happen again." Ladara nodded and wiped a few tears from her cheeks. "I need to talk to Uncle Kovrim for a few moments, though. Alone."

Hetta nodded and turned to depart. Ladara sprang to the older woman's side to assist her. Only Emriana hesitated.

"I need to talk to you," she said, giving her brother a level stare. "Soon."

Vambran nodded and shooed her away. When the two priests were alone in his room, Vambran motioned for his uncle to sit down beside the bed and asked, "What else happened?"

Kovrim shrugged and replied, "Not much more to tell. After you fell unconscious, I laid a few healing spells on you, had a carriage prepared, and had you brought here. You gave me quite a fright, you know."

"That was no casual mugging, Uncle Kovrim."

"How do you know?" the older man asked, worried.

"Because the woman on the roof flat out told me before she attacked me. They weren't after my coin. They were coming after me specifically."

"And you think there's a connection with this and what you saw last night?"

The lieutenant nodded and said, "I'm pretty certain of it. I just don't know how they figured out that I was going to keep snooping around. You're the only person I've told."

"Someone's been following you around, it would seem," Kovrim said with a sigh. "Mayhap reading your thoughts, eavesdropping on conversations." He shook his head in consternation. "You've gotten into something of a hornet's nest, it would appear. You'd better be doubly careful from now on."

"What about the stranger in red?"

"What stranger?"

Vambran frowned. "The figure on the roof, dressed all in crimson. I didn't get to see his face—he had it covered—but he took care of the mage woman while I was fighting with the two brutes on the ground. Didn't he stick around?"

"I never saw a figure in red nor a mage there. Only those two men you were keeping at bay. I wondered how you were burned."

"Right," Vambran said, nodding. "The mage caught me off guard. It was careless and foolish."

"Well, you'll know better next time." Kovrim said, sitting forward as if to rise. "I'm going to go back to the temple and see what I can find out about the two Waukeenar priests. You get some rest."

Vambran nodded and waved good-bye to his uncle, but he was deep in thought about other things already.

Tonight, he decided firmly. I'm going after those fake guards tonight.

CHAPTER SIX

Even if Anista Pharaboldi or her husband are in some way involved in this mess, I honestly don't think Denrick knows what's going on," Emriana said to her brother. She had returned to his rooms right after Uncle Kovrim had left, and they were discussing what she'd learned that day. Vambran paced while she sat cross-legged on his bed. "I was watching him carefully when I told him what we'd seen, and he didn't even react. I made sure I didn't mention any names—well, at the time, I didn't know Jithelle's name—so that if he didn't know, I wouldn't get him riled up. If he was already aware of her death, I think I could have been able to tell, and he didn't blink at all."

"Maybe," Vambran said, still walking back and forth, pulling at his lips in thought. He had dressed in a fresh outfit and seemed none the worse for wear after his ordeal at the *aszraun.* "Or he could just be an incredibly good actor. You took an awfully big risk, testing him that way. If House Pharaboldi wants to keep their connection with the woman quiet, revealing that you know isn't going to help anything."

"I said I was subtle, Vambran. Besides, I did all that before I knew he was bedding her." Emriana rolled her eyes and sighed. "And before I knew about the attack on you. If I had already found out that there was that strong of a connection, I never would have brought it up in front of him. As it was, I pretended to be exhausted for the rest of the afternoon to avoid seeing him again."

"Yeah," Vambran said softly. "I'm sorry you had to find that out, Em."

"Oh, please," she said, forcing a laugh. "You know how I felt about Denrick before. It just confirmed my low opinion of him."

She gave Vambran a wink, but down inside, she had to admit there was at least a little pain. Finding out anyone wasn't being honest with her would do that.

"Do you think the maid who told you all this will keep quiet?"

"I imagine," Emriana replied. "It doesn't help her at all to admit she broke a confidence, especially one her mistress established with her."

"I sure hope so," said Vambran. "You need to be careful, especially now. If Denrick didn't know before, he's going to find out sooner or later. He's still likely to figure that it was Jithelle you were talking about. He may still get suspicious that you know more than you admitted."

"And do what?" Em asked dismissively. "At worst, he thinks I knew who it was during the picnic and didn't tell him. In the strictest sense, that's not true, but he might think that. Even so, what's he going to do? Get angry? Refuse to see me anymore? It's not

like I'm ever going to allow him to think I'm taking
him seriously again. Not when he sleeps with his
family's staff."

"He might not be content with that solution, Em.
From what you've said in the past, Denrick sounds
like the kind of person who's used to getting what he
wants. What if he still wants you, especially now that
his secret mistress is no longer around?"

"It's never going to happen," Emriana said
firmly.

"Or, what if the Pharaboldis are somehow responsible for Jithelle's and Hoytir's deaths? Even if
Denrick isn't in on it, once he finds out and mentions
that you know about it, don't you think they'll consider you a threat to them? Whoever was responsible
for these murders, they won't be afraid to kill again
to keep their secrets intact. They tried it once already,
today."

Her brother was looking at her with a dangerous
glint in his eyes.

"You really think assassins would come after me?"
Emriana asked, trying to sound off-handed, but more
than a bit nervous. "They'd have a hard time getting
in here, with all of Uncle Dregaul's security in place
to keep me from getting out."

Vambran stopped pacing and turned to face his
sister directly.

"Em," he said, "I know you're all grown up now,
turning sixteen in a couple of days, but please listen
to me on this." He reached forward and took his sister
by the shoulders, forcing her to see his face. "You're not
invincible; neither am I. Look what happened to me
today, and I'm trained to expect it. There are people
out there who are capable of a lot of unpleasant things,
and you haven't been around them like I have. Even
though Uncle Dregaul would probably prefer it, you
can't hide in here your whole life. I'm just asking you
to be careful. There's still so much we don't know."

Emriana smiled and leaned forward to hug her brother warmly.

"I know," she said, and held him tightly for a good long time, trying to let some of her worry for him melt away. Then she released him finally and sat back again. "I appreciate it. And I will. But you have to admit, it was a stroke of good fortune, my conversation with Patimi."

"Yes. That's true," Vambran said, pacing once more. "Though I had already heard about the plague story as of this morning, at least we now know who the victims are. I'm not sure where that gets us, though. Maybe we could find out more from the rest of the staff at the Pharaboldis', or from Jithelle's or Hoytir's families."

"Now who's talking about taking risks? How are you going to do that without being noticed by the Pharaboldis themselves?" Emriana sat straighter and reached out to grab Vambran by the hand to force him to stop pacing. "More important, why are we trying to figure all this out ourselves? What good is it doing us to stick our noses in this mess?"

Vambran gave his sister a look that she couldn't read. "Because it's the right thing to do, Em," he said softly. "Because no one else in Arrabar seems at all interested in seeking justice. 'They're just a couple of working class servants,' " he intoned. "Maybe they're even guilty, and everyone has been reading them wrong. But no one has been able to prove it, yet. I can't let that go. Not again."

There it was again, Emriana realized. Those strange comments her brother was making. What was he talking about? She started to open her mouth to ask him, when suddenly, it hit her. The accident! Aunt Xaphira's disappearance! It all made sense, and the realization made her gasp.

"What is it?" Vambran asked, concern in his eyes.

"N-Nothing," Emriana stammered, remembering her vow to keep quiet about the whole affair until the time was right. "Just remembering something Grandmother Hetta told me this morning at breakfast." And, on impulse she added, "About Aunt Xaphira, and an accident."

Vambran stood very still, staring hard at Emriana, his face losing its color.

"She told you about that?" he asked, his voice barely above a whisper.

"Only that something happened," the girl replied, taking her brother's hand. "None of the details. She said the person involved would have to tell me in his own good time," she added pointedly.

Vambran spent so long just staring off into nothingness that Emriana began to worry that she had made a terrible mistake, mentioning her knowledge at all. The realization that it was her brother who had been involved had stunned her too, and she was still sifting through the emotional explosions in her head from that when he finally began to recount the story.

"I was twelve," Vambran began, "and it was the Night of Ghosts festival at the Generon. Adyan, Horial, and I were bored, so we decided to go take some target practice with a brand new crossbow Uncle Kovrim had given to me. We found a spot where we didn't think we'd bother anyone, but it was a stupid, stupid thing we did, because I shot someone."

He stopped there, taking several deep breaths and swallowing. Emriana squeezed her brother's hand reassuringly and nodded, urging him to continue.

"It was Lord Wianar's cousin Rodolpho. It was an accident, but everyone knew that Eles Wianar would bend it to his advantage any way he could. So Aunt Xaphira fixed it. She dressed up like an assassin, hid her face, and managed to get over the walls and out of the city with half the guardsmen in Arrabar chasing her. No one ever figured out the truth."

"Oh, Vambran, I'm sorry," Emriana said, her voice thick. "That must have been horrible for you! And Uncle Dregaul has held it against you ever since," she said, realizing then the origin of the animosity between Vambran and his uncle. "He blames you."

That thought made Emriana feel sick to her stomach. She realized for the first time that she truly hated her uncle.

"He has a right to. Every day since it happened, I've wondered how it must have felt for Rodolpho's family to wonder why someone would want to kill him. I've imagined the pain and hurt that not knowing the truth has caused them." Vambran blinked then and looked at his sister with determination. "I won't be a party to another covered-up killing. That's why I have to do this. I would hope that you would do it just because it's the right thing to do, but if you don't want to . . ."

He shrugged and began to pace once more. It was Emriana's turn to feel hurt.

"I never meant that," she said. "I want to do what's right, too, especially now that I know. I just want to make sure we're doing it for the right reasons, and in the right way. Uncle Dregaul isn't going to like us defying him, especially because of . . . because of what happened."

"I don't care what Uncle Dregaul thinks. I'm through cowering at his feet for my past crimes. I'm making amends, and this is my redemption."

"As long as you realize that he could be right. If by continuing to dig around, we hurt the family business, are we doing more damage than good?"

"Are you saying that preserving the 'business as usual' attitude of Uncle Dregaul is more important than bringing murderers to justice?"

Emriana stared steadily at Vambran.

"No," she said quietly. "I am saying that we should be subtle, in case we're completely wrong, so that we don't unduly hurt House Matrell. Grandmother Hetta is a proud woman, and she deserves that much from us."

Vambran stood quietly, considering for a moment, then he nodded and said, "That's reasonable and fair. All right, I'll make you a bargain."

"Name it," Emriana said, smiling again.

"I'll keep a low profile while I sniff out what's going on, if you'll promise to be careful and not take any unnecessary risks."

"Deal."

"Good. Now, I have something for you."

"You do?" Emriana said, getting excited.

"Yes. This was supposed to be your birthday present, and I guess it still is, but you're getting it a day early, after all."

Emriana couldn't help but smile in glee as Vambran reached into one of his traveling trunks, which had been brought to the estate from *Lady's Favor* by wagon earlier in the day, and pulled out a small pouch made of fine satin. He handed the thing to his sister.

"What is it?" the girl asked breathlessly, pulling open the drawstrings and dumping the item inside into the palm of her hand.

It was a pendant, she saw, a large opal, mostly gray with swirls of mauve, orange, and green, in a teardrop shape. The narrow end had a fine gold chain threaded through it. It took Emriana's breath away.

"Oh, it's beautiful!" she breathed, holding it up to let it shine in the light. She lunged at her brother and wrapped him in a big hug. "Thank you so much!" she gushed.

"Hang on," Vambran laughed, freeing himself from her. "Remember the message I sent you?" he asked. When Emriana nodded, perplexed, he pointed to the pendant. "I did it with that."

The girl's eyes widened even more.

"Oh, show me!" she pleaded, handing the gemstone to her brother.

Vambran took the pendant and held it up.

"Once per day, when you are holding it in your hand, you concentrate on the person you want to send the message to, and speak the message."

"Oh, I want to try it, right now!"

"No, wait a minute. Listen to me. I said once per day. If you try it any more often than that, it won't work. You have to hold it and concentrate on the idea of speaking a message to them. If you do that, it will work, no matter how far away from you that person is."

Emriana just smiled and slipped the chain around her neck.

"It's wonderful," she said, feeling her eyes welling up with tears of happiness. "Thank you, Vambran."

"The person on the other end of the message can talk back to you, if they want. But remember to keep the message short. You can't ramble on and on, because only the first handful of words will go through."

Emriana nodded and said, "I'll remember."

"If you ever get in a bind and need my help, use it to get my attention. I'll get to you as quickly as I can."

"All right," the girl replied, smiling and wiping her eyes with her hands. She considered it the best birthday present she had ever received.

Finally, after Emriana had regained her composure, she returned to the topic at hand.

"So, what's our next step?" she asked, feeling conspiratorial.

"Nothing, for the moment," Vambran replied. "I need to spend some time with the company. There's payroll to be distributed, plus I promised Adyan and Horial I would meet them tonight for drinks."

"Oh, you're no fun," Emriana said, pouting. "I was hoping for some real spying tonight."

"Not a chance," Vambran replied. "If nothing else, you're still under Uncle Dregaul's eagle eye at the moment. So you're not going anywhere." When she started to protest, Vambran wagged a finger at his

sister. "Ah, ah, ah! You just got through saying we
needed to keep a low profile. That goes for you, too."

"Fine," Emriana harrumphed. "You take all the
fun out of this."

"I'm sure that there will be plenty of chances for
you to play spy tomorrow," her brother said. "Your
birthday party that Hetta is throwing for you is
tomorrow night."

Emriana smacked herself in the forehead and
groaned, "Oh, Waukeen, that's right. I completely
forgot. And I'm supposed to be escorted by Denrick!"

The girl made a disparaging sound in her throat
and rolled her eyes in misery. The thought of spend-
ing any more time with that self-inflated buffoon,
especially once she knew his true character, was
repulsive.

"You have to act like nothing is wrong," Vambran
warned. "You can't give him or anyone in his family
a reason to be suspicious."

"I know," Emriana sighed, "but I don't have to
like it."

...

The Crying Claw got its name from the sound of
its sign—depicting a single bird's claw—squeaking
as it swung in the wind that blew in off the bay to
the west. The front doors of the place actually faced
northeast, away from the harbor, and it maintained
a sizable taproom just inside the entrance. That was
only a small portion of the whole, though, for the
bulk of the property rested on the side of a rather
steep hill that sloped its way down toward the docks.
It was there, off the back of the establishment, where
the majority of the patrons gathered whenever the
weather permitted. The entire hillside had been
terraced, carved into wide, tiled patios connected by
sets of ramps and stairs and filled with tables, most

of them open to the sky but a few protected by wooden scaffolding draped with brightly colored awnings. Of course, there were the prerequisite planter boxes, trellises, and wooden railings generously placed to divide the space up, all overgrown with the tropical plants and vines that were so common in the Reach. The architecture created the effect of a hillside vineyard in the middle of the city.

The Crying Claw was hopping when Vambran got there, which was typical. It was one of the most popular taverns near the waterfront of Arrabar, and every ship's officer, mercenary captain, middling merchant, and sword-for-hire frequented it whenever they were in the city. Even the inside was busy, and it took the lieutenant a few minutes to squeeze through the morass of patrons and get to the wide arched doorways that led out into the back. The bar had been set up to face two directions, one side open to the interior of the establishment and the other at the top of the terraced patios. Jenis Glowarm, the half-elf proprietor with the ever-present smile, was behind the bar, just as she was every night, along with three assistants. A full complement of servers moved endlessly between the tables and the bar, making their way up and down the stairs and ramps to serve drinks. Anyone wanting a job working for Jenis had to be physically fit.

Vambran slipped into a bit of open space at the bar, and when Jenis spotted him, she gave him a quick wink, for he had been a customer there for a long time.

"Be with you in a minute, hon," Jenis said, scurrying to the far side to serve some customers who were clamoring for more beer.

Vambran gave the proprietor a wave of acknowledgement and kept his coin pouch safely in his hand while he waited.

He turned and let his eyes roam over the length of the terraced hillside, looking to see if any of his

companions had beaten him there that night. Of
Horial and Adyan, there was no sign. That was not
surprising, though, for he was a bit early. He turned
back where he could keep half an eye on the front
doors and the other half on Jenis, wanting to make
sure she remembered that he needed a mug.

The lieutenant considered again his plan for the
evening and asked himself for perhaps the tenth time
whether or not it was really a good idea. The notion
of using his familiarity with Emriana's dagger to
magically find the thugs who had impersonated city
watchmen felt right, but everything that had happened since the previous evening was giving Vambran
a sense of foreboding, as though he were standing on
the precipice of something much larger and more
sinister than a simple murder. He just couldn't put
his finger on it.

Of course, that in and of itself wouldn't be enough
to dissuade Vambran from following through with
his intentions. Adyan and Horial were good friends,
made closer by the unfortunate secret they shared,
and the lieutenant knew they would happily aid
him. But he knew some might question whether it
was proper for him to appropriate his own men to see
the task to its end. He certainly had a high level of
discretion regarding how he put the resources at his
disposal to use, but for what he had in mind, he was
completely on his own.

Vambran was still rationalizing his decision when
he spotted the two sergeants entering the Crying Claw
and peering around uncertainly. The lieutenant put
his fingers to his mouth and gave a shrill whistle,
which not only caught the soldiers' attention, but just
about every other patron within fifteen paces. There
was a brief lull in the conversations as several people
glared at him and wiggled their fingers in their ears,
then the issue was just as quickly forgotten. Vambran
waved to the two mercenaries.

Horial and Adyan waved back and pushed through the throngs until they reached him, though there was no more room at the bar.

"Evening, Lieutenant," Horial said, clapping Vambran once on the shoulder. "I see you're planning to buy the first round," he added, nodding as Jenis sidled up to where Vambran stood, his elbows resting on the bar.

Vambran chuckled and waved the other two men toward the terraces.

"Go find us a table," he said. "I'll bring us three tall, frothy ones."

The other two men nodded in hearty agreement and departed, peering through the openings in the lush, green walls in search of an empty spot. Vambran turned back to Jenis and ordered three mugs of her finest dark ale. Soon enough, he had the drinks in his hand and was working his way through the various patios, seeking his companions. He finally spotted them in a corner around a table meant for two. Shrugging, Vambran set the drinks down and grabbed an unused chair from another table and squeezed in beside them.

"Here's to gold weighing my pockets down," Adyan drawled, hoisting his own mug up to clink it against the other two before downing a long gulp.

"And to the ladies we spend it all on," Horial added, winking as he slurped from his own mug.

"Hear, hear," Vambran agreed, smiling. After each of them had savored the taste of their ales, Vambran settled back in his chair. "Did the men get their payments?"

"Aye," Horial said, drawing his finger through a wet spot on the surface of the table. "All except Ludini, who had to tend to some family matters in Mimph and caught the ferry there first thing this morning. But I already knew he wouldn't be around for several days. I put his share away for him."

Vambran nodded and replied, "We may have a job in a tenday or so, not sure yet. Will Ludini be back by then?"

"Should be," Horial replied, sketching something with the moisture. "What sort of job?"

Vambran rolled his eyes.

"Oh," he said, "some merchants the temple has been using keep complaining that the competition is bullying their caravans whenever they try to use a certain waypoint on the Golden Road. We may tag along on their next run to see to it that it stops."

Adyan snorted into his mug.

"Merchants," he scoffed.

Vambran raised a single eyebrow at the sergeant who, realizing he had just insulted all three of their families, raised a hand in placation.

"Oh, not our Houses, sir," he said quickly. "I just meant the foolish, no-sense kind."

Vambran couldn't maintain the glare though and broke into a grin.

"That's all right, Sergeant Mercatio, you just keep right on insulting my family. You'll make captain in no time."

Horial guffawed as he was drinking and nearly choked.

"Adyan never met a man he couldn't insult sooner or later," the man said, wiping foam from his nose.

The three of them chuckled a moment longer before Vambran grew serious.

"Listen, you two," said the lieutenant. "I have something weighing on me that I need some help with."

"Name it," Adyan said, setting his empty mug down. "I'm there."

"Absolutely," Horial added. "Whatever you need. We've been friends a long time, Vambran."

Vambran nodded, having known to expect the two men's willingness. "Yes, we have. And we've been through some rough scrapes along the way," he said, looking at each of them intently. "Some things we don't even talk about anymore." The lieutenant raised his eyebrows to emphasize his point. "This may be one of those times before the night's through."

Both men's faces turned solemn.

Good, Vambran thought. They understand.

"We're your friends," Horial said. "Whatever's going on, nothing's changed in all these years. Not even that."

"We'll help you any way we can," Adyan drawled, frowning. "Just tell us what you need."

"Are you both sure?" Vambran asked. The two sergeants nodded. "All right, then," the lieutenant continued. "Last night, Emriana and I ran up against some fellows who I think were pretending to be city watchmen. These thugs killed two people, supposedly in the line of duty, but I think there's something else going on. Today, I got jumped by three vermin who definitely weren't after my coin. Someone is hiding something and is awfully intent on keeping me from finding out what it is. But that's exactly what I intend to do, and I need someone to watch my back."

"Sounds like a mighty good time to me," Adyan drawled, popping his knuckles and grinning, emphasizing the diagonal scar on his chin. "What's the full story?"

After flagging down a barmaid and ordering another round of drinks, Vambran proceeded to explain his tale to his two friends. When he was finished, they nodded.

"Hey," Horial said, "I already told you I was your man, but after hearing that, you know we have to set things right."

Adyan nodded in agreement. "If nothing else, you'll be wanting that dagger back," he joked. "When do you want to kick their door in?"

"Tonight," Vambran said. "As soon as you two are ready to go."

Adyan looked forlornly at the half-finished ale sitting in front of him. "Might want to finish my drink, first," he said hopefully.

Vambran rolled his eyes and laughed.

"I think we have time for that," he said.

The trio sat and conversed for a little while longer, finishing their drinks, and set out to begin their night's work. As they departed, Vambran glanced skyward and noted that clouds had rolled in off the Reach, obscuring the waxing moon and bringing the smell of rain with them.

It would be a good night for hunting, the lieutenant decided as he withdrew his sacred medallion with Waukeen's profile graven on it. Closing his eyes briefly, Vambran drew upon the divine blessings of his goddess, visualizing his sister's dagger in his mind and concentrating on discerning its location. He felt an urge to travel west, toward the docks. Nodding, he set out, leading the way.

None of the three noticed a single figure lurking among the deeper shadows of a doorway across the street from the Crying Claw. As the three friends made their way down the street, the figure cautiously stepped out of those shadows and began to follow them.

...

"Yes, I was the one who sent the two Halanthi priests down to the city watch station house with instructions to burn the bodies," Grand Trabbar Lavant said. "How is this a concern of the Sapphire Crescent?" he asked Kovrim, who stood in the Waukeenar high priest's offices, staring at the rotund man with the pudgy fingers, each of which sported a gold ring, heavy with diamonds, sapphires, rubies, and emeralds.

"Then you interfered with an investigation of murder!" Kovrim replied angrily, ignoring for the

moment how unbecoming it was for him, a mere Syndo
priest in the temple's hierarchy, to speak to the Grand
Trabbar that way. "Why would you do that?"

Lavant smiled. "Please, Syndo Lazelle, calm yourself. If you will hear my explanation and give this
matter a moment's thought, I think you will come to
understand the importance of seeing the events play
to this conclusion. But I will not abide you raising
your voice to me."

Kovrim bowed his head in acquiescence.

"Of course, Grand Trabbar," he said. "I was out of
line. My apologies."

"Not at all, my brother. It is often a narrow and
treacherous line we must walk in order to ensure a
bountiful return on our spiritual investments. The
Merchant's Friend would have everyone enjoy the
windfalls of shrewd trade, taking us ever closer to the
golden age that lies ahead, but there are many poor
investments that beckon to us during our dealings.
We all struggle from time to time, allowing anxieties
over whether or not our coin has been spent wisely to
cloud our judgment. You speak from the heart, and
that is good, but you must remember that only cool
heads can prevail at the bargaining table."

"Of course, Grand Trabbar. Thank you for helping
to guide me in my spiritual commerce. May you have
many returns on your investments in me."

Lavant smiled, nodded, and said, "Now, to the issue
of the two unfortunate victims of last night's crime.
What occurred was a result of some very delicate
business negotiations that had hit a snag along their
course to completion. Those deaths were an inelegant
and short-sighted solution, and if I had been privy to
the plans from the beginning, I would have counseled
strenuously against it. But what was done was done
and, by the time I found out about it, could not be
reversed. Rest assured that those responsible have
been harshly dealt with.

"But there was no sense in throwing the baby out with the bath water. It serves no purpose to publicize the events, or to expose those who are tied to, but not guilty of, the crimes. A strategic business alliance hangs in the balance, and destroying potential commerce for the sake of disclosing the details does far more harm than good. The truly guilty have been punished, and the profits to be earned from staying the course can still be realized."

Kovrim nodded, not satisfied, but understanding the situation. He respected Grand Trabbar Lavant, not just as a spiritual leader, but as a man who could prioritize the needs of various individuals or groups in the scope of Waukeen's greater plan for a golden age, when all would find the bounty of wealth. Still, it was sometimes a little too easy for the man to turn a blind eye toward injustices in the name of wealth. Particularly when the temple itself stood to benefit from the endeavor. Kovrim had no doubt in his mind that that was the case with those particular circumstances. Otherwise, he knew, Grand Trabbar Lavant would not be rationalizing his actions in such a way. Kovrim decided he would need more time to contemplate his position on the matter. Alone, where he could really think and pray.

"Well, sir, you have certainly cleared that up for me," Kovrim said finally, rising to go. "I wish that it had not come to such, but I will take comfort in the fact that you believe this was the right course of action, even if I do not completely understand its importance myself."

"Indeed I do, Syndo Lazelle. If there's anything else I can do to assuage your concerns, please don't hesitate to speak up."

"Not at all, Grand Trabbar. You've calmed my fears and concerns admirably."

Kovrim turned to depart.

"Oh, uh, Syndo?"

Kovrim stopped and asked, "Yes, Grand Trabbar?"

"I realize your nephew is also trying to determine what truly went on," the high priest said. Kovrim nodded fervently, working hard to mask his surprise. Lavant continued, "As he is serving under you in one of our esteemed companies, it would behoove you to speak with him and get his attention on something else. It really doesn't sit well with the Overgold of the temple to have one of their own working against them, however inadvertent and well meaning it may seem."

"I understand, Grand Trabbar. I will see to it immediately," Kovrim replied, his mind racing. How had they discerned Vambran's involvement so quickly? Was Grand Trabbar Lavant responsible for the suspected eavesdropping? Perhaps even the attack at Dark She Looks Upon Me? One thing was for certain; they were keeping closer tabs on the situation than Kovrim had previously thought.

"Yes. Perhaps something to occupy his time with? Say, a new assignment?" Lavant suggested.

Kovrim frowned slightly and said, "It would be difficult at this late juncture to shuffle the schedule of services for the Crescent, but I can look into it."

"Something else, then. A little entertainment, perhaps. Is he in need of fresh companionship?" The Grand Trabbar was drumming his fingers on his belly as he said that. "If he already has someone at his arm, then maybe the two of them just need a special time together. Something we could help arrange. With a suitable amount of leave time?"

"I can try to find out, sir."

"I'm only making suggestions that will help ease him off this scrutiny. It's for his own good, you realize."

"Of course," Kovrim said, really wanting to be finished with the conversation. "I will take care

of it, Grand Trabbar. Don't fret over it for another
instant."

"Thank you, Syndo Lazelle. I knew you were a man
to be counted upon."

...

Vambran, Horial, and Adyan stood before the
front entrance to a large warehouse connected to
a meat- salting business. It sat at the end of a cul-
de-sac at one end of the wharf. The cloudy weather
had turned into rain, a light, misty drizzle that
really only made the cobblestones slick but didn't
feel wet to anyone caught in it. The air felt mildly
cooler because of the sprinkle, and the shadows a
little deeper due to the lack of a moon, but that was
about it.

It had taken the lieutenant three castings of his
divine magic before he had been able to pinpoint the
location of Emriana's dagger. The three of them had
wandered through the streets, having only a direction
to go on, working their way closer and closer to the
harbor before turning to one side and finally finding the place. It was completely dark and shuttered,
a business that catered to ships wanting to restock
their supplies for sea travel. Vambran had ordered
salted pork and beef from the place for some of his
own excursions on more than one occasion, and he
knew the proprietor to be a fair and friendly business-
woman. She had continued to run the place even after
her husband and son had died, and her dried meats
were quite good.

"Well?" Horial said, looking at Vambran expectantly. "You're sure it's in there?"

Vambran nodded and said, "No doubt at all. And I'm
thinking these men are in there without the consent
of the woman who owns the shop. I don't think she'd
let a bunch of thugs live in her warehouse."

"They might be paying her rent," Adyan suggested, frowning as if he didn't believe that possibility himself.

"No miscreants I ever ran across paid for anything they didn't have to," Horial said with a mild snort. "They've got a secret way in and out, and your shopkeeper knows nothing about it."

"That's what I'm thinking, too," Vambran said. "Let's find it."

The three soldiers began to circumnavigate the place, examining every wall for a hidden or concealed door. They also checked the various windows, which were open arches covered with broad awnings to keep the weather out and sealed off by strong steel grates.

At the fourth such opening, Horial discovered that the grate was loose and could swing wide of the wall.

"Here we go," the man whispered. "This is probably how they're coming and going."

Vambran nodded and motioned for the mercenary to proceed. Horial went first, followed by the lieutenant, and Adyan brought up the rear. As Vambran set his feet down, he could tell by the feel of it that the floor was hard-packed earth. Other than that, he could discern nothing. Once all three were inside, they stood together in the darkness, trying to let their eyes adjust to the gloom. As they waited, Vambran listened intently for any telltale sounds that might provide a clue as to whether the thugs were there or not. It was totally quiet. Even after several minutes, it was still too dark to see anything clearly, but Vambran felt confident there was no one besides the three of them inside the building.

Vambran reached into his coin pouch and pulled out a single Sembian raven, then he found by feel the gold emblem of Waukeen he wore on the chain around his neck and grasped it firmly.

"Watch your eyes, boys," he said softly. "I'm going to shine a little light on things." He uttered the words of a quick and specific prayer, directing the magic onto the silver coin in his other hand, and instantly, the surroundings were bathed in soft white light, as if the lieutenant held a torch high in his hand.

The trio of mercenaries were standing in a jumble of crates and barrels, stacked haphazardly all around them and high enough that they couldn't see anything beyond the containers. A narrow walkway filed between two stacks and deeper into the environs of the warehouse. Vambran motioned for them to continue, and Horial filed into the gap and wound his way along the path, the other two close behind.

Perhaps ten paces through the walkway, it emerged on the other side of the stacks, right in the central part of the warehouse. The rest of the place, or as far as the dim light would reveal, was filled with more of the same. Rows of crates, boxes, and barrels lined either side of the long, narrow building, with a wide path running down its center and a row of thick square posts in the middle of that to support the ceiling high overhead. On the near end, where the trio stood, all the equipment needed to salt meats was spread out. Overhead, an assortment of already-cured meats hung from the rafters, ready to pack for shipment. A small door was set into the wall nearby. Vambran assumed that it led into a large smokehouse, and indeed, he could detect the odor of wood smoke strongly there.

"So? Where are they?" Horial asked softly as he and Adyan fanned out, peering among the stacks of boxes and crates. "You're absolutely sure it's in here," the sergeant asked again.

"Yes," Vambran said, pointing toward the far end of the warehouse. He could still sense the dagger's location through the use of his divine magic. "It's down that way," he said.

Nodding, Horial set out in the direction Vambran had indicated, and the other two fell into step with him, still watching and peering everywhere the light reached.

"They must have dumped it and lit out," Adyan drawled as they advanced. "Because there's no one..."

The words died in the man's throat as the first body came into view.

"By the Lady," Horial gasped, staring down at the corpse.

The body was of a man, and Vambran thought it might have been one of the thugs from the previous evening, though he couldn't tell for sure, because its skin was covered with hundreds of tiny, bleeding wounds. Each mark was in the shape of a three-sided star, no larger in diameter than the girth of Vambran's index finger, but the blood that leaked from them pooled around the victim. The man's skin was sallow when it wasn't stained crimson, and his form looked emaciated.

"Something sucked all of his blood out," Vambran said grimly, stepping closer.

The light from his silver piece revealed the next corpse, a little farther on. It was in the same condition. As the lieutenant advanced along the broad walkway between the corpses, he spotted two more. One was draped across a single crate, the man's back exposed through a shredded shirt, and the other was slumped in a sitting position next to the crate, a club lying next to his outstretched hand.

"What in the Nine Hells would do that to a man?" Horial rasped, nudging one of the bodies.

Adyan made a strangled sound as he held his nose and asked, "What's that wretched smell?"

The hair on the nape of Vambran's neck prickled. He spun back to Adyan and tried to call out, "Watch yourself!" but he wasn't quick enough.

A dark form, its whole shape writhing, lunged out of the shadows from between two stacks of crates. It grabbed at the mercenary. It took Adyan in both arms and hugged him tightly, dragging the man backward into the darkness.

CHAPTER SEVEN

H elp him!" Vambran shouted, even though
he didn't think he could be heard over
Adyan's screaming.

The bulky thing that had gotten a hold of
the soldier was backtracking steadily, obviously strong enough to keep Adyan in a bear
hug and drag him at the same time.

Horial leaped forward, yanking his short
sword free, and tried to get in close enough
to stab at the creature, but the path between
the crates where it was retreating was too
narrow, and Adyan's body served as a shield.
The sergeant advanced, keeping his blade
ready for any opening.

Cursing his stupidity, Vambran looked for
some way to get over or behind the monster
that had a hold of his friend. The stacks of
crates were high there, but not too far down,

he could see where they were staggered. He might be able to work his way to the top, but if he ran off with the light, Horial wouldn't stand a chance of getting in close and pulling Adyan free.

Deciding quickly, Vambran tossed the glowing coin into the press so that Horial could fight on, and he sprinted in the direction of the lower crates, pointing a finger up near the top of the stacks and speaking the phrase that would summon the flaring light. Instantly, the warehouse was a little bit brighter, and Vambran had no trouble finding his way. Reaching the nearest low crate, he launched himself on top of it and sprang to the next stack, jumping hard and grabbing at the edges to pull himself higher.

Adyan was still screaming, though his voice was both weaker and more muffled than it had been initially. The lieutenant was running out of time. He worked his way up and up, then finally reached the top of the crates and leaped from stack to stack, causing some of them to wobble dangerously. As quickly as he could, Vambran advanced toward a gap in the stacks he could see against the wall. The sounds of the struggle emanated from that point.

When he finally reached the edge of the closest stack and peered down, Vambran realized that he was a good fifteen feet above the floor. The thing was there, humanoid in shape, but the lieutenant could not spot any sort of skin. Instead, the beast was covered in a writhing mass of black, slimy worms. It was thick and bloated, with a rotund stomach bulging out in front.

No, not worms. Leeches, Vambran realized, and saw to his horror that dozens of them were attached to Adyan as he slumped in the monster's arms. That was what had attacked the thugs, sucking their blood and leaving them as drained husks. Horial was there, bobbing and weaving, looking for a good opening with which to lunge in and stab at the creature with his sword.

"Let go of him, you stinking thing!" the sergeant shouted and darted in, thrusting once, quickly, and backing away again.

The creature retreated a step, and Horial, emboldened thinking that he had hurt the thing, tried his attack again. The next time, though, the beast was expecting it and swung one of its huge, writhing arms out and bludgeoned the mercenary in the face. Horial staggered backward from the blow, and the monster advanced another step, dragging a now-limp Adyan with only one arm.

Vambran saw his chance. He crouched low, his sword out and held point downward with both hands, and dropped over the edge of his stack of crates. He plummeted toward the monster, aiming the tip of his blade at the base of the thing's thick neck. He had aimed perfectly, and it looked like a solid strike, but somehow, the creature sensed that he was there and sidestepped out of the way, swinging Adyan's form around to protect itself.

Vambran was forced to jerk his blade out of the way at the last second, ruining both his aim and his fall. He hit the floor hard, bouncing sharply to one side and tumbling onto his back. He grunted from the impact, losing his breath. Gasping, the lieutenant scrambled backward, dragging his sword with him to get clear of the threat.

The leech-covered monstrosity flung Adyan's body aside and turned to face Vambran, advancing toward him. The thing had no face. There was definitely a head-shaped bulge at the top of its shoulders, but that was the extent of its humanoid appearance. There were only the writhing, wriggling leeches where eyes, a nose, and a mouth ought to be. And the fetid stink of the thing was gagging.

Vambran lurched to his feet as the monster

advanced, drawing his sword up and gripping it with
both hands. He kept the point level with the thing's
chest, but it didn't seem to care. It simply ambled
forward, and Vambran stepped into a smooth, strong
swing that slashed the beast across the chest and one
forearm. Blood and ichor sprayed from the gash, but
the creature didn't slow down one whit. Eyes wide,
Vambran rebalanced and tried for another hard hit,
but he wasn't fast enough.

The creature lunged at Vambran, trying to get its
huge, slimy arms around his neck. He ducked, causing the beast to miss with its bear hug, but it still
managed to kick at him as he rolled out of the way.
He grunted in pain from a sudden burning sensation
across his forearm and managed to come up to his feet
again in another corner. Vambran glanced down at his
arm and saw that his shirt sleeve had been shredded,
and there were numerous tiny scratches across the
surface of his skin, all of which were bleeding steadily.
Shaking the burning sensation off, Vambran readied
for another lunge from the thing.

Out of the corner of his eye, the lieutenant saw
movement and glanced that way. Horial was struggling to his feet, his face bloody from where the
creature had decked him earlier, and the sanguine
flow seemed to be dripping into his eyes. Vambran
recognized an opportunity for his companion to get
behind and maybe surprise the beast, so he stepped a
little closer and began to stab and slash at the thing,
feinting rapidly, hoping to keep its attention fixed
on him.

The beast, apparently heedless of the danger it
was in, sidled forward again, taking a gash from
Vambran's blade in the process, and tried to wrap its
huge arms around the lieutenant once more. Horial
took advantage of that moment to come in quickly
and silently from behind, his blade drawn back for
a severe strike.

Again, though, the creature seemed to sense a foe near it, even coming from the rear. It spun at the last moment and lashed out. Horial, caught off guard by his enemy's sudden defensive move, was unable to dodge the blow and took another solid hit, that time in the shoulder. Worse yet, the creature simply let its own momentum carry it around, bringing its other appendage to bear on the sergeant. In a single, smooth motion, it had Horial wrapped in a death-grip. As the scores of leeches all over the beast's body began to sink their tiny fangs into the mercenary, he threw his head back and howled in agony, thrashing to get free all the while.

Vambran dived straight at the thing, yanking quick cuts across its back, shoulders, and rump with his blade. He seemed to be scoring some serious injuries, but the creature didn't seem the least bit fazed. It merely retreated from the attacks, spinning around so that Horial was between it and Vambran.

"Damn you!" Vambran cried out, feinting and lunging, trying to get clean hits on the beast without harming his companion. Horial was already unconscious, slumped limply in the creature's grip. Vambran faked to the right, then spun his way back to the left, cutting across the beast's flank with his sword. He scored another hit, but he also nicked his sergeant. It didn't seem to matter, though. Horial didn't flinch, and the creature ignored the blow.

Breathing hard, Vambran was beginning to despair. Even though it was clear that his strikes were injuring the creature in some way, it seemed impervious to the wounds' effects. And both Horial and Adyan were quite possibly dead, or very near to it. He was running out of ideas. As the creature lumbered toward him, keeping Horial up as a makeshift shield, Vambran had a sudden inspiration.

Desperately, he reached for his holy coin hanging from the chain and held it forth while he began to recite the words of another special prayer. Calling on the favor of Waukeen, he jerked and darted his hands in front of himself, moving the coin in a complex motion. He finished the prayer in a shout, thrusting the coin forward once more.

A thunderclap resonated outward from the coin, aimed directly at the monster right in front of the lieutenant. The noise was horrid, more so because of the confines of the space where they had been battling. The cacophony seemed to shake it, though, for it jerked stiffly at the sound and dropped Horial, then spasmed and retreated from the perceived threat, cowering in the corner, up against the crates.

His own ears ringing, Vambran took advantage of the few moments he knew the creature would be stunned to grab Horial and drag him away, part of the way down the narrow path leading into the secret hollow among the crates. He dropped to one knee beside his sergeant, not even bothering to see if the man was still alive, and placed his hand upon Horial's chest. He murmured a quick prayer of healing, just a simple orison that he hoped would stop the blood loss and stabilize his companion. Then he rose again, stepped back over his friend's fallen form, and readied himself to face the monstrosity once more.

"Let's see how you do without my sergeant to protect you," he spat at the creature.

As if understanding it was time to engage its foe again, the beast lumbered forward, ready to battle. Vambran sidestepped warily a few times, watching to see if the creature had any new tricks, but it seemed intent solely on closing in and trying to grab at the lieutenant. When Vambran was certain he understood its tactics well enough, he began to press the attack, slashing and carving his way inside the creature's reach, laying some particularly harsh wounds across its writhing, unnatural body. After five such blows, the mercenary was forced to step back, out of breath.

The leech-thing came on just as strong as ever, and Vambran groaned. When the beast reached for him again, he tried to parry the blow away, but his strength was failing him, and he didn't quite get the blade completely between himself and his opponent. A meaty fist sneaked through and pounded Vambran across the side of the head. The strike snapped his head sideways and he could feel the dozen or so tiny bites on his skin. He knew that the wounds themselves weren't too bad, but the bleeding would slowly drain him of his energy and could quite possibly blind him.

The lieutenant staggered backward, keeping his sword up as protection, but the creature lunged in again, and Vambran was too tired to fight it off. The blows knocked him to the floor, his sword skittering off to the side, out of reach. He shuddered and watched as the creature loomed over him, reaching down with both huge arms. The leeches wriggled and writhed, straining to latch on to Vambran, to suck at his blood. He was going to die there, feeding the horror. He groaned and tried once more to move clear.

"Move it!" a feminine voice called suddenly from above. "Get out of the way!"

Blinking in confusion and unable to see much of anything past the creature, Vambran didn't react immediately, but the beast did. It stood up, ignoring its potential meal, and staggered back half a step, all of its attention on whoever was overhead. Vambran took advantage of the chance to drag himself clear.

The beast jerked and tried to move farther away, but the wounds Vambran and the others had dealt to it hindered it sufficiently that it was not fast enough. As it staggered across the floor, a cascade of white spilled down over it, like fine white sand spilling free of a broken hourglass. Vambran looked up and saw a flash of red cloth, along with a barrel being tipped over onto its side, more of the white stuff tumbling out in an ever more rapid flow.

Salt, Vambran realized. And it was burning the creature. The beast shivered and flailed madly about, trying to shake free of the powdery substance, but its slimy exterior simply let the salt cling to it, and everywhere the stuff touched the monster, there was a sizzling sound. The creature jerked and spun, trying to bat away the salt as it continued to cascade down, and it was on the floor, jerking, spasming, burning. As the last of the salt poured out of the barrel, Vambran's red-clad savior let the container slip over the side and tumble down to land atop the monster, shattering.

The beast lay still. Vambran heaved a great sigh of relief and sagged to the floor, gasping in exhaustion. He tried to wipe the sweat and blood from his face, but his arms felt like lead.

"Please," he called out, "I need help. My sergeants might be dying."

There was no response from above.

Vambran couldn't walk, so he forced himself to crawl across the floor toward Adyan. It was a monumental struggle. Finally the lieutenant reached his companion and, with the last vestiges of his strength, he slipped his hand atop the other man's chest. Vambran sank his head down on his arms and closed his eyes. Then, in barely a whisper, he murmured a healing prayer, not even knowing if it was already too late. As the last words passed his lips, he felt the magic flow from him and to the sergeant, then he let blackness wash over him and settled into unconsciousness.

•••

"Uncle Kovrim!" Emriana called from the shadows. She could see the priest walking furtively toward the warehouse her brother and his two companions had entered nearly an hour before. The priest was accompanied by five other figures, one of whom was a stout dwarf, and by the light of the lanterns they carried as they approached, the girl quickly recognized the emblem of the Sapphire Crescent on their tabards.

"I'm over here," she said, making herself visible.

Kovrim and his retinue quickened their steps and closed the distance with her. When he was near enough, Emriana ran to her uncle and hugged him tightly.

"They haven't come out, yet," she told the priest, pointing to the window the three mercenaries had used to get inside. "I heard fighting, and now nothing. Something terrible has happened, I just know it!"

Kovrim gave his niece a calming pat on her head. "It's all right. We're here, now. You did the right thing, summoning me." He looked to the five mercenaries and jerked his head. "Get in there and see what's what. And be careful."

The dwarf, a sergeant in the company named Grolo Firefist, gave a quick nod.

"Yes, sir," he said in a deep, resonating voice. He turned to the other four and began to give orders. "All right, you heard the man. Let's get in there. No, not the window; I'm not climbing through that. Find the front entrance and let's get the doors open. Move it!"

As the soldiers leaped to obey, Kovrim stepped back and eyed Emriana up and down, his lips pursed in a frown. She blushed slightly in the semidarkness, feeling very foolish at the moment. She was dressed in her dark clothing, a snug black shirt and a pair of breeches. She also had a very fine crossbow that was diminutive in size but could be slung easily onto her back by a long leather strap. Kovrim had actually given her that when she was a few years younger, a delicate weapon that she could cock and fire as a youth.

"I knew he would do something like this," the girl told her uncle, trying to divert his attention away from her.

"And so you did exactly the same thing?" he asked, but she could hear no real recrimination in his voice.

Emriana simply shrugged and turned back to the soldiers making their way around the building. She watched the soldiers looking for an easier way inside, and she and Kovrim followed them, the priest with his arm around her shoulders. It didn't take long for the mercenaries to break inside the warehouse and begin to check for threats. Kovrim and Emriana waited outside.

Finally, Grolo returned to the entrance and called, "It's all clear."

The girl darted forward the moment she heard the dwarf's first words.

"Is he all right?" she asked, not stopping to wait for an answer as she scampered inside.

She never saw the sergeant's nod.

Emriana found Vambran lying face down, being carefully examined by one of the other members of the company. She dropped down next to her brother, looking for some reassuring sign from the man tending to him.

"He'll live," the soldier said, "though he needs treatment from the priest. Same for the other two," he added. "Though how they lived, I don't know. They're each hanging by a thread."

Emriana began to shake her brother, calling to him. Vambran regained consciousness as she rolled him over onto his back.

"Hello, Em," he said, blinking in confusion in the light. "What are you doing here?"

"Shut up," Emriana scolded as she hugged her brother. "If it weren't for me, you'd probably be dead by now."

Kovrim knelt down beside Vambran.

"Let me look at you," he said, gently moving Emriana a little to one side so he could see how severe the lieutenant's wounds were.

Vambran didn't complain as his uncle checked him out. Gently, Kovrim settled his palm on Vambran's forehead and reverently spoke a prayer of healing. Some color returned to Vambran's face, and he began to breathe easier. Emriana found a bit of cloth the other soldier had left beside her brother, picked it up, and began to dab at his face with it. She wiped the blood from his eyes and sat back.

"You'll live. That's twice today, Vambran," the priest said, shaking his head. He rose to his feet. "And now my attentions are needed elsewhere."

"Adyan? Horial?" Vambran asked weakly, looking at his sister.

"The dwarf said they made it," Emriana said. "Though he doesn't understand how."

"Good," Vambran said, and he closed his eyes in relief as the girl continued to wipe the blood from his face. "I didn't know if I got to them in time. I led them here, into a trap, and they nearly paid for my foolishness with their lives."

He shook his head in anger as he struggled to sit up.

Emriana glanced over to where the dwarf was standing, staring down at the remains of something, holding his nose as he inspected it. He nudged it once with the toe of his boot.

Kovrim moved over to what the sergeant was looking at and made a face.

"Leechwalker," he said distastefully. "Don't see that in the city every day. Someone brought it here."

"So that was some quick thinking, calling Uncle Kovrim," Vambran said, "even though you're supposed to be at home."

"This pendant isn't such a bad birthday present," Emriana said, grinning and ignoring her brother's scolding.

Vambran looked up at his uncle and said, "The red stranger was here tonight, too."

"The one from today, who assisted you at lunch?" Kovrim asked.

Emriana looked around.

"Maybe he's still here," she added, worried.

"I doubt it," her brother said. "And it's a woman, not a man. She spoke this time. Whoever she is, she doesn't want to be found. But that's strange. Really strange. She's apparently following me."

Shaking his head, Vambran looked at his sister again.

"And what are you supposed to be?" he asked, nodding at Emriana's outfit. "A spy? Where's your mask?"

"What? You don't like it? I thought I looked rather sinister. Came in handy enough to keep you from noticing me following you."

Vambran rolled his eyes and asked, "And why were you following me?"

"Because I know you. Even though you say there's no chance to go investigating, I figure that's exactly what you've got planned. Only you're going to go with your buddies instead of me. So I decided to tag along."

"You followed me all night?" The lieutenant asked wearily, finally climbing to his feet. "Dressed like that?"

"Hey, it worked. And yes, to the Crying Claw and over here."

"If Uncle Dregaul finds out, he's going to—"

"Don't start lecturing me," the girl retorted. "You're just as guilty of sneaking off as I am. I thought you were only going to take care of company business tonight."

Vambran groaned and said, "Well, I did. This just happened to be part of the evening, also."

"Well, I was right not to trust you to be honest with me, so you've got no right to yell at me."

"Fair enough," her brother replied, and Emriana was surprised that he didn't put up more of a fight than that. "But you still should have worn a mask." She looked at him sharply, and he gave her a side-long glance accented by a smug grin. "The question is, can you sneak back inside without Uncle Dregaul noticing?"

"The only way Uncle Dregaul finds out is if you tell him, in which case you have to tell him what you were doing here, too. And I don't think that's something you're quite ready to confess, is it?"

Vambran sighed and waved his hands in surrender.

"All right, you win. But you're on your own if you do get caught."

Emriana didn't say anything, just gave her brother a smug look.

"Well," Vambran continued, changing the subject, "someone sure didn't want me to talk to these thugs. I should have realized whoever is behind this would kill again to protect their dirty little secret."

"Vam," Emriana said, giving her brother the most serious look she could conjure. "You scared the hells out of me tonight."

Vambran nodded and said, "I know. I'm sorry. It was a blunder of me to underestimate these people. Twice." He eyed her right back, his expression severe. "You realize that, if I had let you come with me instead of them, it would be you and me lying here bloodless, right?"

Emriana gave a little shudder as she considered the possibility. She shook her head.

"And there would have been no one watching your back to come to the rescue," she said. "But that's not how it ended up. We're all alive, and the thing's dead."

"Right, thanks to some mysterious red-clad bene-factor. Em, this is getting out of hand."

"You don't know the half of it," Kovrim said, coming to stand beside the two siblings again. "This whole thing does indeed have temple connections."

"What?" Vambran blurted out, drawing a sharp look from the mercenaries, who were in the process of carrying out the still unconscious sergeants. "How do you know?"

"Because," Kovrim replied grimly, "I had a conversation with Grand Trabbar Lavant tonight. He didn't deny it. I was surprised, to say the least."

"How can he justify murder?" Vambran said, his voice a bit softer, but no less vehement.

"He didn't. At least he claimed not to condone it. But let's not talk in here. Eavesdroppers might be about. It's already happened at least once, I think."

Emriana spun around, staring wide-eyed into the darkness. "I thought your men said it was all clear!" she said, trepidation making her shake. "Who's still here? Vambran's mysterious rescuer?"

"Calm down, Em," Kovrim admonished. "I meant magical eavesdroppers. Scrying and the like. I'll explain why when we're a safe distance away."

The trio took a walk, leaving the rest of the clean-up business to the mercenaries. Vambran stopped quickly before they departed the warehouse, fetching Emriana's dagger and returning it to her. Then they began to walk through the misty evening, making their way in the general direction of the temple.

Kovrim continued his revelation as they strolled.

"What Grand Trabbar Lavant told me was, the temple is on the verge of negotiating a very lucrative business opportunity, and the murders were an ill-advised cover-up on someone else's part to eliminate something standing in its way. He assured me that the guilty parties were being suitably punished, and he just felt that there was no good reason to bring the authorities into it, drag the whole thing before the public eye, and ruin the chance to complete the deal."

"That's absurd," Vambran said, shaking his head. "The Lady herself would never approve of such underhanded business tactics."

"I agree," Kovrim said, "but the fact remains that you're inadvertently butting heads with the temple, now. Regardless of the morality of your actions, you're taking your career's future in your hands. You need to be very careful how you proceed."

"Are you suggesting that I stop? Give it up and trust the Grand Trabbar to see to it that justice is served?"

"Not necessarily," Kovrim began.

"Good, because there's no way I'm leaving this alone now," Vambran replied angrily. "The man and woman who were murdered were servants of House Pharaboldi. Her name was Jithelle, a kitchen maid, and his was Hoytir, a stable hand. Apparently, Denrick Pharaboldi was seeing her on the sly. Em found that out today."

Kovrim whistled and said, "That sheds some unusual light on the whole affair."

"Exactly," Vambran replied. "And seeing as how our two Houses are so friendly right now—Em was, in fact, there for a social tea—I think it behooves me to make sure we as a family are not getting involved with someone untrustworthy or willing to commit murder to further their business causes."

Kovrim nodded and said, "I agree. But you still need to be particularly cautious. You don't want to draw any more of the temple's attention to yourself in this way."

"It's a little late for that, don't you think?" Emriana said, nodding back the way they had come. "You brought a squad of mercenaries who answer to the temple with you tonight. Word is bound to get around."

Kovrim looked at the girl with surprised admiration.

"Very good point, Em." He smiled and continued, "But in this case, not a worry. Those are some of my most trusted soldiers. We already discussed the need for silence on this matter. They are working tonight strictly freelance."

"Excellent. And Adyan and Horial know to do the same," Vambran said. "At least, once I get a chance to talk to them. Perhaps we can make sure Grolo takes care of that."

"I'm sure we can arrange that," Kovrim answered. "I'll speak to him later. But for now, here's what I think you should do next. If this is the same Jithelle I think you're talking about, I know her mother, Nimra Skolotti. A sweet old woman, and likely wondering what really happened to her poor daughter. She might know something useful, so I think you two should go visit her tomorrow and see what you can find out."

Vambran nodded and Emriana said, "Oh, the poor woman. Maybe it would make her feel a little better if she knew someone was trying to clear Jithelle's name."

"Precisely," their uncle said. "In the meantime, I'll do a little more digging—very subtle digging, mind you—to see what I can find out about potential business opportunities with House Pharaboldi. If I turn anything useful up, I'll let you know."

Vambran turned to face his uncle. "Thank you, sir, for everything you've done so far."

Emriana stepped in and gave the priest a hug.

"Yes," she said, "thank you so much for coming tonight. I don't know what I would have done if I hadn't been able to reach you."

"You two just be careful," replied Kovrim. "This isn't a game we're playing, here."

...

"Damn it!" Grozier snarled as he watched Kovrim, Vambran, and the girl exit the warehouse. "Follow them!"

The wizard Bartimus shook his head.

"I can't," he said, shrinking away from his employer's angry gaze. "I focused the spell on Dressus; it goes where he goes."

Grozier threw up his hands in frustration and began to pace.

"Well, that clinches it, then," he said. "They're uncovering far too much, and furthermore, they know that we're watching them. You heard the priest say as much."

Bartimus nodded, though he didn't think that Grozier saw the gesture, and furthermore, didn't care. The less attention paid to him, the better, as far as the wizard was concerned.

"I've got to talk to the others. That damned mercenary is proving more resourceful than I expected, especially when he has so many friends and family to aid him. He's got too many resources."

"Pardon, sir," Bartimus said, wondering why he would dare to question his employer's logic. "But why don't we take those resources away from him?"

"What?" Grozier asked harshly, scowling and looking at the wizard as though he had just noticed him for the first time. "What are you talking about?"

Bartimus took a deep breath, then said, "The high priest outranks all of them. I'm sure he could arrange it so that the mercenary can't draw on fellow soldiers or his uncle for help. In fact, that may have been what Lavant intended from the beginning, and we didn't give him a chance to put it into motion."

Grozier cocked his head, regarding the wizard with approval.

"Why don't you offer up these kinds of insights more often?" he asked.

Bartimus cringed, but said, "Because you usually just yell at me when I do."

"Yes," Grozier replied with a sigh. "I suppose I do. All right, I'll try to control that. You just keep doing more thinking. I like it."

"All right," Bartimus said, stunned.

"In the meantime, I think we need to move up our meeting. Let everyone know."

"Yes, sir," Bartimus replied, already moving through his study to fulfill his employer's request.

CHAPTER EIGHT

Vambran strolled along inconspicuously, following the woman as she made her way carefully through the market and holding on to the younger woman's arm who was escorting her. The mercenary had been following the pair for a while, watching as they shopped for fresh vegetables in the lines of stalls that filled the open square. The day was bright and crisp, somewhat cooler than it had been the day before, but still the sun was warming to the lieutenant's skin as he kept pace with his quarry.

Vambran had tracked down Jithelle's mother easily enough from the instructions Kovrim provided him the night before, getting up early and making his way to the east side of the city, where the less affluent neighborhoods were. He had no trouble finding the

small house, really an apartment on the second story
of a rug merchant's shop, where Nimra Skolotti and
her youngest daughter Mirolyn lived. Initially, he
intended to just visit the woman directly, but then
caution got the better of him, and he decided to wait.
If he was being followed, or watched in some other
way, perhaps it would be better not to draw undue
attention to the grieving mother.

The mercenary did not have to wait long before
Nimra and her daughter appeared on the street.
The pair of them headed first to the bakery where
they purchased a single small honeyed bun to split
between the two of them, then they made their way to
the market, nibbling at their breakfast and chatting
softly as they strolled. Nimra maintained a steady
grip on Mirolyn's arm. It took Vambran a few minutes
to realize that Nimra was blind.

The mercenary watched as the two women examined some melons, Nimra picking up one then another,
squeezing them with her hands and smelling them.
They selected one and paid the merchant, then moved
on, toward a stall that sold peppers. Vambran smiled
to himself, wondering if those might have been the
very same peppers he'd helped make their way across
the Sea of Fallen Stars aboard *Lady's Favor*. Nimra
and Mirolyn chose a small handful of the peppers and
completed their purchase.

When they reached a corner next to a small kiosk
selling hot tea, Vambran approached them. He stepped
up next to the younger woman and spoke softly.

"Excuse me, but I would like to speak with you and
your mother for a moment."

Mirolyn turned to face the mercenary in surprise,
but Nimra only cocked her head to one side and said,
"I wondered how much longer you were going to follow
us before you showed your intentions."

Vambran did a double take.

"You . . . you knew I was following you?" he asked.

"Certainly. Not too many big, strapping fellows in some sort of armor make a habit of strolling behind me at the same distance all morning long."

Mirolyn looked from her mother to the man in front of her and shrugged.

"Nothing wrong with her hearing," the girl said, a wan smile emerging briefly.

"I guess not," Vambran said. "I assure you, I have no malicious intentions, here. But I need to speak with you for a few moments, someplace where we won't be bothered. It concerns your other daughter, Jithelle."

At the mention of their slain family member, both women's faces turned ashen, and Mirolyn closed her eyes, swallowing a sob.

Nimra turned her sightless eyes toward Vambran and said, "Who are you, bringing pain to an old woman by speaking that name?"

Vambran swallowed and frowned. He knew it would be a difficult subject to bring up, but it was unavoidable.

"I'm sorry for your loss," he said, "and for reopening the wounds of her passing, but if you will give me a moment of your time you will see that—"

"I'm sorry, but we have nothing more to tell you, soldier," Nimra interrupted. She took hold of Mirolyn's arm and began to tug her away. "It was watchmen who killed her, and I will not help you besmirch her name further."

Vambran shook his head, then remembered that Nimra couldn't see his gesture.

"I'm no watchman, milady, as your daughter will certainly testify. I am a soldier, true, but one who is trying to find the truth, not bury it."

Nimra hesitated and turned back.

"What purpose do you have in tracking me down?" she asked.

Beside her, Mirolyn looked at Vambran with eyes already brimming with tears.

"I was witness to your daughter's death," Vambran said quietly, eliciting a gasp from both women. "I don't believe the charges leveled against her, and I want to discover who would see her dead."

"Why do you care what happened to a commoner?" Nimra questioned quietly, reaching a hand out to take one of Vambran's. "Yes, I suspected as much. You may have the calluses of a swordsman, but you still have the voice and bearing of a wealthy man."

"The gold in my family's vaults does not affect my desire to see justice," Vambran replied. "I cannot stand to see murder done, any more than you, though Jithelle was no one I know." As he spoke the word "murder," the lieutenant saw both women flinch again. "But we must not talk here," he continued. "It is not safe. Where can we go for a bit of quiet conversation?"

"The cheesemaker's on Slake Street," Nimra said quickly. "Mirolyn works there, and the proprietor will let us visit in his room upstairs. Do not follow us," the woman added. "Meet us there at the next bells."

And with that, the two women turned away and crossed the square, continuing their shopping, though their pace was a bit quicker and more urgent to anyone who might have been watching. Vambran observed them both go, then turned and took a different route, weaving in and out of the crowds of people at the market. He headed surreptitiously toward Slake Street, approaching it finally from the opposite direction from the market, and when he ducked his head inside, found only a single customer being served.

The proprietor, Neely, if the name on the sign outside was accurate, gave Vambran an appraising look, then shrugged and finished filling his customer's order.

When the woman left with her block of cheese, the man turned to Vambran and asked, "What can I serve you today, good sir?"

Vambran smiled and cast a quick glance around, then said, "Nimra Skolotti sent me here. I am supposed to meet with her in a few moments, and we needed a private place to gather. She suggested that you might make your family room available for a few minutes."

At the mention of the woman's name, Neely smiled, but the grin vanished again just as quickly.

"Is there a problem?" he asked. "Mirolyn is a fine girl and a hard worker for me, and I would hate to see anything happen to either of them, especially after—"

"Nor would I," Vambran interrupted, "which is why I would ask you not mention what you were about to bring up, or me, to anyone else."

The man gave Vambran a long, hard look before he finally nodded.

"You can wait upstairs in the parlor. Straight back there"—he jerked his head behind the counter and into the back room—"up the stairs, first doorway in the right-hand corner."

Vambran thanked the man and slipped past the end of the counter and strode into the back part of the house. There, he found that the whole building was a large square, with a very small open courtyard in the middle. The courtyard was surrounded on all four sides by two stories of open balcony, literally covered with climbing plants and hanging baskets. In the middle of the courtyard was a single large rain barrel. One set of stairs rose up along the back wall, and Vambran made his way there, climbing them quickly. At the top, he went to the right, as the man had instructed, and found a small patio that opened back out onto the front, where the street was. He cast a quick glance down the lane in both directions, then retreated into the shade and settled into a wooden chair to wait.

The mercenary did not have to wait long. Shortly after nine bells, he heard voices emanating from below, in the courtyard, and slow, methodical footsteps on the stairs. Soon, Nimra's graying head appeared, accompanied by Mirolyn's, and the pair of women made their way into the little tiled parlor. Mirolyn helped her mother to a seat and settled her there before moving to a chair of her own.

Vambran simply sat and watched the blind woman for a moment, waiting to see her demeanor before he began to speak. He had no doubt that she knew he was there, for whether Neely the proprietor had informed her that he had preceded them or if she could merely hear him breathing, he was confident she was waiting for him to speak first.

"I know it must be hard for you, speaking of your daughter, but I'm trying to find out anything I can about her, anything that might clue me in as to who would want her dead."

Nimra nodded and asked, "Can you give me some idea of where to start?"

"Well, how about first telling me if she ever thought of pretending to wield arcane power, ever intended to thrice mark herself in public."

"Never," Nimra said. "My daughter was a good, law-abiding girl who wouldn't dream of such a foolish and dangerous thing."

"Was she secretly delving into magic somehow? Is it possible she really did know some arcane tricks?"

"Jithelle didn't even know her runes, sir. She didn't know how to read or write, much less how to cast a spell. If she was found with marks on her head, as they say, then someone else put them there."

"I see. Mrs. Skolotti, did you daughter ever mention seeing someone? Perhaps where she was working?"

"She was not having relationships with the stable boy," Mirolyn said. "No matter what everyone says about finding them together, she wasn't seeing him."

"Hush, girl," Nimra said. "Jithelle's personal affairs are just that—personal."

Vambran shook his head, again forgetting that his counterpart couldn't see him.

"No, Mrs. Skolotti. I need to know these things. It's very important, if you want me to be able to prove that your daughter didn't commit those crimes and didn't deserve to die."

Tears began to flow down the woman's cheeks then, and she reached up with a gnarled hand to brush them away.

She sniffed once, softly, and said, "How will such a discovery make anything better? I already know the charges against her are untrue. Letting the rest of the world know will only make it hurt more, for then I will hear an endless string of apologies and sympathies from everyone, none of which will bring her back to me."

Nimra sobbed quietly then, as did her daughter.

Vambran found it difficult to swallow, his throat thick with emotion.

But he forced the sadness down and said, "I understand, Mrs. Skolotti. But if the criminals who wronged your daughter are never caught, they will feel emboldened enough to perhaps do it again. Don't you want to see them punished for their crimes?"

"Punishment is far too convenient an excuse for the things men do to one another," Nimra replied, her voice steady again. "But I would see that the people who took my poor Jithelle from me never have the opportunity to make anyone else hurt the way I do right now."

"Then please," Vambran pleaded, "you must tell me anything you can think of that might help me. I have already heard that she was sharing a bed with one of the Pharaboldis. I just want you to tell me anything else that might give a hint about whether or not her employers would wish to see her dead."

Nimra sat very still for a moment, her sightless eyes gazing straight at the wall before her.

Finally, she sighed and said, "So you know about her relationship with her noble lord. Do you also know that she carried his child?"

Vambran's eyes widened.

"No, I didn't," he said. "You know this for certain?"

"That's what she told me," Nimra replied. "And she was overjoyed. When she came to visit and revealed it to us, she went on and on about how she and her baby would have a better life, how her nobleman was going to take good care of us all."

"Of course he was," Vambran muttered.

"What?" the woman asked, cocking her head to listen more intently.

"I'm sorry," Vambran replied. "I just don't believe that Denrick Pharaboldi was ever planning to provide that kind of life for a bastard."

Nimra sniffed in disdain, obviously nonplussed at Vambran's reference to her lost grandchild's birth status, but the woman said nothing. Mirolyn, however, glared openly at the mercenary.

Vambran ignored it.

"Mrs. Skolotti, Miss Skolotti, I think I have a pretty good idea of what happened to your daughter. I think she got in the way of some very powerful people who had big plans for themselves. The fact that she was with child not only makes the crime that much more tragic, but it also may very well be the reason it was committed in the first place."

"You think they killed her so that she couldn't have the child?" Nimra asked softly.

"I do."

"Then that baby made the mistake of having the wrong father. What will you do, now?"

"I will confront the man who sired that child and find out whether he cared so little for his own offspring that he would be a party to such an act. And if he didn't do it and doesn't know who did, I will keep searching until I do find the criminals."

"Why would you do this?" Nimra asked again. "Why does it matter to you whether or not two commoners died in the streets of this city? How does it ruin your life that the men who committed the crimes roam free?"

Vambran thought for a long time before he answered, "I could tell you, Mrs. Skolotti, that it is because I believe in seeing justice done. I could tell you that my piety and my morals dictate it. And that would be true. But it also just happens that I have a sister, a young woman who will turn sixteen tomorrow, in fact. But for the grace of Waukeen, it could have been her in that alley the other night. That, and the man who led your daughter astray with his lies is also courting that sister of mine."

Nimra sat very still.

"A man of candor. I like that," she said. "I pray then, sir, that you make sure they never hurt anyone again."

•••

"It's time, sir," Bartimus said, nodding toward Efusio's in the center of the plaza. "The others are ready and waiting."

Grozier nodded and said, "Good."

He stepped down out of the carriage and crossed the cobblestone lane and headed toward the cafe, which faced the plaza and had a large open patio in the front. A series of small tables were arranged on the patio, which butted right up to the street, and people could gather to enjoy a strong cup of Tashalaran coffee—or perhaps a good ale imported from afar, such as Mulhorandi dark—and a smoke, for Efusio offered a wonderful variety of *balaumo* to be put into a pipe, including numerous fruit-infused blends, such as cherry, apricot, and apple. Grozier felt in his pocket for his long-stemmed pipe and smiled.

The head of House Talricci picked a table to one side of the patio, but he put his back to the street and settled into the chair and relaxed. It wasn't long before a plump serving girl with olive skin and lustrous black hair approached.

"Sir?" was all she said, and Grozier had to stop for a moment to admire her very black eyes.

The man finally shook himself back to the matter at hand and said, "Just a cup of Tethyrian tea and some *balaumo*. Uh, peach and grapewood, if you have it."

"Yes, sir," the serving girl replied and scurried away.

Grozier stretched his legs out under the table and waited, letting the mid-morning breeze ruffle his hair. The warm dampness of the day before was gone, replaced by a cooler, dryer bit of weather. The last vestiges of spring still clung to the Reach, appearing on occasion.

The girl brought Grozier his tea and a small silver bowl filled with the pipeweed for which he'd asked. He pressed a gold dinar into her hand and waved her away, then he began stuffing his pipe enthusiastically. It had been a couple of days since he'd enjoyed a good smoke.

Are we all linked? came a voice in Grozier's head. It was Bartimus.

Yes, Grozier responded. *Am I the last?*

You are, came a second voice, belonging to one of the two Houses in the alliance. *We are all linked now. So, why the urgency? Why couldn't this wait?* The voice held a hint of irritation, but Grozier ignored it.

The mercenary won't go away, he thought, sending his own irritation through the mental connection to the others. *He is persistent, and the little trap Bartimus and I laid for him last night didn't work. I need other ideas.*

I think you're devoting much too much time to him, a third voice chimed in, that of the individual of the third House. He *will go away soon enough, when his company is called to duty again. The Grand Trabbar will see to that.*

I don't think you understand, Grozier insisted. *He is getting very close to finding out who was behind the incident in the alley, and I think he means to come after us, regardless of the revelations. He has his uncle involved, now.*

There was a lengthy pause then the second voice suggested, *We need to threaten him more openly. We need to send him a message he'll understand once and for all.*

I agree, Grozier replied, *but what will faze him? What can we hold over his head?*

His family, the third voice said firmly. *We make it clear that others around him may not survive his meddling.*

That kind of tactic never works, Grozier responded, letting disappointment bleed into his thoughts. *His kind always take that as a personal challenge to push back harder.*

But he doesn't make the decisions for the family, the third voice said confidently. *We know who does. This is simply a perfect excuse to finally rein in him in, forcefully if necessary.*

Grozier considered the possibility.

Yes, he conceded after a moment. *I think you're right.*

Of course I'm right, the third voice said. *You plan the threat, and I'll make sure we get the proper response from Hetta.*

Done, Grozier said. *And the uncle? All of Matrell's friends? What do we do about all of the aid he's receiving?*

Let Lavant take care of that. Get a message to him, today if possible.

All right, Grozier replied. *We're close, now. Remain patient.*

Who's not patient? the second voice answered. *Just take care of this. Do it tonight. Then everything will be in place.*

Agreed. See you tonight, Grozier thought, then he told Bartimus to break the link.

When he was certain the mental connection with his business partners and his wizard had been eliminated, he smiled and lit his pipe.

Tonight, he thought, is going to stun them all.

...

Emriana didn't know whether to laugh or cry. On the one hand, she was incensed that Uncle Dregaul had insisted that she remain in her rooms, with Jaleene to keep a watch on her, so that she wouldn't spoil any of the surprises for her party later that night. The girl was beside herself, wondering what Vambran had learned from Jithelle's mother. On the other hand, it was her sixteenth birthday, and the extravaganza being planned was making her almost wriggle in delight. She paced endlessly back and forth in her rooms, going from the patio to the foot of the bed and back again.

"Will you stop that?" Jaleene finally chided Emriana. "You're making me dizzy."

"Oh, I'm sorry," Em replied, full of exasperation. "I just can't stand all this waiting. And I hate being cooped up."

"It's no picnic being here with you, that's for sure," Jaleene muttered.

Emriana scowled at her maid, then she giggled.

"Come on," she said, "Give me some hints about what's going to happen tonight."

Jaleene shook her head vehemently.

"Please," Emriana begged, moving to sit down on the bed beside her companion. "Pretty please?"

"Mistress Emriana, even if I did know something—which I don't, so quit asking—I wouldn't tell you. You get to be sixteen once in your life, and I'm not going to be the one who spoils anything for you. Trust me, you'll thank me later on."

"Highly doubtful," Emriana said, folding her arms beneath her breasts and pretending to pout.

She looked out of the corner of her eye to see if Jaleene was reacting, but the handmaiden was studiously ignoring her charge's attempts to guilt her into revealing tidbits.

"All I'm saying is you're going to be amazed," Jaleene said. "Don't you remember the big to-do for your brother when he turned sixteen?"

"Jaleene, I was nine. They made me go to bed halfway through the evening. You were the one who had to drag me back here, remember?"

Jaleene giggled in spite of herself.

"I tried to forget," she teased. "You were worse when you were that age than Quindy and Obiron are."

"Oh, be quiet," Emriana said playfully, then jumped up from the bed and began to pace again. "By Waukeen, I wish Vambran would get back here. I can hardly stand this."

"And what would you do if I never came back?" Vambran said, suddenly standing in the doorway off her patio.

"Vam!" Emriana shouted and jumped up to pull her brother inside.

Jaleene scowled and said, "Master Vambran, you shouldn't approach Milady's chambers unannounced. It's not proper."

Vambran gave the handmaiden a low bow. "Of course not," he said, "but I hope you will forgive me in this one instance. I had a feeling she would pop if I didn't come here immediately upon returning."

Jaleene rolled her eyes.

"You don't know the half of it," she muttered, but she dismissed his apology with a wave of her hand. "So long as you don't make a habit of it," she insisted, to which Vambran bowed again, more deeply.

"Oh, stop with the formalities and tell me what you found out!" Emriana demanded, guiding her brother to a single chair in the corner before moving to sit on the bed opposite him.

Vambran glanced sidelong at Jaleene, but Emriana shook her head.

"It's all right. She knows most of what you were doing already," the girl explained. "And besides, good luck getting her to leave. She's terrified I'm going to sneak out again."

"And shouldn't I be?" Jaleene retorted. Then the handmaiden grew serious. "Mistress Emriana, Master Vambran, I must tell you both that it makes me terribly nervous, what you're doing. If Master Dregaul finds out, there's going to be a firestorm in this house."

Vambran returned the woman's look with a grave one of his own.

"I understand," he said, "but do you know what it is we're trying to do? A woman was killed the night before last because some very powerful people wanted her out of the way. Just like that"—and he snapped his fingers—"because she was a commoner. I mean to see to it that they don't get away with it."

"I know, sir, and I admire that about you. You and Mistress Emriana, the whole Matrell family, have always been very good to me, and I respect my good fortune. I would just hate to see something awful happen to either one of you."

"There's always that risk," Vambran conceded. He set his jaw and continued, "But I am going to see this through to the end, and I think Em feels the same way."

Emriana nodded solemnly and said, "I have no intention of giving Denrick Pharaboldi any reason at all to think there's a future between us, but I want to know for sure just what he's guilty of before I tell him to his face."

"And you will. I promise," Vambran replied. "Tonight, I think."

"So, what did you find out?" Emriana asked, leaning forward. "Did you meet with Jithelle's mother?"

Vambran sighed.

"I did," he said. "It broke my heart, too. Did you know that Jithelle also had a sister?"

"No. Did you meet her, too?"

"I did. Her name is Mirolyn. I sat and talked with both of them for a good long time."

"And?" Emriana asked. "What did they say? Anything useful?"

"I don't know if I would call it useful, exactly, but I did learn one very important thing."

"Spit it out!" the girl insisted. Her brother's stalling was making her crazy.

"Jithelle was pregnant with Denrick's child," Vambran said.

Emriana sucked in her breath in shock when she heard her brother's words. It took her another moment to fully register them in her head, to make sure she understood what he was telling her. She finally let out a long, slow breath and clenched her hands together to keep them from shaking from her anger. She glanced over at Jaleene and saw that her handmaiden was crying, a single tear trickling down the woman's face from glassy eyes.

"We must make him pay," Emriana said finally. "It's more than just breaking off my relationship with him. He must understand how base he is, how utterly cowardly a person he really is."

"Assuming he was in on it," Vambran cautioned. "We don't know that for certain."

"Then we find out, once and for all, tonight," Emriana said. "At the party. It will be our best chance to confront him, when he's not hiding behind the guards on his estate."

"All right," Vambran said, nodding. "You will maneuver him into a private corner, and I will drop in on the pair of you and have a nice long, pointed conversation with the young man."

"I can do that," the girl said with conviction. "I can do that very easily."

...

Vambran walked with a purpose as he entered the barracks of the Sapphire Crescent, which were bustling with activity. It surprised him. It was obvious that troops were preparing to depart, packing gear and standing in groups, talking in that excited way when they know they're about to go on an assignment. Vambran frowned, wondering what might be up.

The lieutenant's steps were quick, his demeanor businesslike, but he still offered a wave or arm clasp for those men who knew him and greeted him as he went by. Those men were professional soldiers, but many of them, like Adyan and Horial, had become friends. He wondered if, put into a position of having to make a choice between doing their duty to the temple or following him out of personal loyalty, they would aid him. He hoped he wouldn't have to find out, but he feared that such a moment might be drawing near. If things came to a head with the conspirators behind the murders, Vambran might need men he could trust to fight for him. He prayed it wouldn't come to that, but he was smart enough to anticipate and plan for the worst.

In the meantime, he had an appointment to keep, one for which he was very late. Captain Vertucio, Vambran's commanding officer, had sent a summons to him while he'd been visiting with Nimra Skolotti and her daughter. The lieutenant had not received the message immediately, even after returning to the Matrell estate, because of two things. The first, of course, was the fact that the entire household was in something of an uproar, preparing for Emriana's birthday party. The second reason was because Vambran had been careful to avoid being seen by too many people, particularly the rest of the family, when he'd returned from his excursion to the east side of the city. The less Uncle Dregaul knew of his whereabouts, the better.

Vambran made haste to the captain's office, hoping the meeting would not last long. It was already growing late in the day, and Emriana would be devastated if Vambran wasn't in attendance for the beginning of the party. He'd promised to be her escort during her presentation to the guests, and he had no intention of letting her down. If he could be in and out of the captain's offices in only a few moments, he should still have plenty of time to get back, clean up, and be ready to go.

Vambran rounded a corner and nearly stumbled into Grand Trabbar Lavant, who was coming from the opposite direction.

The lieutenant stopped himself from scowling and stammered, "I—oh! Grand Trabbar!" He bowed and continued, "You don't make your way down here into our part of the temple very often. What brings you here today?"

The Grand Trabbar looked Vambran over with a critical eye, and the mercenary began to grow uncomfortable under the high priest's gaze. It was apparent that the older man was studying him, and Vambran knew that Lavant was aware of his involvement in the aftermath of Jithelle's and Hoytir's murders. He wondered if the Grand Trabbar was on to him, if the high priest knew that Vambran had continued to seek out answers even after Kovrim's warning to be subtle.

Finally, Grand Trabbar Lavant smiled and said, "Vambran Matrell, I was just beginning to wonder if you were going to appear at all today. Your captain sent that message out quite some time ago."

Vambran sucked in his breath and replied, "My apologies, sir. I was indisposed for most of the morning, and tonight, my House is celebrating my younger sister's sixteenth birthday. You can imagine what sort of chaos is taking place today as everyone in the household prepares."

"Yes," the Grand Trabbar said coolly. "I had, in fact, heard that. Well, we must be quick. There's no time to waste."

"Of course, sir," Vambran replied, trying not to appear wary, though he was feeling very suspicious.

There was no reason why someone as high in the temple's hierarchy as Lavant would bother to sit in on a meeting between officers of the mercenary company. That told the lieutenant that the Grand Trabbar was up to something, and he was pretty sure it had to do with getting him out of the way of the cover-up of the murders. He smoothed his expression as the pair of them entered Captain Vertucio's office.

The captain was seated behind a desk, looking over some roster lists, when the high priest and the lieutenant arrived. His eyes brightened at the sight of Vambran.

"Ah, good, he found you!" the officer said. "I was beginning to think I was going to have to send out a search party."

Vambran smiled slightly and said, "I'm very sorry, sir. As I explained to the Grand Trabbar, things are just a little bit manic at our estate right now. My sister's birthday party is tonight."

"Ah, right!" Captain Vertucio said. "I remember you mentioning that. Well, then, I'm sorry to pull you away from your family affairs, but I've got important news. We're going to be shipping the entire company out at first light tomorrow. I'm putting you in charge of logistics. You need to get started immediately."

CHAPTER NINE

Kovrim closed his eyes and pinched the bridge of his nose between his thumb and forefinger in frustration. He held that for several moments, massaging the flesh to stave off the headache he could sense was coming. The priest let out a long, slow sigh, trying to relax his whole body, and the effect was startling. He hadn't realized how tense his shoulders were until he consciously relieved them.

The Syndo was getting nowhere in his search for some evidence that would reveal who was involved in the business deal at which Grand Trabbar Lavant had hinted. Whatever Lavant had going on that might be connected to the deaths of the two commoners, no one knew anything about it, and there was no record of it in the temple's business logs, current or archives. The high priest had done a good job of hiding it, if it did exist, which Kovrim was beginning to doubt. He was about ready to throw his hands up in despair and tell his nephew that there was nothing to pursue. Or, that Vambran would have better luck following up other leads, such as with the dead girl's mother.

Then Kovrim considered a possibility that hadn't occurred to him before. It made him feel ill at ease, for it was far from honest.

Then again, he told himself, if there's something going on, do I not have a responsibility to expose it before it brings woe to the entire temple?

The argument didn't feel terribly convincing. Claiming that the ends justified the means had never held much water with Kovrim, and he certainly didn't like falling back on it simply out of convenience then. Still, he felt a sense of urgency to do whatever it took to uncover the truth. If that meant a tumble from grace, then so be it. He could atone later, if that was what was required, or suffer the persecutions otherwise. He had to exercise every available option given to him. For Vambran's sake.

After all, he thought, I gave him that crossbow when he was twelve.

Nodding as if to convince himself, Kovrim scurried out of the records room and back to his own offices. If he was going to do it, he would have to know beforehand that it would offer up results. He shut the door and slid the bolt home, locking the portal securely. Then he sat down at his desk and took several deep, calming breaths. Afterward, he pulled his ceremonial prayer accoutrements out of the drawer of his desk and arranged them carefully on its surface.

First, Kovrim lit a taper from one of the lanterns in his office and used it to light some incense, which he placed in an open bowl. Once the smoke from that began to fill the room and he was sure it would not go out, the priest poured a bit of water from a stone pitcher he kept handy into a second bowl, a larger one, and set that right before him. He pulled a pouch open and dumped a handful of gold coins, five-sided Sembian nobles, out onto the desk, which he began to drop into the bowl of water one by one. As each coin splashed and tumbled to the bottom of the bowl, Kovrim spoke a word of thanks, or of offering, or a plea for divine favor. When twenty-five coins were piled in the bowl, Kovrim closed his eyes and began to pray.

The priest sat that way for a very long time, murmuring his entreaties to Waukeen, fervently asking for guidance in what he was about to do. He formed the question he wanted answered in his mind, thinking only of it, letting the words of the prayer fall from his lips by rote, focusing every other part of himself on divining the answer. He willed himself to perfect calmness, let the odor of the incense and the joyous presence of his deity wash over him. He was at peace when he prayed, whether he was simply acknowledging his goddess's favor with appreciation, or he was drawing on the Merchant Friend for miraculous magic. That was his life, his dedication, and he felt no fear, no doubt, when he was in such a state.

After an indeterminate amount of time had passed, but which Kovrim knew was perhaps ten minutes from watching others perform such a prayer, he spoke the question aloud, calmly but firmly, requesting his goddess grant him guidance through its answer.

"Tell me, Lady of Trade, if I shall invade the sanctuary of my quarry and discover the confirmation I seek. Reveal to me, O goddess of coin and barter, if I peruse my adversary's private records, shall I discover the proof I need? Will I find a record of his secret business dealings?"

Almost immediately, a voice, an angelic voice—no, it was beyond angelic; it was power and love and wisdom itself—spoke to him, filled his mind with the answer.

*The light of veracity will shine upon all that is
hidden from you. Your heart will know the truth it
seeks.*

All at once the voice, the presence Kovrim had
felt, the spirit of his deity, was gone, and he was left
sitting alone in his office. He opened his eyes and
peered about, feeling displaced for a moment, like
he wasn't where he had expected to be. His fervent
prayers always left him feeling that way, and it was
comforting, in an odd sort of way, for it confirmed
that he was totally devoted to Waukeen at those
times, and let nothing else intrude on his deference
and dedication.

The bowl with the coins and the water was empty,
the sacrifice taken, as Kovrim knew it would be. Nodding in satisfaction, he took hold of the incense and
carefully, almost reverently, ground it out, tapping
the ash free of the remainder. Then he put his accoutrements away, setting them back in the drawer.
Once he was finished, he sat back, staring at the wall
for several moments, considering the answer to his
prayer. He would find the answers he sought if he
went and ransacked Lavant's personal things in his
office. Now he knew that evidence existed, and that he
would find it if he had the courage to follow through
with his plan.

But should he? Kovrim wondered, still having
doubts even after his divination. He supposed he
should have expected to still feel reluctant, considering what was at stake. On the one hand, he still
had no certain knowledge that the evidence would
show anything other than that Lavant had arranged
a business relationship between the temple and some
merchants or similar partners. It might not give any
credence at all to the suspicion that Lavant was actively covering up crimes. Indeed, Lavant might be
truly guilty of nothing other than bad judgment in
picking business partners.

On the other hand, if the high priest was guilty of much more than simple poor assessment of his associates, Kovrim felt a need to expose it, before it caused severe damage to the temple as a whole, both spiritually and financially. Regardless of the risk to himself, Kovrim had to know for sure. If he was wrong, then he might simply look the fool and receive punishment for invading the high priest's personal quarters unbidden. But if not . . .

Quickly, before he could change his mind again, Kovrim got up and unbolted his door. He slipped out and padded through the brightly lit corridors of the temple, making his way toward Grand Trabbar Lavant's offices. He knew the high priest would not be there during that time of the day, for it was common knowledge that he retreated to the gardens below to pray and meditate.

Kovrim chuckled, because what he knew that few others did not was that Lavant's "meditations" were actually simply an excuse for an afternoon nap before evening services commenced. Kovrim had no personal problem with the idea of resting when one could. He just thought it humorous that the Grand Trabbar was vain enough that he needed to fabricate a reason to cover up his rest. Either way, Kovrim felt safe in choosing that particular time of the day to skulk into the high priest's offices.

Though his heart was beating rapidly, Kovrim made a deliberate effort to nod and smile to anyone he met along the way. To do otherwise would cast suspicion on him, he knew, for his reputation as one of the more jovial and warm priests of the temple was strong. Indeed, he found that no one paid him a second glance so long as he maintained the facade of a merry priest strolling though the corridors on official business.

At last, he reached Lavant's office. Noting that there was no one around to witness him sneaking inside, Kovrim let himself in through the door and shut it softly behind him. Then he turned to the desk, where the high priest seemed to continually maintain a stack of parchment, records of numerous financial reports, business transactions, and proposals from underlings about potential deals the temple could make. Lavant was responsible for a great many things the temple was involved with monetarily.

Scratching his head, Kovrim realized he didn't really know where to begin. He'd thought it a simple enough matter to simply go through the records, but once he looked at them, he saw that there were a great many. He would have to eliminate some of them, or he would never make it through the entire search without getting caught. The priest decided to ignore proposals and balance sheets for the moment. He doubted that anything related to what he was looking for would be at either of those stages of development. Instead, he would concentrate his efforts on the piles that held business plans.

The priest sat down and began to rapidly sort through the appropriate piles, scanning each page quickly for some recognizable text, particularly the name of House Pharaboldi. Of course, as he worked, his nerves were on edge, and every sound out in the corridor, every person walking by, every thump from an adjacent office caused Kovrim to nearly leap out of the chair, a half-formed explanation on the tip of his tongue. After the fifth such incident, the priest chastised himself for his cowardice and redoubled his efforts.

Finally, when he was on the verge of considering other places to dig, he found something. It wasn't much, just a document containing some estimated figures of the full ranks of the mercenary armies the temple either controlled or had strong ties to. And there, at the bottom, was a note, scribbled quickly, showing another set of figures, and the names of three merchant

Houses beside each figure. Kovrim recognized the figures themselves as financial. They were substantial
amounts, the kind of wealth the merchant Houses in
Arrabar might pay to hire an army. The Houses that
would pay that kind of coin for a professional army
usually spent those amounts when they expected to
keep them around for a while, or when they foresaw
particularly bloody confrontations in their future. It
was the kind of wealth a House spent when it believed
it was about to fight a minor war.

There were three Houses listed in a column,
each one of them with a figure beside it, each figure
enough coin to hire a mercenary army to fight such
a war. Together, the funds were substantial enough
to do something really serious, like invade another
country or conquer a city. Pharaboldi was one of the
three Houses, the name that had originally caught
Kovrim's eye. But beneath that were the names of
two other Houses. It was the third name on that list
that made Kovrim freeze, made him reread the words
three times to make certain he saw it correctly.

The third name was House Matrell.

...

Vambran paced like a caged animal in the barracks
where his men were busily organizing supplies for the
impending departure. He wanted to pound his fist
against a wall, wanted to scream at someone. Captain
Vertucio had refused to grant him any time to return
to his estate, not even long enough to tell the family
what was happening. The officer had explained, and
rightfully so, Vambran had to admit, that the need to
get the company ready had to be the lieutenant's first
priority. If, after everything needed for the upcoming
trip up the coast was readied—Captain Vertucio said
the destination was confidential for the moment, and
all Vambran needed to know was that they would be

marching overland—perhaps Vambran could sneak away for a quick good-bye.

But those were not ordinary circumstances. Vambran realized that the change in orders, the accelerated pace of the departure time, even his own additional responsibilities to handle logistics for the entire unit, were all suspiciously convenient means of keeping him from pursuing the murderers' identities. Grand Trabbar Lavant knew enough to arrange it so that Vambran would have no choice but to abandon the investigation.

Unfortunately, that also meant that Vambran could not aid Emriana, nor could he warn her to back off without him there. His sister would be on her own against Denrick Pharaboldi that evening, plotting to wrest the truth out of the young man and falsely thinking that Vambran was nearby should she need him. And that didn't even take into consideration how devastated she would be that he'd missed her birthday party. It had all gone horribly wrong, and Vambran was at a loss as to how to manage both crises at once.

The irony of having come full circle was not lost on the mercenary. It had only been two short days before that he'd stood on the deck of *Lady's Favor*, hesitating to go home, loving the freedom and excitement that serving in the mercenary company afforded him. And yet, there he was, about to muster out again, on the verge of another interesting campaign with his soldiers, his friends, and he wanted more than anything to get clear of it, to run home. It nearly made him laugh, except that he was seething at the injustice of it.

"Sir, we're going to need to procure additional horses for the supply wagons," one of the young soldiers said, saluting Vambran as he stepped near.

The lieutenant sighed.

"How many?" he asked. "And what happened to our regular supplier?"

The soldier shrugged.

"I don't have a clue, sir. Sergeant Grolo just told me I should pass that message on to you. He says to come to the stable yard immediately so the two of you can assess the situation."

Vambran paused in his pacing and turned to regard the soldier delivering the message.

"Did he, now?" the lieutenant asked.

"Yes, sir."

Vambran tried to hide a smile.

"Very well," he said, "I'm on my way. Get back to what you were doing, soldier."

The younger man nodded and ran off to whatever task he'd been about before the dwarf had interrupted his work.

Vambran began to head toward the stables, which were clear on the other side of the compound from where the barracks were. Grolo was the last officer Vambran would have put on horse detail; the dwarf hated horses and couldn't ride one to save his life. He would be a poor choice for making decisions about them when it came to supply logistics. Something else was going on.

Vambran worked his way across the compound and to the stables. When he got to the yard, he found the dwarf standing outside the large building, huddled with a number of other men, all soldiers who served in Vambran's platoon. He strolled up to them, noting that they didn't seem to be paying any attention to any horses at the moment.

"I got a message that we have a horse problem," Vambran said casually, eyeing the small group.

Grolo turned to face the lieutenant.

"More like a priority problem," the dwarf replied, and he stepped aside and let Vambran get a better look at the rest of the group. Hiding in the midst of the others were Adyan and Horial.

Vambran broke into a quick grin at the sight of his two sergeants.

"What are you two up to?" he asked slyly.

"We've just been explaining our little problem to Sergeant Grolo here," Horial said, tilting his head sideways to indicate the dwarf. "We explained how this latest campaign is likely to turn out rotten, what with our lieutenant distracted by events going on at home and all."

"He thinks that's bad for morale," Adyan drawled. "He doesn't want a lieutenant who isn't fit for battle heading up any part of the company."

"And you, sir, aren't fit for battle right now," Horial remarked. "At least, you aren't so long as your family's in the middle of some trouble."

Vambran turned to look at Grolo, who stood with his thick arms folded across his stout chest.

"And you believe these two no-good, worthless soldiers?" he asked the dwarf.

Grolo spat on the ground and said, "From what I hear, you're the best thing that ever happened to these two, and most others who have served under you." At that, there was a murmured chorus of assent from the rest of the group. "And, after what I saw last night at the warehouse, I'm pretty much figuring they're right."

Vambran gave the dwarf a shrug of placid acceptance.

"They're good men," he said in all candor. "I'm honored to have them in my unit."

"When the politics of the temple starts getting in the way of the effectiveness of the Crescent, something's wrong," Grolo said, spitting on the ground again. "And I'm thinking something's wrong."

Vambran nodded again, still unsure what the dwarf was getting at.

"We'll cover for you as long as we can, Lieutenant," Sergeant Grolo announced. "You go take care of what you need to, and we'll make do here while you're gone."

Vambran's smile became a much larger grin, then. He reached out a hand and clasped the dwarf's.

"You have my gratitude," he said sincerely. "I owe you for this. All of you," he said to the whole group. "I can tell you now, though, that by stepping into the middle of this mess with me, you're putting yourselves directly in front of the temple's scowling eye. There may very well be severe repercussions."

"Ah, we'll repercuss when the time comes," Adyan said, his country accent stronger than normal. "They can't do much without an army, can they?" he added, laughing, and the rest of the men nodded their assent.

"All right, then," Vambran said, turning to go. "I'll try to get word to you or get back here as soon as I can."

"Ah, sir?" Horial said, causing Vambran to pause and turn back. "You forgot your ride," the sergeant told him.

Vambran didn't understand until one of the men led a saddled and bridled horse out into the yard from the stables. Then he grinned anew.

"Very clever," he said, moving to the animal and mounting up. "Thanks again."

He urged the horse into a trot out through the gate, and very quickly, Vambran was riding at a rapid canter toward his family's estate.

...

Kovrim stepped out through the great front doors of the Temple of Waukeen and made his way down the broad steps to the pathway below, which led to the street. Instead of following the path, though, the priest turned to the side and began to walk across the great lawn that surrounded the temple. As he walked, he studiously observed his footfalls, avoiding the temptation to glance around to see if anyone was watching.

Even though the priest believed he had restored
Grand Trabbar Lavant's office to its original condition, he was fearful of being discovered. A sense of
dread pervaded his mood, made him worry that he'd
forgotten some minute detail, some crucial piece of
information that would make none of his concerns
real. But every time he examined it, Kovrim came
to the same conclusion. He had the information that
had been eluding him and his niece and nephew for
the past three days. He knew who was behind the
murders of Jithelle and Hoytir, the two servants
who'd worked at House Pharaboldi. Not only that,
but he had a pretty good idea just what the three
Houses were plotting, and it made his stomach heave
to contemplate.

Just considering the possibility made Kovrim
quicken his steps, and he had to force himself to slow
down to avoid looking suspicious. He continued across
the grass, past the tall trees and the benches in the
little groves, down the hill toward another boulevard
that he could take up to the next district, and he would
cut across a small plaza and head directly toward the
merchants' district. He had to let Vambran know.

The priest kept telling himself that he had a perfectly good explanation in case anyone stopped him
and demanded to know where he was off to. After all,
he actually was supposed to be attending Emriana's
birthday party that evening. Of course, he had put off
departing until the last minute, and it was those final
precious moments that had allowed him to discover
the truth. He would have to hurry to avoid being late,
but at the same time, he sensed that hurrying too
much would draw unwanted attention.

His thoughts swirling back and forth with all of
his knowledge, Kovrim didn't at first notice the pair
of figures standing casually at the far end of the path
he was following through the gardens. When he did
glance up, he did a double take. It was a pair of Ha-

lanthi priests, apparently wrapped in conversation.
He carefully avoided directing his gaze straight at
them, looking for an inconspicuous alternate route.
It was too late to turn aside and avoid them, though.
He would either have to continue on, coming face to
face with them, or double back, making it clear that
he was trying to avoid them. His hands trembled,
fearing that he'd been found out.

Despite his desire to avoid looking guilty, Kovrim
faltered a step. Were they really waiting for him? It
was possible that they just happened to have been on
a walk themselves, out for a stroll and stopping for
a respite. He could walk right by them, he thought.
But in his heart, Kovrim knew they were not there by
chance. Some premonition told him they were there
specifically to waylay him. Lavant knew that he had
discovered the Grand Trabbar's secrets. The high
priest had sent those two to intercept him, prevent
him from revealing what he knew.

Whether his fears were accurate or he was just
losing his nerve, Kovrim made the decision to turn
away. He could not be caught. He had to warn Vambran. He stopped and half turned around, snapping
his fingers, hoping he made it appear that he had
simply forgotten something. It was a feeble hope, but
he could think of nothing else.

The moment it became clear to the two priests that
Kovrim was not going to walk any closer to them,
they both came alive, watching him overtly. He spun
completely away, ready to sprint back down the path.
But two more Halanthi were blocking his exit, about
equidistant from him. His heart sank. They had him
cornered.

Kovrim considered just turning and running into
the midst of the gardens, losing his pursuers in the
lush undergrowth of vines, bamboo, and trees. But
the four priests were much younger than he, and he
doubted he could outrun them, even if he did manage

to vanish from their sight temporarily. The other option was to confront them, try to browbeat them to back off, but he doubted that would work. They had their instructions, and Lavant undoubtedly made it clear that they were to prevent him from leaving at all costs. That left just one more possibility. And despite the fact that he was more advanced than any of the other four, and his divine magic powerful enough to rebuke them, given enough time, their advantage lay in their numbers. Kovrim doubted he would be able to cast more than twice before they incapacitated him.

Hells, he thought, they don't even have to get close to me. They can just stand back there and take their shots.

When it came down to that, the priest knew he only had one choice. He spun and scrambled into the thick cover of the garden.

Behind Kovrim, back on the path, the four priests began to shout. He ignored them, pushing his way through the dense plant life, struggling to find a way to freedom before they either caught up to him or circled around. His heart was pounding, and a sense of panic welled up in him that he was about to be caught.

Suddenly, Kovrim felt a tingle of magic wash over him. One of the four was attempting to stop his flight magically, and he believed he knew the type of holding magic the Halanthi was using. He steeled himself mentally, fighting to resist the spell, and thankfully continued to churn his legs, moving forward. He knew that he was making noise, that the crashing of the foliage was giving away his position, but he had no choice. If he stopped, they would be on him.

Another wave of magic passed over Kovrim, and he heard an insistent voice from behind him, ordering him to halt. The urge to follow that instruction was too great to resist. Despite his own inner voice screaming at himself to keep going, he pulled up, panting and swaying breathlessly, waiting. He was doomed. The four Halanthi priests would surround him and grab him. He groaned, hanging his head.

But the priests did not catch up to him, and after a moment, Kovrim was willing to run again. Only then, he didn't charge full force through the bushes, but instead began to creep through them, listening to the sounds of pursuit. There was the occasional shout, sometimes from behind, sometimes from up ahead. Whenever he heard such, he altered his direction, angling always to keep clear.

Something in the back of the priest's mind told him that they were herding him, that he was being driven right toward another of their group. One who was being quiet and waiting for Kovrim to stumble onto him. He stopped moving, then, listening to the sounds around him, and he began to believe more earnestly that it was exactly his pursuers' plan. They were on three sides of him, slowly trying to drive him in the direction he'd been going. He would try to outwit them by doubling back.

Just as he turned to retrace his steps, one of the four Halanthi priests jumped up from behind a barricade of shrubs only a few feet from where he was about to pass by.

"Syndo Lazelle," the priest said, gesturing for Kovrim to stand down. "You can't escape. Please," he said, looking expectantly at his quarry.

Kovrim sighed despondently, and briefly thought of bolting back into the brush, fleeing again. But the Halanthi, whose name was Javoli, the Syndo remembered, shook his head as though reading the older man's intentions.

"He's here," Javoli called out to the others. "We've got him surrounded." He turned his gaze back to Kovrim. "You see? You only make it more difficult for yourself."

It was at that moment that a figure cloaked in red flashed into view, smacking Javoli in the back of the head with a sap. Kovrim heard the solid thunk and watched the junior priest drop to his knees with a groan and topple over and lie still.

He turned to look more closely at his savior. The figure had a cowl wrapped around his face so that the priest couldn't see it. The hands were gloved in red, and the figure wore soft boots of the same color.

Ah, Kovrim thought, Vambran's savior. And perhaps mine, now.

"Come on," the figure insisted, and it was the voice of a woman. "We have little time."

Kovrim cocked his head sideways in confusion. The voice sounded familiar.

"Who—?"

"Not now," the woman responded, motioning frantically. "In due time."

Nodding, Kovrim stepped forward and began to follow the figure, the memory of her voice tugging at the back of his mind. The memory was a good one, one that made him feel safe. He felt very close to figuring it out.

CHAPTER TEN

Emriana's breath nearly caught in her throat as she first stepped out onto the high balcony overlooking the gardens of the Matrell estate. The open lawn in the middle had been filled with tables, and party guests mingled everywhere throughout the grounds. Colored lanterns hung from every tree, sat on walls and banisters and the tables themselves, swaying in the gentle breezes. On one porch looking down on the festivities, a full orchestra played lively tunes, to which numerous partygoers danced in line, laughing and clapping in time with the music as they did so, on a second large patio directly below the musicians.

The scents of lamb and eel roasting over a large fire pit dug near the spread, as well as peppers and turnips, made Emriana's mouth

water. She could also see platters of cheeses, saltfish,
a variety of spicy sauced meats and vegetables, and
more kinds of sweets than she could imagine. She
was already craving some of the custard pastries she
loved so much. In the middle of the tables set with
the food was a large pedestal with a magnificent ice
sculpture atop it, an image of a mermaid lounging on
a rock. The sculpture glowed somehow from within,
and spellcraft also kept the frozen wonder from melt-
ing in the warm evening air.

Servants roamed through the guests' tables with
pitchers of wine, ale, and cool fruit juices, keeping
every visitor's cup or tankard filled to overflowing.
Everyone had put on their most dazzling attire for
the evening, and Emriana nearly jumped for joy at
the number of attendees. She thought she would pop,
and she imagined that the silly grin on her face must
have made her look six years old, but for once, she
didn't care if anyone accused her of such. The girl
made up her mind right then and there that, despite
the events of the past several days, she was going to
thoroughly enjoy the party in her honor.

She looked to her left, where her brother stood,
thankful that he was beside her at all. The lieutenant had arrived only moments before the first guests,
coming to her straight away. Despite Jaleene's protests,
Emriana let him into her rooms, where he proceeded
to tell her what was going on with the mercenary
company, and how he'd managed to sneak away.

"I don't know how long I'll be able to stay," he
explained, "so we can't waste any time tonight. The
first chance you get, suggest a private walk and take
Denrick where we agreed. I'll be there and we'll get
the truth out of him."

The realization that Vambran might be gone by
morning made Emriana shudder. She hadn't even
considered the possibility that he would disappear
again before the two of them managed to uncover the

details of the mystery behind the two murders, and yet it was looming in front of her. The girl shook her head, refusing to let those worries spoil her evening. Instead, she focused her attention on the fact that her brother was there right then.

Vambran was decked out in a most regal outfit, his officer's uniform. He wore a finely tailored pair of dark blue breeches, loosely tucked into his crisp black boots, which came almost to his knee and were then turned down to a wide cuff. A snow-white silk shirt billowed over his arms, with tiny slashes in each sleeve designed to show off the blue silk layer underneath. His black leather riding gloves made a nice contrast to the shirt. Over all of it, the lieutenant wore his ceremonial breastplate, all polished silver with gold highlights, including the family crest, a bas relief tiger's head facing directly forward. He had even buckled on his crossbow, which hung from his belt on the opposite side from his sword.

"You look dashing," Emriana whispered to her brother. "Especially the breastplate."

Vambran smiled and whispered back, "It was Xaphira's, you know. She gave it to me the night she disappeared. I had to have it adjusted for size a bit, of course. You, by the way, look radiant."

Emriana giggled and looked down at her own attire. She and Jaleene had spent most of the afternoon preparing her for the evening, and for the first time, she was glad for it. She wore a dress the color of sea foam, creamy white with just a hint of green highlights in it. Over it, her entire upper torso was bedecked in an elaborate vest of fine gold filigree that hugged her bosom snugly, enhancing her figure. From the wrought mesh of gold hung emeralds interspersed with tiny bells and chimes. Every move she made caused the little instruments to tinkle gaily. Even the girl's boots, hidden beneath her dress, were festooned with strings of bells that jangled sweetly when she walked.

Emriana's hair had taken the longest, for it had been pulled up and piled stylishly atop her head, with individual ringlets hanging down at each temple. Though she found it difficult and occasionally frustrating to walk elegantly and keep still so that it would not come loose, she felt very regal. Jaleene had even applied some face paint, highlighting her cheeks and darkening the area around her eyes. When the girl had seen herself in her wall mirror, she felt that the last vestiges of her childhood had faded away.

"Shall we?" Vambran asked, offering his sister his arm.

Emriana smiled and looped her own wrist around his crooked elbow, and together they descended the steps to the party.

At that moment, the orchestra stopped in mid-song, and Uncle Dregaul appeared on the balcony next to the musicians, directly above the crowd.

"Lords and ladies," he began, gesturing for quiet. The general conversation dropped to a low hum, with only a few murmurs still rolling through the guests. "Tonight is a very special occasion, for many reasons. We have several delightful surprises in store for you throughout the evening. But before we can let the party truly begin, let's all welcome our guest of honor tonight." He gestured, open-palmed, toward where Emriana and Vambran stood at the bottom step of the last staircase. "Tonight," Dregaul said, "Let us celebrate her passing into adulthood. Let us envy her, and try to remember what it was like to be sixteen." That drew more than a few chuckles from the crowd. "I present Lady Emriana Matrell!" Dregaul finished with a flourish.

The partygoers gathered close, clapping and cheering cordially for the girl.

As Emriana and Vambran approached the garden, guests hovered around the siblings, and every last one of them greeted her, calling out good wishes for a happy birthday. The first to meet her at the base of the

stairs were, of course, her own family. Grandmother
Hetta was standing in the front, with Ladara right
by her side, as usual. Emriana smiled brightly at her
grandmother, and she thought she would begin to cry,
she was so happy.

Hetta leaned down and gave Emriana a kiss on
her cheek.

"My little Em is all grown up," the elderly woman
said, a glow in her eyes of absolute pride. "Dazzle
them, dear."

Emriana's mother gave her daughter a tight hug.

"My baby," she said, then stepped back.

Evester and Marga were next, with the twins by
their sides.

Evester gave Emriana a quick hug and whispered,
"You've made us all very proud."

Then he was stepping back again, letting his
wife in.

Marga beamed as she took Emriana's hands in her
own. She smiled for a long time.

"Just look at you," she said softly. Then she finally
crushed the girl in a tight hug. "It's wonderful having
you as my sister-in-law."

Marga kissed Emriana on the cheek, and Emriana
flushed with emotion, genuinely happy.

The twins both hugged their aunt at the same time,
wrapping their arms around her waist.

"You look beautiful," Obiron said.

Emriana smiled down at her nephew.

"If you promise to behave, I'll dance with you later,"
she told him.

That brought a huge smile from the boy, who
nodded and looked at his mother.

"Can I eat, now?" he asked.

Marga rolled her eyes and shooed him away with
a, "Yes, but don't get anything on your clothes."

Quindy was feeling the fabric of Emriana's dress
and said, "Can I wear this when I turn sixteen?"

Emriana gave a mocking groan and grabbed her niece in a second hug.

"Sweetheart," the older girl said, "You'll have your own dress that's twice as pretty as this one."

When Quindy grinned, Emriana tussled her hair and stood up.

"All right," Hetta commanded, "let her through. She has guests to greet."

The family parted to allow Emriana and Vambran to pass through them and meet everyone else.

The birthday girl beamed as she strolled among her well-wishers, smiling and thanking them with a word or a nod. She didn't feel at all like herself at the moment, but like she was hiding in someone else's body, a member of the royalty with everyone in attendance at her beck and call. She took a deep breath, getting her proverbial feet back under her and firmly on the ground.

It's just a party, she told herself. No one made you queen.

There were guests in attendance from numerous other merchant Houses. Many folk she knew, at least by sight and reputation, if not personally. There was Ariskrit Darowdryn, the matriarch of House Darowdryn, one of the oldest and wealthiest merchant clans in all of Chondath. Ariskrit was probably nearly as old as Grandmother Hetta, and Emriana had seen them together on more than one occasion at parties, visiting like old friends. Ariskrit's nephew, Tharlgarl, was at her side, a huge bear of a man with great white mustaches that hung down below his chin. Everyone called him "Steelfists," and the nickname fit, for he was wearing the most pompous suit of full plate mail Emriana had ever seen, fully stylized with gold highlights. It must have weighed as much as Emriana herself did, the girl thought, and she could only imagine how stifling it would be inside the suit in the warm and sticky clime.

Both of them smiled and took her hand, offering
her congratulations, as though turning sixteen was
some sort of accomplishment that she had worked for,
rather than simply a passing of years.

A little farther on, Emriana shook hands with
several members of the Elphaendim household,
including the patriarch of the merchant family,
Thalammose, who stood quietly with his grandniece,
Cauvra. Cauvra was only a couple of years younger
than Emriana herself. Cauvra looked positively bored,
but as Emriana caught her eye, the other girl smiled
and waved. The girls had played with one another on
the handful of occasions when the two Houses gathered together for some event or another, though in
more recent days, the word in the gossip circles was
that Cauvra was a budding young wizardess and her
great-uncle Thalammose, an accomplished arcanist
himself, would no longer let her far from his side. "The
Old Elf," as many referred to him derisively behind
his back, apparently feared to let her out into the
world, where her potential talents could easily be
enslaved or misused.

Brastynbold Elphaendim was also there, though
he was about as far from his uncle in temperament
as possible. Whereas Thalammose was a quiet, timid
lover of books, "Oldhelm," as people knew Brastynbold, was a boisterous fellow with a huge love of
wine and a fair brawler in his own right. Few people
in Arrabar had not heard the story of the time he'd
hurled a greatsword across an entire courtyard—after
downing nearly a smallkeg of fiery wine by himself,
so the story claimed—squarely striking a thief in the
back as he attempted to escape by climbing over an
estate wall. Looking at the immensely tall, barrel-
chested man, Emriana no longer doubted the veracity
of the story, especially after he took her hand in his
own with a riotous laugh and brought it to his lips
for a kiss. He nearly took her arm out of her socket,

but she turned the grimace into a smile and politely curtsied, then moved on.

Some other guests, Emriana did not know. She smiled at them just as sweetly and thanked them for attending just as sincerely. In addition to the necessity to show her genteel upbringing and avoid embarrassing Uncle Dregaul in the eyes of anyone he might have business dealings with, Emriana was genuinely grateful for the attention she was receiving that evening. Over the course of the years, the Matrells had been invited to a good number of coming-of-age birthday parties themselves, even though in the greater scheme of things, their House was not high in the rankings of the politically powerful or prestigious clans. The girl knew that political success was primarily due to her grandmother's shrewd business dealings and connections with greater Houses. That same acumen was respected in social circles, and most of the people there that night were honoring Emriana because Hetta had always dealt fairly with them. Most of them were.

Denrick Pharaboldi was standing near the end of the crowd as Emriana and Vambran approached. He had dressed in lavish style, with breeches and boots of similar fashion to Vambran's, though his were maroon in color. Instead of a billowy shirt such as her brother wore, though, Denrick wore a greatvest that hung down nearly to his knees. The vest was open, and the girl could see several crisscrossing chains of gold coins adorning his bare chest. When he saw her approaching, the young man went into an elaborate and superfluous bow, with his forehead nearly touching his bent knee and his arms spread wide.

Emriana suppressed a groan and curtsied slightly in response. Vambran squeezed her hand subtly, where no one else would notice, but the message from her brother seemed clear: I'm here with you, so calm down and act the part. Emriana widened her smile as Denrick looked her up and down appraisingly.

"You are a sight," the young man said, and the way in which he gazed at her figure, coupled with his words, made her feel vaguely like a piece of live-stock at market.

Emriana curtsied again and said, "Thank you, Denrick. You are looking well tonight, too."

Denrick's eyebrows arched slightly in surprise at her choice of words, but before any more could be made of it, Vambran said, "I have the privilege of the first dance, Em," loudly enough so that several people could hear. "Come on, before your line of suitors grows too long." To Denrick, Vambran said over his shoulder, "Sorry, good sir, but you'll have to indulge me."

Denrick smiled, somewhat sickly, Emriana noted, but nodded and waved them toward the patio where the dancing was taking place, as though it was of course the absolute correct sequence of events, and he wouldn't have dreamed of intervening.

When they were together on the dance floor, turn-ing and stepping to the notes of a new tune, Emriana gave Vambran a relieved look.

"Thank you," she whispered as they moved in time, weaving in and out of the other couples in a sequence. "I just wasn't ready to face him, yet."

"It's all right," her brother replied, "I could tell you were still working up your courage. But he's already coming over here, so get ready."

Emriana nodded and took a deep breath as she and Vambran finished the complex steps and moved to the ends of their respective lines.

Soon enough, Denrick stepped in and whispered something to Vambran. Emriana saw her brother nod, and he moved aside to let the Pharaboldi heir take his place. With one last, piercing glance at her, Vambran strolled off, falling in with a crowd of other folks close to his age, all of them wanting to hear about his latest exploits with the Sapphire Crescent.

Denrick was an excellent dancer, Emriana had to admit, but her mind wasn't really on the steps, and more than once, she got fouled up during the moves. Finally, Denrick pulled her out of the line and off to one side.

"Are you all right?" he asked, looking very concerned.

The girl tried to smooth her expression to one of complete innocence and said, "I'm fine. This is all just a little overwhelming, that's all."

Denrick nodded sagely, giving her a look that said, "I know exactly what you're going through." His eyes brightened.

"Let's take a walk," he suggested.

Emriana had to swallow the lump that rose suddenly in her throat. Unsure of her own voice, she simply nodded. Then, steeling herself to trust in the plan and in her brother, she took the older boy's hand and led him away from the main party, through the garden and along one of the meandering paths between stands of trees, bushes, and vines. The couple walked for a little while, Denrick apparently happy to let his counterpart lead the way and probably thinking that she was taking him to one of her favorite secluded spots in a far corner of the garden. For her part, Emriana tried to make it seem as though she was simply strolling with a companion, though she wanted more than anything just to drag Denrick to the location she and Vambran had agreed upon before the party had begun.

After a few moments, Emriana turned down another path that led back in the general direction of the house. Denrick hesitated, tugging on the girl's hand.

"Wait," he said. "Where are we going, now? I thought we were going to come out here and be alone," he added, smiling and flashing his eyes at the girl in the semidarkness of the moonlit night.

"There's a great view of part of the city over here," Emriana lied, struggling to control her panic. *He knows we're on to him!* her mind screamed. *He's figured it out!*

"Oh," Denrick replied, easing up. "As long as we can enjoy the view by ourselves," he added, his voice husky.

Emriana didn't answer as she resumed her trek through the greenery, winding her way up the sloping hill to the estate. When they broke free of the garden path and began to cross the lawn, she could hear the sounds of the party on another side of the house. She longed to be back there, among the colorful lanterns and the smiling people. She had felt safe there, admired and honored. Where she was, there was only Denrick, and despite her private mental admonitions to be strong, she feared him.

Shaking off the feeling of dread that was washing over her, Emriana led the older boy to a set of steps that climbed to a higher part of the house, a wide patio that surrounded a cistern built into the structure for catching and storing rain water. The pool was filled at the moment with cool, clean water almost to its brim. There was a single doorway leading inside, but the path was dark there, for it led into a part of the house that was little used at the moment. They were alone.

Denrick nodded in satisfaction and strolled casually around the perimeter of the cistern, staring at its surface, which was undulating gently in the warm night breeze that blew in from the harbor to the west, carrying with it the smell of the ocean and the scents of the blossoms from the garden below. Emriana stood and watched him, wondering what he thought was about to happen. She wondered if he even had an inkling.

"So, where's the city?" Denrick asked. "I thought you said you had a good view of it from here."

"I—" Emriana began, stammering. She hadn't thought he'd care one way or another, once she got him there and showed him that they were ostensibly alone. "I meant that—this isn't the right spot. It's a different place where you can—"

"You were fibbing to me, weren't you?" Denrick said, coming around the corner of the cistern toward the girl.

She blanched—though he couldn't see the blood drain from her face in the near-darkness—and barely stopped herself from fleeing back to the party right then and there. He was calling her bluff. He knew what was going on.

"You don't come up here to see the city. You just wanted to have me all to yourself," the older boy said, smiling wolfishly at her. "It's all right; you can admit that you want to be with me here. It's just the two of us, now, no one around to pretend that you're still all prim and proper."

Emriana took a step back, confused, but nonetheless wary of the advancing figure.

"What?"

"I said, you don't have to pretend that you're still the innocent little girl," Denrick replied. "I know how you look at me, and I feel the same way." He took another step closer. "Up here, where no one else is around, you can let down your guard, be the woman I know you are. You've turned sixteen, now. You look all grown up to me."

Another step.

"Denrick," Emriana began, backing up another step, until suddenly, she was against the railing and had nowhere else to retreat to. "I'm not . . . I mean, it's a little too fast to . . ."

She couldn't get the words out. She kept seeing Jithelle Skolotti's face, kept imagining that that must have been how Denrick had tried to woo her, too. What had he said that would have made the woman get into his bed?

"Em," Denrick said, taking another step closer, close enough to reach out to her, and he started to. "Quit pretending you don't want me to do it," he said, taking her by the waist and drawing close to her. "I promise you, I'll make you feel so good. Trust me."

Suddenly, Emriana couldn't maintain the pretense anymore. She shoved Denrick backward from herself, hard. Then she darted to the side, out of the corner in which he had apparently been trying to trap her.

"Is that what you told Jithelle before you had her killed? To trust you?" she spat as she maneuvered herself around to the opposite side of the cistern pool from the older boy.

"Jithelle? What?" Denrick said, shaking his head and trying to guess which way to circle the pool to reach Emriana.

Every time he stepped in one direction or the other, she would counter it, keeping the pool between them.

"Stop this, Em," he demanded, taking a firm couple of strides to his left.

"No," the girl replied, moving in concert with the older boy. "I'm not letting you near me. I know about Jithelle, Denrick. I know about all of it."

Denrick stopped then, staring hard at Emriana in the gloom.

"Well, I guess that proves it, then," he said quietly.

"What do you mean?" Emriana asked, watching the boy for some sign of attack, some indication that he was going to come after her.

Where is Vambran? she wondered desperately, berating herself for letting slip her suspicions before he had arrived.

"What I mean is, you're not the innocent little girl you've been pretending to be," Denrick replied. "Yesterday, at the picnic, you knew already, didn't you? All those questions. You were setting me up, weren't you?"

Emriana was already shaking her head before
Denrick even finished his accusation.

"No," she said. "Not when I first arrived. I only
figured it out later, when we went to get the picnic
basket. And even then, I didn't know you were bedding
her, you lecherous bastard."

Even in the darkness, Emriana could see Denrick
wince at her revelation and scathing words.

"Em, you don't understand," he began. "I didn't
know, then. I only heard it later, last night."

"Liar," came a voice from overhead, on the roof of
the entryway into the house. Vambran crouched there,
looking down at both of them. Emriana sighed in
relief, nearly collapsing against the railing. Denrick
whirled around in shock, backing away from the edge
of the house several steps to get clear of any attack.
"Em and I think there's more to your story that you're
not telling, Denrick Pharaboldi."

"Vambran," Denrick began, regaining his composure
somewhat. "What are you doing here?" He looked again
at Emriana. "You set this up," he growled, folding his
arms across his chest. "You two are working together."

"That's right," Vambran said as he swung himself
over the edge of the roof and dropped down to the
tiles of the patio, landing softly. "We planned the
whole thing."

He began to walk around the perimeter of the pool,
like Denrick had done before, and the younger man
would have been forced to move in the same circular
direction to keep the lieutenant away from him. But
Vambran simply stopped when he stood next to his
sister. Emriana reached out for her brother's hand
and gave it a squeeze, just a silent way to thank him
for showing up when he did.

"So, go ahead," Vambran said. "Tell us again how
you didn't know about Jithelle's death beforehand.
Tell us how you're just as distressed as everyone else
about her death."

"That's right," Denrick replied. "That's what I was trying to tell Em. I didn't have her killed. She was slain by the city watch, running from them after trying to impersonate a mage. I had nothing to do with it," he insisted. "If you were there, as you claimed yesterday, Em, then you know this already."

"That's pretty convincing," Vambran said, "but I'm not buying it. Those weren't city watchmen that night. They were hired killers dressed up like thugs, sent to kill your mistress."

"What? No," Denrick said, practically whining. "The watchmen said she was a criminal. I couldn't believe it. She'd never done anything like that before," he babbled, and Emriana felt sick to her stomach. Whether he was telling the truth or not, the thought of him wanting her, to have her in his bed with him, was making her sick.

"Liar," Vambran said again. "You had to get her out of the way so you wouldn't have an illegitimate heir running around."

"What?" Denrick said quietly, stiffening in the faint moonlight. "What are you talking about?"

"She was with child, Denrick," Emriana said. "*Your* child. You killed your own child!"

"No," Denrick said, crumpling down to the tiles, his voice cracking. "I didn't—she was pregnant? I was going to be a father? Oh, gods!" he whimpered.

Vambran crossed the distance between them and loomed over Denrick as the younger man drew his knees up under his chin and wrapped his arms around them. Emriana watched from where she was, still safely on the opposite side of the cistern from both of them. Despite his crumbling demeanor, Emriana found no sympathy in her heart for him. She simply looked on him as a pathetic, despicable person. There had never been a time when she was truly enamored of him, despite his obvious interest in her, but knowing what she more recently did, she regarded him with loathing. He may very well have been innocent of the crimes against Jithelle, but she doubted he had as much regard for the servant as he was pretending. He had been far too eager to become intimate with Emriana that night for her to believe that.

"I'm not convinced of your innocence," Vambran said, towering over the huddled Denrick. "You're going to have to try a little harder to prove it to me."

Denrick craned his neck, looking up at his tormentor.

"I told you," he mumbled, "I had no idea of any of the things you're—"

There was a scream from the other side of the house, a loud, piercing sound of terror and anguish. Vambran jerked upright, cocking his head. Emriana felt her heart leap into her throat.

"Who was that?" the girl asked, trembling.

"I don't know, but I'm going to go find out. Come on," he said, turning and taking the stairs two at a time back down to the garden.

Emriana was right behind her brother, leaving Denrick and all thoughts of his transgressions behind. Together, they sprinted in the direction of the sound, which seemed to have come right at the edge of the party. Emriana was a fair runner, but it was impossible for her to match Vambran stride for stride, and the lieutenant very quickly left her behind. Still, she hoisted the dress she wore high enough to keep it from tripping her up and kept going, terrified to think of what might have befallen one of her guests.

When she finally caught up to the scene, Vambran was already kneeling down, a crowd gathered around him. Ladara was right next to her son, sobbing, and Emriana knew that it had been her who had screamed before. Someone else was shouting for everyone to move back, to give them some room. As Emriana drew closer, she nearly sat down in the grass right there, horrified. It was Hetta.

Em watched helplessly as Vambran worked on their grandmother, who was lying in the grass on her back. Vambran was turned away from his sister, so she could not see what he was doing. His concentration was focused on the elderly matriarch's legs. With a sudden jerk, Vambran's arm came up, and he held half a crossbow bolt in his hand, the metal head dripping blood. At the same time, Hetta lurched in pain, issuing a feeble cry of suffering. Emriana cringed but closed the rest of the distance and knelt down next to her grandmother.

Hetta's eyes were open, but they were staring off at the darkened sky, glazed over and seeing nothing. Her breath was rapid and shallow. Her calf had been hit, and Vambran was pulling the rest of the bolt out, having already snapped off the head to avoid further pain and injury. Then, ignoring Ladara's panicked sobs for him to do something, the mercenary placed his hands on the wounds on either side of his grandmother's leg and began to chant a prayer.

Emriana squeezed her own eyes shut and prayed right alongside her brother, begging Waukeen to let Hetta live. She know that her own pleas were insignificant compared to the true divine power inherent in Vambran, but she didn't care. No amount of fervent, sincere entreaties would hurt the cause.

To the girl, the waiting seemed to go on forever. She opened one eye to look down at Hetta, still with that glazed look in her eyes, then she glanced over at her brother. He was still in the midst of his prayer, face smooth and serene. She couldn't imagine how he could remain so calm, but then, she reminded herself, he had seen such horror before, on the battlefield.

Hetta gasped and tried to sit up.

"So cold!" she blurted out, tossing her head from side to side and casting her gaze, which was quite clear and focused again, around.

She cried out, reaching for her leg as though suddenly realizing she had been injured.

"Easy, Grandmother," Vambran said, grasping Hetta by the hand and moving closer to her head. He gently forced the elderly woman to lie back down. "You're going to be fine."

Ladara let out a sob, but it was one of relief. His mother grabbed at Vambran and hugged him, then put a trembling hand to her mouth as she patted Hetta on the cheek.

Only upon hearing her brother's words did Emriana allow herself to relax. She realized she had been holding her breath the entire time and exhaled sharply. She felt tears of relief running down her cheeks. She reached up and put a thankful hand on Vambran's shoulder to reassure him, and nearly jerked her hand back again, startled.

The muscles in the mercenary officer's shoulder were tight, corded, and felt like steel. Emriana watched as he slowly stood, looking around.

"Who saw what happened?" he demanded.

Several people began to speak at once, all clamoring to be the first to inform the large man, who had a look of death in his eye, what had transpired. From the jumble of words, Emriana somehow deciphered that Hetta had simply been standing there, visiting with several other folk, when she cried out and crumpled to the ground. Then Ladara screamed, and everyone came running.

Vambran must have been able to piece together the story from the cacophony, too, for he finally held up his hands for silence.

"Where did the shot come from?" he said, his voice like ice.

Party guests turned to one another for some sort of support, but no one seemed to know. The lieutenant was answered with a lot of shrugging.

There was another shout, this time from the undergrowth off to the side of the open lawn. Vambran had his sword out, advancing toward the sound, almost before Emriana had turned to see what the commotion was. A house guard came stumbling out of the underbrush, a crossbow in his hand. When he saw the hulking Vambran coming at him, weapon out, he grimaced and held up a placating hand.

"I found it. I just found it," he insisted quickly, frantically trying to calm the mercenary before he was attacked.

Vambran relaxed but then, just as quickly, he lunged forward and snatched the weapon away from the guard. He peered down at it for a moment, then, tossing the thing aside, he sprinted down the path, leaving behind him a wake of startled guests, gasping and looking at one another to try to understand what was happening.

Em rushed over to the crossbow and took a closer look at it. There was a note attached. She unfurled it and read:

Next time, it will be her heart I pierce.

CHAPTER ELEVEN

Vambran reached the wall of the Matrell estate and heaved himself atop it, then he stopped and listened for the sounds of someone nearby, even as he carefully peered into every shadow, stared at everything that might be a figure hiding in the darkness. He heard and saw nothing. Clenching his teeth in determination, he walked along the wall for a while, tuning all of his senses to his surroundings.

Inside, the man burned for vengeance. They had dared to threaten his family. They had come after his whole House, and he would not stop until he hunted them down and made them accountable.

He would not stop.

Vambran kept seeing the image of his grandmother, lying on the grass, her blood

staining her clothes red. He clenched his fists, trying
to control his breathing. He'd never entered into battle
in such an emotional state, and he knew that if he
didn't calm himself, he would make a fatal mistake.
He had to regain control of his feelings, save the sav-
agery, the fury, for later. Then the bloodletting could
begin, he promised himself.

In the meantime, Vambran was also upset that
he had been unable to complete his interrogation of
Denrick Pharaboldi. He had intended to get the boy so
beside himself that he would let down his guard, and
the lieutenant would read his thoughts. He'd hoped
to get some inkling as to whether or not young Pharaboldi was telling the truth, or if he was, as Vambran
suspected, hiding his complicity in the murders. Of
course, Denrick was properly warned that the Matrell
offspring were on to him, and they would not so easily
corner Denrick by himself again. Even if they were
to manage to confront him on favorable ground, he
would be ready for them next time, possibly even have
the presence of mind to mask his thoughts, or worse
yet, to procure some form of protection against just
what Vambran had intended.

The lieutenant paused in the midst of his walk
along the parapet, drawn to some faint sound. He
strained to see if he could hear it again, but there was
nothing. He stood motionless, moving just his eyes,
seeking out that form, that indistinct protrusion of
darkness that was just a little off, was not quite right.
He was looking for that hint of someone hiding close
by. He saw nothing.

He exhaled slowly and was on the verge of turning
around and going back in the other direction when
he heard the sound again. It was nothing more than
a faint scrape, but he was certain he heard it, coming
from the wall itself, just ahead and around a bend,
perhaps. He carefully began to pad forward, trying
to keep as quiet as possible, but with no delusions that

he was a master thief, trained to silence. As he moved, he continued to watch, and he spotted the motion at almost the same moment the intruder realized he'd been discovered.

The shadowy figure was hanging by his hands from the top of the wall, his feet dangling down toward the ground some five feet below. He was in dark shadow where he clung, and he held himself motionless there, as though waiting. As Vambran approached, the figure tilted his head slightly, so slightly, in fact, that if the lieutenant hadn't happened to have been looking directly at him, he might never have seen him.

"Hold it!" Vambran called, moving forward, freeing his crossbow from his belt.

At almost the same instant, the figure let go of the wall and dropped to the cobblestones with an almost inaudible grunt. Swearing, fumbling to load his crossbow, Vambran ran toward where the figure had been.

But the fugitive was too fast, darting across the street in the blink of an eye, and Vambran couldn't get a clean shot off. Swearing again, Vambran swung down off the wall, dropping easily to the street. He took off after his quarry, not about to let that one escape.

The figure dashed down the street and into an alley, a good thirty paces ahead of Vambran, who sprinted after, his long strides making up only a little ground. The mercenary turned the corner to the alley and flinched as a crossbow bolt thwacked hard off the stone of the building only inches from his face. Vambran felt flecks of stone spray his cheek from the impact. He dropped low, making himself a smaller target, and he pressed himself closer to the wall, hoping he wasn't so easy to see.

Already, though, footsteps receded down the other end of the alley. Vambran was up and after the

fugitive the moment he realized he was no longer
a target. He recalled that the alley turned sharply
around to the left a little farther ahead, then split
into two directions at a Y-shaped intersection. He
would have to hurry if he wanted to get there in
time to avoid losing his quarry. His blood pounding
in his ears, the mercenary urged himself to go faster,
lengthening his strides again, heedless of the danger
of another crossbow bolt.

The lieutenant reached the turn and darted around
it, his feet skidding only slightly on the cobblestones.
He spotted his prey in the distance, still running. The
would-be assassin took the left-hand path at the intersection and, as Vambran lumbered ahead, closing
with the man little by little, the shadowy silhouette
vanished.

What the—? the mercenary thought, increasing his
strides and peering around, letting his fury bubble
over again at the thought of having lost track of his
prey.

Vambran nearly didn't see the hole in the street
for all of his careful observation everywhere else. He
nearly stepped right into it, but at the last moment,
he leaped over and clear.

It was a drain into the sewers that ran below the
city, and the grate was flipped open. A slough of
water trickled down the street from both directions
and poured into the sewers, splashing into the runoff
that eventually made its way to the harbor. It was too
dark to see into the pit, but Vambran had looked down
plenty of those drains as a boy and knew that the pas-
sages were certainly large enough for a man to walk
through. A stink rose up from that particular opening, and Vambran wrinkled his nose in distaste.

"Damn it," he growled.

The mercenary cocked his head to listen for signs
the fugitive had indeed gone that way. He heard nothing. He rose to his feet once more, breathing heavily,

drenched in sweat. He peered around the alley, trying
to see some other evidence of to where the figure
might have disappeared. There was nothing. Though
not keen on wading in the muck and waste of the
sewer, he wasn't letting his quarry escape so easily.

On impulse, Vambran pointed his finger in the air
in front of himself and twirled it in a circle as he spoke
a quick arcane phrase, looking away at the last second.
A set of lights sprang into being, as though four lanterns hung suspended in the air in front of him. The
light was blinding, but he sent them with a flick of
his finger circling around himself, using their glow
to peer into the deepest shadows of the alley. When
he didn't see anything suspicious, he sent them zipping down into the opening of the sewer and he peered
down after them. The vertical shaft of the drain was
perhaps ten feet high, certainly an easy drop, but not
so easy to climb out again. If he was going to follow
the figure, he would have to find a better way to climb
back out. At the bottom of the descent, he could see
the passage, filled with murky brown water, flowing
sluggishly parallel to the alley.

Does it look stirred up? the mercenary wondered.

Sighing in disgust, Vambran wrinkled his nose
again and sat, then slipped his feet over the side. He
held that position for only a moment, long enough
to remember the image of his grandmother bleeding on the grass of the estate. That thought erased
any hesitation that lingered. He was on the verge of
dropping down into the slime when he heard a faint
noise behind him and up high. He froze, listening,
and detected it again. It was the sound of soft cloth
sliding over stone.

He twisted around, directing his magical lights up
and out of the sewer and flying back over his head.
As the dancing lights swept up the side of the building, Vambran climbed to his feet, peering intently
up there. It was the back of a shop, and on the second

floor, where a patio protruded out over the larger lower floor, his quarry was just pulling himself up over the edge of the roof.

As the lights reached the height of the wall, Vambran directed them to hover right next to the man, who cried out and flung an arm up to shield his sight. Vambran smiled to himself and mentally set the lights to remain there, dancing around his foe's head, while he reached for his crossbow.

You're not slipping away again, you bastard, the mercenary fumed, fumbling to free the weapon as he kept his gaze trained on his would-be target.

Before Vambran could unhook the crossbow from his hip and cock it, though, the figure somehow managed to pull himself the rest of the way up and over the edge of the flat roof. He was gone. Vambran gave a primal shout of frustration and slapped the crossbow back down against his hip.

I'm not letting him get away from me! he swore to himself. Got to find a way up there.

There were no stairs up to the patio, but a rain barrel sat in a corner formed by the building and its neighbor, and Vambran ran to that, hoisting himself up and balancing on the edge as he stood. The edge of the patio was still a bit out of his reach, and his perch on the barrel was so precarious that he didn't trust himself to try to jump. He strained, stretching up with his fingers, but it was no use. He nearly punched the wall, but managing to hold his rage in check, Vambran jumped down and desperately sought another way up.

The mercenary sent his lights swarming along the edge of the roof in both directions, looking for some sign of his mark, but it was fruitless. Figuring that his foe would try to escape down the opposite side of the clump of buildings, Vambran took off, running the rest of the way through the alley, clinging to the hope that he might yet spot the intruder. He reached the

end of the alley and turned, scrutinizing the handful
of people who were walking there, but none of them
seemed to fit the description of his foe at first glance.
The lieutenant moved from person to person anyway,
giving a quick, rather invasive glance at each face,
apologizing each time but offering no explanation.

Finally, when he was satisfied that none of the folks
strolling along the street were his quarry, Vambran
scanned the roof line again, hoping his prey was still
up there, hiding and waiting for him to give up. He
briefly considered trying to gain access from one of
the shops themselves, though few were still open that
late in the evening. He supposed he could knock, but
he knew his request would seem strange and possibly
threatening, and the last thing he wanted to do right
then was upset the people living there.

Kicking at the cobblestones beneath his feet in
frustration, he looked around for other ideas. He spied
a potential hiding place on a window sill under a broad
awning of a pottery merchant's establishment. It was
a good place from which to observe the roof unseen,
for the sill was wide and comfortable, though barred
from inside by a metal grate. The awning hung well
out over the window, and from there, Vambran could
peer out without being seen much from overhead.

Still feeling absolute rage boiling just beneath the
surface, Vambran settled down to wait, pulling at his
damp, sweaty clothing from time to time.

Let's see which one of us is the more patient, he
thought, smiling coldly in the darkness.

...

Emriana wanted to cry. Hetta was going to be
all right, it seemed, but the girl felt terrible for her
grandmother's sake. It was clear to her that the crossbow bolt had been a warning, and she had no doubt in
her mind that it was directed at her brother and her.

Obviously, she and Vambran had been getting close to the truth, and they had managed to bring their entire family into it, unwittingly and unwillingly. Everyone was in danger, and it was because of her.

Several of the men at the party had set out after Vambran, perhaps in a show of support to help him track down the heinous criminal, but more stood around, ostensibly to protect Hetta from future attacks. They helped her up and inside, where she insisted on being led to her favorite chair in the sitting room deep in the house. It was not a bad plan, Emriana thought, for anyone wanting to get to the older woman would have to sneak pretty far into the building to reach her.

Ladara never left Hetta's side, insisting that Emriana fetch things for her grandmother, when in fact there were numerous servants standing around wringing their hands who could have been put to better use than fretting. Emriana sent them scurrying instead, choosing to stay beside her grandmother as well, at least until Ladara told the girl in no uncertain terms to get the elderly woman's house robe. Shaking her head, Emriana went to fetch the garment.

In the hall halfway to Hetta's rooms, Dregaul caught up to her.

"You insolent brat," he spat, grabbing Emriana by the arm and jerking her so she spun around. "You would defy me at every turn, wouldn't you!" he shouted, his face growing red. He put it right down in front of hers, his eyes bulging in anger. "You and your brother were both instructed—instructed!—to leave this foolish watch business alone, and you chose to ignore those instructions."

Emriana recoiled from her uncle as flecks of spittle sprayed onto her face with every word. She cringed from him, wanting to slip away and run, but he would not let go of her arm, crushing it painfully in his grasp.

"Do you see, now, what your impertinence, your audacity—audacity!—has brought down on this family? This *House?*"

Emriana reached up to try to pry Dregaul's grip lose from her arm.

"Please," she pleaded, "you're hurting me."

"I'm hurting *you?*" he said, his voice a constricted shout. "*You're* hurting? How do you think my mother feels right now?"

"We didn't know," Emriana wailed, the tears flowing. "We only wanted to help. We thought we were doing something important. Something that would set things right. I'm sorry. I'm so, so sorry. . . ."

"Stop that," Dregaul said, jerking her arm. "You're not a little girl anymore, remember?"

Emriana nodded, trying to calm herself, though she felt like a foolish little girl right then, a little girl who had tried to play at being grown up but who was overwhelmed with fear and self-doubt. She took a deep, shuddering breath and wiped her eyes with her free hand.

"You have to believe me. We never expected something like this," she said at last. "Honestly, we know there's something big at stake, and we're trying to work it out, but we never meant to bring any danger down on the family."

Dregaul let go of her arm then and stepped back, shaking his head.

"When are you going to learn that the most important job of any one of us in the family is the preservation of the House? You act out of some noble sense of grandeur, you and your brother, when you should be weighing every action in terms of its effects on House Matrell."

As she listened to her uncle's words, Emriana's sorrow and guilt began to transform into anger. She eyed her uncle with disdain, a look he did not fail to notice. She didn't care.

"With you, it's always the House you're worried most about, rather than the people living under its roof. Sometimes, I think you care more for the name itself than those of us who bear it."

Dregaul got a dangerous glitter in his eye then. He raised one eyebrow and asked, "And do you not think the House is more important than the individuals who are a part of it? Do you not see that the whole is greater than the sum of its parts?"

"Not when such an attitude means that everyone who is a part of that whole is reduced to misery and sadness. Do you really care that Grandmother Hetta was wounded tonight? Or are you merely concerned with the damage the attack has done to our reputation?"

Dregaul's slap was so sudden, Emriana didn't even react to it for a second or two. She merely blinked, taking a moment to register that it had, in fact, occurred. She felt her eyes grow wide, and she brought her hand up to feel her cheek.

"Don't you ever speak that way to me again," the man standing in front of Emriana said quietly, coldly. "I ... will ... not ... tolerate it." He stared straight into her eyes, unblinking. "Do you understand me? If you ever do, I will have you beaten."

Dregaul's words shocked Emriana so completely that she didn't even react to them. She merely stared at her uncle, open-mouthed, and tried to make some sense of his threat. He would have her beaten? *Beaten?* Finally, she was about to ask him just who in the Nine Hells he thought he was, but he didn't give her a chance.

"Now, we're going to go back outside to your party and see if we can salvage some of the evening. You are going to walk out there with me, stand quietly by my side, and smile when I say smile," Dregaul instructed his niece. "If you so much as make one wrong face to my guests, I will have house guards take you below. Are we clear?"

Emriana considered arguing, showing Dregaul
how defiant she could be, but at the mention of the
house guards and "below," she knew he was serious,
and he had the wherewithal to follow through with
his threats. The estate had a very seldom-used prison
cell in one of the basements, a dank hole with no light
that had been built "just in case." She'd played down
there a few times, and it had seemed innocent enough
at the time, but standing there in the hall, thinking
of being locked in there and waiting for her uncle to
come discipline her, she shuddered.

Emriana had no one there to defend her. Vambran
had run off, pursuing the intruder. Her mother would
fuss, but ultimately she would not stand in Dregaul's
way—she had never stood up to him in all the years
since Emriana's father died, so why would the girl
expect her to do it right then? And Hetta was in no
condition to do anything, though Emriana was sure
that, eventually, her grandmother would discover her
son's actions and put a stop to them. The question was,
how long would Emriana suffer her uncle's very real
punishments before that happened? As those demor-
alizing thoughts passed through her mind, Emriana
found herself clamping her mouth shut and nodding
in meek agreement with Dregaul.

"Excellent," the man said. "Perhaps we'll find some
usefulness to this evening, after all."

It wasn't until they were already walking out onto
the balcony overlooking the party that Emriana realized Dregaul had referred to the gathering as his
guests, and not hers. She was beginning to get a great
sense of dread as her uncle started to speak.

"Lords and ladies," the man started, once again
motioning for silence from those below. Emriana saw
that the attendance had fallen off somewhat, as a few
of the guests had made haste to depart. Whether for
their own safety at an obviously unsecured estate, or
simply to rush home and begin gossiping with their

neighbors about the attempt on Hetta Matrell's life, Emriana neither knew nor cared. Most remained, though, and she supposed it was out of both courtesy and concern for her grandmother. They closed in around the balcony, murmuring among themselves, waiting for Dregaul to give them some news.

"Lords and ladies," Dregaul repeated, "I am delighted to tell you that my mother is recovering nicely"—there was a genuine cheer of happiness at those words—"and is going to be fine, thanks to some quick action on several people's parts."

The cheers turned into full-blown applause.

Emriana simply watched, feeling stone faced, even though her uncle had ordered her to smile. She simply could not.

"In addition," Dregaul continued once the uproar had died down somewhat, "House Matrell has some very exciting announcements to make. First and foremost, I would like to pass along the news that we are entering into a strategic partnership with two other Houses, beginning immediately. One of the two, House Talricci, is already tied in a familial relationship with us because, as I'm sure you all realize, my oldest nephew Evester is married to Marga Talricci. We are simply formalizing a bond that already exists."

There was more clapping, though this was more polite than genuine enthusiasm. To Emriana, it seemed that the guests were just as confused as she was as to why Dregaul would choose right then to announce such news. Numerous groups of people began whispering behind their hands to one another, occasionally shaking heads.

Sensing that he was losing his audience, Dregaul raised his voice even more as he proceeded.

"And," he said, giving a slight pause to let the crowd quiet a bit, "the third House that will be joining us in our new ventures will be House Pharaboldi—"

Emriana didn't initially hear the rest of Dregaul's speech, for suddenly, she felt that sense of needing to throw up overwhelm her again. She staggered where she stood, the realization of what her uncle was saying racing through her. He was going into business with the Pharaboldis? That was impossible! She and Vambran had all but proven that House Pharaboldi had somehow been responsible for the deaths of two people, and still her uncle wanted to work with them!

Suddenly, it all began to make sense. Dregaul's reluctance for either of them to remain involved in the investigation was driven by the knowledge of who was behind it. Emriana's own uncle was a part of the conspiracy! The business relationship that the high priest had referred to was right there, under her own nose.

The girl felt unsteady on her feet and thought she was going to have to sit down before she fell down. Then she realized that everyone in the audience was clapping and cheering and looking expectantly at her. Except for Denrick, she realized. He was coming up the steps, Dregaul turning to greet him with an outstretched arm, shaking the Pharaboldi heir's hand warmly.

What was happening? Emriana thought, panicking. What had Uncle Dregaul just said? She made herself go back over what her subconscious had heard, recalling the words. When it came to her, Emriana lost her breath.

"In honor of the commitment of these two Houses to work together in a true partnership, and in order to strengthen those ties, we are proud to announce that Emriana Matrell will give her hand in marriage to Denrick Pharaboldi."

...

Vambran wasn't completely aware of the stranger until the other was almost upon the mercenary. The lieutenant had been so preoccupied with carefully observing the buildings across the street that he had failed to keep a watchful eye on the rest of his surroundings. Thus it was more than a little surprising when the red-attired figure suddenly darted under the awning and sat down across from him on the window sill of the pottery merchant's shop. He couldn't see the person's face, for it was draped in cloth so that only the eyes were visible, though in the near-darkness there, he wasn't even certain he could make those out.

Vambran went to draw his sword, but the figure held up both hands, empty, and said, "Before you run me through, I have some information you might want to hear."

It was a woman's voice, and one he knew.

Vambran stilled his hands, shaking then, wrapping his mind around memories that flooded into him after hearing that voice.

"Aunt Xaphira," he breathed, not sure he could trust his ears. "It can't be you."

The woman chuckled softly, sending a shiver down Vambran's spine.

"It can and it is," she replied, reaching up to undo the mask that covered her face.

Even in the shadows, he could see the long, lustrous black hair and the dusky complexion. She stared hard at her nephew for a moment.

"It really is me," Xaphira said, more softly, and she tentatively reached out a hand to her nephew. "I can only imagine what you're feeling right now, and I'm sorry for that. But it was necessary."

For the first several heartbeats, Vambran simply sat there and stared, having a hard time believing his own eyes. Then, drawing a deep and ragged breath, Vambran grabbed her and hugged her, just letting the emotions wash over him. Xaphira hugged him back, and they simply held that for a long moment.

Everything that had happened, all the guilt and
sorrow he'd felt in the intervening years since the
night she'd left, just welled up inside the mercenary,
and he felt twelve years old all over again. It took
him a moment to realize he had tears in his eyes.

Finally, Xaphira pulled away.

"Now," she said, "I know you have questions, but they
have to wait. I'm with Kovrim. He needs to talk to you.
He's hiding on the porch of a shop over on the next block
and around a corner. There are people after him."

"Uncle Kovrim?" Vambran said, stiffening in
alarm and half rising to his feet. "Where is he?
What's the matter?"

The woman held her hands up and gestured for
Vambran to calm down.

"Easy, there. Keep your voice down." As the lieutenant relaxed, she continued, "He's fine. But we all need
to talk. It's urgent."

Vambran nodded and stood.

"Let's go," he said. "Tell me what's happened on
the way."

"He found out what the temple is involved in," Xaphira said, also rising. "He was trying to get to you
to tell you, and they tried to stop him."

"Is it House Pharaboldi?" Vambran asked.

"Yes, among others," Xaphira replied. "There's a
lot more to this than you realize, but now's not the
time. He's still in danger, and we've got to get him
somewhere safe. I tried to talk him into going into
hiding and just letting me tell you, but he refused.
He wants to talk to you himself."

"Who are the other Houses?" Vambran insisted.

"First we go to him. Then you can talk about the
larger problem."

"Who?" the mercenary demanded.

Xaphira sighed again.

"Ours," she answered quietly. "Matrell. And Talricci. They're all three in it together."

"Oh, hells," Vambran muttered. "Uncle Dregaul . . ." Then, realizing he had left Emriana by herself, he swore again. "I've got to go," he said. "They don't know."

"Vambran, wait!" Xaphira begged, grabbing her nephew by the arm. "You can't fight them all by yourself. Kovrim and I can help, but you have to wait for us."

Vambran stood indecisively, knowing the woman was right but feeling a panicky need to race back to the estate. He'd just left Emriana, left all of them. And they didn't have a clue. His desperation was over-whelming him. But he needed allies. With a great effort, he turned back to Xaphira.

"All right," he said. "Let's get him. And we don't stop until we're back at the house."

The two started walking quickly, Xaphira taking furtive looks everywhere as they traveled. She had rewound her mask around her head and drawn up her hood. Vambran kept pace with her easily, though he wondered why she seemed so jumpy. He had a million questions he wanted to ask her.

"Is Kovrim all right?" the mercenary finally asked.

"He is, but only because of some dumb luck. That, and the fact that I was there to help him."

That relieved Vambran—for a moment.

"Wait!" he said, stopping in the middle of the darkened street. "I know you've been following me since I got back into the city. It was you at the wagon yard, and again last night at the warehouse. But why? You've known something was going on for a while, now."

Xaphira raised her hands and again gestured for her nephew to calm down.

"Keep your voice down," she said, reaching out and taking his hands in her own. "Yes, I have, but I couldn't risk revealing myself too soon. There's so much more going on here, Vambran. I want to tell it all to you, but you've got to trust me that now is not the time for all this. Come on."

They continued on, keeping their pace quick without actually running. When they reached the porch where Xaphira had left Kovrim, he wasn't there.

"Now, where did he get to?" Xaphira murmured, peering in both directions. "He promised me he would stay right here and wait for me."

"Something happened," Vambran said, the panic rising again. "The men who were after him must have discovered him. We've got to find him." The mercenary struggled to keep a clear head. He was torn with fear for both his uncle and the rest of his family. He hated that he was being forced to choose who to rescue first.

"Listen," Xaphira said. Vambran cocked his head, holding perfectly still. There was a shout, muffled but distinct enough that he could tell it was coming from the alley behind the shop.

"Come on," Xaphira and Vambran both said at the same time, jumping off the porch and rushing down the street toward the corner. The pair of them raced around to the back and into the alley.

Kovrim was there, surrounded by perhaps a dozen men. Several of them were pointing crossbows at the priest.

CHAPTER TWELVE

I can't believe he would do this to me!" Emriana sobbed, her face buried in her pillows. "He never even talked to me about it!"

Jaleene sat beside her charge, gently stroking her hair and trying to soothe the girl with soft sounds.

"Your grandmother would never let this happen," the handmaiden said. "When she finds out, she'll put a stop to it."

Emriana sniffed and said, "Grandmother Hetta doesn't seem to know what's going on."

The thought occurred to her then that perhaps her grandmother was in agreement with Dregaul, that the two of them had made the decision together that she should marry Denrick. As ridiculous as that seemed, especially after the conversation the girl had had with the elderly woman only two short days

before, the notion left a cold hole in the middle of her
stomach. She began sobbing again, feeling like her
world was crashing down around her.

When Emriana had first pieced together what her
uncle had announced, she didn't believe it. She didn't
think that she was remembering correctly. But there
was Denrick, climbing the steps and greeting Dregaul
warmly, that sickly wolfish smile on his face. And she
knew. In her heart, she realized that Uncle Dregaul
had sealed the business relationship with her life. He
had promised Denrick that the boy could have her, as
though she were some prized horse or plot of land. And
she understood, too, then, in that terrible moment of
realization, that Jithelle Skolotti had been slain, had
been murdered with Denrick's unborn child in her
womb, because the heir to House Pharaboldi was to
wed Emriana. The poor servant girl had died because
Emriana Matrell was waiting in the wings. It made
her physically sick.

She ran, then, turned and fled the balcony, dashing past both Dregaul and Denrick, who looked on
with a mixture of surprise and amusement. Dregaul
called to Emriana, shouted at her, demanded that
she return and show proper deference, or some such
nonsense, but she ignored him and ran, all the way
back to her rooms.

Jaleene had arrived a few moments later, having
been a witness to the whole thing, and was trying to
calm her.

"Hush, Em," the woman soothed. "It's going to be
all right."

Emriana sat up and looked at her companion.

"How can you say that?" she wailed softly, her
eyes burning with tears. "They killed that poor girl
because of me. Uncle Dregaul probably knew about
it. He probably insisted on it before he would agree
to the merger. What am I going to do? He's already
planned my future for me, with that, that—"

"That what?" came a voice from the doorway to the balcony. It was Denrick, standing there looking in, a faint smile on his face. "What am I?" he asked.

Emriana physically recoiled from the boy, even though he was halfway across the room leaning casually against the frame of the door.

Jaleene got up and moved to stand between the intruder and her charge.

"You shouldn't be here," the handmaiden said, her hands on her hips. "It's not proper to visit a young lady in her private chambers. Leave now, or I'll call the house guards to remove you."

Denrick simply chuckled, making no move to go in either direction.

"Will you, now?" he said. "And do you think they'll respond to you, a servant, when the man they actually answer to is of a far different mind? I've already been told that I was welcome to come up here and visit my fiancée, and that is exactly what I've done. No house guard is going to throw me out, I can assure you."

"Don't you talk to her that way," Emriana said, rising from the bed to stand beside her handmaiden. "You might treat your own servants like dirt, but you will not do so here."

Denrick laughed again.

"You're still convinced I did something to Jithelle, aren't you? Well, my dear, I'm sorry to disappoint you, but I did no such thing." He took a step into the room, interlacing his fingers and thrusting them out, palms downward, to crack his knuckles. "She was a comely one, and I'll admit only to having a weakness for falling into her wonderful eyes and a need to nestle against her other womanly charms from time to time. But that was the extent of it."

"You sorry bastard," Emriana sneered. "The sorrow by the cistern was just an act, wasn't it? You didn't feel anything about her loss, or the fact that she carried your baby."

Denrick smirked.

"She was a diversion, that was all," he admitted. "A man of my tastes has a variety of needs, and she fit some of them nicely, but that was all it was, and all it would ever be. If she believed there would be more to it, that was her mistake, not mine."

Emriana glowered at the pompous man, but he ignored her and continued, "As for the child, I truly did not know about it." A brief grimace passed over his face, but it faded again just as quickly. "But no matter; I'm sure you'll provide me with plenty of children to dandle from my knees," he finished, taking another step into the room.

"I will never lie with you," Emriana snarled. "You can lust for me all you want, but it will never happen."

At nearly the same time, Jaleene stalked forward, with the obvious intention of physically pushing Denrick back out through the door.

"I told you," she said, planting her hands against his chest and shoving, "that it is not proper for you to be here. Now leave, or I—"

Denrick swung a fist up, smacking the servant hard with the back of his hand. The blow snapped Jaleene's head around, and with a grunt, she stumbled backward and tumbled to the floor, sprawling full out. She moaned once softly and lay still.

"Don't ever lay a hand on me again," Denrick said coldly, walking to loom over her. "You need to learn to remember your place."

Emriana gave an animal cry and lunged forward to punch at the callous, hateful man, but Denrick was ready for her, bringing his arm up to ward off the blow, then reaching out and grasping her by her wrists. He jerked her around, twisting both of her arms up behind her back, and walked her forward, toward the bed.

In a flash of realization, Emriana came to understand that he was leading her toward a bed, and

the images of what he would do to her there began
to cascade through her mind's eye. She panicked,
fighting for all she was worth, digging her heels in
and trying to jerk her arms free. In her desperation,
Emriana managed to slam the heel of one of her
boots against the man's shin. He yelped in surprise
and released her.

The girl darted away, thinking to charge out the
door, but Denrick was too fast, and he cut her off, forcing her to turn away from him or be caught again.
She angled away, looking to double back around, but
Denrick simply sidestepped several times, slowly
working her into a corner.

"There's no place to run," the man said, settling
into a position facing Emriana, keeping her pinned
in the corner of the room. "And this time, you don't
have a cistern or your fool brother here to protect
you."

Emriana glanced furtively around, looking for a
means of escape, or a weapon with which to defend
herself, but there was nothing. She glared at the
man, hoping her fiery gaze made it clear that she
would not go down easily, and he would be better
served to find some other woman with whom to
dally. In her heart, though, she feared that it was
only a matter of time. She stole a quick look toward
Jaleene, but her only ally at the moment was out
cold.

"If you touch me, I'll tear your eyes out," Emriana
warned the predator in front of her. "You think you
had problems before, trying to figure out what to do
with Jithelle, but you don't know the half of it, if you
get any closer to me."

Denrick smiled that wolfish grin.

"I have no doubt at all that you mean what you
say, and that you could probably back it up, too. But
why all the fuss? I wasn't kidding before, when I told
you by the cistern that I could delight you. No woman

yet has shied away from me, once she's felt my touch.
I doubt you'll be any different, if you'll just let down
your guard and see what you're missing."

"You unbelievable, smug bastard!" Emriana said,
shaking her head in scorn. "You think you can turn
me to your side just by your touch? How arrogant can
one man be?"

Anger flashed in Denrick's eyes, then.

"Watch your tongue, Em. I won't tolerate that kind
of attitude from my wife."

Emriana's jaw dropped.

"Your *wife!* Do you honestly think this marriage is
going to happen? You're delusional. My grandmother
is going to put a stop to this as soon as she—"

"Your grandmother is on the verge falling into her
grave," Denrick interrupted. "She's in no condition
to do anything about any of this. Now quit stalling,
Emriana, and accept the fact that you are going to be
my wife, and you are going to serve me dutifully, in
any capacity I wish. The sooner you get used to that
idea, the better off you'll be."

Emriana snarled, lunging left and darting back to
the right, running as fast as she could for the door.

She almost made it, too, but Denrick was just a
half-step faster. He dived for her and got a hand in her
dress—the damned dress!—and tripped her up enough
that she went sprawling. She scrambled desperately
forward, opening her mouth to scream for help, but
then someone was standing in the doorway. As Denrick grabbed at her and sat on her to keep her still,
Emriana craned her neck, hoping it was Vambran.
Instead, it was a Matrell house guard, and he was
leering down at what was taking place.

"Help me," Emriana pleaded at the man, expecting
him to come to her rescue.

Surely, no matter what Uncle Dregaul might be
planning, it didn't include her being ravaged against
her will.

"So?" the guard asked, smiling unpleasantly. "You finally figured out a way to keep her from sneaking off, huh?"

Denrick chuckled as he began to wrap something tightly around Emriana's wrists, tying them together behind her back.

...

Bartimus sat quietly in the corner to one side of Grozier Talricci's chair. His employer and the other heads of the three Houses were gathered together in an inner room, a study with a beautiful atrium along one side, discussing some of the business details of the impending merger. The wizard wasn't really listening closely, for the details were not important to him. Nor, for that matter, was any of that his responsibility. He had been brought there solely to keep an eye on everyone else, while Grozier concentrated on the financial aspects.

Bartimus studied each of the other three people in turn, observing their mannerisms, their speech, and the looks in their eyes, for he knew that it would be through those things that he could determine if any of them were nervous or unsure about what was taking place. Those telltale signs were the clues he was responsible for spotting, so that he could warn his employer if there were any potential surprises ahead.

Thus far, Anista Pharaboldi seemed perfectly at ease, but Dregaul Matrell was agitated over the attack on his mother. Bartimus would have thought that the man would have been pleased to see the matriarch of the household, a potential thorn in their sides, eliminated, but instead, the man seemed to be concerned about it all.

Bartimus couldn't say he blamed Dregaul. The whole affair of the servant girl's pregnancy and the ensuing chaos had left everyone on edge. Grozier certainly hadn't wanted to take such extreme measures to deal with the unfortunate discovery by Vambran Matrell of the servant's elimination, but the persistent mercenary officer had left them with little choice. It was even more unfortunate that Vambran was a member of one of the Houses involved, as that created still more problems. Indeed, Bartimus didn't really consider the whole affair settled. Vambran would have to be once and for all permanently removed from the middle of things before the issue was closed.

In the meantime, though, Grozier and the other two needed to move forward on the facets of the deal that really mattered. They had to begin planning how to invest their pooled resources, to get the army they were going to buy early enough in the season that they could get a full summer campaign out of it. Any mercenary bands they still employed in the fall would continue to be able to conduct the business of warfare, of course, but it was a much dicier proposition then. The weather was less likely to cooperate, and cash flow would certainly be a larger problem, as most of the summer trade boom would be past them. There was no more time to delay getting the merger going, regardless of the potential problems looming on the periphery.

The wizard realized he was letting his mind wander and he wasn't watching Grozier's counterparts as well as he should be. He mentally smacked himself for getting distracted and refocused. Dregaul was arguing some point about profit splits, and how much should be reinvested back into the effort, while Anista was suggesting that they diversify those earnings into some war-related businesses that could, in turn, cut costs down the road. Grozier was shaking his head at both of them, trying to get them to understand that there would probably not be much revenue in the first two years.

"The costs of conducting the conquest are going to increase as time goes by," the head of House Talricci explained. "You have to take into account the lengthening of supply lines."

"Ah," Anista said, frowning.

"Why?" Dregaul demanded, seeming to grow upset at that notion. "What drives the cost up?"

Grozier sighed and said, "Because, as I explained before, it gets longer. Either that, or we build a waystation at some point closer to the front and deliver the supplies there ourselves."

"Yes, let's plan to do that," Dregaul said, nodding. "Between us, we have the subsidiaries needed to get that done less expensively, anyway, which of course puts more funds back into our war chest."

"Remember, though," Grozier said, "that a full waystation could be sacked or taken over by the enemy. If that happens, it sets us farther back than if we just pony up the extra coin for lengthening supply lines."

"Hmm, good point," Dregaul said, frowning again.

"That doesn't leave us very much play in the numbers, then," Anista Pharaboldi said, scribbling something on a piece of parchment in front of her. "We'll be running a shortfall for at least—"

The door to the room slammed open, and Hetta Matrell strode inside. The look on her face told Bartimus she was ready to chew through steel, she was so angry. The other three individuals in the room jumped slightly at the sound of the door banging against the wall, Dregaul most of all. Bartimus, however, subtly slipped a hand in his pocket, ready to wield a little magic in his employer's defense, should it come to that.

"Dregaul Matrell," the elderly woman said, "this travesty of a business decision you've made has seen its last day."

Bartimus could see then that she was accompanied by another woman whom the wizard did not know, as well as two house guards.

"Mother, what are you doing here?" Dregaul demanded, turning in his chair, a concerned look on his face. "You should be resting."

"I have no intention of resting while my son is bringing my House down around all of our ears," the elderly woman said. "I would think, after all these years, that you would have figured out by now that I can tell when you're up to something. Did you really think I would approve of such shaky business tactics? Worse yet, did you really think I would allow you to mortgage our finances to their limit so that you could start a war?"

"Mother, the upside to this venture is going to make us ten times the size we are now. When we're finished, we'll be considered up there with the really big Houses. House Matrell will stand tall in Arrabar."

Bartimus looked to Grozier, waiting for some sort of signal that the man would like him to act. For the moment, though, Grozier seemed to be listening intently on the argument in front of him.

"No, Dregaul. I'm sorry. You are not going through with this. I am still the head of this household, and I still have final say on what business ventures House Matrell enters into. I truly am sorry," and she turned first to Anista, then to Grozier, "but the deal is off the table. House Matrell won't be a party to an invasion of another city for profit."

"I'm afraid it's a little too late for that," Grozier replied. "Armies are already hired, marching orders have already been given. Things are in motion now, and not so easily stopped."

Hetta Matrell drew herself up to her full height, then, straightening shoulders that had not always been stooped.

"Then you will just have to find the way to stop these 'things,' or else find other business partners to replace your lost revenue. But you cannot have ours."

"Mother! That's enough!" Dregaul seethed, rising from his chair to fully face Hetta. "You're past your prime, Mother, and I'm sorry to say it, but you no longer have the clarity of thought to see that this merger is important—important!—to our future as a player in Arrabar's most prestigious financial arenas. I think it's time you officially stepped down and handed the reins completely over to me, Mother."

Hetta actually began to laugh then, shaking her head. She had to put a hand out to the other woman for support at one point, until she could get her breath back. Her chuckles only served to anger Dregaul, though, who drew his lips tight and grimaced until her mirth had subsided.

"I should have yanked full control of House Matrell back from you a long time ago," the matriarch said at last. "I could see you had no good understanding of what your father and I had tried to build here, but I kept holding off, thinking perhaps you'd finally figure it out. Sadly, I was wrong."

"And what was that?" Dregaul asked hotly. "What were you and Father trying to build? A second-rate, copper-and-silver operation? Because that's what we got. Hesta, Obril, Xaphira, and I got to grow up being the laughingstock merchant clan. House Matrell was nothing. All the other Houses turned their noses up at us, led by the bastard of House Mestel. Our own kin wouldn't even give us the time of day!

"And now, when I have a chance to do something truly remarkable, to finally let House Matrell make a respected name for itself in all the right circles, you come along and try to ruin it. I don't understand you. Don't you want to leave your mark? Don't you want to go to your grave knowing House Matrell was bigger than when you started it?"

Hetta was shaking her head, obviously hurt and saddened by her son's words. But she stood firm.

"Clawing our way to the top of the heap was never what this family was about, and I'm sorry I didn't do a better job of teaching you that, my son. But the time for lessons is past. I hereby remove from you all responsibility regarding this family's business interests and resume full control of them myself." She half-turned to the pair of guards behind her. "If he will not get up from that table quietly, remove him by force and lock him in the cell in the basement. Then come see me.

"As for the rest of you, I'm sorry it has come to this. I must respectfully ask you to take the remainder of your meeting somewhere else."

With that, Hetta turned and began to exit.

The two guards didn't move.

"I'm sorry, Madam Matrell, but it isn't quite going to work out like that," one of them said. "Please, go back into the room."

...

"Well, I'm glad we finally got a chance to gather for this meeting," one of the thugs surrounding Kovrim said with a laugh. "I've been waiting for this for quite a while." He motioned toward Vambran and Xaphira. "Come on over. Join our little party."

Vambran approached cautiously, freeing his crossbow from the hook on his belt and cocking it in one smooth motion. Xaphira fanned out to the opposite side of the alley, staying even with Vambran but not too close, giving them both room to fight.

"Oh, now, that's not very sociable," the man said in response to Vambran loading his weapon. "You really might want to rethink that. Someone could get hurt."

Vambran could see then that his uncle was unarmed, standing in the midst of the men with his arms stretched out to his sides, as though he had already surrendered to them.

"Uncle Kovrim? You all right?"

Before the priest could answer, the man who'd been acting as spokesman for the rest of the group responded, "Of course he's all right. We haven't harmed a hair on his balding head. Yet." The thug turned and leveled his crossbow at Vambran. "But that might change very soon, if you don't see reason and lay down your weapon."

Vambran halted his advance and studied his opponent, considering. If he gave in to the demand, Kovrim would almost certainly die. The men had no doubt been ordered to hunt him down and prevent him from sharing the information he had with anyone else. But if the lieutenant and his aunt decided to fight it out with them, Kovrim would likely fall within the first moments of the battle anyway. Either choice seemed like a bad proposition for the mercenary's mentor. Vambran chose to stall.

"It's too late," he said, hoping to bluff the thug. "I already know the news. Even as we speak, the alliance of the three Houses is being dissolved. The fight is already over; you just don't know it yet."

The lead thug laughed and said, "That's a pretty good story, my friend, but sadly, I recognize a lie when I hear one. I would know if something was going wrong back at your estate. I'd have heard about such events as quickly as they occurred."

Vambran knew it was a possibility that the fellow was in some sort of magical communication with his employers, but he'd hoped for the outside chance that he wasn't. Still, Vambran refused to diminish any of his family's chances by acting hastily.

"Maybe your lord just can't think straight," said Vambran. "Maybe he got caught so unaware that he never had the chance to warn you."

"Sort of like how I caught you and your grandmother unaware earlier tonight?" the thug responded.

Vambran's eyes narrowed, and his jaw jutted out in anger.

"You," was all he said.

"Me," the thug replied. "It's so easy to assassinate someone when you have the house guards on your side. They just let me through, easy as you please."

Vambran raised his crossbow, sighting down it at the thug, who raised his eyebrows.

"Careful, boy, you might accidentally shoot someone important," the thug said, smiling knowingly. "Wouldn't want that to happen again, would we?"

Off to his right, the lieutenant heard Xaphira gasp softly, but then she said, "Vambran, don't be a fool."

The mercenary only stood there, looking past the fletching of the bolt at the thug who had shot his grandmother, wondering how the man before him might know his secret. He could barely restrain himself from firing.

"You think you can hit me somewhere that will keep me from shooting back?" The thug asked, aiming his own crossbow. "We just might kill each other, but then, where would that leave your uncle?"

"I will see your blood on the cobblestones tonight, one way or another," Vambran said menacingly, but he lowered the weapon.

Pulling the bolt free, he set the crossbow itself down on the street and shoved it away with his foot. Then he slipped his sword free and let it fall, too. Finally, with the bolt in his hand, he took a few steps closer to the thug, his arms out to his sides, showing that he was unarmed.

"You're smarter than I was led to believe," the thug said. "Maybe I'll let you live, give you a chance to work for me," he added, smiling. "But then, you already did. You just don't know it."

He recentered Vambran in his sights.

At that moment, a mist began to rise from the street, much to the surprise and dismay of the thugs gathered in a cluster near Kovrim. Their shouts distracted their leader enough to cause him to turn around to see what the fuss was about. At the same instant, Vambran brought his crossbow bolt up so that it rested freely atop his open palm, with him looking down its length at his opponent. He spoke a quick phrase, enchanting the bolt with arcane dweomers. The bolt flew from his hand, straight toward the leader, just as he was turning around again.

The thug must have had cat's blood running in his veins, for he somehow managed to shift his weight enough at the last possible moment, so that the bolt struck him in the arm rather than squarely in the chest. As the thug reeled from the blow, staggering wide-eyed back a step, he reflexively pulled the trigger on his own crossbow, letting the missile fly. Vambran had anticipated the possibility and slid off to the side, but he'd guessed wrong, turning into the wild shot rather than away from it. The bolt struck him in the shoulder, just below the edge of his armor, sinking into his flesh.

The mercenary cried out, dropping to one knee from the pain. He looked over at the leader and saw that the man had dropped as well, clutching at his own arm. Behind him, there were shouts of confusion and pain, but the other thugs were enveloped in a thick mist that engulfed them completely. Vambran could see nothing. He took a deep breath and rose to both feet again, reaching down with his good arm to retrieve his sword. He grasped it and walked with a purpose over to the wounded leader, who was warily watching him approach.

"I told you," Vambran said, raising high his blade, "that I would see your blood spilled tonight. Too bad you didn't listen." The mercenary officer loomed over his foe, his eyes narrowed dangerously. "Who told you about it?" he demanded.

The thug laughed and said, "No one, foolish boy. I watched it with my own eyes."

Vambran snarled in fury and swung his sword down, aiming for the thug's neck, but at that moment, the man uttered some arcane phrase and simply vanished before Vambran's eyes. The mercenary's blade sliced through thin air.

"Damnation!" the lieutenant screamed, spinning around, trying to see where his would-be opponent had fled.

There was no sign of the man.

At that point, another one of the thugs staggered out of the obscuring vapors and, seeing Vambran, the man hefted his own sword and came at the mercenary. Growling, Vambran turned to fight. As they danced on the cobblestones, the lieutenant tried to ignore the throbbing pain in his shoulder where the bolt still protruded. Several times, the thug lunged in toward that side, perhaps hoping to force Vambran to jerk back out of the way and cause himself pain. On the third such lunge, though, Vambran was ready for it and spun completely around so that he ended up behind the thug, slashing into the small of the man's back with his own blade. Vambran's foe cried out in pain and fell to the street.

Vambran was already turning to look for another opponent to vent his anger on, noticing then that the misty vapors had begun to dissipate, drifting away with the perpetual breezes that blew through Arrabar. The lieutenant could see more figures, many of them surrounding Kovrim, who had summoned a cloud of coins with which to fight. Kovrim kept the glowing, incorporeal weapons dancing before himself, using them exclusively defensively. Vambran also noticed that Xaphira had managed to slip inside the circle of thugs and was standing back to back with

Kovrim, using only her hands and feet to keep the
approaching thugs at bay. Several of the attackers
were lying about the alley, some of them still, others
moaning in pain. Six or seven still stood, though, and
they seemed to have gotten the idea that if they timed
their attacks to occur simultaneously they might get
inside the pair's defenses.

Vambran was just squaring himself to jump in and
attack one or more of the thugs from behind when he
heard a shout from the opposite direction. Turning, he
spotted a host of men at the mouth of the alley running
toward him. He groaned, thinking at first that those
were reinforcements for the thugs, sent to come in from
behind him and keep him from escaping. But then, he
got a better look at the soldiers' markings and saw that
they were members of the Sapphire Crescent.

Most of the mercenaries rushed past him, crashing
into the remaining thugs who, realizing they were
outnumbered by a sizable margin then, turned and
fled. Vambran doubted any of them would reach the
far end of the alley.

Two of the mercenaries pulled up short, though,
stopping to face Vambran and salute him.

"Looks like you needed a bit of help, sir," Adyan
drawled, that scar on his chin glowing in the moonlight. "Glad we happened to hear your scuffle."

"We've been sent to bring you back to the temple,"
Horial added, a smirk on his face. "I couldn't think
of a better reason to gather the platoon and come see
if you needed some assistance."

Vambran looked back and forth between the two
men and started to laugh.

"Well met," he said, offering his hand. "Well
met!"

CHAPTER THIRTEEN

Emriana continued to tug against the strips of cloth that Denrick had used to bind her into one of the high-backed chairs in her own room. He'd torn them from her dress, which lay in a discarded heap on the floor nearby. Wearing only her chemise, she glared at the young man, who was sitting on the edge of her bed, watching her with a glare of his own and rubbing a spot on his forearm where she'd managed to bite him. That was before he'd wedged a thick knot of more cloth into her mouth and tied it in place with yet another strip. So she was confined to the chair, her legs and arms strapped down. Denrick had managed it with the guard's help, of course.

"That wasn't very nice," Denrick grumbled, examining his wound.

Emriana had barely broken the skin, but watching her captor fuss over the flesh wound gave her some small level of satisfaction. She glanced over to where Jaleene sat next to her, tied to another chair in a similar fashion. The handmaiden's eyes were wide with fear, and she'd said nothing since awakening. Emriana pitied the woman a bit, but not so much that she had forgotten to be afraid for her own well-being.

Despite her bravado, Emriana knew that she was helpless against whatever Denrick ultimately wanted to do to her, and his intentions seemed pretty clear as he studied her, that wolfish grin slowly returning. She desperately wished the dress were still on, no matter that it had been a rather uncomfortable thing to wear. She refused to let her fear show through, though, and kept her malevolent gaze right on his face the entire time.

Denrick stood up and began to pace back and forth in front of the two women. He placed his hands behind his back as he did, as though deep in contemplative thought. He began to speak.

"If this marriage is going to work at all, we're going to have to establish some ground rules. You know, some guidelines by which you can keep from getting into trouble, which you most definitely are in right now."

Emriana simply snorted through her gag, showing what she thought of the older boy's guidelines.

"Deride them if you want, but at your own peril," Denrick said. "For I might begin to grow tired of you if this foolish resistance keeps up for much longer. I had hoped for a more amicable marriage, but I will take what I need from you less amicably, if necessary."

The girl lowered her eyes for the briefest of moments at Denrick's not-so-veiled threats, feeling her heart pound. He seemed perfectly capable of following through with sating his despicable lust. She could see it in his eyes. The look had always been there, had always been a part of Denrick Pharaboldi's visage, for as long as she'd known him, and it was what was always so off-putting about the man. Emriana had just never realized what it truly signified until just then.

"So, whether you begin to recognize the value in making me happy, or I have to extract my enjoyment from you the hard way, I will get my satisfaction from you. It was promised to me from the start of this little venture, and I will have you."

Thinking of her uncle negotiating with such a man and using her body as part of the offer incensed Emriana. She began to thrash, jerking on the strips of cloth that pinned her to the chair, grunting in fury and desperation. Her rage washed over her, and she wanted nothing more right at that moment than to lunge at the glowering, smirking cretin and scratch out his eyes. She wanted to ram her knee up between his legs as hard as she could. She wanted to cry.

"Excuse me, Master Pharaboldi," came a voice at the door to Emriana's rooms.

Denrick spun around with a sigh of exasperation.

"What is it, Bartimus?" he asked, impatient.

The man standing there was slightly paunchy, with a round face and a flat nose on the end of which sat a pair of spectacles. The man's hair was sort of greasy and white. He seemed to be working very hard to be ingratiating to Denrick, for he wore a silly grin, but at the same time he appeared distracted, as though he was thinking of something completely separate from the discussion at hand.

"Master Talricci and Master Matrell have finished dealing with everyone else at the meeting. And the house is secure."

"Excellent," Denrick said, nodding. "And my mother?"

"She is waiting with the others. Master Talricci would like to know if you want to deal with her yourself."

"Hmm," Denrick said, thinking. "Yes, I suppose I owe her that. All right, tell them I'll be right up to explain things to her."

"Of course," the man named Bartimus said, then he turned and ambled off.

Denrick came back around to face Emriana.

"Well, I guess you've earned yourself a short reprieve. If I were you, I would spend it giving careful consideration to the repercussions of continuing to defy me. My patience is growing thin, and you must realize that, sooner or later, I will get what I want. You might as well make it easy on yourself and not anger me further."

He spun on his heel and left the room, walking confidently and quickly out the door.

As soon as their tormentor was gone, Jaleene burst into tears.

"Oh, Mistress Emriana, I'm so sorry! He's a wretched man, but you mustn't be afraid. He'll do what he's going to do and be finished, and it's only one moment. Don't fight him and make him angry, Em. Just let him finish and he'll leave us alone."

Like hell I will, the girl thought, and she screamed through her gag as loudly as she could, forcing Jaleene to stop her chattering. The handmaiden looked at Emriana, her eyes wide with fear.

"Mmph," the girl vocalized, then jerked her head down toward her arm, which was bound by the cloth.

"What is it?" Jaleene asked. "What do you want me to do?"

"Mmph!" Emriana yelled, rolling her eyes.

She gave her companion a look of patience and, taking a deep breath, she began to rock her chair from side to side. Jaleene watched her, confusion still obvious in her visage, but Emriana had to concentrate on her own movements. Slowly, steadily, she got a rhythm going, making the chair tip just the slightest bit each time she shifted her weight. As she worked, she made the rocking grow a little with each pass, until soon she was riding up on two legs each time, making the chair lean way over from side to side.

Finally, Emriana threw her weight as hard as she could toward Jaleene, causing the chair to tip once more, hanging in the air on two legs, and her center of balance shifted enough. The chair continued over, and it would have fallen completely sideways, had it not come to rest against Jaleene's chair. Emriana's hand and Jaleene's were close enough that they could touch.

"Mmph!" Emriana said, reaching for Jaleene's wrist.

She didn't have a lot of room to work, as her own arm was lower than her handmaiden's, but she had enough play in her bonds that she could begin to work on the knot that held Jaleene immobile. Desperately, ignoring the ache growing in her fingers, Emriana pulled at the knot, trying to loosen it and free the woman. At first, the tie wouldn't budge at all. The girl delivered a number of frustrated grunts and moans as she worked on it. Then, slowly, she began to feel some progress. Frantically, sensing that at any moment Denrick could return, she jerked at the knot, feeling it slip little by little. Suddenly, Jaleene was able to slip her arm free.

"Oh, thank goodness!" the woman said, reaching over to untie her other hand. "If Waukeen is with us, perhaps we can slip out through the porch and into the garden. You'll have to show me how to sneak, of course, but—"

"Mmph!" Emriana screamed in exasperation, wanting Jaleene to stop her prattling and pay attention. "Mmph," she repeated, wiggling her own arm.

Please, she thought, free me first.

Jaleene stared at Emriana like the girl was being intractable.

"Yes, of course I'll untie you next. I'm not going to leave you, you know."

Emriana rolled her eyes and gave the best exasperated sigh she possibly could with a gag wedged into her teeth.

"Mmph!" she ordered, wiggling her arm again.

"Oh, all right, don't get into a snit," Jaleene grumbled, reaching over and working on Emriana's knot. "I thought it would be better to get me completely free, first, so I could perhaps get away and get help if he came back before both of us were undone, but goodness gracious, you still act like the spoiled child sometimes."

As soon as Emriana was able, she jerked her arm free and reached up to tug the sour-tasting gag out of her mouth.

"Hush," was all she said as she took hold of the opal pendant Vambran had given her.

Closing her eyes and concentrating, she envisioned her brother's face and, when it was clear in her mind, she felt a stronger connection between herself and the mercenary.

"Vambran, help me! Denrick has taken us prisoner! They have the house guards on their side. Jaleene and I are tied up in my rooms—" and the connection shifted somehow, and Emriana knew that the rest of her plea was not getting through.

Almost immediately, though, she heard her brother's voice, as though he was sitting beside her, talking to her in a soft tone.

Hang on, Em. We're coming. Stay strong.

And that was it.

Except that it wasn't. Just as Emriana was letting go of the stone and trying to start untying her other arm, Denrick returned.

"Hey!" he shouted, seeing that his prisoners were about to get free. He charged across the room as Emriana and Jaleene both struggled frantically to jerk free of the last bonds. He was by far the quicker. Grabbing at Emriana's free wrist in his painfully strong grip, Denrick jerked her hand away from the knot she'd been struggling with and pinned it down against the chair arm again, righting the seat in the process. Then he got his face right down in hers.

"I warned you," he said. "You just won't listen. If you're not careful, I'll let them do to you what I had them do to Jithelle."

Emriana swallowed hard as she tried to lean back, away from her captor's vicious gaze. His eyes told her he was not lying.

...

"I was afraid you wouldn't be able to find me if I left the porch," Kovrim explained as the entire group of people, including the platoon of mercenaries from the Sapphire Crescent, headed closer to the Matrell estate. "But I didn't see any choice. Those were some of Grozier Talricci's men, and they were sniffing me out pretty well."

"Well, we did find you," Xaphira said, "and Vambran here is going to get us inside the estate, right?"

Vambran nodded grimly. Having heard Kovrim's full tale—Houses Matrell, Talricci, and Pharaboldi were all pooling their resources to fund a professional army and launch an attack on one of the other city-states in old Chondath—he was more fretful than ever about getting back to their family. If Dregaul was actively courting the other two Houses, that meant he was aware of a great many things that he hadn't been letting on. And the fact that Grand Trab-bar Lavant was keeping the whole alliance a secret seemed to suggest that not everything was on the up and up, which Vambran obviously already knew. It was then just a matter of how hard the heads of the three Houses were going to work to keep everything quiet. How many more deaths would there be before all was said and done?

At the same time, the thug leader's cryptic words and maddening disappearance were also weighing heavily on the lieutenant's mind.

How could he know about it? Vambran wondered. And what did he mean about already working for him?

The thought gave Vambran a cold sensation in the pit of his stomach.

"Vambran," Xaphira said. "Are you listening to us?"

"Hmm?" the mercenary said, coming out of his thoughts. "I'm sorry, I was thinking. What did you ask me?"

"We were just discussing the fact that we don't really know the state of things at the house," Kovrim said. "It might behoove us to let you go in first, playing innocent, and see just what's happening."

"No. Remember," the lieutenant replied, "the leader back there admitted that the three heads of the households were gathering to seal the deal. And with his escape, I fear we may be too late to—"

Vambran, help me! Denrick has taken us prisoner! They have the house guards on their side. Jaleene and I are tied up in my rooms—

Vambran nearly stumbled as the words echoed in his mind.

"Hang on, Em. We're coming. Stay strong," he replied. To all the puzzled faces around him, he said in a tight voice, "All hell's broken loose. Em's been taken captive by Denrick Pharaboldi. The house guards have been turned. Dregaul may be part of it. We have to hurry."

And he took off in a near sprint.

"Vambran, wait!" Xaphira called from behind. "Now, more than ever, we need a plan."

When he wouldn't stop, she called after him, "If you just go barging in there without knowing what's going on first, you're only going to risk their lives."

The mercenary officer closed his eyes and grimaced as he slowed his pace. He knew his aunt was right. He just couldn't stand the thought of delaying any longer. He stopped in the middle of the street and hugged his own arms, bending over and breathing hard, trying to regain some composure.

If only I hadn't run off, he berated himself. If only I had stuck around long enough to get a better read on Denrick. Damn it!

He mentally screamed, punching at the air in frustration and pacing around in a circle.

The rest of Vambran's companions caught up to him. Xaphira took him by the shoulders, forcing him to stop pacing and look at her.

"Stop blaming yourself," she told him, looking him directly in the eyes. "You have done everything possible to fight this, and now, whether you realize it or not, you're in a better position to put a final stop to it once and for all."

"This is where your military training must come to the forefront," Kovrim said. "Now is the time to put your skills and resources to work. We can surprise them, but only if we keep our heads."

"They don't know we're coming," Horial said as he and Adyan gathered in with the rest of them. "They think only you're likely to come back."

"Assuming they don't know I defeated the thugs that were after Uncle Kovrim," Vambran argued. "The leader got away and could easily warn them, and he said that he had some sort of mental connection with his superior, that he would have known if something was going wrong at the estate. That link very well could have worked both ways."

"Maybe," said Xaphira, "but he vanished before the Sapphire Crescent showed up. So even if the conspirators know that the three of us might be on our way, they still don't know that the platoon is coming, too. We've got to use that to our advantage."

Vambran considered their words, looking for anything he could anchor his emotions to and find some calm. He realized they were right. They had the element of surprise, but they had to make sure they could use it correctly. What they needed, he decided, was some on-the-sly scouting.

"We've got to get a peek inside the house, and maybe around the grounds, and see just how bad it really is," the lieutenant said.

"I can do that," Xaphira said. "Since I know the place, I can scout everything out without the chance of getting lost or cornered if something goes wrong."

Kovrim nodded and said, "All right. But I have another idea that might help. Xaphira can look for a way to get me and the mercenaries inside the walls without being seen. In the meantime, Vambran, since you would like very much to get up there now and check on your family, especially Em, let me do something that will get you there quickly and without notice."

Vambran was all for it and readily agreed.

As the group neared the Matrell estate, they finalized their plan. Kovrim began to pray, taking a talisman out of his robes and clasping it tightly as he closed his eyes. He uttered the words of a sacred prayer to Waukeen, then touched Vambran. When Kovrim opened his eyes, he looked at his nephew.

"You now have the ability to walk on the air," the priest said, gesturing for Vambran to try it. "Just imagine that you're walking up a steep hill, planting your feet on the air in front of you."

Vambran took a tentative step forward, trying to visualize himself following a sloping path upward. His foot settled solidly on something invisible maybe two feet off the ground. The mercenary took another

step, and another, and suddenly, he was standing at a
level higher than his companions' heads.

"This is magnificent!" he said, taking a few strides
more. "What wonderful magic."

"You can walk levelly or come back down, just by
imagining it," Kovrim explained.

Vambran strolled along for several steps, hovering
a good fifteen feet above the street, then he began to
descend, just as his uncle had described.

"How long will it last?" the lieutenant asked
Kovrim.

"More than an hour," the priest replied. "Plenty of
time to get high in the air and walk in well over the
grounds without being spotted."

"But remember," Xaphira warned her nephew, "you
are not invisible up there, and the moon is bright tonight. You should try to go in from the south side,
where the garden is the most overgrown."

Vambran nodded.

"I'm going to Em's rooms, first," he declared. "If I
get into any trouble, I'll send up a flare."

Everyone else wished the mercenary luck.

"We'll be working our way in from a different direction," Kovrim said. "I don't have a way to contact
you when we begin, but I think you'll know when we
set our plan into motion."

Vambran shook hands with them all and set out. He
tried to stick to the shadows as much as possible, gaining
altitude quickly by imagining the slope as being quite
steep. Very soon, he was high in the sky and looking over
the grounds of his own home, trying to figure out a way
to smuggle himself inside without being seen. The irony
was not lost on him, but he spared no time worrying
about it. Instead, when he was satisfied that he was far
enough over the ground that no one would be likely to
spot him, Vambran leveled off in his walk.

He took a quick glance around and, despite the
urgency of his goal, had to stand for a moment and

simply appreciate the beauty of the entire city spread out before him. Arrabar had always been an amazing city to the mercenary's eyes, though he usually only gazed across it during the daytime. At night, it took on a different but no less enchanting demeanor, with its twinkling lights spread out in undulating waves across the gentle hills stretching from the perimeter walls down to the bay. The water there glowed in its own right, the shimmering light of the bright, nearly full moon glimmering across its glassy surface. It was a magnificent city.

Vambran shook his head, refocusing his thoughts on the task at hand. He began to move toward the interior of the estate, peering down. He moved slowly, keeping an eye out below for any potential threats, but it was as Xaphira said; the garden was at its densest and most overgrown there, with lots of trees to obscure the night sky from anyone down below.

As he got in closer, Vambran began to angle into a very gradual descent, heading for the highest point of the house, the observation deck upon the flat roof, to start. He figured that he could step off the invisible pathway at the apex of the estate and work his way down from above. Anyone inside who was waiting to ambush him would not likely expect him to come from overhead.

As he walked, Vambran thought about what Emriana had said in her desperate message. The house guards had turned. Denrick had her held prisoner in her own rooms. He wondered if anyone else had put up a fight, had tried to resist. He feared for Hetta, and for his mother. He wondered about Evester, Marga, and the twins. It was hard for him to imagine his uncle Dregaul turning on all of them, but the evidence was damning.

Dregaul had certainly strayed into murky territory with his latest decisions. Vambran thought about how little he and his uncle had seen eye to eye over the past few years. They had rarely gotten along, especially because of the death of Rodolpho Wianar, but the lieutenant never remembered seeing evidence of his uncle straying so far from the righteous path before. Perhaps the tragedy at the Generon all those years before had tainted Dregaul differently than it had Vambran. Perhaps, in being a part of the cover-up, Vambran's uncle had blurred the lines of right and wrong in his own head more and more in the intervening years. The shooting had been the crux, and Vambran and his uncle had taken opposite paths from it. They had become opposites themselves, apparently. So different in their takes on life.

The lieutenant's most recent visit home had seemed to bring those differences to the forefront. It seemed like a hundred years had passed since he was standing on the deck of *Lady's Favor*, hesitating to step off, just so he could avoid facing Dregaul for a little longer. How he had wanted to avoid such unpleasantness! He and Dregaul had found an uneasy peace when he stayed away.

But there the two men were, on opposite sides of the most divisive conflict in the history of the family, and Vambran was preparing to bring his uncle down, once and for all. He was perhaps the whole family's last hope. The thought didn't make him feel particularly proud, only sad that it had come to that, and he didn't even really understand why.

Vambran realized he had reached the observation deck. He settled his feet softly to the flat surface, willing the pathway of air to evaporate then he considered where he was in relation to the interior of the house. Emriana's rooms were almost exactly below him, a couple of floors down. If he had some rope, he could get there straight from the observation deck, but he was no mountain goat and wasn't about to try to climb down unaided. Instead, he could reach there easily if he went around to the west and dropped down at the cistern.

Thinking of that patio made the lieutenant pause briefly, bitterly, as he was reminded of his failed attempt to get a true read on Denrick. The arrogant brute had certainly lied as smoothly as could be. Though Vambran had sincerely believed the younger man was a ne'er-do-well, Denrick had actually convinced him for a time that he had been innocent of the crimes against Jithelle. Too late, Vambran knew better.

The mercenary shook those distracting thoughts out of his head and forced himself to concentrate on the matter at hand. From the cistern, he knew he could either go inside the house and work his way through some of the servants' quarters, or he could slip around onto another patio that connected to his grandmother's rooms, and from there leap or shimmy across a narrow wall to Em's patio. Of course, all of that assumed that the various porches were unoccupied. If not, then he would have to deal with whomever he encountered. He hoped he could do it quietly enough not to arouse the suspicions of anyone else.

To Em's first, Vambran decided, and the rest of the family afterward.

He moved across the rooftop to the spot where he had appeared before, over the cistern. Looking down, he saw the reflection of the moon in the water's surface. It made him realize how much his white shirt stood out, and how much his highly polished breastplate glimmered in the faint light.

He slipped down to the tiles next to the cistern and held there, listening through the doorway that led inside. He heard nothing coming from that part of the house, so he skirted the pool and went to the balcony overlooking the west gardens. Climbing carefully up onto the banister, he swung over the side there and lowered himself down to the next level, dropping softy to the next porch down. From there, he dropped down behind a large rain barrel

and several planters that had been filled with some of
Hetta's favorite blooming plants. There were no lights
burning in his grandmother's rooms beyond the patio,
and no sounds coming from inside. From down in the
garden, however, Vambran heard the telltale sounds
of men talking.

Carefully, watching where he placed every hand
and knee, the lieutenant crawled over to the railing,
where he could peer through the balustrade and down
to the lawn below. A group of three men—guards, it
looked like in the moonlight—were huddled together,
talking and laughing softly. One of the three was
smoking a long-stemmed pipe. That right there
was a good indication that something profound had
changed with the house guards' loyalties, for Hetta
had never permitted the soldiers they employed to
smoke while on duty. She considered it distracting to
their concentration.

Vambran backed away from the railing and moved
carefully across the patio to the other side. There was
where his efforts would become tricky, he thought at
first, for the gap between Hetta's porch and Emriana's
was thirty feet or more wide, and there was only a
large trellis attached to the wall, overgrown with
creeping vines, for him to traverse in order to reach
the other side. Beyond the difficulties in keeping his
balance, the mercenary also feared making noise or
otherwise being noticed. The only other choice he
had was to descend one set of steps that led into the
gardens and scoot over to head back up the other staircase, which connected to Emriana's porch that way.

He nearly snapped his fingers in disgust, refrain-
ing from that foolish gesture at the last second when
he remembered he was trying to be quiet.

The magic Uncle Kovrim bestowed upon me should
still be functioning, he realized.

He could use that easily enough to cross the void
between the two balconies, and never have to set foot

down in the grass at all. The only problem there was the three guards. As long as they stood around talking, he doubted they would think to look up, over twenty feet above their own heads, to watch for intruders. But any motion out of the corner of someone's eye, any flutter of fabric in the breeze, or clank of the joints in his breastplate, would alert them that he was there.

I either wait until they move on, he thought, or else I risk it. Unless I just decide to shoot them right now, he thought snidely, considering it a punishment too kind for their traitorous dispositions.

But he knew he would not attack a man unaware. He was just going to have cross the gap and hope they didn't see him. Cautiously, starting several steps back and in the shadows, Vambran attempted to ascend the air. The magic still functioned. Nodding in relief, the mercenary started toward the edge of the porch, stepping perhaps four feet above the tiles, plenty of room to clear the railing. He tread carefully, one slow step at a time, trying to minimize any unnecessary movements. One foot in front of the next, he moved out over the drop-off, then proceeded, watching the three guards, who seemed right next to Vambran, but who were in reality a good fifty paces away.

A muffled grunt from ahead made Vambran freeze. It had come from Emriana's rooms, and it was followed by a second grunt. They both sounded as though someone was in discomfort. The lieutenant had to resist the urge to speed up, to jump forward and dash into the rooms beyond. But his other fear was that the noises coming from inside would attract the attention of the three guards below, who would naturally look up to see what was going on and spot him.

In desperation, Vambran moved on, continuing to set one foot in front of the other as quietly as he could, until he was over the railing guarding Emriana's patio. At that point, he angled his descent sharply,

reaching the tiles in two steep strides. He let his momentum carry him forward, to a pillar, and stepped
close to it, trying to blend with its shadows.

From there, Vambran could see through the gauzy
material of the drawn curtains into the interior of
his sister's rooms. Emriana was there, all right, as
was her handmaiden, Jaleene. The two women were
tied in chairs, and Emriana had been stripped to her
shift. That alone made Vambran's blood come near to
boiling, but then he saw Denrick. The pompous ass
was still dressed in the same clothes he had worn to
Emriana's birthday party earlier in the evening, only
he had removed his jacket and preened in front of
the women, bare-chested. Next to him stood a rather
pudgy man with disheveled white hair and a set of
spectacles perched on the end of his nose, who was
peering at Emriana and Jaleene with a mixture of
interest and timidity.

As Denrick walked around to stand in front of
Emriana, his words made Vambran's blood turn to
ice in his veins.

"Yes, use your magic to make her drawn irresistibly to me. I want her to desire me and take me
willingly to her bed."

CHAPTER FOURTEEN

Kovrim refused to admit it to anyone but himself, but he was growing fidgety. Xaphira had probably not been gone all that long, but to the priest, it seemed like it had been an eternity. He paced back and forth in the shadows near the mouth of the alley across the street from the Matrell estate, anxious for her to return.

In contrast to him, the soldiers that made up Vambran's platoon within the Sapphire Crescent mercenary company seemed calm and relaxed, though Kovrim knew that it was a technique practiced by many professional mercenaries. Inside, they were probably just as restless and eager to get started as he was.

They just hide it better, Kovrim thought with a wry smile.

For perhaps the tenth time, the priest halted his pacing and crept forward to the very edge, peering around the corner to where the wall of the estate came closest. It was still a good forty paces away on the other side of the street, and it was where Xaphira had climbed over and disappeared into the compound. There was still no sign of her.

Kovrim was just turning to head back into the alley when a soft voice called from above him, "What's wrong? Are you worrying about me?"

The priest nearly jumped out of his skin, but when he realized it was Xaphira, he let out a long, loud sigh and looked up.

The woman was just dropping down from a second-story railing that ran around the entire perimeter of that particular building, front to back. As her feet hit the hard-packed dirt of the alley, she tucked her knees to soften the blow, then came smoothly up again. Kovrim moved closer to her so they could converse quietly.

"Yes, I was beginning to worry about you," the priest admonished. "Allow an old man to fret a bit."

Xaphira chuckled softly.

"It's nice to know someone still cares," she said. "All right, I've reconnoitered the entire perimeter of the place, as well as a couple of potential points farther inside the walls where I think we can get through unhindered. I have an idea of how we can go about getting this brouhaha started, but it requires that we split the troops into two squads."

"I'm listening," Kovrim said, "but let's get the two sergeants involved in this. Their men are the ones on the line here, after all."

The two of them receded into the alley and gathered the officers to them, and Kovrim motioned for Xaphira to begin explaining her plan. When she finished, and they had discussed and adjusted a few minor points, she peered at each one there.

"All right, then," Xaphira said. "Are we in agreement?" Everyone gathered at the discussion nodded in turn. "Then let's get started."

The mercenaries jumped up as soon as the word was given that things were about to start happening. The sergeants quickly had them divided into two equal groups, with each officer commanding one unit. Both sets of soldiers were led to their respective spots, and Xaphira went with first one, then the other, slipping over the wall again to double-check that the locales were all clear, or to take a guard out who might have been too close. That left Kovrim by himself to get through the gates and provide a distraction.

The priest waited for a while, a set time that they had all agreed to beforehand, gauging the passage of time by the moon. He hoped that all of it would work, not just because failure would mean chaos for the soldiers who were trusting their lives to a couple of people they hardly knew, but also for the sake of the Matrells inside. Kovrim tried to imagine how he would feel if he were in Vambran's shoes, or Xaphira's, for that matter. He doubted he would be holding up nearly so well. He had to admire that about them.

Finally, it was time to go. Taking one slow, calming breath, Kovrim prepared a couple of spells that he would use to both capture his foes' attention and protect himself. He walked toward the gates, his talisman of Waukeen in his grasp, and called on the favor of his goddess to ward him from attack. He felt the protective magic settle into place around him just before he reached the gates, which were closed.

A pair of guards stood on the other side, and as they noticed the priest's approach, they leaped to action, coming close to the wide gates and demanding to know who it was.

Kovrim simply smiled and began to weave the second bit of magic he had in store for the men, speaking as he did so.

"On this night, of all nights, we are blessed by the serenity of the moon, and the breeze off the harbor," he said, just rambling, knowing it really didn't matter what he spoke of, so long as he kept up the speech for the duration. He watched the two guards closely to see if they were drawn into the mesmerizing words. They both seemed to be, for they relaxed and settled their gazes on him quietly.

Still speaking, Kovrim reached through and unlatched the gate, opening it just enough to step through. The guards didn't react to that, for they were attentively listening to his speech, which had become a diatribe concerning the evils of hoarding coin and how that held Waukeen's golden age of plenty at bay. Farther up the path, though, someone shouted, and three more guards rushed down toward the gates to see what was going on. As they neared and began to hear the priest's speech, they too stood still to listen. Kovrim smiled as he continued, pleased to see even more of the guards running in his direction.

...

Emriana made a strangled cry and shook her head vehemently as she heard Denrick's words suggesting that the wizard, Bartimus, might ensorcell her into desiring the man. The thought horrified her, was more terrible to contemplate than the notion of being taken by force. The idea that her free will could be taken from her so that she would give Denrick what he wanted sent her spiraling down into a dark pit of despair.

Denrick noticed the girl's reaction, and he smiled.

"What, don't you think it would be better like that?" he asked Emriana. "At least you'd be fooled into looking forward to it," he added, that wolfish grin growing more feral by the moment. He turned back to the diffident wizard. "Well? Can you do it?"

Bartimus nodded and replied, "I can, but these things are never guaranteed to work, and there are always unintended side-effects. I'm giving you these warnings so that you will be fully aware of them and not blame me later if it doesn't all turn out as wonderfully and romantic as you're envisioning right now. Furthermore, I have to say that—"

"Are you quite done?" Denrick asked, cutting off the babbling man. "I don't want a full lecture on the details. I just want to know if you can do it or not." The wizard simply nodded. "Good, then get on with it."

Emriana sobbed and began to thrash in her bonds again, shaking her head violently back and forth, mmphing through the wad of cloth shoved back in her mouth, pleading with Denrick not to go through with his foul game. The young man simply gestured expectantly toward her while staring down the wizard.

Bartimus walked cautiously over to stand near Emriana, shoved his glasses farther up his nose, and said, "All right; we've got a couple of choices here. I think perhaps . . . yes, that should do nicely."

Emriana whined plaintively at the man, trying to make him see her side of things, but Bartimus was effectively cowed by Denrick and he totally ignored her, other than to begin the casting.

That's when Emriana began to rock her chair back and forth again. She had been moved farther away from Jaleene so that they couldn't help one another escape again, and the handmaiden had been gagged, too. But Emriana wasn't trying to reach her companion in the hopes of getting her knots untied. She simply wanted to tumble over, fall flat on her back, knock herself unconscious, perhaps. Anything was better than being magically charmed into crawling into bed with Denrick right at that moment.

The girl heaved her weight around, trying to increase the motion. As she got into a rhythm, Denrick came around and grabbed the chair, halting it. Emriana whimpered in absolute disconsolation. Then Denrick slapped her, once, hard enough to cause her to grunt again. He leered at her.

"All right," Bartimus said, "I think I'm ready to begin. Are you sure you want to go through with this?"

Denrick stepped back from Emriana's chair and replied, "Yes, use your magic to make her drawn irresistibly to me. I want her to desire me and take me willingly to her bed."

Bartimus opened his mouth to begin, but he never got even the first words out, for both his and Denrick's attention were suddenly drawn to something behind Emriana. They were looking in the direction of the doorway leading out to her patio.

The girl turned her head, straining to see behind her, but the chair's angle and high back made it impossible.

"If you don't shut your mouth right now"—it was Vambran—"I'll plant this crossbow bolt right into the middle of it."

Em closed her eyes in relief.

"Damn you!" Denrick cried as Bartimus stammered, mumbled, and backed away. "How the hells did you get past the guards?"

Vambran advanced into the room and into Emriana's view. She could see that he carried a crossbow, which he had leveled at Denrick's chest.

"Hello, Em," Vambran said, giving her a smile, though he never took his eyes off his target. "I came as soon as you called."

Emriana gave her brother a steady stream of joyous, thankful, but incomprehensible gibberish through her gag, though she knew he understood the gist of it.

He made it, she thought, and not a moment too soon.

"Well," Denrick snarled, glancing down at the girl. "You managed to do a little more than untie your hands while I was gone, I guess." He backed away from Vambran, who was slowly closing the gap between the two of them. "And you managed to show up where you weren't wanted all over again," he said to the mercenary. "Just like the other night, when you had to go dashing in to save poor, pathetic Jithelle. You messed everything up!"

"And you're a sad, spoiled little boy who never learned that the world and the people in it don't belong to you just because you're wealthy," Vambran replied. "Now, you're either going to drop down to the floor and plant your face on the tiles, or else I'm going to put this bolt right in your nose. Your choice. What's it going to be?"

In response, Denrick grabbed Bartimus, who had edged over by the merchant's son, and he thrust the wizard between himself and Vambran. Denrick gave Bartimus a good shove to send him careening in the direction of the mercenary then he took the opportunity to dart out the door.

Vambran cursed and stepped forward, apparently intending to chase the fleeing man, but the wizard hindered him just enough that it was obviously a fruitless exercise, and Vambran held up after only a couple more steps.

Instead, he turned back to the wizard and snarled, "Get over there and untie my sister, you lecherous little worm."

Bowing and holding his hands up in front of his face, as though trying to ward off Vambran's anger and the impending bolt that might be fired at him, Bartimus scurried over to where Emriana sat and went to work on the knots.

As soon as one hand was free, Emriana yanked the gag free of her mouth once more and drew in a deep, fresh breath.

"Oh, thank Waukeen you got here when you did!" she gushed, wanting to get up and hug her brother. She grew impatient with the wizard's fumbling fingers and knocked his hands away.

"Go untie her," she ordered Bartimus, pointing toward Jaleene.

The wizard nodded and ran over to comply, leaving Emriana to free herself. The girl finally managed to get the last of the bonds undone, and she leaped up and hugged her brother with every once of her strength. She didn't want to let him go.

That's when Jaleene screamed. Emriana released Vambran just in time to see a huge black hound materialize right in front of the chair where the hand-maiden was still bound. The beast wasn't quite there, but seemed instead to be made of shadows. Even so, its huge fangs and glowing red eyes were visible enough. The hound, a mastiff, growled low in its throat and reared back to lunge at the helpless Jaleene.

At the same time, Bartimus was waving his hands through the air and murmuring in a low voice. As Vambran reacted, raising his crossbow to fire at the wizard, a blue, shimmering curtain of light formed next to the pudgy man. The curtain parted to reveal a doorway, and Bartimus leaped through it, the crossbow bolt glancing off his cloak. The doorway winked out.

Emriana stared, dumbfounded, as Vambran rushed forward, dragging his sword free of its scabbard in one smooth motion. Just as the shadow hound was about to bite Jaleene, Vambran got between them, slashing down with his blade.

The huge dog howled in pain and leaped away, landing in the corner. It turned to face Vambran, who was closing with it, his sword held defensively in front of himself. Warily, the two of them began to circle one another, the hound snapping and biting at the blade, Vambran feinting and thrusting back.

Emriana ran over to Jaleene, who was trembling. The girl began to work on the knots that still held the woman tightly. After several moments of frantic tugging, she managed to free her companion and pulled her out of the chair.

At that moment, Emriana turned to see her brother lunge at the hound again, drawing thick, black blood. In response, the dog opened its mouth wide and let out an ear-splitting bay that chilled the girl to the bone and made her want to flee right out into the night. She and Jaleene together ran to the opposite side of the room and cowered in the corner, watching Vambran combat this magical creature of shadow.

He didn't seem fazed by the unearthly howl. He slashed down again, cutting a deep furrow into the dog's shoulder, which caused the dog to turn and jump into the shadows, disappearing.

Emriana gasped.

"Gods, what is that thing?" she whispered as Vambran searched for the beast, poking and prodding at the spot where the dog last stood.

"I don't know, but when I catch that wizard again, I'm going to thrash him," her brother responded. "I shouldn't have let my—"

Vambran's words were choked off as he suddenly discovered the shadow dog again. The beast leaped out of the shadows where it had hidden and charged at him, knocking him down.

The lieutenant had to roll to the side to avoid having his throat ripped out by the shadow hound's snapping jaws. He managed to swing his sword around and slice at the creature once more, sending a spray of black blood everywhere. The dog howled in pain and backed off.

Vambran managed to climb to his knees, but before he could stand, the shadow hound charged forward again. That time, though, the mercenary was ready, and when the dog leaped forward, Vambran had his

sword positioned perfectly to run it through. The
creature gave one last, whimpering howl and sagged
down. As it dropped to the floor of Emriana's room,
the dog vanished.

"Conjured creature," Vambran explained. "The
wizard brought it here with a summoning spell."
Then recognition lit in his eyes. "I'll bet he was the
one responsible for the leechwalker that jumped us
in the warehouse."

Emriana nodded mutely as she continued to stare,
wide-eyed, at where the dog had vanished. The baying
had unnerved her, and she couldn't shake the sense of
panic it had caused, even though she knew Vambran
had dispatched it.

"Em," Vambran said, walking over to his sister
and pulling her up by one arm so she could stand.
"Get dressed. We have to get to the rest of the family.
It's time to track down Denrick and pay him back for
what he did to you."

...

Kovrim's voice was growing hoarse, but he dared
not stop speaking. He had managed to gather perhaps
fifteen or twenty guards around him, all of them
except two listening in rapt attention to his speech.
The two who'd managed to resist the enthralling
influences of his magic had tried to get the priest
to stop, first by shouting at him, then by charging
forward. But to their surprise, both of the soldiers
discovered that they just couldn't bring themselves
to attack the man who had enraptured all of their
companions. Such was the magic that Kovrim had
employed to keep himself protected.

Fortunately, the whole diversion had worked about
as well as the priest had hoped. He could already see
that the mercenaries had taken the house, and a squad
of them was marching down the path toward where

he continued to orate on anything that came to mind. He was running out of energy, though. He prayed that the Sapphire Crescents would hurry.

Just about the time Kovrim's voice was giving out, the squad of mercenaries reached the back side of the gathering of house guards. With a sigh of relief, Kovrim finally trailed off, ending the spell. The guards, realizing he was finished, blinked and began to get their bearings again, realizing just how captivated they had become in the priest's mesmerizing words. As they remembered that they were supposed to be preventing intruders from gaining the grounds, more than a few of them grew agitated, and several of them readied their weapons.

It quickly became clear, though, that they had allowed themselves to be tricked, and they were outnumbered and unprepared to battle the mercenaries. The guards surrendered without a fight, making Kovrim's smile even larger. As the Sapphire Crescents relieved guards of their weapons, the priest strolled past them toward Adyan, who had led the "attack" down the hill.

"Easiest engagement I've ever been a part of," the sergeant drawled, giving Kovrim a grin and slap on the back. "We need you on the battlefield more often."

"I was there in my younger days," Kovrim informed the mercenary. "It was only after I grew too old and soft to put up with the hardships of the campaign trail that I retired and took up an administrative position within the temple."

"Well, if you ever decide to un-retire, I'm sure Vambran'd be able to find a gentle horse and a good use for you," the sergeant replied in his easy accent.

Adyan ordered a small detail to mind the prisoners and he, Kovrim, and the rest of the troops moved back up the main path to the house, ready to rejoin the other half of the Sapphire Crescents.

Once they were together with the rest of the
troops, the Crescents broke into smaller squads
and prepared to move through the house room by
room, not sure how strong the resistance would
be, but clearly understanding that members of
Vambran and Kovrim's family were in potential
danger inside. As the Crescents entered the house
and fanned out, Kovrim realized for the first time
that Xaphira was not with them. He worried for her
briefly, but then the priest dismissed such thoughts.
The woman had been able to take care of herself for
quite a long time, and her skills were formidable,
as she had already demonstrated several times in
the past couple of days. She was lurking somewhere,
ready to spring out when she was most needed, he
decided.

The priest accompanied Adyan and two other mercenaries as they moved into the large dining room of
the Matrell estate. One of the soldiers had a lantern,
but otherwise, the room was dark, which Kovrim
found disturbing. Normally, the servants would have
lit lanterns and candles to brighten every room in
the house, but thus far, the Crescents had found everything dark and silent. The priest was just about
to suggest that they move on when a cry rose up from
the kitchens, just through the next door, followed by
the sounds of battle.

Weapons drawn, the mercenaries rushed through
the portal. Kovrim was in the rear, but he saw that
another group of Crescents had stumbled onto a con-
tingent of house guards who were accompanying two
other men moving through the kitchen, perhaps to
sneak out the back way onto the grounds. The guards
engaged the mercenaries, leaving their charges to
retreat to safety.

"Don't let them escape!" Kovrim called out, and a
pair of Crescents pushed through the swirling fight
to pursue the men.

Kovrim picked his way more carefully, dodging a sword swipe in the process, and finally reached the door that led out onto the tiled patio off the kitchen. The two soldiers were facing off against one of the men, whom Kovrim recognized as Grozier Talricci. The other man, a somewhat shorter, flabby fellow, cowered behind Grozier, watching the whole skirmish through a pair of spectacles that were slipping off his nose.

Suddenly, the timorous fellow reached into a pocket and drew forth a handful of something that Kovrim couldn't see. He knew well enough that he was watching arcane magic, though, and tried to shout a warning. The paunchy wizard was too quick. He popped something in his mouth, casting his spell before the priest could make the mercenaries aware of the danger. Raring back, the wizard suddenly belched forth a spray of something, thoroughly covering one of the two mercenaries in the liquid. The man began to scream and claw at his own body, and Kovrim watched in horror as the substance, obviously some sort of acid, began to burn him.

Without thinking about it, Kovrim darted across and approached the man, who was down on the tiles, rolling in misery, his clothing half-burned away and his flesh covered in open sores and smoking. The priest grasped his talisman of Waukeen and knelt beside the anguished mercenary, praying to the goddess for the power of healing. Heedless of his own danger, Kovrim placed his hand upon the burned man's chest and let the healing energy flow. The spell didn't completely counteract the effects of the acid, but it was enough to ease the mercenary's pain and keep him breathing.

A commotion right behind him drew Kovrim's attention once he was finished applying his divine magic, and he realized that he was right in the wizard's line of sight. The priest dived across the body of

the now-unconscious soldier, hoping to buy himself a
moment or two to recover his wits and defend himself.
As he tumbled across the tiles and turned back to
face whatever danger might be coming toward him,
Kovrim was relieved to see that several more Crescents had arrived and were quickly surrounding the
wizard.

"Watch it!" Kovrim warned. "He's spraying acid
from his mouth!"

One of the mercenaries gave the priest a funny
look, but the wizard didn't attempt his deadly trick
again. In truth, Kovrim had doubted it could be done
more than once per use of the spell, but he didn't want
to take any chances.

"Bartimus!" Grozier shouted when it was obvious
the two were quickly being overmatched. "Get us out
of here!"

The wizard simply shook his head and held his
hands up, indicating that he was out of ideas and
would no longer resist. With a resentful snarl, Grozier
threw his weapon to the side and surrendered, too. The
mercenaries quickly kicked the weapons clear and
forcibly took hold of the two men, some patting them
down for hidden weapons, others pulling bits of rope
out of belt pouches and restraining their prisoners.

Kovrim approached the head of House Talricci.

"How did it come to this, Grozier?" the priest asked.
"The murder of innocent people, just for the sake of
profit? Waukeen has her limits, you know."

The other man simply glared at him.

...

Vambran crouched at the corner of the hallway,
listening. Behind him, Emriana made no sounds as
she hovered, waiting to see what her brother was
going to do. Jaleene had been sent to find the other
servants and get out of the house, if she could. The

woman had not wanted to be separated from her charge, apparently still fearing for the girl's well-being, but Emriana had insisted. Vambran was thankful for his sister's courage. He wanted her with him, both so that he could keep an eye on her and so that she could be there when Denrick went down. But having her personal maid along would have been too much. Jaleene was a kind woman and cared very much for Emriana, but the servant was in no condition mentally to resolve the situation, and it was better off for all of them if she got out of the middle of it. She had left with one last teary-eyed look back at Emriana.

The house was strangely empty, which worried Vambran more than a little. Even when many of the family members were not at home, he could recall numerous staff and the occasional house guard moving about, taking care of their appointed duties. At that moment, it was like a tomb. He did not care much for that analogy. He tried to consider where Uncle Dregaul might have taken the rest of the family if he intended to usurp total control of the house. Most likely, they would be confined to their rooms, but he had not found any of them there. It was possible, though unlikely, that his uncle had sent the lot of them down into the basement to be locked in the old cell that had been built. Vambran didn't want to consider that a viable possibility until he had exhausted all the others, though. It was simply too base for him to believe.

Then again, he told himself, Dregaul has lost his faculties.

Vambran still had a hard time believing that the man would stoop to taking his own family hostage and offering up his niece's flesh for the sake of an alliance in order to run the House the way he wanted. Dregaul had always been an intense man, but that just seemed too out of character.

When Vambran was satisfied there was no one in the main sitting room, he crept forward. He could barely discern Emriana padding along behind him. Vambran considered whether he should check the basements after all. The only places in the main part of the house he hadn't yet searched were there, the kitchens, and Dregaul's study.

He would leave the basement for last, the mercenary decided. He had to deny that choice for as long as possible. The study it was, then. He turned to follow a new hallway to a flight of stairs that led up to a balcony surrounding the sitting room. That's when he heard the shouting.

It was muffled, coming from behind a closed door, but it was clear enough to make out that someone was arguing vehemently in the study. Vambran nodded to himself in satisfaction and turned to his sister.

"They're up there," he whispered, pointing toward his uncle's sanctuary. "I don't know who all is there, but I can hear arguing."

"Then let's go," the girl replied.

"Not so fast," Vambran said, holding up one hand to stay her. "The study opens onto the atrium, right?" Emriana nodded. "You think you can get up there?" She nodded again. "Then let's come at them from two directions. We've got the element of surprise here. Let's take advantage of it."

Emriana leaned over and kissed Vambran once on the cheek and whispered, "Thanks for trusting me to help you. I'll wait for some sort of signal before I go in."

She slipped off down the hall to head to another part of the house, where stairs could get her to the next floor above the study.

Vambran turned his attention back to the closed door. The shouting had subsided for the moment, and he knew that he should wait for a little while to give

Emriana some time to get into position, but he just
couldn't. He had to find out if his family was all right,
and he had to confront his uncle.

Peering around once more to make sure he
wasn't missing someone hiding nearby, watching
him, Vambran stepped out and began to work his
way through the sitting room, heading for the
spiral staircase on the far side that would take
him to the balcony overhead. The doors to the study
opened onto that balcony. Then, on impulse, the
lieutenant tried to step high, seeing if he could
still walk on air. He could. He angled himself
upward and began to climb through the sitting
room, heading up and directly toward the study
doors. He ascended all the way over the banister
of the balcony and settled to the tiles. Just as he
was about to crouch near the portal for a listen,
the doors opened and Denrick stormed out, a sword
belted to his hip.

The younger man had his back turned to Vambran at the moment, and the lieutenant could
have easily gotten a quick and surprising strike
in, had he wanted to, but it was what he saw just
beyond the man, over his shoulder, that stayed the
mercenary's hand. Anista Pharaboldi was lying
across the large table in the center of the room, a
dagger jutting up from her chest. She didn't move,
and her eyes, still open, were glazed over as they
stared up toward the ceiling. Beside her, Dregaul
Matrell was in a similar pose. Vambran's gasp gave
him away.

Denrick spun around then, and when he saw
Vambran standing there, a malevolent grin spread
across his face. "Your uncle was easy, but I thought
you'd be more difficult to kill. I guess I don't have
to hunt you down in order to finally do it, after all,"
he said, pulling his blade free and settling into a
fighting stance. "I'll finish you off, first, then find

that wildcat of a sister of yours and finish what you interrupted."

Vambran unsheathed his own weapon.

"Not a chance," he said.

CHAPTER FIFTEEN

Emriana moved fluidly, soundlessly, through the darkened house, making her way up to the third floor, to the high chambers that had once been her grandfather's library. That section was little used anymore, but her grandmother insisted that all of her husband's old books be left where they were, kept clean but otherwise undisturbed. Emriana didn't think it was some strange clutching at the past, but rather a desire on Hetta's part to keep the innumerable tomes available, should someone else in the family ever choose to take up reading as a pastime. The girl had come there occasionally as a youngster just to stare at the countless books, and a few more times more recently when she needed to get away from everyone, especially the twins.

Unlike most of the rooms in the house, it was completely enclosed, without the usual

open arched windows, to better preserve the books
inside. There was still access to the outside, though,
through a pair of doors that had windows of leaded
glass set into them. The doors led to yet another balcony, a small one that sat at the top of a three-story
light well in the middle of the house. The atrium at
the bottom was filled with climbing plants on trellises, and Emriana felt confident she could make her
way down to the level below, to the small balcony off
the study, by descending one of the wooden lattices.

She opened the doors to the library and quietly
slipped through, pulling the doors shut behind her.
She stood there for a moment, peering around, but the
chamber was completely dark except for the glow of
moonlight shining in through the leaded glass windows in the doors on the opposite side of the room. That
was her destination, but she would have to practically
feel her way across the open floor, because she literally could not see any chairs or tables that might be
standing between her and that portal. She had not
come there often enough or recently enough to remember the layout of the furniture with any clarity.

Slowly, her hands in front of herself so she could
feel her way clearly, Emriana began to walk toward
the far doors. Each step was short and gentle, because
one wrong move, any instance of bumping into the
furniture, would alert anyone in the chamber underneath her. Her fingers brushed the edge of a chair, and
she remembered that it was clear to the right of it, so
she sidestepped slowly and advanced again.

The girl was perhaps halfway across when she got
the sudden sensation that she was not alone in the
room. The hairs on her arms and the back of her neck
prickled in alarm. She froze, straining to listen for
any telltale signs that someone else was with her.

Quietly, as if realizing it had been detected,
a shadow separated itself from the surrounding
darkness and moved out into the open. Emriana's

heart leaped into her throat. The form shifted over to stand in front of her, becoming a silhouette against the backdrop of the windows. Emriana took a step backward and bumped against the chair she had so carefully circumnavigated before.

"I had a feeling you'd come this way tonight," the form said, "just a hunch, really, that you might think of sneaking into the study through the atrium."

It was Evester.

Emriana nearly dropped to the floor, she was shaking so hard, but she sighed in relief.

"Waukeen, Evester!" she hissed, moving toward her oldest brother. "Do you intentionally make a habit of scaring the life out of me? What are you doing here?"

"Waiting for you," Evester replied as Emriana closed with him to give him a hug.

Evester returned the embrace—and the girl was flipping over sharply, off balance against her brother's hip. She landed on the floor with a solid thud, her arms pinned behind her. The breath was knocked out of her.

As Emriana gasped and tried to make sense of what had just happened, she felt her brother cinch her arms together with rope. Her heart sank, realizing that something was terribly, terribly wrong.

"Uncle Dregaul should have paid more attention to your antics," Evester said, finishing his knot work and starting on Emriana's legs. "He would have realized, like I have, what a clever little rogue you've turned into, sneaking out all the time."

"Evester," Emriana said, "what are you doing? What's happened to you?"

"Oh, plenty," Evester replied. "I woke up and realized if I waited around for Grandmother Hetta to die and Uncle Dregaul to finally retire, I'd never gain control of this family and its assets. So I decided to take matters into my own hands."

"Why?" the girl asked in a small voice, horrified that her older brother was behind all of what was going on. "What could you have possibly wanted that you couldn't already have?"

"Oh, little Em," Evester said with a chuckle, "you are still so innocent. Sixteen tonight and thinking you understand life, but you don't. There's so much more. The real power to be had in this city is there for the taking, if people are just willing to step up and grab it. Denrick and I see that. Someday, maybe you will, too."

"It was *you!*" Emriana said suddenly, realizing that Evester and not Uncle Dregaul had promised Denrick he could have her. "You told that lecherous worm that he could violate me! You gave him permission to *take* me!"

She struggled to get up, then began kicking to try to break free, but it was too late; her brother had already bound her tightly.

Evester chuckled and said, "I was just being a good businessman, Em, taking full advantage of the resources at my disposal. Remember what I said the other night about risk and reward, and how none of the Houses in Arrabar would take chances with each other? I had something Denrick wanted, so we struck a deal. It was just business, sister, just business. It's a fearless man's game, running a great House in Arrabar, and I'm just the fearless man to play it. With my two trusted partners, of course."

"Vambran won't let you get away with it," Emriana said, trying to sound convincing, for her own sake as much as for her brother's.

Evester laughed again.

"Vambran?" he said. "Unlikely. Not when the rest of his family is in danger. He's just a little too idealistic for his own good, little sister. He and Dregaul are just alike, more so than either would care to admit. Both of them spent all these years protecting the family, hiding Vambran's dirty little secret from the world, though for very different reasons. He's not about to jeopardize his kin to stop me, sis. He'll sacrifice himself thinking he can save you, just as Aunt Xaphira did for him. Problem solved. It'll be a pleasure to be rid of his brooding, self-righteous presence."

Emriana could not speak, she was so furious, hurt, and stunned. She would never in a hundred years have imagined that Evester could be so callous. She felt tears begin to well up in her eyes, saw in her mind's eye her world crashing down around her once again.

"Well, it's time to go downstairs," Evester said, pulling a magically illuminated rock from some hidden pocket and lighting the room with its pale, pearly glow. "I'm sure Denrick will be happy to see you've been rounded up once more."

With that, Evester stooped down and hoisted his sister up over his shoulder. He carried her back out the door of the library.

...

Vambran blocked a quick stab at his head and backed up a step, then jumped to his left as Denrick slashed low with his sword. The lieutenant planted his feet against the wall and pushed back the other direction, going high, and parrying another rapid slice with his own blade. He landed on the banister of the balcony, then had to swing out over the sitting room a story below, one arm wrapped around the closest column, to escape yet a third slash from Denrick. Vambran came back around to the banister again, with that column between him and his opponent. Denrick's blade smacked sharply against the column as Vambran jumped down to the balcony again.

"I guess all that service with your soldier buddies was good for something," Denrick scoffed, advancing

again. "You may not fight worth a damn, but at least
you're good at the acrobatics."

Vambran ignored the other man's jibes and concentrated on matching his moves. The lieutenant had
to admit that the Pharaboldi whelp was an excellent
swordsman. He had already pushed Vambran back
three times, and the mercenary officer was beginning
to wonder if there was a way inside the man's defenses.
Though Vambran's blade was a bit longer, Denrick
was very fast with his, and he always seemed have a
parry in place when Vambran attacked.

"Come on," Denrick said, "the night's not getting
any younger. If I'm going to have any time left for
your sister's charms, we've got to finish this sometime
in the next few hours."

Vambran knew the man was just trying to rattle
him, and he worked hard to tune out the scathing
words. But every time Denrick mentioned Emriana,
the lieutenant wanted to smash his head against
a wall. The first time Denrick had taunted Vambran with his carnal intentions, Vambran had let
his emotions get the best of him and jumped in for
a fierce series of slashes and cuts, thinking to put
the upstart down then and there. But Vambran was
rudely awakened when he took a cut across his wrist.
It was a glancing blow, and Denrick's blade wasn't
turned at precisely the right angle, but it had opened
Vambran's eyes to just how cunning and talented his
foe really was.

As Denrick closed for a new attack, Vambran
dropped down and sliced at the man's feet. Denrick
leaped over the swing and used his momentum to turn
a back flip back out of the way as Vambran came up
suddenly, thrusting into the air where Denrick had
been a split-second before.

Vambran's rush carried his center of balance a
little too far forward, though, and Denrick came
back in with a downward stroke, trying to cleave

Vambran's head in half. The lieutenant rolled to
one side, grabbing at a pedestal with a bit of ancient
Netherese pottery displayed atop it. Vambran pulled
the pedestal down and around, clipping Denrick's
knee as the scoundrel's blade clanked off the pottery,
shattering it. Vambran rolled away and spun around
again.

Denrick smiled as he came closer again.

"Arm getting tired?" he asked casually. "I can cut
it off if it is," he added, smirking.

Vambran noted that members of the Sapphire
Crescent were gathering below, and several more of
the mercenaries were ascending the stairs, coming
to aid him. Denrick would quickly be outnumbered.
Though he suspected the man could take a soldier or
two down before he himself dropped, Vambran would
prefer not to lose any of his men.

"Your time is up," Vambran said to his foe. "It's
only a matter of time before we drop you. Let's spare
both of us a lot of pain and end this sensibly. You don't
want to die, do you?"

"No, but I want you to die," the younger man retorted, charging in on Vambran again. The lieutenant
was forced to spring to the side of the new rush, and
he slammed against the railing of the balcony again,
overbalancing and tumbling over the top of it.

For an instant, Vambran seemed to hang in mid-
air, flailing as his body tilted awkwardly, his sword
spinning out away from him. Then he managed to
grasp hold of one of the spindles of the railing, jerking himself to a stop, but wrenching his shoulder in
the process. He dangled there for a moment, his arm
twisted painfully over his head, and let go, dropping
down to the sitting room below, just as Denrick lunged
out over the banister to try and stab at him.

Vambran's escape permitted several of the mercenaries watching the melee from below to get in a
clean shot with their crossbows, and Denrick took two

hits as he tried to straighten back up. One bolt grazed his arm, marking a clean line diagonally along the forearm, and the other sank deeply into his thigh. The young man howled in pain and staggered back from the railing, sinking down onto his backside in a whimper.

Vambran heaved a sigh of relief as several more soldiers moved in around Denrick, taking him prisoner. The lieutenant looked up and saw Kovrim, Adyan, and Horial among the troops, and he smiled at them.

"Good timing," he said. "I owe you, boys."

Kovrim nodded, and Horial started to say something as the men upstairs forced Denrick to his feet and began to march him back toward the stairs. But everyone stopped short as a clear, calm shout echoed through the sitting room.

"Vambran!" It was Evester. He stood at the railing of the highest balcony, one level above the study, where Old Obiron's library was. Beside him, standing stiffly, was Emriana. She had a sorrowful look on her face, and Vambran suddenly realized that she was bound.

The lieutenant shook his head.

"Evester?" he called out, "Are you all right?"

"No," the mercenary's older brother called down, a hard edge to his voice. "No, I'm not. You've ruined everything, you stupid lout."

"I did what?" Vambran said, moving to a different spot where he could see better. "What are you talking about?"

"It wasn't Uncle Dregaul, Vam," Emriana called forlornly. "It was Evester. He's behind it all."

Vambran's breath caught in his throat as he heard his sister's chilling words.

"What are you doing, Evester? What is this about?"

"It's about me taking my rightful place as the head of the family, about getting things done that no one else can do. And it's about you interfering with all of it."

"How did I do that, Ev? What did I interfere with?"

"My alliance, you idiot! You came home and promptly shredded the whole plan to pieces. Because you had to stick your nose into something that had no effect on you at all."

"Oh, so because it wasn't anyone I know, I shouldn't care what happened to her?"

"By the gods, Vambran, save your concern for the people who really matter! If you devoted half as much of your noble concern worrying about how your actions affect your family as you do worrying about some stupid, common wench, we wouldn't be here right now."

"That's pretty funny, coming from the man who has usurped the family seat, practically sold his own sister into slavery, and is going to—to do what, Ev? Are you going to get rid of us? Me? Em? Grandmother Hetta? You think all of that is showing concern for your family?"

"Shut up," Evester said, pulling a dagger and placing it against Emriana's throat. "What would you know about it, anyway? All you ever managed to do was shoot the Lord of Arrabar's cousin and let someone else take the blame for it. Not only did you put the whole future of the House—*my* future—in jeopardy, but then you couldn't even stick around and take your lumps like a man. No, you had to run off and join a mercenary band while I stayed here and learned the business. And everything that Uncle Dregaul and I tried to get you to do to help improve the family's station, you railed against. So how would you know what's good for the family?"

"Waukeen, Evester," Vambran said quietly, "you think I didn't regret that every single day of my life? You think I didn't wish I could take it back? That's the very reason why I wouldn't let this go. Maybe Jithelle Skolotti was just a 'common wench,' but I couldn't stand by and watch another person's family wonder what really happened, like I did to Rodolpho's."

Evester shook his head.

"I'm through talking with you," he said. "Just get up here. And Denrick. Both of you climb up here now, or Em slips and falls over the side."

And, just to show he meant it, Evester grabbed his sister by the shoulder and shoved her forward, making her lean out over the railing.

Emriana yelped in fright and struggled to back away from the drop, but Evester had all the leverage, and he just kept pushing her, forcing her farther and farther out.

"Vam! Help me!" the girl shrieked. "Please, stop it!"

"Get up here, Vambran," Evester said. "I'm not kidding."

All around him, Vambran heard the murmurs and grumbles of his men, angry at the situation and talking bravado about knocking Evester down a peg or two or giving him a good swift sword in the gut, but Evester had them bested, and everyone knew it. The lieutenant eyed Denrick, who was grinning malevolently at him, and he nodded to the men holding the prisoner. Understanding, they let the younger man go, and he jerked his arms free indignantly, then turned and demanded his sword. Reluctantly, the soldier holding it handed it over.

"You see?" Denrick said to Vambran. "In the end, you can't beat us. You're a fool to even try. The city belongs to us, Vambran. Not to the old fools who hoard their gold, or the small-time thinkers like your uncle or my mother. Only people such as Evester and me truly understand how to wield the power of coin."

"I hardly think it takes a lot of brains to take the cowardly road, Denrick," Vambran said. "And you're not out of here free and clear, yet. So I wouldn't go flapping my mouth off too much if I were you."

Denrick just glared at Vambran, who gestured for the younger man to go first. Denrick limped forward, taking the lead, and the pair of them began to ascend to the top floor.

When Vambran arrived, Evester was standing behind Emriana, holding the blade to her throat once more and using her as a shield.

"First, you're going to heal him, Vambran. Then, you're going to let him tie your hands behind your back, and the four of us will walk out of here."

"And go where, Ev? The whole city will be hunting for you after this. There's no place you can retreat to and still sit atop your ill-gotten perches."

"Nonetheless, you're going to do exactly what I just said, or I will slit her throat and throw her over the side. Do you understand me?"

"Sure, Ev," Vambran said, defeat making his words quiet. He knelt down, ready to examine the puncture wound in Denrick's leg. He cast one last glance up, about to tell Evester that he would cooperate and be their hostage if they would let Emriana go right then, when he spotted the faintest hint of movement from behind his older brother.

Xaphira.

Apparently, Denrick hadn't seen her, so Vambran quickly averted his eyes downward again, not wanting to betray the potential rescue. He directed his face toward the end of the bolt still rammed in Denrick's leg, but he watched carefully out of the corner of his eye for some sort of telltale sign that she was acting. He saw her take the first subtle step toward Evester, and he reacted.

Reaching out, Vambran gripped the end of the bolt and slammed it sideways, twisting at the same time. The howl of pain as Denrick stumbled backward was loud and piercing. The younger man staggered backward, reaching feebly toward the pain, as Vambran stood up again and turned back toward his brother.

Evester held a look of shock on his face as he watched what Vambran had just done, and he let his hold on Emriana sag slightly, dropping his guard. Xaphira timed it perfectly. She stepped in behind the man, snaking her arm underneath the one of his that held the dagger and leveraging it out, away from his hostage's face. At the same time, she shifted her weight under his, shoving him up off the ground with her hip and spinning him over backward. He landed with a thud on the balcony, well away from Emriana.

Emriana sank down to the tiles, for she was still bound hand and foot. Vambran moved to her, ready to help free her, when her eyes grew wide.

"Look out!" she cried, and Vambran instinctively dived to one side as Denrick's sword whistled over his head.

The force of the strike sent Denrick staggering forward, for his leg had no strength in it, and he could not easily recover his balance. He stumbled forward, right at Emriana. She rolled backward, even as he came at her, and Vambran could see what the heir of House Pharaboldi was about to do. The lieutenant willed his body to lunge forward, to stop Denrick's forward progress, but he was much too slow. There was nothing he could do to stop Denrick from slipping his blade right into Em's chest as he fell on top of her.

Curiously, though, the wounded man didn't reach the girl. As he fell, she rolled backward, bringing her feet, which were still tied together, up under him. She used his momentum against him, hoisting him high and shoving as hard as she could, sending him completely past her, over her, and toward the railing.

Vambran watched the sequence as if time had slowed down somehow. Denrick, still flying forward, was headed over the railing. He was twisted awkwardly, unable to stop himself, and he flailed about desperately for something to grab hold of, anything at all that would keep him from falling to his death.

The one thing that was there, within reach, was Evester. Somehow, Vambran's brother had managed to get to his feet and was circling with Xaphira, when Denrick went tumbling by.

The oldest son of Ladara Matrell never saw his companion coming, but Denrick managed to grab hold of his shirt. As he fell over the railing, Denrick hung on to Evester, refusing to let go, and the force of his momentum pulled Evester right over the side with him. The last thing Vambran saw of his brother was one arm, fingers extended, grasping futilely for the banister. There was a shriek of terror, and a moment later, one large thump that Vambran felt even at the top of the house.

...

"I knew Dregaul was beginning to slip into a maniacal notion that any business deal, no matter how questionable, whether financial or ethical, was all right," Hetta said.

They were all gathered in the sitting room. The elderly matriarch of the Matrell family was in her favorite chair, and Ladara was beside her, as usual, though Emriana's mother was obviously more subdued than usual. The girl couldn't really blame her; she had lost a son and a grandson, after all.

After Denrick and Evester's deaths, the rest of the family had been found, unharmed, locked in the cell in the basement. Marga had not handled her husband's death well, though in the end, after some magical calming ministrations from Kovrim, she at least began to see that she and her twin children had probably been spared a lifetime of misery under a tyrant's rule. Still, she was left in a quandary. Her own House was devastated, just as House Pharaboldi was. Her only true family seemed to be the Matrells. The three of them were resting quietly in their rooms while the rest of the family discussed how to honor their dishonorable dead.

"But I had no idea he was teaching those same reprehensible qualities to Evester," Hetta continued quietly, sadly. "If I had, I would have taken control back a long time ago."

"But Grandmother," Emriana asked, "why in the world didn't you do that anyway?"

"Because I needed Dregaul to do something that would get him in over his head," the woman replied. "I needed to be able to show to everyone, you included, that I was still sharp and that he was the one unfit for running the family business."

Emriana nodded, though she didn't see how Hetta would think that anyone wouldn't trust her. To her, the woman seemed to have the most sensible head on her shoulders of all of them.

"That's not the only reason you let it go on, though, is it?" Xaphira said, sitting off to one side and studying the family.

Emriana still hadn't gotten used to the idea that her long-lost aunt had returned from her self-imposed exile. She had heard the story about the woman's disappearance only a couple of days before, and yet there she was, in the flesh, and Emriana had a chance to get to know a new member of her family. The thought excited her, especially after the conversation she and Hetta had had. Such a newfound mentor, coupled with the loss of Dregaul and Evester, caused the girl's emotions to be in turmoil at the moment.

"No," Hetta said, answering Xaphira's question. "I also needed to see who would recognize that the House was on unstable ground and do something about it. I had to see who I could trust."

Emriana realized that her grandmother was looking at both her and Vambran then. She cocked her head to one side, not understanding.

"If Dregaul wasn't suitable to manage the Matrell

family affairs, then who would be?" Hetta explained. "You are, my dear," she said, smiling at her grand-daughter.

As what Hetta was saying began to dawn on her, Emriana looked over at Vambran. He seemed just as apprehensive as she felt.

"Us?" she asked quietly, uncertainly.

"Yes," Hetta affirmed. "You and your brother did far more than I had ever imagined for the sake of the family—not the House, the *family*. Of course, I never envisioned having to stop Dregaul from forcing you to marry, or for us to need to be rescued from a trio of misguided fools," she added wistfully.

Emriana felt her chest tighten, then, for she knew that Hetta grieved for her lost son and grandson.

"You two have a lot of thinking to do," Hetta continued. "I know you're not ready to assume control of the House yet, but it will be time, soon. I'm not going to be around forever, you know."

That sobering thought just added to Emriana's poignant mood. She went to her grandmother and gave the woman a long hug.

"You can't leave us too soon," she said in a fierce whisper. "You still have too much to teach me."

Hetta laughed and replied, "I'm sure that whatever wisdom I fail to impart to you, Xaphira can more than make up for."

Emriana turned and smiled at her aunt.

"I'd like that," she said, and Xaphira smiled back. She looked over at her brother, then, and saw him still brooding. "What are you thinking about?"

Vambran sighed and said, "That everything is changing. The House, the family responsibilities.... I don't even know how much longer I'll remain a member of the Sapphire Crescent, with all that's happened."

"You still have a bright future there," Hetta said. "Your captain was more than understanding when you abandoned your post."

Vambran grimaced. He had received a disciplinary rebuke for his actions, a symbolic punishment and nothing more. He claimed that he was ultimately thankful for the light punishment, but Emriana could tell that he had become somewhat disillusioned with his service in the mercenary company. She wondered whether he would stay a part of it. He seemed to love it so much, and he excelled at his craft. But he was faced with becoming the head of the household, and perhaps some of the things he liked doing most would have to be set aside, for the sake of the family.

Of course, Em thought, I'm facing the same thing. Who would have thought that turning sixteen would carry so much responsibility with it?

Things had definitely changed at the Matrell estate. As Emriana looked around at her family, she wondered just how many more changes were on the horizon.

"You know," Vambran said to Xaphira during the lull, "you still have some explaining to do to me. Why have you been following me the past few days? And what have you been doing all these years?"

"She's been working for me," Hetta cut in. Everyone turned to look at her, shocked. "That's right, I've kept some secrets, too. The truth is, Matrell holdings are actually ten times the size that you all think they are, thanks to Xaphira. Even after she disappeared, we kept in contact. Never mind how, just trust me that we found a way. She's been my business partner for the past eleven years, and together, we've managed quite a few shrewd investments." When everyone still gaped, the matriarch feigned indifference. "What? Did you think I was going to trust all of our assets to Dregaul? If I had, we'd be a very poor family right now."

"And the other?" Vambran asked. "Following me?"

Emriana watched her aunt not say anything for several moments.

Finally, taking a deep breath, Xaphira said softly, "I told you last night that there was more to this than you could fathom, and there is. I'm still only beginning to put all the pieces together. But you should know that I'm almost certain you didn't shoot Rodolpho Wianar twelve years ago."

Emriana gaped at her aunt, then at Vambran. Her brother's mouth hung open.

"What?" he said quietly, as though he couldn't understand what he had just heard.

"Let me show you something," Xaphira said.

She walked over to where her red cloak hung near the door and removed a small bundle from a pocket inside it. The bundle was long and thin and wrapped in oilcloth, and when she unrolled it, Emriana could see a pair of crossbow bolts.

"This one," Xaphira said, holding up the first, "was in the quiver you gave me that night a dozen years ago before we parted ways. I dumped everything else into the sea once I was well out of port."

Xaphira took up the second bolt. Emriana could see that it was darkened at the tip, stained.

"This one," her aunt said, "was one I pulled out of my leg that night, after I ran from you."

The woman held them up, side by side. They were identical, right down to the blue fletching.

"What?" Vambran said again. "How can that be?"

"Because someone who was shadowing me that night, following me as I ran from the watchmen, had it in his possession. He shot me with it while I was fleeing, down near the docks."

"But, where did it come from?" Emriana asked, confused.

"It was stolen from my quiver at the Generon, before Adyan, Horial, and I ever started shooting," Vambran said, his tone cold. "Someone used my own bolt to assassinate Rodolpho Wianar, making it look like I did it."

"Exactly," Xaphira said. "And that someone is the same man who has been behind the scenes, working for Grozier Talricci, Denrick Pharaboldi, and Evester. It has been that man who has tried to thwart you at every turn when you started digging into the kitchen maid's death."

"The thug who confronted us last night, in the alley, during the fight for Uncle Kovrim!" Vambran said, his face lighting in recognition.

"Yes. His name is Junce Roundface, and he's a very skilled assassin."

"You knew this, and you didn't say anything?" Vambran asked, looking squarely at his aunt.

"We had more important things to take care of," Xaphira replied just as firmly. "First your uncle, then your sister, were in trouble. I didn't want you distracted with my news when you needed a clear head to save everyone else."

Vambran nodded, understanding his aunt's reasoning.

"After all these years, you still understand me too well," he said, a slight smile creeping onto his face.

Emriana noticed that Xaphira smiled, too.

The woman continued, "Besides, all of my suspicions are just that, still—suspicions. I don't have any other proof than these two bolts. And I've only recently managed to connect him to the shootings that night. I was following him to get some sort of additional proof of who he's connected to, who might have been behind the attack that night."

Hetta cut in: "And by following Junce, you began following Vambran, simply by extension."

Xaphira smiled at her mother.

"Something like that," she said warmly. "Once I saw that Vambran was getting involved in activities Junce was behind, I decided to keep on eye on my nephew full time, just to be nearby if he should need me."

"But that means that whoever is behind Junce's actions—and Grozier's, Denrick's, and Evester's—was also behind the murder of Rodolpho Wianar twelve years ago," Emriana said, understanding at last the connection.

Her stomach was fluttering.

"Yes, it does," Xaphira replied. "I don't know what the connection is, but there is one there. You're involved in it from both ends, Vambran."

Emriana's brother nodded and said, "It's all connected somehow. Grand Trabbar Lavant is still looking to manipulate events to broker an alliance, I'm sure. And he'll find other Houses willing to rally to his cause. Uncle Kovrim and I are going to have to stifle him politically, because we have no real proof that he's behind any of this."

"You couldn't prove that he and Grozier Talricci were working together?" Hetta asked.

Vambran shook his head.

"No," he answered, "we haven't yet begun truth-reading either him or Bartimus. They're both very good at masking their thoughts, so we're going to have to bring in more powerful magic to break them down. And Uncle Kovrim can't actually say that he rooted out Lavant's involvement by going through the high priest's personal records. Those have undoubtedly been destroyed or moved, so it would be his word against the Grand Trabbar's and I think we all know who's side the temple would take in that instance. So, we're going to have to deal with this one subtly."

"What about the four Halanthi priests who tried to waylay him yesterday?" Xaphira asked. "Can't you make a connection between them and Lavant?"

"I wish we could, but they have all disappeared. The temple is in turmoil over all this, and of course, the Grand Trabbar is screaming longest and loudest for justice on Uncle Kovrim's behalf."

"Of course," Xaphira replied.

Emriana's brother didn't say anything for a long time. Finally, as the silence grew uncomfortably long, the girl asked shyly, "How did you get into and out of the warehouse without me seeing you?"

Xaphira laughed and said, "You're going to be quite the little sneak when you get some more seasoning. It wasn't easy, but I've learned a few tricks that you don't know about yet."

"And aren't going to learn about any time soon," Ladara said firmly, stirring from her spot beside Hetta. "You are only sixteen, and you have no business sneaking out like that all the time. Do you understand me?"

Emriana opened her mouth to protest, but then she caught a look from her grandmother out of the corner of her eye and she repressed a smile.

"Yes, Mother. I won't do it anymore."

To herself, Emriana thought, As far as you know.

She stole a glance at Aunt Xaphira, who was hiding a smile of her own.

The girl's thoughts were interrupted as a figure appeared in the sitting room doorway. It was Uncle Kovrim, ushered in by one of the servants.

"Kovrim, welcome," Hetta said, smiling and rising to greet their guest.

The priest wore a dark frown as he said, "I wish my visit were for a happier purpose, but I've got unfortunate news."

Vambran sat forward in his chair.

"What's wrong?" he asked.

"Grozier Talricci and Bartimus the wizard escaped custody during the night. They were helped by someone on the outside, someone very good at getting in and out of the watch headquarters where they were being held."

"Junce Roundface," Vambran growled, standing. "This isn't over, yet. We have to find them."

"Why you?" Ladara asked quietly. "Why do you have to be the one to do this?"

"Because whoever is behind it has made me live

with unnecessary guilt for twelve years, and I owe them a little payback."

"It won't be easy," Kovrim said. "They know we're looking for them, and they have powerful magic at their disposal to aid in staying hidden."

"Perhaps," Vambran said, "but we have to try. Junce Roundface is working for someone even more powerful in this city. Apparently, they all are."

"Someone who wants to start a war," Xaphira said.

Emriana looked at her family, from face to face. They all wore the same grim expression.

They're all thinking the same thing, she realized. House Matrell is still in danger.

To be continued in

The Scions of Arrabar Trilogy, Book II
THE RUBY GUARDIAN
November 2004

R.A. Salvatore's
War of the Spider Queen

Chaos has come to the Underdark like never before.

New York Times best-seller!

CONDEMNATION, *Book III*
Richard Baker

The search for answers to Lolth's silence uncovers only more complex questions. Doubt and frustration test the boundaries of already tenuous relationships as members of the drow expedition begin to turn on each other. Sensing the holes in the armor of Menzoberranzan, a new, dangerous threat steps in to test the resolve of the Jewel of the Underdark, and finds it lacking.

Now in paperback!

DISSOLUTION, *Book I*
Richard Lee Byers

When the Queen of the Demonweb Pits stops answering the prayers of her faithful, the delicate balance of power that sustains drow civilization crumbles. As the great Houses scramble for answers, Menzoberranzan herself begins to burn.

INSURRECTION, *Book II*
Thomas M. Reid

The effects of Lolth's silence ripple through the Underdark and shake the drow city of Ched Nasad to its very foundations. Trapped in a city on the edge of oblivion, a small group of drow finds unlikely allies and a thousand new enemies.

FORGOTTEN REALMS

The Hunter's Blades Trilogy

New York Times best-selling author
R.A. SALVATORE
takes fans behind enemy lines in this
new trilogy about one of the most popular
fantasy characters ever created.

THE LONE DROW
Book II

Chaos reigns in the Spine of the World. The city of Mirabar
braces for invasion from without and civil war within. An orc king
tests the limits of his power. And *The Lone Drow* fights
for his life as this epic trilogy continues.

Now available in paperback!

THE THOUSAND ORCS
Book I

A horde of savage orcs, led by a mysterious cabal of power-hungry
warlords, floods across the North. When Drizzt Do'Urden and
his companions are caught in the bloody tide, the dark elf ranger
finds himself standing alone against *The Thousand Orcs*.